PRAISE FOR THE DETECTIVE SHERIDAN HOLLER SERIES

'An excellent crime novel, full of humour and pathos as well as utterly realistic action. A stunning debut.'

—Elly Griffiths

'Make way for the brilliant Detective Sheridan Holler! Urgent and artful storytelling for die-hard fans of crime fiction and new blood alike.'

—A. J. West

'A thrilling debut . . . If y   one
set in the mean streets o

nah

'T. M. Payne has hit th   ead.
Gritty, well-paced and p

—M. W. Craven

'A gripping and gritty start to what promises to be an excellent new police procedural series.'

—David Fennell

'An evocative, brilliantly plotted debut which I defy you to put down. I promise it will haunt you long after the end.'

—Graham Bartlett

'A brilliant debut.'

—Steve Cavanagh

'A twisty, compelling, page-turning cracker of a debut. Full of great characters, T. M. Payne's *Long Time Dead* is so absorbing you'll miss your bus stop AND stay up past your bedtime. Perfect for fans of Val McDermid and Michael Connelly.'

—Chris Merritt

'Dark and gripping, expertly plotted, and full of warmth and humour – you won't want this book to end.'

—Mel Sherratt

'A propulsive and character-driven mystery woven with authenticity and aplomb.'

—Victoria Selman

'A brilliant and compassionate new detective joins the scene.'

—Claire McGowan

'Such a great series. DI Sheridan Holler is one of my all-time favourite detectives. Written with warmth and humour, as well as a dark and twisty tale.'

—Jo Callaghan

'T. M. Payne's 18-year career in the criminal justice system brings authenticity to every page of *This Ends Now*. An expertly woven plot combined with the warmth and wit of the main character, DI Sheridan Holler, make this second book in the series a must-read for all crime fiction fans. A cracking police procedural. Don't miss this one!'

—D. S. Butler

'T. M. Payne is one of the most exciting new voices in crime fiction. In *Long Time Dead*, she crafts a richly textured thriller that brims with authentic detail. I loved the humor, the poignancy and the intricate rendering of Liverpool in all its heart and grit. The comparisons to Val McDermid are well earned indeed.'

—Kia Abdullah

'T. M. Payne is one of the most talented storytellers of our time. The gripping and authentic storytelling, clever and deeply satisfying plot and superb characters make *This Ends Now* my standout novel of the year and puts Payne at the top table of crime writers.'

—Graham Bartlett

'Good twists, and plenty of red herrings, and the book builds to a very tense and unexpected conclusion, with some neat stings in the tale . . . a really quick and engaging read.'

—*Deadly Pleasures – Mystery Magazine*

'Worth every interminable minute it takes to wind down.'

—*Kirkus Reviews*

COUNT
THE
DEAD

ALSO BY T. M. PAYNE

COUNT THE DEAD

A DETECTIVE SHERIDAN HOLLER THRILLER

T. M. PAYNE

THOMAS & MERCER

Text copyright © 2025 by T. M. Payne
All rights reserved.

Published by Thomas & Mercer, Seattle

www.apub.com

Amazon, the Amazon logo, and Thomas & Mercer are trademarks of Amazon.com, Inc., or its affiliates.

EU Product Safety contact:
Amazon Publishing, Amazon Media EU S.à r.l.
38, avenue John F. Kennedy, L-1855 Luxembourg
amazonpublishing-gpsr@amazon.com

ISBN-13: 9781662532535
eISBN: 9781662532528

Cover design by Dan Mogford
Cover image: © Matilda Delves / ArcAngel Images; © Rolandas Grigaitis © Inga_Ivanova © EmilioZehn / Shutterstock

Printed in the United States of America

For Susie
Whenever you are in danger, I will always stand in front of you
Whenever you need my support, I will always stand behind you
And for everything else, I will always stand by your side

Who is this monster that you seek, what even is
his crime?
Take heed for he will never stop, and you're
running out of time
He'll lead you down to darkness, where broken
candles lay
Such is the shame, he'll win the game, unless
you dare to play

You know not what he looks like, although he's
shown his face
He'll take his time for his perfect crime,
dropping crumbs for you to trace
If he feels that you are closing in, he'll stay one
step ahead
And now he's dining with the devil, while you
go and count the dead

PROLOGUE

Saturday 22 July 2006
Edge Hill train station, Liverpool

Annette Lennon removed her headphones, tucked them into her pocket, and glanced down the platform before checking her watch. 9.47 p.m. Taking a step forward, she stared down at the track. She'd read the poster situated behind her – a contact number for the Samaritans, with the message that read 'You're not alone, we are here 24/7' – twice, and wondered how many lives it might have saved. How many lost souls before her had considered jumping, but found the courage to pick up the phone and speak to a stranger? Her heart felt heavy, as a momentary sadness enveloped her. It was too late for her to pick up the phone.

The station was empty apart from a young couple on the platform opposite. Annette watched as they kissed and then quickly looked away.

She had spent the evening with her best friend, Clara – her only friend – and their conversation still echoed in her ears. Usually, they talked about how they would go on a diet, join the gym, take themselves clothes shopping in normal stores, not the ones that sell outsize clothing. And then meet the man of their dreams.

But on this last visit, Clara had told her that she'd met someone. Clara's excitement had been obvious in the way she described all the things they planned to do together. It was a bombshell for Annette. Although she was pleased for her friend, she realised that everything would change between them. She could already see a difference in Clara, and knew she was going to be cast aside now she was no longer needed. Like she had been for most of her life. She'd hidden her inner sadness from Clara; she was well practised in hiding.

Glancing back at the Samaritans poster, she knew that talking to someone was the last thing she could ever do. If she couldn't be honest with her best friend, then how could she tell a stranger that her life was miserable? She sometimes wondered why she bothered getting out of bed in the morning.

Her train was due in eight minutes, but there was a non-stop service that would fly past a few minutes earlier. Annette had made the decision before she left Clara's house, leaving herself enough time to be on the platform as the fast train came. She probably wouldn't feel any pain, all she had to do was just step off the platform and it would all be over. Would anyone really miss her? Closing her eyes, she felt a strange but welcome sense of peace wash over her. Was this it? Could it really be that quick and easy? Opening her eyes, it suddenly smacked her in the face. She was ending it. Right now. Right here.

She glanced down at the track again; any minute now the fast train would come and take her with it. Dark thoughts pulled her closer to the platform edge, the tips of her shoes now overlapping with the yellow line. Just then, out of the corner of her eye, she spotted a guy in a hi-vis vest using a litter grabber to pick up an empty crisp packet that had been discarded on the platform. As he got nearer, he smiled at her.

'I love this part of the job; picking up after messy folks,' he said, cheerfully.

Annette didn't reply. He walked slowly towards her.

'You waiting for the 9.55?' he asked, still smiling.

Annette nodded. She studied his face under the dim glow of the fading July light. He was probably in his forties, short brown tidy hair, his teeth were perfect, and he looked smart in his uniform of dark trousers, jacket and hi-vis vest, his shoes polished and shining as if he was a proud soldier ready to go out on parade.

'Best not stand too near to the edge, the fast train will be passing through in a minute.' He stepped a little closer to her.

Annette looked past him and was sure she could see the lights of the approaching train. If she backed out now, how many more times would the thought go through her head? How many more times would she find the strength to end it? It had to be now. It had to be *right* now. The train appeared around the distant bend of the tracks and when it was almost upon them, she closed her eyes.

'Best step back, eh?' She felt his hand on her arm. 'Miss?'

Annette opened her eyes and just as the front of the oncoming train hurtled towards them, he squeezed her arm a little tighter and, as it flew past, he grabbed her and wrapped an arm around her throat.

Suddenly Annette felt an excruciating pain in her cheek and the hotness of her own blood pouring down her face. She tried to scream, but his gloved hand was clamped hard across her mouth. Over and over, he stabbed at her forehead and face with the handle end of the litter grabber, and she could feel blood in her eyes and down her neck. She tried to grab his arm in a desperate attempt to stop the onslaught, but he was too strong for her. Blinded by the blood in her eyes, she closed them, her muffled cries drowned out as the train passed by and disappeared down the track.

She felt his warm breath by her ear.

And then he spoke. Quietly, but clearly.

'Tell them I'm just making a point.'

CHAPTER 1

Present day
Sunday 20 June 2010
Hale Street Police Station, Liverpool

Detective Inspector Sheridan Holler almost knocked over the uniformed officer as she raced past him up the stairs, heading to her office.

'Sorry,' she called, as she barrelled forward.

Just as she reached the top stair, she nearly collided with Detective Sergeant Anna Markinson.

'What's wrong?' Anna asked as Sheridan caught her breath and without stopping or answering, ran down the corridor. She followed Sheridan and reached her office, just as Sheridan emerged, flying past her.

'Sheridan? What's happening?'

'I can't stop. I have to get back down there,' Sheridan called, taking the stairs two at a time.

Anna, realising that Sheridan might need her help with whatever the emergency was, chased after her.

As she reached the bottom of the stairs, she spotted Sheridan who had finally stopped at the vending machine.

'What the hell is going on?'

Sheridan rifled through the change she'd grabbed from her desk drawer, then pushed a pound coin into the slot. As it dropped, she made her selection on the keypad.

'Watch this,' she said to Anna, and a moment later, three bars of chocolate dropped down into the tray. Sheridan smiled broadly. 'It's having a wobble. This bastard machine has robbed me so many times and now it's gone into some sort of meltdown and it's chucking out three bars every time.' She put her hand up to high-five Anna, who crossed her arms.

'You silly cow. I thought there was some sort of bloody emergency.' Anna kept her arms crossed, leaving Sheridan hanging. Anna shook her head.

'Did you not hear what I just said?' Sheridan continued. 'It's throwing out three bars of chocolate, *every* single time.' She pushed another pound into the slot. 'Go on, choose something.'

Anna frowned. 'Thanks to you, I'm now late for a meeting with CPS. It's Taylor the tyrant, and he's going to do his bollocks.'

Sheridan wasn't listening, instead watching intently as the machine churned out bar after bar.

Anna turned to walk away, shaking her head. 'You're mental,' she muttered.

'Do you want three KitKats?' Sheridan called after her.

'No. I bloody don't.' Anna reached the stairs, then hesitated before calling back. 'I'll have three Twixes – you can leave them on my desk.'

Sheridan grinned and placed Anna's order.

'Sheridan?' The voice came from behind her. Sheridan turned to see Andrea, the public enquiry officer, walking towards her.

'Have you got a sec?' Andrea asked, pulling a face at the sight of Sheridan, who'd turned around with her arms full of enough chocolate to stock a sweet shop.

'Bit busy,' Sheridan replied.

'Jesus. That'll rot your teeth.' Andrea pointed a finger. 'When you've finished schnaffling that lot, can you come and speak to a guy in the PEO?'

'What does he want?'

'He's asking to speak to someone high up, although he looks like a vagrant.' Andrea bent to pick up a Twix that Sheridan had dropped.

'I'll be there in five minutes.' Sheridan winked and made her way back to her office with her haul.

Five minutes later, Sheridan walked into the public enquiry office to find Andrea dealing with a man who was standing in front of the protective glass screen with his hands raised above his head, looking up to the ceiling.

'We are all here only because God allows us to be,' he said loudly. His hair was gelled up into a frenzy, and his long goatee beard was twirled at the end of his chin. Blue tracksuit bottoms swung above his ankles and his long dark coat looked two sizes too big. He turned sideways, still looking up, and repeated the words. 'We are all here only because God allows us to be.'

Andrea replied, 'Yes. I'm sure you're right, sir. But if you can step aside, I have other people to deal with.' Her voice was calm and controlled.

The man kept his hands raised and turned his back to her, head held high. 'We are all only here because God allows us to be,' he repeated.

Each time he turned he repeated the phrase, much to the amusement of everyone in the PEO. Sheridan knew that all sorts of characters came into the station – some aggressive, some in distress, while others were just plain bonkers. Like this one. She knew that

Andrea had seen it all before, too, and would deal with the God man in her own way.

Sheridan looked at the sea of faces waiting to be seen, trying to find the vagrant who had come in to speak to a senior officer. Hoping very much that it wasn't weird God guy, and that Andrea was just winding her up. Among the crowd at the back of the room she saw several faces that stood out to her.

One was a heavily built man in shorts and a T-shirt that barely covered his belly, taking pictures on his phone of the preacher.

Standing by the counter was an elderly couple who watched in horror, the man holding his wife's arm.

A tall, painfully thin lad with pebble-dash skin started laughing as the God guy began singing 'We are all only here because God allows us to be.'

Finally, sitting on the bench secured to the wall was a middle-aged man with one leg crossed over the other, dressed in beige trousers and a light short-sleeved top. He sported a thick beard and his hair was combed flat over his forehead. His blue-rimmed glasses were perched at the end of his nose as he squinted at the preacher with a look of amusement on his face. The man looked at Sheridan and raised his eyes to the ceiling, smiling. Sheridan smiled back.

Andrea was beginning to lose her patience. 'Okay. That's enough.'

God man stopped and stared at her. 'We are all only—'

'Yes, yes I know, we're all only here because of God and all that but you've got three seconds and then you'll be meeting him in person.' Andrea folded her arms. 'One, two . . .'

He continued chanting. Andrea looked pleadingly at Sheridan, who took it as her cue to intervene.

'Is this my guy?' Sheridan mouthed to Andrea, who shook her head, before pressing the buzzer to let Sheridan into the public area.

'Sir, can I help you at all?' Her voice was calm and commanding.

'Who are *you*?' God man asked, tilting his head to one side.

'I'm Detective Inspector Sheridan Holler.' She stepped closer to him and whispered, 'I'm sure you're just exercising your right to free speech . . . but maybe you could do it quietly? Somewhere else?'

'Are you going to arrest me?' he whispered back.

'Only if you don't leave now,' Sheridan replied.

He thought for a moment. 'Fine. I shall leave. I'm getting hungry anyway. I think I'll go and get myself a piece of pie.' And with that, he left.

'Right, who's next?' Andrea called out, and the elderly couple stepped forward.

Sheridan waited as Andrea buzzed her in, noticing the man in the beige trousers had dropped his glasses and was trying to reach them under the bench. Sheridan bent down and picked them up, handing them to him.

'Thank you, Detective Inspector Sheridan Holler.'

'Are you the chap that's here to see me?' Sheridan asked, a slight frown on her face. This guy didn't look like the vagrant Andrea had described.

'No. I heard you introduce yourself to the man who just left.'

'Oh, right.' Sheridan rejoined Andrea at the desk. 'Where's the guy who wants to speak to me?'

Andrea scanned the room. 'Oh. He's gone.'

'Did he say what it was about?'

'No.'

'Okay, well give me a call if he comes back.' Sheridan left, rather pleased that the vagrant had moved on, because she had an appointment with a vending machine.

CHAPTER 2

Thursday 24 June 2010

As Sheridan locked her car, she bit the chocolate off her ice cream and looked up to see DCI Hill Knowles walking towards her.

'I'm off to a meeting and I'm late,' Hill snapped, the comment coming without invitation.

'Everything okay?' Sheridan asked.

'Yep. All Q in there. Keep it that way, I'll be back before the end of your shift.' Without slowing her stride, Hill added, 'And change your bloody shirt.'

Sheridan frowned, puzzled, before looking down and spotting a huge dollop of ice cream rolling down the front of her shirt.

'Bollocks,' she said loudly.

Having an uncanny knack for dropping food down herself, she'd learned to always keep spare clothes in her locker. Now all she had to do was make it upstairs to her office and get changed before anyone else saw her.

Sneaking in the back door, she was grateful to find the corridor was void of people. As she put her foot on the first stair, a call came from behind. 'Sheridan.'

She turned to see Andrea peering around the corner. 'Sorry but that guy's back, the one who was in the other day asking to speak to someone high up, I just saw DCI Knowles leaving before I could grab her, but to be honest she scares the shit out of me so I'm glad I missed her.' Andrea hardly took a breath as she spoke.

Sheridan grinned. 'I didn't think anyone scared the shit out of you, Andrea. Most of the officers are actually scared of *you*.'

Andrea beamed proudly at the comment and winked. 'I like to keep up my reputation. I think I've already frightened the new PEO. He's only been here a couple of weeks, and I've had to shout at him at least three times.'

Sheridan raised an eyebrow. 'Poor fella.' She instinctively lifted the file she was holding in an attempt to hide the ice cream that had now seeped through her shirt on to her skin. 'Anyway, this guy who wants to speak to someone . . . did he say what it's about?'

'No. But . . .' Andrea whispered. 'Can you speak to him *now*? I'm not being funny but he's proper stinking the place out, and we're rammed in there.'

'Stinking out the place, how?'

'By just being there – he really, really stinks. I think he's a tramp, a vagrant, homeless.' Andrea screwed up her nose. 'Whatever I'm supposed to call him. I can't keep up with all the correct terminology these days.'

Sheridan followed Andrea to the PEO and was surprised to see the place so packed with people – some were familiar faces, those who were there as part of their bail conditions to report to the police station daily, but there were others she didn't recognise. A young woman scooping her baby out of its pram and rocking it back and forth, trying to stop it from screaming blue murder. A drunk swaying back and forth, slurring incomprehensible nonsense about seagulls. A suited woman, flicking through a file, probably a solicitor waiting to be called through to custody to represent a prisoner. Two young lads hovering in the doorway, shouting to someone outside on the street and looking as dodgy as fuck.

'Sorry – it's chaos in here,' Andrea said, raising her voice over the noise and nodding towards her colleague, who was asking the drunk to step aside for a moment. 'This is Marcus, he's the new guy.'

Sheridan nodded at Marcus, who nodded back, a faint, almost desperate smile flickering across his face, before he took a deep breath and called the next person in line to come forward, ignoring the drunk who was now flapping his arms up and down and making bird noises.

Sheridan's eyes scanned the sea of faces. 'Which one's my guy?' she asked Andrea.

Andrea pointed. 'Over there, standing in the corner,' she answered in a whisper. 'The one everyone's trying to keep away from.'

Sheridan studied the alleged tramp. His clothes looked especially grimy in the light coming through the large glass doors. It was blisteringly hot outside and beads of dirty sweat sat on top of his ragged beard. She could smell him from where she was. 'Great,' she said under her breath.

He spotted her and she beckoned him to approach with a swift flick of her hand. He shuffled over and put his face up to the glass.

'How can I help you?' Sheridan resisted the urge to clamp her thumb and forefinger to her nostrils to stave off the stench.

'Are you from the murder department?' he whispered in a thick Scouse accent.

'I'm Detective Inspector Holler from CID,' she replied. *Jesus, you stink*, she thought. 'And you are?'

He glanced behind him and then back at Sheridan. 'My name's Bobby. I need to speak to you in private.'

'Can I ask what it's about?'

'My mate, Kenny James. I need to tell you something about him, but I don't want to say it out here.'

Sheridan very reluctantly buzzed him through the door and into the corridor. 'So, what about your mate, Kenny?'

'I've just found out that he's dead. They reckon he slashed himself, committed suicide.'

'I'm sorry to hear that.' Sheridan kept her answers short, trying to hold her breath.

'There's no way he killed himself.' Bobby shook his head as he spoke.

'Why do you say that?' Sheridan asked.

'It was literally impossible for him to have done it like they said.'

CHAPTER 3

An hour later Sheridan was in the custody suite, having changed out of her ice-cream-stained shirt and persuaded the custody sergeant to accommodate Bobby, by letting him use the prisoners' shower and finding him some clean clothes that were kept spare for detainees. The tracksuit bottoms were a little on the large side, and bright yellow, but beggars couldn't be choosers, and Bobby wasn't going to complain.

He'd gratefully tucked into a microwaved meal and six slices of bread and butter, washed down with two cups of coffee.

When he emerged, escorted by the detention officer, Sheridan hardly recognised him. He was fresh-faced and clean-shaven, his blue eyes sparkling through the longest eyelashes Sheridan had ever seen.

She showed him into an interview room, and he sat opposite her, biting into the last of his bread and butter. 'Thanks for the shower and the food, miss. Nice one. Proper bread as well.' He smiled, and Sheridan was surprised that his teeth were in good order.

'Proper bread?' Sheridan asked.

'Yeah.' Bobby showed her the remains of his slice. 'The posh stuff, got seeds in it. Lovely. Might make it a regular thing eh, if I can get decent grub in here?' His eyes twinkled as he spoke.

'You'd have to be arrested to make it regular, Bobby,' Sheridan replied with a smile, before laying a notepad on the table in front of her. 'Right, let's start from the beginning. Tell me everything you know about Kenny James.'

Bobby settled in his seat and told her his story.

Bobby had first met Kenny five years earlier. Both homeless, they'd got talking and shared a doorway one night, tucked up to their chins in sleeping bags, watching revellers file past, high on drink and singing arm in arm down the street. That same night, one of the revellers approached them and threw a pound coin at Kenny before urinating on him. Some prick in a suit.

After emptying his bladder, he'd laughed loudly and called Kenny a lazy piece of shit while zipping up his trousers. What the prick in a suit hadn't bargained for was the group of Scouse women who were out on a hen night and all dressed up as Paul O'Grady's alter ego, Lily Savage. They chased the prick down the street, throwing their chips at him.

Bobby remembered the incident clearly because, after dishing out their retribution, the hen party returned and had a whip-round – giving forty quid to Kenny so he could buy himself a new sleeping bag. He'd joked with the girls, telling them that he'd rather they'd given him their chips instead of lobbing them at the prick in the suit. And the girls did what Scouse girls do: had another whip-round and bought Kenny and Bobby the best chippy meal they'd ever had.

In the years that followed, Kenny and Bobby often shared a doorway. They became friends. Shared their life stories. Bobby had started taking drugs when he was still at school and tumbled into a life of stealing to pay for his habit. His mother threw him out after he nicked her lecky money for the umpteenth time and found himself on the street. He learned quickly that the streets were dangerous, and he often slept during the day because it was safer than sleeping at night.

Kenny's story was not a million miles from Bobby's. Like Bobby, Kenny was an only child. He'd been quiet and gentle with a mild personality disorder. When Kenny's mother died, he couldn't cope and went to live on the streets of Liverpool. Unlike Bobby, Kenny didn't do drugs, but he did drink. A lot. Anything he could get his hands on.

And that's what Bobby recalled about him the most; his hands.

It was one night when they were sharing a bottle of cheap shit wine that, after taking a swig, Bobby handed the bottle to Kenny, and it slipped from his grasp. He'd made light of it, but later confessed to Bobby that he was losing the feeling in his hands.

Bobby had suggested he went to the hospital to be checked out, but Kenny wasn't having any of it. He hadn't been to the doctor's for more years than he could remember, and he hated hospitals, so resigned himself to the fact that whatever was wrong with him was just the result of his lifestyle. As the months went on, Kenny practically lost the feeling in the fingers of his right hand, making even everyday tasks difficult.

Sheridan listened intently as Bobby spoke. 'Kenny coped with it, but he started to drink even more and that's why we lost contact. It was the reason I ended up back in prison. I was on a suspended sentence, but Kenny needed a bottle of wine, so I offered to go and nick one for him. Most of the store detectives and security staff knew who I was, so I tried to disguise myself a bit. I used to have a bright red coat that I always wore, so I swapped it with Kenny's black one and went to get his wine. But I got caught anyway, and went to prison for a few months. When I got released, probation sorted me out a hostel. But I was a dickhead and didn't stick to the rules, so I lost my bed there. Then a couple of weeks ago, I thought I'd look for Kenny and see how he was getting on, but he wasn't in his usual place.' Bobby took a sip of his now cold coffee. 'Anyway, I was talking to another fella a week or so ago and he told me Kenny was dead. Killed himself. Apparently, they found him in some derelict building on the Dock Road last year. I was proper upset, I felt bad that I hadn't been there for him. We were really close, people even used to ask us if we were brothers, we were so similar in a lot of ways, even physically. Anyway, this fella tells me that Kenny had slashed himself and I knew something wasn't right. That's when I thought I'd come and speak to the bizzies, to check if you've looked into his death.'

'You came in a few days ago, but left before I could speak to you . . .'

'Yeah, sorry about that.' Bobby leaned forward slightly. 'He didn't kill himself.'

'Did he ever talk about suicide to you?' Sheridan asked.

'No, never. I heard he slashed his arm with a razor blade. But, I'm telling you, there's no way he could have done that. Not with his right hand being the way it was.' Bobby sighed. 'Look, I know people will just think he's some homeless nobody, but he was a mate, and I think someone did this to him.'

CHAPTER 4

Sheridan made her way to the CID office and headed straight over to DC Rob Wills' desk.

He nodded at her. 'Your shirt buttons are done up wrong.'

Sheridan looked down. 'For fuck's sake.' She undid the buttons and re-dressed herself. 'I've already managed to throw an ice cream down myself and it's not even lunchtime.'

'You having one of those days?' Rob grinned.

'Yeah.' Sheridan waved as if swatting away a fly. 'Anyway, can you do something really quickly for me?'

Rob leaned back in his chair. 'On or off the record?'

In the years that Rob had worked with Sheridan, he'd become her 'go-to' detective. She trusted all of her team and they in turn trusted her implicitly, but Rob had proved time and again that he could be trusted to keep her secrets when she needed something done on the QT.

Sheridan smiled reassuringly. '*On* the record. Can you have a look at a suicide from July last year, a guy called Kenny James. He was found dead in a derelict building on the Dock Road, slashed himself. I just need to know the circumstances.'

'Sure. Can I ask why we're looking at it?'

'His mate's just been in, says it wasn't suicide. He thinks someone killed him.'

'What makes him think that?'

Sheridan told Rob about her conversation with Bobby.

'Okay. I'll do some digging.'

'Cheers, Rob.' Sheridan tapped the desk then headed to her office.

◆ ◆ ◆

Two hours later, Rob was at her door. 'Got a bit of info on the Kenny James suicide.' Rob perched himself on the edge of the desk and referred to his notes. 'Kenny James was forty-nine years old, born in Formby. A few arrests for theft, drunk and disorderly, nothing major. He'd been homeless for about seven years. He was found by a couple of kids in a disused building on the Dock Road on Friday twenty-fourth of July. He was known to sleep in the building regularly. Cause of death was suicide – he basically cut his brachial artery with a razor blade.' Rob pointed to the inside of his own arm as he spoke. 'This artery here. He would have bled out pretty quick. No other injuries.' He looked up from his notes.

'Any suicide note?' Sheridan asked.

'Nope.'

'Which arm did he cut?'

Rob looked back at his notes. 'His left.'

Sheridan sat back. 'Can you get me the file, everything, photos, any CCTV that was seized, medical records, the whole lot.'

'Sure. You thinking he really couldn't have slashed himself?'

Sheridan raised her eyebrows. 'Not with a redundant right hand he couldn't.'

CHAPTER 5

Sheridan was standing in front of the fan in her office, trying to cool down, when Rob walked in. 'Got the file on the Kenny James suicide. I'm just waiting for the CCTV.' He dropped the file on the desk and joined Sheridan at the fan.

'Budge up.' He leaned into her and nudged her out of the way. 'How come you get the best fan in the building, and we have to put up with the shit one that sounds like a helicopter taking off?'

Sheridan grinned. 'Because I'm the DI and you lot are mere DCs.' She playfully nudged him back.

Rob shook his head. 'I'm going to put in a complaint,' he mumbled, heading for the door.

'No, you're not,' Sheridan called after him, before settling behind her desk and picking up the file on Kenny James.

A minute later, her phone rang.

'DI Holler.'

'Yes I am,' Rob's voice whispered down the phone.

'Dickhead.' She put the phone down, smiling to herself.

Opening the file, she began to read.

Kenneth Michael James DOB 04/04/60 (age at death 49). Born in Formby, Liverpool. No Fixed Abode. Only child. Father, Maurice James – deceased (died of a stroke

1975). Mother, Beryl James – deceased (died 2002 – throat cancer).

Kenneth James (Kenny) believed to have lived on the streets since his mother died in 2002. Known as a loner with few friends. Found deceased in a derelict building (formerly 'Tony's Tyres' a tyre recycling warehouse situated on the Dock Road, Liverpool), on Saturday July 24th 2009 by two young boys (aged 10 and 11) who had entered the building to play inside. They had spotted Kenny and walked over to him, immediately noticing a considerable amount of blood on his clothing, the wall he was sitting against and on the ground next to him. They did not touch the body. Police and ambulance were called to the scene, and it was quickly ascertained that Kenny was deceased.

Kenny was dressed in blue jeans, a blue T-shirt and black trainers. A red coat was on the floor next to his body.

The scene was forensically examined and photographed. A razor blade was found on the ground, near his left arm. A single deep cut was visible from just below his axilla (armpit) down to the middle of his left palm, severing his brachial artery.

Blood loss resulting in death would have likely been within 2-5 minutes.

The case was referred to the coroner and a post-mortem examination showed he died from significant blood loss and had been deceased for approximately two days before he was found. It also showed he had late-stage heart failure and cirrhosis of the liver.

Kenny had not seen his GP in over 14 years prior to his death and had only once attended hospital as a child when he dislocated his collar bone. His medical records showed that he had not therefore been diagnosed with heart failure or cirrhosis.

The razor blade found at the scene had no DNA on it, other than the deceased's, and only his fingerprints were present.

The deceased's head, hands and feet were bagged at the scene to preserve evidence. Examination showed that no other DNA was found.

The scene provided no evidence of other weapons, and the deceased had no other injuries – there was no indication of foul play.

Cause of death: Suicide.

Sheridan turned to the photographs taken at the scene.

Kenny was sitting on a flattened cardboard box, his legs outstretched in front of him. His dark, greying hair was stuck to his forehead and his face was covered in blood. He was surrounded by empty bottles, a milk carton and a carrier bag from which a sandwich packet was protruding.

She noticed the red coat – the same coat that Bobby had mentioned swapping with his own the day he was arrested.

She noticed a significant amount of blood spray up the wall, which partly covered the graffiti of faded paint-sprayed symbols and tags, likely left there by the local kids.

As she studied the picture, she noticed that just above Kenny's head, hidden among the graffiti, were the initials JT. At first glance, they didn't look out of place. But as she looked closer, something about them looked odd.

As she looked through the other photographs, her colleague DS Anna Markinson appeared at her door.

'Rob wants to know if you're going out anywhere today.' She walked in and bent forward over Sheridan's fan, pulling her shirt open to cool down.

'Why?' Sheridan asked, still studying the photos.

'Because he's going to nick your fan for the CID office.'

Sheridan stood up. 'I am actually going out. Wanna come?'

'Where are we going?'

'To a derelict building where a homeless guy was found dead last year.' She scooped up one of the photos.

Anna frowned. 'What case is this? I don't remember anything about a homeless guy crossing our desks.'

'I'll tell you on the way.'

CHAPTER 6

Sheridan parked up outside the long-abandoned Tony's Tyres building. The afternoon sun was relentless, and the heat smacked her in the face as soon as she was out of the air-conditioned car. Anna followed her inside. 'You take me to all the best places,' she said, stepping over a dead pigeon.

Sheridan walked to the wall where Kenny James had been found. The cardboard box he'd sat on and the surrounding bottles were long gone. A broken wooden pallet was propped up against a pillar, with a filthy duvet draped over it. She looked at the wall. All the graffiti was still there, albeit slightly faded now. All *except* the initials, JT.

She leaned in closer, noticing that the initials hadn't just faded; the section of the wall they'd been written on had been scraped away, leaving no evidence that the initials were ever there.

Anna appeared at her side. 'What've you found?' she asked, waving a persistent fly away from her face.

'That's odd.' Sheridan held the picture up. 'Someone's removed the "JT" mark that was here – but none of the other graffiti has changed.'

Anna wiped a bead of sweat from her upper lip. 'Maybe it was rubbed off when the cleaning team washed the blood away?'

'Maybe,' Sheridan said. 'But look.' She pointed at the wall. 'It's been *scraped* off, part of the brick has been gouged out where the initials were.'

Anna nodded in agreement and stepped back, observing Sheridan as she just stood, as she always did, taking in the scene.

Anna knew that at times like this, Sheridan was best left alone with her brilliant mind; the mind that worked so differently from any other detective's that Anna had ever known. Sheridan saw things that others didn't. She inhaled a scene, memorised it, picked out the unusual details that were often missed.

'JT,' Sheridan finally said under her breath. 'JT.' She turned to Anna. 'Why do the initials JT seem familiar?'

Anna blew out her cheeks. 'Don't know, mate,' she replied, flapping the top of her shirt, trying to cool down in the overbearing heat.

Sheridan looked back at the wall. 'That's going to bug the shit out of me.'

'So, what do you want to do?' Anna asked.

'I need to figure out where I've seen those initials before.'

CHAPTER 7

Sheridan and Anna walked into CID, Sheridan immediately spotting the fan that Rob had commandeered from her office. 'I'm having that back,' she muttered to him as she passed his desk.

Making her way to the front of the room, she stuck the photograph of the scene where Kenny James had been found on to the whiteboard. Then, checking no one was on the phone, she got her team's attention.

'Right, everyone. I know it's almost home time, but I need you to rack your brains.'

She told them about her and Anna's visit to the derelict building and the missing JT initials.

'I've seen these initials before, so can anyone think where? Is it a job we've dealt with? A shit-bag maybe?' She looked around the room.

Rob piped up. 'I can't think of anything, but I can get intel to check and I'll speak to PNC, maybe that'll throw something up.'

'Cheers, Rob.'

Hoping that the intelligence unit and police national computer system would provide something for them to go on, and with no other suggestions or ideas from her team, Sheridan was about to leave when DCI Hill Knowles walked in.

'What's going on? What's *that*?' Hill snapped, stabbing a finger towards the picture.

Sheridan took a deep breath and began to brief the boss.

She was halfway through explaining when Hill interrupted her. 'So, I go to a meeting and everything's nice and quiet. I come back . . . and now we have a possible bloody murder to deal with?' Hill crossed her arms. 'So, why does this Bobby fella think his mate didn't kill himself?'

Sheridan chewed on her bottom lip. 'He told me that Kenny *couldn't* have sliced his own arm, because he was losing the feeling in his hands. There was no way he could have held a razor blade in his right hand.'

'And this Bobby's an expert witness, is he?' Hill asked, in her usual style: abrupt.

'No. He's a mate who knew Kenny really well.' Sheridan sighed. 'Look, I just want to do some digging. I know I've seen the initials JT before and . . .'

Hill put her hand up. 'Fine. I'm too fucking hot and bothered to argue.' She turned on her heel. 'I've got another meeting to go to.' And with that, she left.

Sheridan smiled at her team. 'That was easier than I thought.' She turned to Anna. 'Okay, Anna, Rob and I will look into this job, the rest of you stay on your current cases. But keep trying to think of those initials: JT.'

She walked over to the stolen fan, unplugged it and carried it out of the office, whistling merrily.

CHAPTER 8

Sheridan pulled on to her drive and could see Maud, her cat inside, trying to catch a fly at the window. She carried on watching as she got out of the car and screwed her face up as Maud stuck her tongue on the windowpane, trapping the fly, before eating it.

'That's going to give you the shits,' Sheridan said under her breath as she walked into the house.

Her girlfriend Sam was in the kitchen. Sheridan kissed her on the cheek before opening the fridge, immediately attracting Maud who legged it into the room and pushed her head against Sheridan's leg. Maud *loved* the fridge.

Sheridan bent down and picked her up, kissing her head.

Sam pulled two glasses from the cupboard. 'How was your day?'

'I spent it with a stinky tramp who thinks his mate was murdered. Dropped ice cream down my shirt, managed to piss Hill off and dragged Anna round a derelict building.' She placed Maud on the floor. 'She ate a fly by the way, so she might get the squits.'

Sam screwed up her nose. 'Why did Anna eat a fly?'

Sheridan laughed. 'Not Anna – Maud.' She poured the wine.

'Oh,' Sam replied, smiling.

'How was *your* day?' Sheridan took a large glug of her drink and immediately felt her shoulders relaxing.

'Typical teacher stuff. Nothing exciting. My car's playing up, it's making a weird noise and it smells funny.'

'Why didn't you take it to the garage?'

'I was almost home. I'll take it in at lunchtime tomorrow.' She took Sheridan's hand and led her into the living room. 'Anyway, fuck all that . . . tell me about this stinky tramp.'

Sam and Sheridan had met over five years earlier when Sheridan was investigating the shooting of two women, one of whom ended up in a nursing home where Sam's best mate, Joni, worked as a carer. There was an immediate attraction between them, and that spark had turned quickly into a committed relationship. Sam always loved hearing about the cases Sheridan was working on, as she thought Sheridan's stories were more interesting than her own from the classroom. Hearing about a decaying body found buried in a back garden was always more fascinating than talking about some kid in class who'd got Plasticine stuck up their nose.

They sat top and tail on the sofa, with Maud plonking herself on Sheridan's lap. Sheridan told Sam about her visit from Bobby Stover and how she knew she'd seen the initials JT before but couldn't remember where.

'Do you really believe he was murdered?' Sam asked, downing the last of her wine and getting up to refill their glasses.

'If what Bobby says is true, then yes, I do.'

CHAPTER 9

Friday 25 June

The next morning, Sheridan could feel a scratching tiredness in her eyes, having lain awake thinking about the initials JT that had been removed from the scene. She and Sam left the house together and Sheridan was about pull away when she saw that Sam was struggling to get her car to start.

'Stupid heap of shit.' Sam tutted as she climbed into Sheridan's car. 'Can you drop me at the station? I'll get the train.'

After Sheridan pulled up outside Birkenhead Park station, she leaned over and kissed Sam. 'Have a great day – we'll sort your car out later. You be okay getting the train home?'

'Yeah, no worries. See you later. Love you.'

'Love you, too.' Sheridan watched as Sam walked through to the ticket office, glancing at a tall skinny lad whose eyes shifted between the flurry of people heading through the entrance. Sheridan watched closely as Sam fixed her eyes on him as she passed, letting him know that she'd clocked him. Sheridan smiled as Sam disappeared around the corner and the lad skulked off down the road.

She reversed out of the parking spot and as she sat at the lights, it hit her.

She remembered where she'd seen the initials JT before.

DCI Hill Knowles was in her usual foul mood as she stormed into CID. 'Where's Sheridan?'

'I'm here,' Sheridan replied as she walked in with Anna. 'And I need everyone's attention.'

Making her way to the front of the room, she grabbed the photo from the whiteboard and pointed to it.

'JT. I remembered where I've seen those initials before.'

Hill crossed her arms and listened, as did the whole team.

'It was about four years ago, a young woman standing on the platform at Edge Hill train station one night. She was attacked by a guy who pretended he worked in the ticket office. He stabbed her in the face with a litter grabber and when she was at the hospital, having the wounds cleaned and stitched up, it was clear that they were in the shape of two initials.' She pointed at the picture again. 'JT.'

She looked at Hill. 'I want to re-look at both cases, the young woman and Kenny James.'

Hill inhaled, looking hesitant. 'I'm not *entirely* convinced they're linked based on that . . .' She put her hand up just as Sheridan opened her mouth, ready to object. 'But, I do agree we should look at them, just in case.'

'Cheers, boss.' Sheridan pointed at Rob. 'You know the drill.'

He nodded. 'I'll get the file on the Edge Hill stabbing case.' He tapped his pen on the desk.

Sheridan went to her office, Anna following close behind.

'You've got a weird memory,' Anna said as she hovered in the doorway. 'What made you remember the girl on the platform?'

Sheridan told her about dropping Sam at the train station and the lad who was watching people, and how she'd remembered that, after the girl was stabbed, women in the area were terrified to be alone at night, especially on train platforms.

'So, if Kenny James *was* murdered, you think it could be the same guy who attacked the girl?' Anna asked.

Sheridan sat back. 'A sharp implement was used on both victims, both victims were alone and both have a connection with the letters JT. I think that's more than a coincidence, don't you?'

'Yeah, possibly. But they're three years apart, the MO is different, and he didn't kill them both.'

Sheridan shook her head. 'I still think it could be the same guy. We just need to figure out who or what JT is.'

CHAPTER 10

Rob Wills walked into Sheridan's office. 'Annette Lennon,' he said, placing a file on the desk.

Sheridan snapped her fingers in recognition of the name. 'Yes, that's it. The girl at the train station. Is that the file?'

'Yup,' Rob replied. 'You okay to start going through it? I've got a meeting with CPS about an aggravated burglary job.'

Sheridan picked up the file. 'Of course. Good luck.'

As Rob left the room, she opened the file on Annette Lennon and read the summary of the incident.

> *Annette Lennon is a single 29-year-old library assistant who lives alone in her flat near Liverpool city centre. On Saturday 22nd July 2006, she walked a short distance from her friend's flat to Edge Hill train station, where she planned to catch the 9.55 p.m. train to Liverpool Lime Street. She arrived 10 minutes early and waited on the platform alone. The station was quiet and she only remembers seeing two other people on the platform opposite: a young couple.*
>
> *She was approached by a male, who she described as white, approximately 5'9", medium build, short*

brown hair, in his mid-forties. He was dressed in dark clothing apart from a high-visibility vest, dark shoes which she remembers were 'very clean'. He was picking up discarded rubbish and began talking to her. She believed he was working at the station. He asked her if she was waiting for the 9.55 train and he knew there was a non-stop train that was due before hers. He was quietly spoken.

As the train approached, he warned her to stay back, but as the train was passing through, he grabbed her around the throat and then using the litter grabber, he began his assault. She stated that she suddenly felt excruciating pain to her right cheek and realised she had been cut. The male then proceeded to stab her in the face several more times. Before he left the scene, the male, while still holding her around the neck, said to her, 'Tell them I'm just making a point.'

She did not turn around at first and did not see where the male went to. After a short while, believing he had left the scene, she called out to the couple on the platform opposite for help. The couple alerted a member of staff, who from the position of the ticket office, could not see any of the platforms and was unaware that the incident had occurred. Emergency services were contacted and attended the scene.

Annette was taken to the Royal Liverpool Hospital where she was treated for her injuries. She was released two days later.

The consultant at the hospital noted that the injuries appeared to have been caused by multiple blows to the face with a sharp instrument.

The incident was captured on CCTV but the male's face cannot be seen due to the location of the CCTV cameras and poor quality of the recording.

From the footage, it was clear that Annette was standing right on the edge of the platform and was asked if she was suicidal, which she denied.

Still holding the litter grabber, the attacker left the scene by scaling a high wall to the rear of the platform. He was captured on CCTV a moment later where he was seen to enter an alleyway. CCTV footage ends there.

Annette was visited at the hospital by police, who noted that together her injuries appeared to resemble the letters JT, something that Annette herself had also noticed.

Annette described the man's accent as 'Soft Scouse'.

Her clothes were forensically examined but no other DNA was found.

Sheridan looked through the photographs of Annette that had been taken on the night of the incident, the following day and several weeks later. All showed the shape of the injuries to her face, cheeks and forehead made a clear J and a clear T.

She played the CCTV from the platform that showed the male walking along, picking up litter. The images were of poor quality, but the male could be seen to be keeping his head down most of the time. Sheridan watched him approach the victim and the interaction between them before he grabbed her. She replayed the recording several times, noticing that as he walked along the platform, he hesitated before sidestepping to his right as he neared the victim. After the assault, the male scaled the high wall behind the platform and disappeared down an alleyway.

CCTV from the surrounding area was checked at the time and no further sightings of the male were found, including in the weeks leading up to the incident.

Sheridan made a note: *He knew the train timetable. He's confident. Planned it, possibly seen her before? Maybe he's followed her in the past. Went prepared – wore a hi-vis vest and used the litter grabber to attack her – likely adapted the handle to make it into a weapon. He's physically fit – jumped over a high wall to escape. Keeps his face hidden from the CCTV. Takes a step to the side before he reaches the victim to further avoid CCTV. Gave the victim a message: 'Tell them I'm just making a point'. Tell who? Police? He wanted her to report it. Why? JT. Are these his initials? Annette possibly suicidal. She looks down at tracks several times and stands very close to platform edge. Both victims (Annette and Kenny) were attacked in July. (Annette attacked 22nd July 2006; Kenny killed 24th July 2009.)*

Sheridan sat back, thinking. *Who the hell is this guy?*

CHAPTER 11

Sheridan and Anna were sitting in Annette Lennon's tiny living room. 'Nice little place you have here.' Sheridan smiled, trying not to stare at the horrific scars on Annette's face. Even though they had clearly faded over the years, the JT initials were still visible.

Annette coughed, clearing her throat. 'It's okay. It's better than the last place I lived in. I couldn't stay there anyway, not after what happened.' She was softly spoken, making little eye contact, appearing awkward. She eased herself down into the armchair opposite Sheridan and Anna.

'So, you said that you're re-looking at my case?' she asked, briefly looking at Sheridan, before focusing on the floor.

'We're looking into another incident where we think it may be the same attacker,' Sheridan replied.

Annette swallowed before asking, 'Did he attack another girl?'

'No, and I'm really sorry, but I can't give any details I'm afraid.'

Sheridan noticed Annette touching one of the scars on her face as she spoke. 'I hope you catch him.'

Annette went on to tell Sheridan and Anna that even before the attack, she had been shy – socially awkward even. She kept herself to herself and only really had one close friend, Clara, whom she had visited on the night of the attack. She admitted that sometimes life got her down and she often turned to food for comfort. Her doctor had warned her that she was morbidly obese and offered her a referral to a weight loss clinic, but Annette had declined. Food was the only thing that made her happy, euphoric even, and without it, she felt she had little else in her life.

After the assault, she had become practically a recluse and rarely left her flat. Terrified that her attacker might have discovered where she lived, she gave up her tenancy and moved back in with her parents temporarily, until she found herself the flat she lived in now. She gave up her job at the library, feeling vulnerable in a public place, and started working at a food factory, until she was dismissed due to her sickness record.

'So, I don't work at all now. I don't really go out anywhere, I just stay here all the time.' She glanced towards the window.

Sheridan had noticed the heavy curtains were closed apart from a slight gap, allowing little light into the dark and dreary room.

'I still think he could be watching me.' She wiped a rogue tear from her face. 'I'll never get over it, not until he's caught.' She looked at Sheridan. '*If* he's caught.'

Sheridan chose her words carefully, broaching the subject as delicately as she could. 'Annette, I've seen the CCTV of the incident, and I wondered why you were standing so close to the platform edge.'

Annette took an age to answer. 'No reason,' she eventually said, her voice almost inaudible.

Sheridan, not wanting to push her, went on to ask Annette if she remembered anything else from the night of the attack.

'Not really. I told the police everything I remembered at the time.' She touched her cheek again. 'The consultant offered me plastic surgery to make the scars look less, well, look better. But I said no.'

'Why?' Sheridan asked.

'Because if the man who attacked me is ever caught, I want him to see my face. I want him to see what he did to me.'

Her comment hung in the air for a moment, before Sheridan said gently, 'Do the initials JT mean anything to you?'

Annette shook her head slowly. 'No. I've thought about it since it happened, what with the scars looking like those initials. But, no.' She momentarily made eye contact with Sheridan. 'I know you can't tell me anything, but I'm guessing the other person he's attacked has the same scars as me.'

'No. It's not the same kind of attack as yours.'

After assuring Annette that they would keep her updated, Sheridan and Anna left and made their way back to their car.

'Do you think she was suicidal?' Anna asked.

'Yeah. I'll show you the CCTV, she looks like she's going to jump on to the track.'

'And you still think it's the same guy?'

'I think so. It's the JT that's the link.'

Anna tilted her head. 'Is that enough of a link, though?'

Sheridan started the engine and then turned it off. 'Fuck. I've just thought of something else. I need to look at the Kenny James file again.'

CHAPTER 12

Sheridan flicked the pages over in the Kenny James file and ran her finger down the text. Stopping at one point and re-reading it. *Post-mortem examination showed he died from significant blood loss and had been deceased for approximately two days before he was found.*

Sheridan looked up as Anna walked in and tapped the file as she spoke. 'Both victims were attacked on the twenty-second of July, three years apart.'

Anna stepped over to the desk and arched her neck to read Sheridan's notes, before responding. 'It's not the same date. Annette was attacked on the twenty-second of July, but Kenny was found on the twenty-fourth—'

'Yes, but he'd been dead for two days. So, he died on the twenty-second,' Sheridan interjected.

Sheridan dialled Rob Wills' extension and summoned him to her office.

A minute later, he slowly peered around her door, pulling a face. 'I guess I'm not going home, am I?' he pouted.

Sheridan grinned. 'Yes, you are going home today. But tomorrow I need you to go back to 2007 and 2008, and check if there were any suspicious deaths reported on or around the twenty-second of July. Especially suicides.'

She updated him about her theory that whoever was behind the two attacks had carried them out on the same date.

'Why suicides and why go back to 2007?' Rob asked.

'Well, if it's the same guy, then I think Annette was his *first* victim. He didn't kill her because he wanted her to give us, or someone, a message. Then, he killed Kenny. And as for suicides.' Sheridan moved her mouse and beckoned Rob and Anna to look at her screen. She pressed play. 'This is the CCTV from Annette's attack. Watch it and then tell me what you see.'

She sat back, allowing them to view the footage.

When the footage had run, Rob said, 'She looks like she's going to jump on to the track before he walks up to her.'

Sheridan smiled. 'Exactly.' She glanced at Anna who was nodding slowly in agreement. Sheridan linked her fingers together. 'Kenny James's death was made to look like suicide, so the perp clearly didn't know him, because he didn't know that he had no feeling in his hands. I think he spotted that Annette looked like she was about to jump. So, there's a possible link here with suicide.'

Rob stood up straight and stretched his back. 'But he could have pushed her in front of the train and made it *look* like she jumped.'

Sheridan shook her head. 'No, he couldn't. He knew he was on CCTV. That's why he kept his head down, away from the camera. He wanted her to survive. He gave her a message: "Tell them I'm just making a point." He wanted her to report the attack.'

'Yeah, but why?' Anna said.

'I don't know.' Sheridan sighed, looking up at Rob. 'Anyway, get yourself off home. Make a start on it tomorrow. Anna and I are on a rest day, but ring me if you find anything.'

When Rob was gone, Sheridan switched off her computer and grabbed her bag. 'You got plans tonight?' she asked Anna.

'Nope.'

'Wanna come to ours?'

'Only if you can guarantee that Sam's not cooking.'

Sheridan grinned. 'I'll text her now and tell her we're picking up a takeaway.'

Sam had, over the years, proved beyond any reasonable doubt that she couldn't cook. Being aware of her culinary shortcomings, she had enrolled in a cookery class in an attempt to improve. But even then, she had eventually been asked to leave by the tutor. In a nice way. Her best friend, Joni, had then suggested she enrol on a first-aid course, and Sam had questioned why. Joni had explained that the day would likely come when Sam's atrocious cooking would be a risk to life, either from food poisoning or choking to death. Sam had agreed, and completed the course. Much to everyone's relief.

As they drove towards the Kingsway Tunnel – Anna having left her car at the nick – Sheridan asked how things were going with her ex-partner, Steve.

Two years earlier, Anna had thrown Steve out after he had hit her. And it wasn't the first time he had raised a hand to her – although she had never shared that fact with Sheridan.

Sheridan had, over the years, doubted Anna's denials that Steve had ever been violent, but hadn't wanted to force her on the subject, out of fear that it would push her best friend away.

Since they'd split up, Steve had slowly been tricking his way back into her life with his lies. He was happy to bide his time, but ultimately, he was going to get Anna back. One way or another. Whatever it took.

During the journey, Anna told Sheridan that she and Steve were still friends, and even met up on occasion – but just for a drink.

'Do you think you'll get back together?' Sheridan asked, trying to hide the concern in her voice.

Anna sighed. 'No. I don't think so. I still hate living on my own, as you well know. There are times when I really miss him and a bit of me thinks we could make it work, but I think, at least for now, we're better off as mates.'

'Are you not interested in finding someone else?'

'I'm not sure.'

Sheridan didn't respond as she pulled into her drive.

Anna lifted the takeaway food from the footwell, and they made their way inside.

Sam was in the kitchen, setting the table.

After they'd eaten and settled in the living room, all three of them heady from the wine, the conversation turned to Anna and she drunkenly agreed that they would set her up on a dating website.

Two hours later, they were huddled round Sam's laptop, flicking through the potential candidates, or 'victims' as Sheridan had called them, the comment earning her a slap from Anna.

'What about *him*?' Sam pointed at the screen. 'He's got a nice smile.'

Anna leaned in closer, reading out the man's profile. 'Forty-six, five foot ten, accountant, non-smoker, non-drinker, likes healthy eating, vegan. Dislikes swearing, coffee, Christmas, loud women, allergic to cats.' She shook her head. 'Fucking hell, he sounds like marriage material. Set me up with him immediately.'

They all laughed loudly, the alcohol adding to the fits of giggles as they carried on searching. Sheridan went upstairs to use the bathroom as Anna clicked on the next profile, her shoulders dropping as she flopped back on the sofa cushion.

Sam looked at her. 'Oooh, this one's got your attention.' She grinned and started reading out the man's profile. 'Forty-two, loves the outdoors, non-smoker, non-drinker, gentle type, quiet and kind. Loves . . .'

Anna sat back up. 'You can stop there, Sam.' She bit her lip, then said quietly, 'That's my ex. That's Steve.'

CHAPTER 13

Saturday 26 June

Sheridan was in the kitchen, waiting for the kettle to boil, when she felt Sam's arms around her. 'Anna's still asleep, I won't wake her.'

Sheridan turned around and kissed her gently. 'Good idea. She was probably awake half the night thinking about Steve being on that dating site.'

'You think she's upset that he's put himself back out there?' Sam whispered.

'Possibly. I hope he does find someone else if I'm honest—'

Sheridan stopped talking as she heard Anna coming down the stairs, appearing at the kitchen door with Maud in her arms.

'Oh, shit. Did she wake you?' Sheridan grimaced.

'A little bit.' Anna grinned. 'She managed to open the bedroom door, climb on the bed and sit on my head.'

At that moment, Sheridan's work mobile rang.

'DI Holler.'

'Sheridan, it's Rob.'

'Hello mate. You okay?'

'I've found a suicide.'

Sheridan shot a look at Anna. 'Go on.'

'2007. A lad called Jake Hannigan. Nineteen years old, jumped off Thurstaston Cliffs on the Wirral.'

'What date?'

'Twenty-second of July.'

'The same date as the others.' Sheridan ran a hand through her hair. 'Any suicide note?'

'Sort of. He was an amateur artist and was up there painting the scenery. When they found his stuff, he'd painted a message on the picture saying he couldn't take any more. The file states he was autistic and sometimes struggled with it.'

'Had he ever mentioned suicide before?'

'No. But he did have bouts of depression.'

'Cause of death?'

'Broken neck, fractured skull and multiple internal and external injuries.'

'Have you got the scene photos?'

'Yeah.'

Sheridan felt her stomach flutter. The same date, 22nd July. The suicide link. Could this be another case involving the same man? She thought for a moment, before answering. 'I'm coming in.'

Sheridan and Anna made their way to CID, Sheridan having taken the opportunity on the journey to ask Anna about the night before. Anna told her that it made her realise Steve had moved on. What she couldn't tell Sheridan was how she'd wanted to scream when she'd read his profile, describing himself as a 'gentle type, quiet and kind'. Even though a part of her still loved him, she couldn't forget the times he'd hurt her – when he'd punched her in the ribs, knocked her tooth out. When she'd laid in bed the night before, thinking about how it felt to see his profile on the app, she'd found herself worrying about the next woman in his life. Would he hit her too? Anna hadn't told a soul about his violent tendencies, although she wasn't convinced that Sheridan didn't have her own suspicions. If that was the case and she and Steve did get back together, Sheridan would never forgive her. And her friendship meant more to Anna than anything else in her life.

As they walked into CID, Rob was at his desk, Sheridan's fan whirring quietly in the background.

Two other DCs, Dipesh Mois and Bridie Sexton, were on the weekend shift, working on their own cases.

Dipesh, known for his impeccable dress sense, was showing off his new suit to Bridie who was nodding in all the right places as he invited her to feel the quality of the material.

Sheridan and Anna pulled up two chairs and sat on either side of Rob.

'So much for having a day off,' he commented. 'It might be nothing, so apologies if I've dragged you in for no reason, boss.'

Sheridan shrugged her shoulders. 'It's fine, I'd rather be sure.' She glanced at Rob's computer screen. 'Have you got the pictures?'

Rob clicked on the file. 'Yeah. They're not pretty,' he said, opening the first image of Jake Hannigan's broken body in situ at the bottom of Thurstaston Cliffs.

From the photographs, Jake looked to be slightly built, wearing jeans and a yellow T-shirt; one of his trainers was missing. His fringe was swept across his eyes, which were partially open. His head showed significant injuries, his legs were tucked awkwardly under him and an obviously broken arm was outstretched at his side. As Rob flipped through the pictures, he came to the one showing Jake's easel, positioned near the edge of the rock. His paint palette stood on a small folding table next to an empty stool where Jake had been sitting while he painted a canvas.

Sheridan studied the image. Jake appeared to be a gifted artist, his delicate, sweeping brush strokes detailing a sky of varying shades of blue, with a rogue cloud captured perfectly, small sailing boats on the River Dee and the outline of North Wales in the distance. It was beautiful and hauntingly tragic at the same time. Across the skyline, Sheridan noticed that something was written in a lighter shade of blue. The words were hard to make out. She leaned closer and read them out loud. 'Just can't take any more.'

She sighed heavily.

'What do you think?' Anna asked.

Sheridan screwed up her face. 'I'm not sure. This looks like an *actual* suicide to me, so it doesn't really fit. The only thing that's the same is the date and the fact that he was on his own. There's nothing to suggest it *wasn't* suicide.' She sat back in her chair, placing her hands behind her head.

'Okay,' she eventually said. 'Can you get me the file anyway, Rob? I'll take a look at it tomorrow. And can you keep checking for any more suicides or suss deaths on the same date?' She stood up and placed a hand on his shoulder.

Rob nodded. 'Will do. Sorry about fucking up your day off.' He pursed his lips.

'You didn't, mate.' She smiled broadly. 'Because now we're here, Anna's going to treat me to a very expensive lunch.'

CHAPTER 14

Sunday 27 June

Sheridan blew on her coffee as she looked through the file on Jake Hannigan's suicide. A moment later, DCI Hill Knowles walked in and flopped down on the chair opposite her.

'What's happening?' Hill asked.

'Rob found another suicide. Young lad jumped off Thurstaston Cliffs on the twenty-second of July, 2007. But I'm not sure it's connected – it looks like an *actual* suicide.' She sighed.

'Have you thought about the fact that the two incidents we have aren't linked?' Hill rolled her shoulders back. 'Maybe you're trying to see something that isn't there, Sheridan.'

'It's the JT thing. I just can't dismiss it.' She sipped her coffee. 'I'm going to go and see Jake's parents. I want to get a feel for him.'

Hill stood up. 'Fine. Keep me updated.' And with that, she left.

Sheridan rang the doorbell of Jake Hannigan's mother's house, having called ahead to let her know she wanted to discuss Jake's death. It was a large, detached property on the outskirts of Thurstaston Common, standing boldly in the middle of a lawn in need of mowing. Skirting the lawn was a thick, overgrown beech hedge, and the path leading to the house was lined on either side with an array of plants and herbs growing wildly in terracotta pots.

After inviting her in, Jake's mother, Stephanie, showed Sheridan into the bright and airy living room. A large table, covered in magazines and paperwork, stood by the window. Sheridan spotted photographs of Jake practically everywhere. Several hung on the walls, more stood in silver frames along the mantelpiece, while others were displayed on the sideboard.

'Can I get you a cup of tea, or coffee?' Stephanie asked. She was a slight woman with neatly cut, shoulder-length hair streaked with white. Her hazel eyes were warm, if a little tired-looking, and crevasses of worry lined her forehead.

Sheridan politely declined, before explaining that she was looking into suicides that had occurred within the last few years on the same date, carefully not giving anything away.

She sat on the sofa while Stephanie took the armchair opposite. After she was seated, she clasped her hands together, giving Sheridan her full attention.

Sheridan cleared her throat. 'I'd just like to know a little bit about Jake, if that's okay? What sort of person he was. I see from the file that he was autistic. Can you tell me how that affected him? I know every case is different.'

A gentle smile fleeted across Stephanie's face as she glanced at one of the framed photographs of her son.

'His autism was fairly mild. He was fiercely independent, loved being on his own and spending time painting. He was very good at it,' she replied.

'Did he have a lot of friends?'

'No. Jake was a loner, didn't mix too well with other people. Except us.'

'Did he visit the cliffs regularly?'

'Yes, he used to go every Sunday and sometimes during the week. He found it very peaceful, and he loved the views.'

'Did he ever mention talking to anyone while he was there?'

'No. Why do you ask?'

'I just wondered if anyone had seen him there, before he died, maybe they spoke to him in the time leading up to his death.'

'He never mentioned anyone, and no witnesses came forward after it happened. Apart from the young couple who found his body.' Stephanie's voice broke. 'Apparently, they were in a terrible state. It must have been so awful for them.'

Sheridan gave her a moment before she broached the subject. 'Did Jake ever talk about suicide?'

'No. He used to get frustrated with his condition and would sometimes say he hated his life but he never . . .'

Sheridan could see the pain on Stephanie's face. 'I'm sorry if this brings it all back.'

Stephanie looked her in the eye. 'It never goes away. Losing a child and finding out they were so unhappy that they couldn't face life any more. It eats away at you. It's there every second of every day.' She took a tissue out of her pocket and blew her nose.

Sheridan continued gently. 'You said on the phone that you're separated from Jake's father?'

'Yes. We'd had problems for years. Frank never understood Jake's condition. He never bonded with him, even when Jake was little. Frank saw him as imperfect and not the son he'd dreamed of having. I tolerated him for *so* long, but when Jake died, I was so angry with Frank, I blamed him and . . . well . . . he left. So, now it's just me and Jake's sister, Juliet.'

As Stephanie spoke, Sheridan glanced around the room. The place was cluttered, with books stacked next to a glass-fronted sideboard. Inside there were more books, arranged haphazardly.

Stephanie continued. 'Frank was a difficult man. He was controlling and everything had to be in its place. It was like an obsession, and he'd get frustrated if the lawn wasn't perfect, or the curtains didn't hang a certain way. Literally everything had to be just right.'

That explains the clutter. Now he's gone, you've let things go because you can, thought Sheridan. 'I see,' she said.

'Frank was the same with Jake. He couldn't handle having a son that didn't fit his idea of perfection.' Stephanie sighed. 'I should have protected Jake better. He knew his dad didn't love him like I loved him, and I should have been stronger.'

'And what about Juliet?' Sheridan asked.

'Frank adored her. He called her his princess.'

'Does Juliet still live here?'

'Yes. She's out at the moment. Sorry, but you said you were from CID. Is there something about Jake's death that you're looking into?'

Again, Sheridan chose her words carefully. 'I'm just looking into suicides or suspicious deaths that occurred on the same date that Jake died . . .'

The living room door opened, and Sheridan looked up to see a tall, slim, dark-haired young woman walk in.

'Oh, hello,' she said, smiling.

'This is DI Holler.' Stephanie gestured towards Sheridan. 'She's just asking some questions about Jake.'

Juliet Hannigan stared at Sheridan. 'What kind of questions?' She walked over to Stephanie and perched on the arm of the chair, looking at Sheridan the whole time.

Sheridan briefly explained what she had told Stephanie.

Juliet folded her arms. 'So, you think that Jake might not have killed himself?'

'Not exactly . . .'

Juliet flicked a look at her mother, before going on to describe her relationship with her little brother and admitting that he had outbursts of frustration, even anger about how his autism affected him. She said she didn't believe at first that Jake had jumped, but when the message on his painting was revealed, she had to accept that her brother had ended his own life. A fact she had lived with, always feeling she had let him down.

Sheridan asked them if the initials JT meant anything or had any connection to Jake. She knew that JT had to be the link between the cases, if there was one, but Stephanie and Juliet both stated the initials meant nothing to them.

'Why do you ask about those initials?' Juliet said.

'It's just something that came up.' Sheridan looked at Juliet. 'Both your and Jake's name begin with J, do you have middle names?'

'No,' Juliet replied, clearly puzzled, but didn't question it further.

As Sheridan got up to leave, Juliet walked her to the door, and stepping outside, she placed a hand on her arm. 'I know you're not telling us something. The police don't send a detective inspector round to talk about a three-year-old suicide unless there's more to it.'

'There's nothing to worry about, I assure you of that. I just want to make sure nothing was missed.'

Juliet looked unconvinced.

'How did your dad take it when Jake died?' Sheridan asked.

'He was devastated. Him and Jake weren't that close, but Dad lost it when he found out Jake had killed himself. I've never seen him like that before. He wasn't the kind of man who showed emotion, especially when it came to Jake. He never coped with the fact that Jake wasn't *normal,* as he put it. It was like he was embarrassed of him. He hardly even mentioned to people that he had a son, it was like Jake didn't exist.'

'But *you* had a good relationship with your dad?'

'He adored me, called me his bloody princess. I hated it. I hated it because he should have adored Jake as well, but he didn't. He resented him.' Juliet sighed.

'I'm sorry to ask, but did your dad ever hurt Jake?'

'Oh God, no. He was never violent. He'd get frustrated with Jake, but he would never hurt him physically.'

Where was your dad on the day Jake died? Sheridan thought, but she didn't ask the question out loud. She had to tread carefully so as not to alienate the family. 'So, the day that Jake died, were you all at home when you got the news?'

'Mum and I were here. Dad was playing golf with some friends.'

'So, your dad only knew about Jake's death when he got home?'

Juliet sighed. 'Yeah. We tried to get hold of him, but he didn't answer his phone, so the first he knew about what had happened was when he got home and saw the police car on the drive.'

'And are you still in touch with him?'

'No. He met someone else, and they moved to Spain.'

'Okay. Well, I'll be in touch if I need to speak to you again. Thanks for your time.' Sheridan smiled and walked back to her car.

Juliet watched as the detective drove away, then took out her phone and sent a text.

> *Hi Daddy. A detective was just here asking about Jake. I told her we're not in contact, so in case they try to call you. I didn't give them your number. Are you in the country? xx*

Her phone pinged with a message back from her father: *Hi princess. I'm in the country, down south on business. What was the detective asking about?*

Juliet replied: *She said something about wanting to know if Jake spoke to anyone around the time he died.*

Frank messaged: *Why did she want to know that?*

Juliet texted back: *No idea. We'll talk when I see you. Love you. xx*

Frank signed off: *OK princess. Love you too. xx*

CHAPTER 15

As Sheridan made her way back to Hale Street, she thought about Jake and the circumstances around his death. The way he got frustrated with his condition. He was a loner. He'd left a message saying he couldn't take any more. It fitted. It all smacked of suicide. So, why couldn't she shift the feeling that something wasn't right?

Her mind wandered from Jake to her own brother, Matthew. And the mystery surrounding *his* death.

Over thirty-three years earlier, when he was twelve years old, Matthew Holler had been found dead, his naked body buried under a pile of leaves in Birkenhead Park. His clothes had never been found. And neither had his killer.

Back in 2005, Sheridan had finally plucked up the courage to approach Matthew's best friend, Andrew Longford. The friend he'd been playing football with the day he died. Andrew had had his own worries over the years, including the loss of his father, cancer, and subsequent health issues. He had also been racked with guilt his whole life about what had happened to his best friend. It was while Sheridan had been going through old photographs of Matthew and Andrew playing football that she'd spotted a man watching them. A name had been put forward – Stephen Tubby. An officer from the cold-case team – DC Ruth Manning – had located Tubby, who denied being anywhere near the park that day, although Ruth Manning eventually discovered that Stephen Tubby *had* been working locally at the time and had lied about his whereabouts. All she had to do was prove that there was a link between Tubby and Matthew's murder.

In the many years since Matthew had been gone, Sheridan had seen her own parents go through the intolerable pain of losing their son. And today, she'd seen a familiar pain in Stephanie Hannigan's eyes. Matthew had been murdered – he hadn't taken his own life, like Jake – but his killer was still out there.

Sheridan often wondered if maybe something had been missed during the investigation into Matthew's killing. Policing was very different back then, the investigative tools available now weren't even invented in the seventies. Sheridan had studied Matthew's case, scrutinised the scene photographs, looking for anything that might have been overlooked at the time. The way she did with every case she worked on, including Jake's death. She had to be absolutely certain that Jake's family wouldn't be left believing their son and brother had jumped to his death if that wasn't the case.

As Sheridan pulled into the backyard of Hale Street nick, she tried to shake off thoughts of her beloved brother, feeling a tightening in her stomach. As she parked her car, Juliet Hannigan's words rattled around in her head. *'So, you think that Jake might not have killed himself?'*

Yes, I do, Sheridan thought. *And I don't know why.*

Sheridan was at her desk re-examining the file on Jake Hannigan's suicide. Trying to find something, anything, to place some doubt on the initial verdict that he had taken his own life.

She glanced up from her notes when Anna walked in. 'I'm off, are you nearly done?'

Sheridan pushed her chair back and stood up. 'Yeah. You off home?'

Anna chewed the inside of her cheek. 'I'm meeting Steve for a quick drink.'

'Oh. Right.' Sheridan realised immediately how her response sounded, and tried to sound nonchalant as she continued, 'Did he ask you or . . .'

'No, I called *him*.'

'Are you going to ask him about the dating site?'

'No. That's his business,' Anna replied.

'Fair enough.' Sheridan summoned the best fake smile she could manage.

'Right. See you tomorrow.' Anna peered at the file on Sheridan's desk before leaving.

Sheridan cleared her things away, then went home. As she drove, her thoughts were pricked again by Jake Hannigan. There had been a sadness in his sister's eyes as she had spoken about him. Sheridan knew that feeling; she knew what it was like to lose a brother, albeit in very different circumstances.

Ignoring the turning leading up to her house on Bidston Hill, she carried on, feeling an overwhelming need to visit her own brother's best friend, Andrew Longford.

Being in Andrew's house and sitting with him over the years had always given her a strange sense of comfort. Andrew had been the last person to see Matthew alive – apart from his killer – and Sheridan felt close to Matthew when she was with Andrew.

She parked outside his house and walked up the path to his door. She hadn't visited him for several months, but he always made her feel welcome, no matter how long it had been between visits.

When he answered, Sheridan was taken aback by his appearance. He had lost a significant amount of weight, and his face was grey and gaunt.

'Hello, Sheridan. This is a nice surprise.'

As they walked into the living room, Sheridan moved a pile of magazines from the sofa and then sat. She watched Andrew ease himself gingerly down into the armchair.

'It's good to see you.' He smiled a gentle, sad smile.

'You too. Sorry I haven't been round for a while, work's been busy. How are you?'

Andrew took a long, deep breath. 'Not so good.' He reached for the glass of water on the table next to him.

'Oh. What's wrong?'

'The cancer's back, Sheridan.' He took a sip of water, before placing the glass unsteadily back on the table. 'And it's going to beat me this time.'

Sheridan swallowed. She felt a knot in her stomach as she tried to find the words to respond. 'I'm so sorry.' She hesitated. 'So, what have they said?' She instinctively moved forward in her seat and placed a hand on the arm of his chair.

'They've offered me end-of-life care in a hospice, but I've told them I want to be here in my home when it happens. So, I'm getting a palliative care nurse, she'll come every day until . . . well, you know.'

Sheridan bit her bottom lip, desperately fighting back tears. 'I don't know what to say.'

'It's alright. I've accepted it.' He gave a reassuring smile. 'It's just one of those things. I guess God works in mysterious ways, as they say.'

As Andrew talked about his prognosis, Sheridan felt a sad foretaste of the grief that lay ahead. Andrew Longford, her brother's best friend, was dying. He was the last link, the last person, apart from herself and her parents, to have a connection with Matthew.

An hour later, she got up to leave and as they stood at his front door, she wrapped her arms around him and kissed him on the cheek. 'Is there anything I can do? Anything I can get you?'

'No. But thanks, Sheridan.' He placed a hand on her shoulder. 'You take care.'

And with that, she left and drove slowly home.

Sheridan was still trying not to cry when she walked in her front door. Sam was in the kitchen, singing. She stopped as soon as she saw the look on Sheridan's face.

'What's wrong?' she asked, immediately pulling Sheridan towards her.

'Andrew Longford's got terminal cancer.' Sheridan finally let the tears fall and Sam pulled her even closer.

'Fuck.' Sam sighed. She knew instantly that Sheridan would be even more desperate now to find Matthew's killer. Not only for herself and her parents, but for Andrew Longford, the friend who had carried his guilt with him all these years. Guilt that he had got home safely that day. And Matthew hadn't.

CHAPTER 16

Monday 28 June

Sheridan got into work early and, after logging on to her computer, she dialled DC Ruth Manning's mobile.

Ruth answered immediately and listened as Sheridan told her about Andrew Longford. 'I'm really sorry to hear that.'

'How are things going?' Sheridan asked.

'Slow, I'm afraid. I'm still trying to find witnesses to place Stephen Tubby at the building site at the time Matthew was killed. I just keep coming up blank.' There was a momentary silence, before she continued. 'I know how frustrating it is for you, and now with Andrew being so ill . . .'

'I just want to get to the truth before he dies.'

Anna walked in and sat down, frowning at Sheridan's words.

Ruth replied, 'I know you do, Sheridan. Trust me, I'll do everything I can, I promise you that.'

'Thanks, Ruth.' Sheridan ended the call.

'Want to get to the truth before *who* dies?' said Anna.

Sheridan told her about Andrew Longford.

'Oh, mate. That's shit.' Anna sat forward. 'Have you told your parents yet?'

'No.'

She looked up to see Rob Wills' face appear around her door. 'Morning, boss.'

He smiled and stepped into the office. 'I've got the CCTV from the Kenny James job, and I've had a really quick look through it. There's a few people captured on a camera from the building opposite, but the angle's not good. They just walk past, as far as I can see. I've sent the images to you.'

'Cheers, Rob.' Sheridan tried to focus and push Andrew Longford out of her head.

Rob perched on the edge of Sheridan's desk. 'I've also spoken to PNC about the initials, JT. They're looking at it, but in fairness, there'll be tons of nicknames and initials on there, so it's going to take a while to try and narrow them down. I've also spoken to Intel. The only mention of JT they can find is the Annette Lennon stabbing case, but they'll keep looking.'

Sheridan puffed out her cheeks. 'You *have* been busy. Thanks, Rob, you're a star.'

He got up and patted himself on the back. 'I know.' He grinned and left.

Sheridan sat back in her seat. 'We'll talk later, eh?' she said to Anna, who walked around her desk and hugged her.

'If there's anything I can do, you just shout.' She squeezed Sheridan's arm. 'Love ya.'

'Love ya too.'

When Anna left, Sheridan closed her eyes for a moment, struggling to stop herself thinking about Andrew and Matthew. Then she sat upright and started looking through the CCTV that Rob had sent her.

An hour later, something on the recording caught her eye.

Sheridan rewound it and watched it again. And again. There was something familiar about the man in the image, which then drew her to re-watch the recording of Annette Lennon's attack.

'Well, fuck me.' She called Rob's extension and summoned him and Anna to her office.

They sat on either side of her as she played back the first recording of the man who had attacked Annette Lennon from the moment he appeared on the platform, noticing the slow, deliberate steps he took towards her, the slight sidestep before he reached her. Then she played the recording of a male seen near the derelict building two days before Kenny James was found. The same slow walk, with his head down, the same sidestep to the right, just before he disappeared off camera.

Anna was the first to speak. 'Christ. It could be the same guy.'

'That's what I'm thinking,' Sheridan replied, freezing the image on her screen. 'And in both recordings, he keeps his head down.' She sat back in her chair. 'I think this guy knows exactly where the CCTV cameras are and changes the direction he's walking in slightly. He knows how to avoid being seen.'

Rob crossed his arms. 'You're right. That really could be the same guy. His hair's different, but he's the same build . . . looks like the same height, too.'

Sheridan nodded slowly. 'Bear in mind the date he attacks his victims, maybe it's his birthday or something.'

'I'll update PNC and Intel with this new info.' Rob headed out the door.

Anna stretched out her legs. 'How about we get this picture out to the press? See if anyone recognises him. We could put it out that he might be a witness to something, try not to spook him if he sees it.'

'That, my friend, is a very good idea.'

Anna got up. 'Well, to be fair, I was due one.'

She chuckled at her own comment and Sheridan nodded in agreement. 'True.'

Anna left and Sheridan stared at the image. 'Who *are* you? And who are you trying to make your point to?' she said under her breath.

CHAPTER 17

Monday 5 July

DCI Hill Knowles stood at the front of the CID office with Sheridan. The whole team were all now working on the case. DC Dipesh Mois and DC Bridie Sexton had joined the investigation, tasked with sifting through calls from members of the public who had seen the image on the local news the previous Wednesday. They'd had to weed out the time-wasting cranks from the potential leads, which was time-consuming and frustrating. Names that had been put forward had been checked, but none had provided anything substantive yet. As the days had gone on, fewer and fewer calls had come in.

Rob had not yet found any other cases of suspicious deaths or suicides that involved lone victims.

'So, to summarise,' Sheridan said, scanning the room. 'We have our man – let's call him JT – attacking Annette Lennon, a lone female, on the twenty-second of July 2006. Giving her the message, "Tell them I'm just making a point." So, let's say this is his first victim and he wants her to send us or someone a message. Now, we've looked at Jake Hannigan's death, on the twenty-second of July 2007. A lone male who jumps off Thurstaston Cliffs. To be fair, this is probably not connected to our suspect, but I want to keep an open mind.' She paused. That niggling doubt about Jake's death rattled in her head. It was a doubt she couldn't explain but she wanted to leave it out there so her team didn't dismiss the possibility of a connection. She pressed on. 'Then we move to the twenty-second of July 2009, Kenny James, our homeless guy. This is very likely JT. Kenny could *not* have caused the injury to himself that led to his death. So, if our suspect is attacking lone victims, say, one year apart on the same date, twenty-second of July, then we need to find a lone victim who died on the twenty-second of July 2007 and the same date in 2008.'

After the briefing, Sheridan headed back to her office and met the public enquiry officer, Andrea, in the corridor.

'Ah, Sheridan, can I give you this?' She handed over an envelope marked 'CID, Hale Street Police Station'.

'Thanks. You okay?' Sheridan asked.

'Yeah, fine. Just mental downstairs. And the new guy's doing me head in.'

Sheridan grinned as she watched Andrea take the stairs two at a time, mumbling to herself about being 'too old for this shit'.

Sheridan walked into her office and opened the envelope. It was handwritten. Her eyes widened as she read the words on the note inside.

> *I'm surprised it's taken you so long. How many clues does it take to figure it out? You have the key to the answer. I'm sure at some point you'll turn things around. Then all you need to do is fill in the gaps. JT*

Grabbing a pair of gloves and placing the note and its envelope into evidence bags, she hurriedly returned to CID.

The team listened in stunned silence as she read it out.

'This *has* to be from our suspect. He's signed it off "JT" and we haven't released that information.' She handed the evidence bags to Dipesh. 'Can you get this to Forensics? I need it fast-tracked.'

As she drove home, Sheridan thought about the note. She'd had a photocopy made so she could study it better without interfering with evidence.

Was the answer in the note? What did he mean by 'you have the key'? What kind of key? Key evidence or a physical key? Had he left a key at the crime scenes? Had it been missed? Or was he just playing games with the police?

Her thoughts turned to Jake Hannigan. His was the only suicide that occurred on the 22nd of July in 2007 in the Merseyside area. She thought about that fact and wondered if maybe JT wasn't targeting his victims on the same date every *year*. Maybe it was every *three* years. Annette Lennon in 2006 and Kenny James in 2009. Maybe the date in July was coincidental.

As she drove through the Kingsway Tunnel, she wondered if she had missed something in the file on Jake Hannigan's death. Did he really jump, or was he pushed? He'd left a suicide note: *Just can't take any more.*

No, that wasn't right. The words were right, but something about the way they'd been written . . .

Just can't Take any more
Just can't Take . . .
Just . . . Take . . .

'Fuck,' Sheridan said out loud, as it suddenly hit her. Maybe Jake Hannigan *hadn't* committed suicide.

CHAPTER 18

Tuesday 6 July

Sheridan and Anna were heading to CID, ready to brief the team. As they passed DCI Hill Knowles' office, the door suddenly opened and the chief constable appeared. Without stopping, he marched past them down the corridor and made his way downstairs.

'Nice to see you, too,' Sheridan said under her breath. A moment later, Hill came up behind them.

'Everything okay?' Sheridan asked her.

'Fine. Everything's fucking fine,' Hill snapped, overtaking Sheridan and Anna, before disappearing into CID.

'What do you think's going on?' Anna whispered.

'No idea. But the chief looked like Hill's just chewed his balls about something.'

As they walked in, Sheridan noticed Hill sitting at the back of the room with her arms folded.

She pinned up the photograph of the painting Jake Hannigan was working on just before his death.

'Right, everyone,' Sheridan began, 'take a look at this picture. What do you see?' She pointed behind her, but kept her own eyes front to watch as the team studied the image. Her phone pinged and she looked at the screen. A text from DC Ruth Manning from the cold-case team. Distracted, Sheridan read the message: *Nothing to report, but just checking in to see how you're doing.*

Sheridan quickly texted back: *I'm fine, thanks Ruth catch up soon*

She put her phone away and noticed that Dipesh had stood up and was now taking a closer look at the image she had shown the team. 'Not sure what we're looking at, boss.' He frowned as he continued to study it.

She stepped over to the picture, her index finger pointing to the words written across the painting. 'Just can't take any more. A simple message that could be construed as a suicide note. But look closer at the J and the T. The J is capitalised and if you look closely, I think the T is too. JT.'

One by one, the team made their way to the front of the room and the picture. Sheridan could tell by their faces that they weren't seeing it.

'I think it's just the way the blue lettering looks against the blue sky. I mean, it *could* be a capital T, but it's not really clear.' Rob grimaced.

Sheridan looked back at the painting. Was she seeing something that wasn't there? Was she making it fit? No, it wasn't clear, she accepted that, but it also *could* be there.

When everyone had returned to their seats, Sheridan looked around the room. Determined to push her theory, she continued. 'What if it wasn't Matthew who wrote this? What if he was pushed and then our man JT wrote the suicide note on the painting, leaving the same initials there as with the other two victims, Annette Lennon and Kenny James? Matthew's handwriting was compared at the time to the message he'd left on the painting, but it hadn't been conclusive due to the way the words had been written with a paintbrush, so . . .' Noticing a sharp change of atmosphere in the room, Sheridan stopped. All heads had gone down, except Hill's. Sheridan took a moment, and then realised she had mistakenly referred to Jake as Matthew.

She cleared her throat. 'I mean Jake . . . sorry.' She felt her face flush.

Now Hill stood up and made her way to the front of the room, briefly placing her hand on Sheridan's shoulder before looking at the picture. She stared at it for a moment before turning round. The awkwardness in the room was tangible; everyone in the room knew about Sheridan's brother and silently their hearts went out to her.

Hill brought them back to the here and now. 'I'm not saying you're wrong, Sheridan. But if that's not a capital T, then it might *not* be our suspect. I know you want it to fit with the others, and I get that, but I think we need more evidence than this to be sure there's a link between Jake and our mysterious JT.'

Sheridan nodded. 'Fair enough, but let's at least see if there's a link between these cases.'

Hill sighed. 'Okay.'

Sheridan aimed her comments at Dipesh and Bridie. 'Can you two look at Annette, Kenny and Jake. See if there's a link between them all, other than being socially awkward loners, and potentially shy. Did they know each other? Did they go to the same school? Anything.' She turned back to Hill. 'I'm going to re-look at Jake's death anyway, and if I can prove he was murdered, then we have three victims. Annette Lennon in 2006, Jake Hannigan in 2007 and Kenny James in 2009.' She breathed in before continuing. 'If we then find another victim from the twenty-second of July 2008, then we know this guy is striking every year on the same day.' She paused. 'And if that's the case, then we're dealing with a fucking serial killer. And, if we don't stop him, then he's probably going to kill again, in just over two weeks' time.'

After the briefing, Hill followed Sheridan back to her office, closing the door behind her.

'Are you alright?' Hill asked.

'Yeah . . . I'm fine.' Sheridan paused. 'So, what did the chief want? I saw him coming out of your office earlier.'

'Nothing important,' Hill replied. 'You seem distracted.'

'Do I?'

'You just said Matthew's name twice instead of Jake's. What's going on?'

Sheridan sighed. 'Andrew Longford is dying of cancer.'

Hill dropped her arms to her side. 'Oh. Bollocks. I'm sorry.' Her voice was now tinged with genuine empathy. 'Have the cold-case team made any recent progress?' she asked softly.

'Not really. I just . . .' Sheridan swallowed. 'I just want Andrew to go to his grave peacefully, knowing that Matthew's killer is behind bars. He's suffered too and now he's going to die of fucking cancer before I have the answers.' She chewed her lip and pulled herself back together. 'Anyway, thanks for asking.'

Hill perched herself on the edge of Sheridan's desk. 'This JT job is a heavy one, do you need to take some time out—'

'No.' Sheridan cut her off immediately. 'I just want to get on with it. So can we please get off the subject of Matthew?'

Hill nodded. 'Sure. Well, if that's the case then I'll say this.' She stood up, pinching her forehead between her thumb and fingers. 'I don't completely disagree with where you're going with Jake Hannigan's death. But, let's be careful that we're not seeing something that could be easily explained. Yes, the message could indicate a capital J and a capital T, but I don't want us to go off on one and start forcing things to fit our profile. It makes me the bad guy if I challenge everything, and I'm fine with that, but let's not give Jake's mum and sister a reason to start worrying about how he died. Jake's death was more than likely suicide, Sheridan. Even *you* must realise that. There is absolutely nothing to suggest foul play. I don't want Jake's family suddenly doubting everything about his death.'

'I'm not forcing it, Hill. It's there on the painting. "JT". As clear as bloody day.' Frustration seeped into Sheridan's voice.

'Alright,' Hill said, 'but let's be sure to not see something that isn't there. We need to stay focused. *You* need to stay focused . . .'

Hill stepped towards the door. Hesitating, she turned to Sheridan. 'I know you're distracted and I totally understand the reason why, and I also know I'm not very good at this sort of thing. I don't do emotion, but my door's always open if you need to talk.' And with that, Hill left.

Sheridan stared at the doorway, as if Hill was still there. Hill Knowles had lost her own family in a horrific car accident twenty-seven years earlier, on Hill's twenty-sixth birthday. Her husband and six-year-old twin girls had been wiped out when their car swerved to miss a cat on their way to pick up Hill's birthday cake. Hill hadn't been with them but had spent the last twenty-seven years wishing she had been. She had once told Sheridan, '*I'm angry, I'm angry at everything and I can't get past it. I should have been with them in the car, we should have all gone together. We were all so happy and now I wake up most mornings and think of a reason not to end it and the only thing that stops me is the job.*'

Hill hadn't spoken about her family since then. None of the team, except Anna, knew of Hill's story. The story that defined her. She presented herself as hard, emotionless, even, relying on self-preservation to get herself through the day. She distanced herself from everyone, threw barriers up whenever she thought someone was getting close to her. She refused to get emotionally involved, because to do that would put her at risk of having to go through loss again. And Hill Knowles could never let that happen.

Sheridan let out a heavy sigh. Hill had become the person she was now because of her own tragedy, and Sheridan wondered what she'd been like before her family had been killed. Would she ever see a different side to Hill? Sheridan closed her eyes. Everyone had a story to tell.

CHAPTER 19

Sheridan was studying the file on Jake Hannigan, scanning the pictures taken at the time. She grabbed her bag and headed to the door, just as Anna came out of the ladies toilet.

'Where are you off to?' Anna asked.

'Thurstaston Cliffs. Wanna come?'

Anna shrugged her shoulders. 'Sure.'

The torturous July sun was beating down on them as they made their way to the place where Jake Hannigan had spent his final hours. Anna stopped to catch her breath, while Sheridan forged on, having bet Anna twenty quid that she'd reach the spot first.

'Stupid bloody bet,' Anna mumbled to herself breathlessly, as she bent down and rested her hands on her knees. The muscles in her legs were screaming and she made a mental note that she really needed to get herself in better shape.

By the time she reached Sheridan, she had already found the exact location where Jake Hannigan had set up his easel and was standing motionless, taking in the scene.

'The next time you invite me to traipse along a cliff top in fifty degrees heat, remind me to tell you to fuck off,' Anna said as she puffed out her cheeks.

Sheridan grinned. 'It's only thirty degrees. Oh, and you owe me twenty quid.'

They stood for a moment, looking across to North Wales. It was a beautiful scene, and one that Jake had captured so perfectly in his final painting. Sheridan opened her bag and took out the photographs, holding one up, while Anna rested against a large rock. She didn't fare well with heights and even standing back from the edge was making her feel queasy.

A welcome gentle breeze blew against their faces as Sheridan looked down and then back to where Jake's easel had been positioned. Taking it in. She held the photograph up again. Anna watched as she stepped back and navigated around the rock, disappearing from Anna's view.

A few moments later, she called out. 'Anna, come here a sec.'

Anna reluctantly joined her. 'What?'

'Look at this.' She held up the image of his painting. 'Jake was set up in this spot when he was painting this picture, before he jumped. What do you notice?'

Anna looked from the painting and then across to Wales. She turned to Sheridan. 'What am I looking at?'

Sheridan nodded at the picture. 'Give it a second. You'll see it.'

CHAPTER 20

Sheridan and Anna walked into CID to find Hill leaning over Rob, looking at something on his computer.

'I need to brief the team,' Sheridan blurted out.

'You found something?' Hill straightened herself up.

Sheridan walked to the front of the room and stuck up the pictures she'd taken with her to Thurstaston Cliffs.

Pointing to the first picture, she said, 'This is the painting Jake was working on the day he died.' She pointed to the next picture. 'And this is where his easel was found.' Then she held up a third picture. 'There's a huge rock here obscuring his view, even if he was standing up, he couldn't see Wales from this angle, he would have to have been . . .' She indicated to another image. 'Here. About ten metres to the right.'

'What does that prove?' said Hill.

'If Jake had jumped, then why did he move his easel and all his painting equipment?' Sheridan's eyes hit everyone in the room. Confused faces stared back at her.

'What do you mean?' Hill had asked the question that was on everyone's lips.

'Okay. Jake was painting *this* scene.' Again, Sheridan pointed to Jake's picture. 'If he suddenly made the decision to jump over the cliff, he couldn't have done it from where he was situated. There are thick brambles just below where he was painting, so if he'd jumped, he would have just landed in the bushes and not gone all the way to the bottom, which means he would have survived with probably just minor injuries. So, he had to move to where there was a clear drop. If he was suicidal, why move all his equipment before chucking himself over? Why not leave the easel and everything where it was, find a place to jump and . . . well, jump? It doesn't make sense.'

'Maybe the bushes weren't there at the time,' Hill interjected.

'Yes. They were, I've looked at the scene photos.'

'Okay. But hang on,' Hill piped up. 'Why is that suspicious? It doesn't mean *anything*. Maybe Jake was painting the scene, moved the easel and all his stuff around the rock to paint from a different angle and then decided to jump?'

Sheridan pointed to the painting again. 'But if you look closely, Jake had already pencilled the outline of what he was going to paint next and he would have to have stayed in the position he was already in to do that. Something made him move around the rock.'

Hill frowned. 'Like what?'

'I don't know,' Sheridan replied. 'I just know that something's off.'

A silence enveloped the room as the whole team took in this new information.

'Alright,' Hill piped up. 'Everyone, get yourselves home. We'll pick this up again first thing tomorrow.'

CHAPTER 21

As Hill reached home, she noticed a car parked in her elderly neighbour's drive. Gloria lived opposite and rarely had visitors, apart from Hill. Gloria was a character, quick-witted and bright as a button. Their relationship was an unlikely one, but it worked. Gloria was the only person that Hill had really allowed into her life and their friendship had blossomed over the years. Mainly because Gloria was the one person in Hill's life who she felt surprisingly comfortable with. Hill adored her. Not that she'd ever tell Gloria that, of course.

Hill kept a protective eye on her, mainly because Gloria had a habit of inviting anyone into her house – whether they wanted to come inside or not.

Hill got out of her car and walked across the road, letting herself in with the spare key Gloria had given her. When they'd first met, Gloria had given Hill a spare key and told her to never bother knocking, it meant Gloria had to get out of her chair to answer the door and had described it as 'wasted energy'. She was greeted by Gloria's dog, Barney, who wagged his tail so hard he almost fell over. Hill bent down to pat his head, calling out to Gloria.

'It's only me,' she said, pushing the living room door open.

Gloria was sitting in her armchair and opposite, on the sofa, was her friend, Doreen.

Gloria looked up. 'Hello, Hill.'

Hill smiled and turned her attention to Doreen. 'Another new car?' She perched on the arm of the sofa.

'No, it's one my insurance company have lent me, mine got damaged in a hit-and-run.'

'Hit-and-run? Are you alright?' Hill asked.

'Oh, I'm fine. I wasn't concentrating and smashed into a bollard.'

Hill frowned. 'So . . . how was that a hit-and-run?'

Doreen glanced at Gloria, who picked up her teacup and hid a grin behind it.

'I hit the bollard and ran – well, drove – off before anyone saw me. So, it was hit and run.'

Hill put her hand up. 'You do know I'm a bloody police officer. Don't tell me any more.' She stood up to leave.

'Aren't you staying for a cuppa? We're celebrating.' Gloria lifted her cup in the air.

'Celebrating what?' Hill asked, crossing her arms.

'Our thirty-year anniversary.' Gloria air-clinked her cup with Doreen. 'We met thirty years ago today. Been best mates ever since.' She wiped a hand down her front, clearing away cake crumbs. 'Even if she hardly visits me, too busy whizzing around the world on boats and planes, spending her grandkids' inheritance.'

Doreen pulled a face before throwing a cushion at Gloria. 'I'd take you with me, but knowing my luck, your knackered ticker would probably give out and I'd have to bring you home in a box. And you know very well, my grandkids *want* me to spend my money. I'm not doing it out of spite. Honestly, I don't know why I bother. Thirty years I've been your mate and all you've done is moan. Miserable old cow.' She folded her arms in mock annoyance.

Gloria retorted, 'I have a mild heart condition and will probably outlive *you*, you old bat. And don't forget, I know all about your weird skin thing, so don't be bringing up my ticker problem.'

Hill frowned, curiously looking Doreen up and down. 'What weird skin thing?'

Doreen ignored Hill's question and replied to Gloria. 'You'd never have known about that if you'd been paying attention that day. I mean, who goes into someone else's doctor's appointment?'

Hill sat back down. 'What the hell are you two talking about?' she said, intrigued and mildly amused.

Gloria frowned at Doreen and then turned to Hill. 'I was in the doctor's waiting room and heard my name being called out – Gloria Wright. So, I went in to see the doctor, who was a new guy, and as soon as he closed the door, he told me to step behind the curtain and take my blouse and bra off. I thought it was a bit odd, because I was only there for a diabetes check-up. Anyway, I was behind the curtain, half naked, when he asked me to lift my boobs up and said that he couldn't see my rash. I was standing there, holding the girls in the air and I told him I didn't know what he was talking about. He then said that the rash seemed to have cleared up. I told him I didn't have a rash and he quickly checked his notes and asked me if my name was Doreen Wright, I told him, no, my name's *Gloria* Wright and was it okay if I put my clothes back on. Then, when I left, he called Doreen's name, so I knew what she had wrong with her. I waited for her to come out and told her what had happened. We had a giggle about it and went for a cup of tea and after figuring out we're not related, we decided to be friends. And that was thirty years ago today.'

Hill inhaled deeply and looked at the two women. She opened her mouth to speak, but a strange squeaking sound came out, and that set Gloria off. Doreen followed and a moment later, Hill did something she hadn't done for a very long time. She burst out laughing.

CHAPTER 22

Wednesday 7 July

As Sheridan walked into CID, the place was buzzing with activity. Hill had managed to draft in more DCs to help with the investigation. The whole team were working doggedly to find the link between Annette Lennon, Jake Hannigan and Kenny James. She made her way over to Rob Wills and sat next to him.

'How's it going?' she asked.

He leaned back in his chair. 'I'm just looking at a case from July, 2008. Family of four were found dead in their house, a remote place out at Crosby. Elderly couple and their two sons who lived with them. Cause of death was poisoning.' He turned to look directly at Sheridan. 'That's as far as I've got. I'm still reading up on it.'

Sheridan nodded. 'I vaguely remember that case. It nearly came our way but there was nothing suspicious. And it doesn't fit my lone victim theory. Keep looking at it though.'

She stood up, just as Anna walked in and headed towards her. 'Got the results back on the letter that JT sent in. Nothing. A partial print, but not enough for a match, and no trace of DNA.'

'Why doesn't that surprise me?' Sheridan shook her head. 'We're going to run out of time soon. We might only have two weeks to find JT and if we don't, he might kill another victim. What are we missing?'

Anna sat on the edge of Rob's desk. 'We're not getting very far with the JT initials. Dipesh and Bridie are still looking at any links between our three victims, but so far, they have nothing in common. Different ages, born in different areas of Liverpool, different schools, different doctors' surgeries. They haven't worked at the same place, they have or had different lives. Jake's family are very wealthy, Annette comes from a working-class family. And Kenny James was homeless.'

Sheridan absorbed the information. 'So, the victims are chosen at random. They're always alone and he wants to make their deaths look like suicide. He told Annette to tell us he's just making a point. But what point is he making? He talks in bloody riddles, saying we have the key to the answer and all that shit.'

They all remained silent for a moment, until Sheridan broke the silence. 'I need chocolate. Do you two want anything?'

'KitKat,' replied Rob.

'Same. Ta,' said Anna.

They shared a smile as Sheridan left. The vending machine had been fixed – much to Sheridan's disappointment – and was back to its usual working order – stealing her money and giving nothing in return. Anna and Rob didn't hold out much hope of actually getting what they'd asked for.

As Sheridan approached the vending machine, Andrea was walking away from it, holding up a Twix. 'People never cease to amaze me,' she said.

'What do you mean?' Sheridan asked, digging into her pocket for some change.

Andrea showed her a bulging leather wallet. 'This was just handed in by a sixteen-year-old lad. It's full of money and bank cards. It restores your faith in people, doesn't it?' She raised her eyebrows. 'Makes a change from some of the other weird stuff people hand in. Last week this woman rocked up with a carrier bag she'd found next to a lamppost. There were four bananas in it, and she thought maybe someone had dropped their shopping. She got right stroppy when I told her I couldn't take them, and she dumped them on the counter and walked out.' Andrea looked at the wallet in her hand. 'But then you get something like this handed in by a school kid. Anyway, I told him I was so impressed with his honesty, that I was going to buy him a bar of chocolate.' She nodded, smiled, and walked away.

Sheridan grinned to herself, before focusing on her nemesis. 'Right. Play nice and no one has to get hurt.' She dropped the coin in the slot and made her selection.

Then a thought crossed her mind, and she spun around.

'Andrea?' she called after her.

Andrea stopped and turned. 'Yeah?'

'You haven't had a key handed in recently, have you?'

Andrea frowned. 'No, *I* haven't, but I can ask Marcus. Is it yours?'

'No, it's not mine.'

'What sort of key?'

'I don't know. Any sort.'

'I'll check with Marcus and let you know.'

Five minutes later, Sheridan entered the CID office, triumphant that she had managed to purchase three chocolate bars without having to kick the living shit out of the vending machine.

The phone on Rob's desk rang and she answered it, while Rob and Anna tore their KitKats open.

'Hi Sheridan, it's Andrea. Marcus is on his break, but I checked the property log, and a bag was handed in a couple of weeks ago with a watch and a key inside.'

Sheridan took a bite out of her bar. 'Who handed it in?'

'Hang on.' The line went quiet while Andrea checked the log, and then Sheridan heard her chuckle down the phone. 'Sorry, I'm just laughing at this guy's name.'

'Why? What's his name?'

'His surname's Thyme, spelt T, H, Y, M, E, like the herb.' More chuckling.

'Oh right,' Sheridan replied, not seeing what Angela was finding so funny.

'Yeah, but get this . . .' Andrea continued. 'His first name's Justin. Justin Thyme, do you get it?' She laughed.

It was a joke, alright. But Sheridan didn't find it funny.

Sheridan and Anna flew down the stairs and made their way to the PEO. 'The fucker,' Sheridan said out loud. 'Justin Thyme. He's proper playing with us.'

'JT,' Anna said as she followed her into the public enquiry office, which was unusually quiet.

Andrea was behind the counter. 'I'm still laughing at his name. His parents must have had a wicked sense of humour.'

'Can I see the logbook?' Sheridan asked, ignoring the comment. Andrea handed it over, and Sheridan read the entry out loud. 'Tuesday twenty-second June. Small bag containing a watch and a large metal key. Handed in by Justin Thyme. Found under a bench on the Albert Dock, opposite Hale Street Police Station. No contact details left.' She looked at Andrea. 'Where's the bag now?'

'It'll be in the property office.' Andrea glanced down at the log. 'Marcus booked it in. At least I hope he did, he's a bit hit and miss.'

Just then, Marcus appeared at the door, swigging a can of Coke.

'Do you remember this bag being handed in?' Sheridan asked him.

'What bag?' he replied, stepping over to them and looking at the log. 'Yeah. Vaguely.'

'Did you book it into property?'

'Yeah.'

'Brilliant. I'll go to the property office and get it,' Anna said, making her way out of the PEO.

Sheridan continued questioning Marcus. 'What time was it handed in?'

He scratched his forehead. 'I can't remember, possibly lunchtime, maybe around one . . .'

'Okay.' Sheridan picked up the phone and dialled Rob's number.

'It's me. Can you get me the CCTV from the PEO on Tuesday the twenty-second of June? The whole day.'

She ended the call. Placing her hand on the log, she asked Marcus, 'Do you remember what the guy looked like? The one who handed it in? It's really important.'

Marcus flushed a nervous red. 'Not really. We're so busy in here and you deal with so many people, they all blur into one.'

Sheridan nodded slowly. 'His name's quite distinctive. Does it ring any bells? Justin Thyme.'

Marcus blew out his cheeks. 'I vaguely remember him saying his name made people laugh.'

'Did he say anything about the key?' Sheridan pressed on, speaking quickly.

Marcus shook his head, looking at the floor. 'I don't remember.'

Sheridan glanced down at the log again. 'There's no contact details, did you ask him for any?'

'I would have done, we're supposed to, just in case the item's not claimed and we can contact them to come in and claim it themselves.'

'How long do they have to wait before they can claim it?' Sheridan asked.

'Four weeks.' Marcus finished the dregs of his Coke and crushed the can with one hand.

'Okay, this is really important. Did he say anything about coming back to claim it?'

Marcus swallowed. 'I think, if I remember, that he did ask something about that, yeah. I asked him for his contact number, but he didn't want to give me any details. He just said he'd come back after the four weeks was up.'

'What sort of watch was it? I'm assuming it was a decent make for this guy to want to come back after the four weeks?'

'No, it was just bog-standard. Nothing special.'

Knowing that Anna was about to retrieve the bag from the property office, Sheridan decided not to question Marcus any further, for the moment. 'Okay. Well, I'm probably going to need to ask you some more questions once we've got the bag and the CCTV from that day.'

'Have I done something wrong?' Marcus asked, nervously.

Sheridan smiled reassuringly at him. 'No. It's fine.'

When she'd left, Marcus turned to Andrea. 'What's all the fuss about this bag?'

Andrea shrugged her shoulders. 'I don't know. But if DI Holler is interested in it, then trust me, it's important.'

CHAPTER 23

Sheridan was on her way back to CID when Hill met her on the stairs. She told Hill about the bag containing the watch and key being handed in and that Rob was downloading the CCTV from the PEO on the day.

'So, if it belongs to our suspect, we might actually get his face on camera this time,' Hill responded, the hint of a smile on her face.

'It *will* be our suspect. This is a real breakthrough.' Sheridan smiled back, looking behind Hill to see Anna coming up the stairs.

'Have you got it?' Sheridan asked, the excitement obvious in her voice.

'It's not there. It's been claimed,' Anna said, holding on to the banister.

'You're fucking joking.' Sheridan's shoulders dropped. 'When?'

'Last Wednesday.'

'Bollocks.' Sheridan rolled her eyes to the ceiling. 'Who came in to collect it?'

'I don't know. We'll need to ask the PEO staff and check the CCTV. The property office has only got a record that it was collected, not by who.'

Sheridan stepped past Hill and Anna and made her way back to the PEO. She was about to walk in when Marcus came out.

'I was just coming to see you,' he said. 'I've remembered that bag was claimed last week. I'm sorry, I'd forgotten all about it, but I remember now. Some bloke came in and—'

'And you've *just* remembered that?' Sheridan interjected, impatiently. 'It was only last week.'

'I'm really sorry.' He threw a quick glance back at Andrea, who was dealing with a member of the public, before turning his attention to Sheridan.

Keeping his voice low, he looked her in the eye. 'I'm struggling a bit in here. I didn't realise how much there is to do. So many people come in and there's so many forms and procedures. My head's battered by the time I get home. I'm really sorry if I've messed up.'

'It's okay.' Sheridan's voice softened. 'Let's look at the property log and you can tell me about the guy who collected it.'

Marcus described the male as white, medium height and build. He couldn't remember much else, other than he was around thirty years old. Sheridan asked him to describe the key, and he told her it was large, metal, and black in colour. The type you saw hung up decoratively on pub walls or in boxes of collectables found in antique shops. He couldn't recollect much more about it, but reiterated that the watch was cheap-looking and he couldn't remember if it was even working. The bag containing both items was small and made of black cloth. The man had told him that he'd lost the bag while walking towards the Albert Dock. He'd sat on a bench and didn't realise it had fallen out of his pocket. Marcus hadn't questioned his claim because the male had given the same location as the man who had handed it in. He also described the watch and key before Marcus had retrieved it from the property office.

'Okay. I'll probably need to speak to you again, once we've checked the CCTV. In the meantime, if you remember anything else, let me know. Straight away. Day or night.' And with that, Sheridan turned and abruptly left.

Andrea looked at Marcus. 'You okay?'

'I think I've fucked up. And I think DI Holler thinks I'm a dickhead.'

Andrea grinned. 'You *are* a dickhead.'

Rob spent the day looking through the CCTV in the public enquiry office from the time JT had handed the bag in, while Sheridan tasked Dipesh and Bridie to go through the day the bag was collected. The claimant had given the name David Smith and an address: 1 Damsen Drive, Liverpool. An address that the team had quickly discovered didn't exist. He had signed for the bag using his initials only.

It was almost 6 p.m. when Rob finally found the images of the suspect who had handed the bag in. He called over to Sheridan, who was at the whiteboard at the front of the CID office, updating information as it came in.

She pulled up a chair and leaned forward, Anna and Hill standing behind them as Rob played the recording.

The male had walked into the PEO, his head down, clearly to avoid the cameras. He was dressed in a grey suit, a newspaper tucked under his arm and a lidded coffee cup in his right hand. The public enquiry office was packed with people and the male, still keeping his face away from the cameras, appeared to glance over at the counter, where Marcus and Andrea could be seen dealing with members of the public. The male went to one of the benches that lined the walls and sat down. He placed his coffee cup on the table in front of him, opened up the paper and began to read. His face obscured the entire time.

They continued watching as he leaned forward, removed the lid from his takeaway coffee and took a sip, before licking the rim. Then, setting the cup down, he continued reading the paper.

'He keeps his head down the whole bloody time,' Hill said.

They all continued watching as the male eventually approached the counter and handed in the bag. A few moments later, he left the station and walked down the road. His head tucked down towards his chest.

Sheridan replayed the images and suddenly her eyes widened. 'Shit,' she said under her breath. 'That's Bobby Stover.'

'Who?' Hill squinted at the screen.

'Bobby Stover, the homeless guy who came in to report Kenny James's death.' Sheridan pointed at the screen. 'I don't mean he's our suspect . . . But look – that's him there, standing just inside the doors.'

They all carried on watching as Bobby Stover hovered in the doorway, before shuffling off down the road.

'What was he doing there at the exact same time JT handed the bag in?' Sheridan asked.

CHAPTER 24

As Sheridan walked through town looking for Bobby Stover, she sent a text to Sam: *Hi gorgeous, sorry but it's going to be a late one. Please eat and I'll text you when I'm leaving. Big kiss to you and Maud. xxx*

Sam texted back: *No worries. Just stay safe and we'll be here when you get home. I love you. xxx*

Sheridan texted back a single kiss.

After checking the places she knew Bobby generally hung out, and seeing no sign of him, Sheridan headed back to the nick. She spoke to the patrol sergeant and asked that beat officers keep a lookout for Bobby Stover. Any sightings were to be reported to her immediately.

The whole team stayed on late to work through the tasks that Sheridan and Hill had allocated. The DCs who had been drafted in on attachment had been tasked with obtaining the CCTV from local coffee shops and newspaper outlets to see if they could find footage of JT purchasing the coffee he'd brought into the police station on 22nd June. It was a long shot, but one they had to pursue if they were to find any clue as to who this guy was.

The CCTV from the PEO showed the newspaper headline was from several weeks before, so the chances of pinpointing where he'd purchased it from were frustratingly slim.

CCTV from outside the police station and surrounding streets was being scrutinised in the hope of capturing him in the area, and on his journey to and from the police station.

Officers were also checking CCTV from the previous Wednesday, the day the male calling himself David Smith had claimed the bag.

Rob was now back to checking through old cases where suicide was recorded, and it was just before midnight when he walked into Sheridan's office.

'That family we were talking about earlier, the ones out at Crosby in July 2008 who died from poisoning . . .' He paused. 'Accidental death. Not suicide.'

'Remind me of the circumstances, anyway.'

Rob went through the brief details of the case.

Freya and Brendan Barker were a married couple in their early seventies. They lived in a property set within a smallholding in a remote area of Crosby, Liverpool, with their adult sons, Neil and Douglas – thirty-year-old twins, both born blind and with severe learning disabilities.

The family were in financial difficulties but not heavily in debt. They had practically withdrawn from society, keeping themselves and their lives private. Rarely venturing out, they spent their days at home. Brendan tended to the land they owned, while Freya cared for their sons. They were relatively self-sufficient, with Brendan making rare visits into town only to stock up on essentials. Partly due to the constraints of looking after two disabled sons, and partly due to their belief that the Catholic Church had become too liberal, the devout Catholic family rarely even attended church.

The only person they had had any contact with was Freya's sister, Janet Vickers, who spoke to them religiously, once a month. After not being able to get hold of them, and having left several messages on the answering machine, she became concerned and travelled from her home in Cardiff.

She had arrived at the property at just after 1 p.m. on Monday 28 July and found the family dog – a black Labrador – on the front porch. The front door was unlocked, and as she entered, she was met with a putrid smell coming from within the house. She found her sister, Freya Barker, on the sofa. Her husband, Brendan, was upstairs in bed. Their two sons were in the bedroom they shared downstairs. Neil was on the floor, while Douglas was in bed.

Janet called 999 and police and ambulance attended. All four were pronounced dead at the scene.

The house was untidy and generally in poor condition. Human faeces and vomit were found on the floor in both bathrooms, as well as in the bed where Brendan was found. Both sons had soiled themselves. The sofa that Freya was lying on was in a similar condition, with Freya having vomited and defecated where she lay.

Post-mortems were carried out and all four were found to have died from ingesting highly toxic death cap mushrooms. This was only discovered when a bowl of them was located in the fridge and the remains of a meal in a bin. Urine tests were carried out on all four victims, and these proved that they had ingested the mushrooms. A search of the area showed them growing beneath a beech tree on the land.

It was concluded that the family had cooked the mushrooms by accident and consumed them without knowing they were toxic.

Death cap mushrooms are easily mistaken for non-poisonous varieties and even after cooking, they remain extremely poisonous to humans.

It was likely that the family had become ill approximately six hours after consumption. Symptoms would have included vomiting, diarrhoea, extreme dehydration and disorientation. Freya and Brendan were estimated to have died within twelve hours of consumption. Neil and Douglas, being younger and healthier, probably died within forty-eight to seventy-two hours after consumption. Post-mortem results showed all four family members had been deceased for approximately seven days before they were found on 28 July.

The family did not possess mobile phones.

There was no computer in the house.

The landline phone was checked, showing only monthly incoming calls from Janet.

No outgoing calls had been made to any number during the time the family were likely to have become ill. No calls to the emergency services, the non-emergency medical helpline, or any GP surgery.

The family GP was contacted, and she confirmed that the family had registered at her practice some twenty years earlier but rarely attended the surgery. It was believed that after their sons were born, Freya and Brendan Parker blamed their sons' disabilities on the hospital, claiming they were negligent. Medical records showed that the parents were made aware of problems with their unborn twins before they were born, but refused to accept it. As time had gone on and the boys grew older, the family had less and less contact with their doctor.

Freya and Brendan had previously fostered several children. When they last spoke, Freya had told Janet that one of their foster children, now an adult, had recently been in touch and visited them. Janet could not remember his name.

Apart from Janet, the family had cut all ties with relatives and had very few friends. Those they did have rarely saw them and hardly ever visited the house.

Verdict: Accidental death.

After Rob was finished, Sheridan stood up and reached down for her bag, getting ready to leave for the day. 'Doesn't sound like our other cases, nothing to suggest suicide. Anything else in July 2008?'

'Nope. Sorry,' Rob replied.

'The date fits but nothing else. They died on or around the twenty-second, like our other victims. But that's the only thing that links the deaths. I don't think this has anything to do with JT.' She switched off her laptop. 'What happened to the dog, by the way?' she asked.

Rob referred to his notes, smiling. He knew Sheridan was a huge animal lover. 'The dog was fine, Freya's sister took him.'

'Well, that's one good thing. Okay, well, I'm going to check in on the team and send everyone home. We'll crack on tomorrow.' She touched his shoulder as she left. 'Cheers, mate.'

Sheridan traipsed through half-empty streets, looking for Bobby Stover in town. 'Where are you?' she mumbled to herself, finally giving up and tiredly making her way home.

CHAPTER 25

Thursday 8 July

Sheridan was at the front of the CID office, standing next to Hill. Anna was sitting next to Rob. The room was packed to the rafters and tired faces looked up from their computers as Sheridan addressed them.

'Good morning, everyone. Right, let's get straight on.' She turned to Dipesh and Bridie. 'I know you and some of the team have been going through the CCTV from when our suspect, JT, handed the bag in on the twenty-second of June. What have you got so far?'

Bridie cleared her throat. 'I'm having trouble getting the recording to show on the screen for us all to see, but I can go through what we've got so far.' She read from her notes. 'At 11.46 a.m. we see him walking to the nick. He comes out of a side road, where there's no CCTV. He walks slowly past the nick twice, looking in briefly and then the third time, he goes in. He's holding the newspaper and coffee. He goes into the PEO at 11.50 and leaves at 12.12. He takes the same route when he leaves. As soon as he turns back into the side street, he disappears off CCTV. Now that we have a timescale, we're getting CCTV from any premises we can find and we're looking at streets around the area to see if we can pick him up on foot or in a vehicle. Throughout all the footage we've looked at, he keeps his head down the whole time. We get a bit of his profile, but not much else.'

'Okay, good,' Sheridan said. 'Now what about CCTV from when David Smith comes in on the thirtieth of June to *claim* the bag?'

Bridie checked her notes again. 'We've got some CCTV which shows him crossing the road from the Albert Dock at 13.30 hours. He waits outside the main doors of the nick for eleven minutes and goes in at 13.41. Just before he goes in, he checks his phone. The CCTV from the PEO shows him walking in and hanging back. There's only one other person in there, a woman who Andrea's dealing with. Marcus is on the phone. When Marcus finishes the call, David Smith approaches him, obviously we don't have audio, but they have a brief conversation. Marcus then gets what we can only presume is the property log and flicks through it before leaving the PEO. He comes back seven minutes later, after going to the property office, opens the bag, looks at the watch and key and hands them, along with the bag, to David Smith. It's hard to tell if David Smith shows any form of ID, as the image isn't too clear but we're getting it enhanced so we can get a better picture of what the watch and key look like. He then signs for it and leaves. He crosses back over the road and walks towards the Liver Building and keeps walking. He turns down a side road and we lose him from there, but we'll keep looking to see where he goes.'

Sheridan nodded. 'Okay, good work. As soon as you've got the recordings to work better, let me know and we'll all watch them.' She looked around the room. 'I want you all to familiarise yourselves with what these two guys look like.' She turned back to Bridie. 'Send the recordings to me as soon as you can, please.'

Bridie nodded. 'Will do.'

'We know that JT handed this bag in to us for a reason. He refers to the key in his note, so there's something about this key that gives us a clue. The watch? Well, JT gave the name Justin Thyme, so maybe the watch is a message that we're running *out* of time. We also know that he told Marcus that he'd come back in four weeks to claim it, if it wasn't already claimed by the owner.' Sheridan sighed. 'I think JT and David Smith must be working together. Does everyone agree?'

Dipesh raised his hand. 'I think they could be. If I were to hazard a guess, I'd say that JT dropped the key off on the twenty-second of June, then we released his picture on the thirtieth of June, which is the same day David Smith came in to claim the bag. So, I bet JT saw his own picture on the news, panicked that we're on to him and got David to get the bag back. JT knows he can't claim it himself, because he has to wait four weeks.'

Slow nods of agreement from around the room. Sheridan pondered for a moment. 'What time did the images of the man seen near the derelict building where Kenny was found and the man who attacked Annette go out on the news?'

Anna answered. 'First one went out at 9 a.m., then every hour until 13.00.'

'And David came in to get the key at . . .' Sheridan looked to Bridie for the answer.

'13.41,' Bridie replied.

'So, if Dipesh is right, JT sees his image on the TV, contacts David and he comes in to get the bag back.' She turned to Bridie again. 'Did you say that David Smith looked at his phone before he came into the PEO?'

'Yeah.'

'Okay. Well, then maybe David was waiting for a message from JT to tell him when to actually walk into the PEO. I think JT was probably watching the doors. He wanted it to be quiet in there, so

95

that David would be seen to quickly and not on the cameras for too long. What he didn't know was that Marcus was on the phone. So, he sent David in.' She paused. 'Which means that wherever he was watching from, he couldn't see inside the office.' She walked over to the window, pointing over to the Albert Dock, before turning back to face the team.

'Let's do some research on the buildings across the road. Anywhere that JT could have a good view of the doors to the PEO. And let's check out CCTV around the time that David Smith collected the key. Maybe we'll spot JT hanging around.'

After the briefing, Sheridan returned to her office.

She wanted to speak to Marcus again and show him the CCTV from the PEO, in an attempt to jog his memory. He was on a late shift, due to start at 12.00, so while she waited for him to book on, she started viewing the CCTV herself.

At 12.01 she called downstairs and summoned Marcus to her office.

Marcus watched the recordings closely, his leg shaking involuntarily under the desk. 'Yeah, I remember both of them a bit better now. The first guy definitely said he was going to come back when the four weeks was up. And I remember him joking about his name, saying people found it funny. The second guy was just a regular bloke really. Came in, said he'd lost a bag, a watch and a key, he described them and said he'd dropped the bag across the road from the nick and came in on the off chance it had been handed in. The bloke called Justin had said that's where he'd found it, so I knew David Smith was legit. Anyway, I got it out of the property office, he signed for it and left.'

'Did he show you any ID?' Sheridan asked.

'I honestly can't remember.'

'Did you ask him for any?'

'I'm really sorry, I probably did, but I genuinely can't remember.'

Sheridan sat back in her chair. 'Describe the key to me again. In as much detail as you can.'

Marcus described the key as he had before. About the length of his palm, heavy, made of metal and black, antique-looking.

'Did it have any distinguishing marks on it? Any initials engraved on it?'

'I didn't notice anything.' He scrunched up his face. 'Sorry. I didn't really pay much attention to it, it was just an old key.'

'What about the watch? Was it gold? Silver? What sort of strap? Anything you can remember.'

'I think maybe it had a metal strap, but that's really all I can remember.'

'Any engraving on the back?'

'No. I don't think so, I didn't look at it that closely.'

Sheridan moved her mouse and started typing, indicating for him to sit next to her. 'Okay, let's do some googling.'

Half an hour later, having trawled through hundreds of images, he pointed to the screen. 'I suppose that one's the most similar if I had to pick one.'

The key he'd indicated was just as described: the bow was circular, the barrel thick and the bit was a single piece of metal with no teeth.

Sheridan thanked him for his time and asked him to let her know immediately if he remembered anything else.

As he got to her door, he turned. 'Andrea said that if *you're* looking for this bag, then it must be important to you. I really hope I haven't messed up by handing it to that guy, David Smith.'

'It's fine. It's not your fault. But, yes, it's very important that we find it.'

Marcus nodded thoughtfully and left.

Sheridan printed off the picture of the key that Marcus had indicated and went to CID, heading over to the whiteboard, and checking no one was on the phone, she called for her team's attention.

'Right, everyone, just quickly. This is very similar to the key that JT handed in.' She pointed to the picture and indicated the sections of the key. 'This part, the bow, is circular, the barrel is round and thick, and this part, called the bit, is rectangular. The overall size of the key is about the length of your palm.' She noticed Rob was grinning broadly.

'What?' Sheridan asked.

'Bow, barrel and bit . . . didn't realise you knew so much about keys, boss. Been googling, have you?'

His comment sent an unrestrained wave of amusement around the room.

Sheridan deadpanned. 'I thought everyone knew about bows, barrels and bits.' She looked around; the team staring back at her clearly didn't have a clue.

'Oh. Just me then? Fair enough.' She singled out Dipesh. 'I need you to find me an antique key expert.' She glanced at the picture stuck on the whiteboard. 'We need to know what that key's for.'

After the short briefing, Sheridan returned to her office, finding that her desk phone was already ringing as she walked in.

'DI Holler.'

Rob's voice was at a whisper. 'Do you really know that much about keys?'

'No, of course not. I fucking googled it.'

CHAPTER 26

The day had been long and by the time Sheridan logged off and headed home, it was gone 7 p.m., and her head was thumping. As she drove out of Liverpool, her mind went through everything the team were working on. She allowed herself a smile as she recalled the team's faces when she'd described the sections of a key. *Bow, barrel and bit.*

'BBB,' she said out loud.

BBB. It reminded her of when she'd met Sam five years earlier and told her about Matthew's murder and Andrew Longford's description of the man who had been watching him and Matthew that day. All he remembered was that he had a beard, was wearing a brown coat and blue jeans. Sam had said 'BBB' to her: 'Beard, brown coat, blue jeans.' The acronym had stuck in Sheridan's head.

Plenty of things got stuck in Sheridan's head. Minute details, the supposedly insignificant comments people uttered. The tiny specks that no one else saw. Her head was swamped with the inquiry but, remembering what Andrew Longford was going through, she decided to visit him.

As she approached the Kingsway Tunnel, the traffic filing out of the city and over to the Wirral was building up. Coming to a standstill, she sent a text to Sam, telling her where she was going and that she wouldn't be long.

Pulling up outside his house, she noticed his car wasn't there and a sudden wave of panic washed over her. The thought crossed her mind that in the eleven days since she had last seen him, had he lost his battle with cancer?

She walked tentatively up the path and knocked on the door, which was opened a moment later by a young woman probably in her early thirties. The woman was slim, with neatly cut short hair, wearing blue trousers and a matching top.

'Hello,' the woman said, smiling warmly at Sheridan.

Sheridan introduced herself and the woman reciprocated. Her name was Nancy and she was visiting Andrew, having been allocated as his palliative care nurse. She let Sheridan in, and they joined Andrew in the living room. Sheridan had offered to come back another time, but Nancy insisted that she come in, as Andrew had already mentioned Sheridan in their initial conversations.

Sheridan struggled to find any words that didn't sound ridiculous in the circumstances. How could she possibly ask him, *How are you? What have you been up to?*

'Sorry I haven't been round, work's just crazy at the moment,' she said.

Andrew looked at Nancy. 'Sheridan's the police officer I told you about, she's a detective.'

Nancy smiled back. 'Yes, I know.' Her voice was like velvet – warm and calming. Perfectly matching her role.

Andrew turned his head slowly back to Sheridan. 'Nancy and I have been going through my affairs.' He reached for a glass of water and took a sip.

'Is there anything I can do to help?' Sheridan asked.

Andrew put his hand up, giving himself a moment. A rattling cough emanating from his chest. 'Sorry.'

Sheridan waited patiently while he recovered.

'No,' he said, once the fit was over. 'But thank you. We're pretty much there. I've sold my car. The house is rented, and I don't really have any money to speak of. It's just the allotment to sign over now and we're done, I think.' He coughed again. 'The funeral plan's in place.'

Sheridan felt her jaw tighten and she resisted the urge to throw her arms around him. Furiously fighting back tears, she tried to steer away from talking about his funeral. 'I didn't know you had an allotment.'

'Yes. My dad had it from the early seventies. We used to spend a lot of time there together when I was a kid. I took it over when he died. I haven't been there for a while.' He took another sip of water. 'It's the one near you, on Bidston Hill.'

Sheridan raised her eyebrows. 'Oh, yes. I know it, I drive past it every day on my way home. I've probably passed it when you've been in there.'

'Probably.' He ran a hand through his thinning hair.

They talked for an hour about everything other than the fact that he was dying. Matthew's name didn't come up and as Sheridan was leaving, she gently hugged him. 'I'll come and see you soon.'

Nancy showed her to the door, and they stood outside for a moment. Sheridan's voice was at a whisper. 'How long do you think he's got?'

Nancy pulled the door to. 'It's hard to say. He talks about you a lot. He told me about your brother, and Andrew knows you're trying to find his killer before he dies. I'm so sorry, I know this must be awful for you.'

Sheridan nodded once and handed Nancy her card. 'Please call me if there's anything I can do.' She took her keys out of her pocket. 'I'll come and see him as much as I can, work permitting.'

Nancy took the card and watched as Sheridan made her way to her car.

CHAPTER 27

Friday 9 July

Sheridan was at her desk watching the recording of JT leaving the police station after handing in the bag. She played the footage of him turning right and making his way back to where he'd come from. She noticed he walked slowly, with his head down the whole time, and at one point he stopped and hesitated, as if thinking about going back. Before he continued, a woman walked towards him, but he remained still. She glanced at him as she passed, then looked back once. JT didn't look up, but instead moved to his left, then again to his right before disappearing down the side street and out of view.

Sheridan thought back to the images of him at the railway station and near to the building where Kenny James died. The same strange walk.

She pulled up the recording of JT taken two days before Kenny James was found. As he passed one of the many disused buildings, she noticed a cat run across the road towards him. It reached the pavement, slowed to a walk and disappeared into an alleyway. It was at that moment she noticed JT step to the side, hesitate and then carry on.

She made herself a note: *He always changes his position when someone or something is nearby.*

She then watched the recording of David Smith when he came in to claim the bag containing the watch and key. He too kept his head down and while he was standing in the PEO, waiting to be seen, he looked jittery and uncomfortable. He was a little shorter than JT and slimmer, wearing grey tracksuit bottoms and T-shirt, white trainers and a black cap. Sheridan noted that he touched the visor at least twenty times during the time he was in there. 'You both keep your faces hidden,' she said to herself.

She reviewed the images of Bobby Stover as he hesitated by the door. She watched closely to see if he looked at JT, which he didn't appear to. Bobby waited by the door for around thirty seconds, before he left. 'What the hell are you doing there the same time as JT?' she said under her breath.

She looked at the entries made on the property log and made herself another note: *JT had declined to leave a phone number and gave the name Justin Thyme. A play on words. 'Just in Time'. David Smith also didn't provide a phone number, and he gave an address that doesn't exist. Which means David Smith is very likely not his real name.*

The names Justin Thyme and David Smith had been put through PNC and Intel, with no credible results returned.

She flicked back to the images of JT from the PEO. He was dressed in a grey suit and black, smart shoes. Unlike David Smith, he appeared calm and in control. She noted the slow, deliberate way he picked up the coffee cup and read the newspaper.

Dipesh appeared at her door, patches of sweat visible around the armpits of his shirt. The July heatwave was unrelenting and even with Sheridan's window open, the air outside was too hot to allow the breeze to cool her office down. She'd taken a permanent marker pen to the fan in her office and written on it: *I HAVE*

BEEN STOLEN FROM DI HOLLER'S OFFICE. RETURN ME IMMEDIATELY. One of her ongoing jokes with Rob.

Noticing that Dipesh looked a tad dishevelled, not his usual impeccable self, she said, 'New shirt, Dipesh?' and grinned.

'No.' He stepped into the office. 'But the trousers are new, do you like them?' He twirled around. 'My tailor is a genius . . .'

Sheridan jumped in. 'Hang on . . . you have a tailor?'

'Yeah. Of course I do. How do you think I get to look this smart all the time?'

'What's wrong with off-the-rack suits?'

Dipesh shrugged his shoulders. 'Nothing. But me and my wife have a deal. She can spend what she likes on Lego and I can buy myself a new suit every couple of months.'

'Hang on . . . your wife collects Lego?' Sheridan raised her eyes to the ceiling. 'I literally know nothing about you.' She looked at him. 'Anyway, what can I do for you?'

Dipesh held up a piece of paper. 'I've found a couple of local antiques dealers. I'm going out to see them now, hopefully they can shed some light on the key.'

'Great. Cheers, Dipesh.'

When he left, she moved her focus back to the recordings. The common assumption among the team was that JT and David Smith were working together. That theory made sense, but as she sat back and placed her hands behind her head, something in the back of her mind was niggling her – there was something that didn't add up. She closed her eyes. Thinking.

JT handed the bag in on the 22nd of June, saying he'd come back when the four weeks was up, if the owner hadn't claimed it. As he hadn't left any contact details, the only way he'd know it hadn't been claimed was to either ring the station or come in to claim it. Police release an image of him on the 30th of June, the same day David Smith comes in to claim the bag. JT told the public enquiry officer Marcus that he'd found the bag across the road from the nick, under a bench. David Smith tells Marcus that's where he'd dropped it.

Anna walked in. 'Sleeping on the job?' she said loudly.

Sheridan snapped her eyes open. 'Cheeky fucker. I'm thinking.'

'Yeah, right.' Anna sat down.

Sheridan leaned forward. 'Something's bugging me about the theory that JT and David Smith are working together, and I can't think what it is.'

Anna stretched her legs out in front of her and yawned. 'Well, if anyone can figure it out, it's Sheridan Sherlock.' She raised her eyebrows. 'I've just figured something out.'

Sheridan's eyes widened, waiting for what she hoped would be a revelation that would answer the niggling question in her head. 'What?'

'I call you Sherlock Holmes, your name's Sheridan Holler. Same initials.' She put her hand out, palm up. 'How weird is that?'

Sheridan shook her head. 'That's not weird. *You're* weird.' She pointed a finger at Anna.

'Anyway. I'm sure you'll figure out what's bugging you. You always do.' Anna crossed her arms.

Sheridan sighed. 'We know JT is playing with us, leaving initials at the crime scenes, telling us in his note that we've got the key to the answer and all we have to do is fill in the gaps. Then he gets David Smith, or whoever he really is, to take the key and watch back before we realise he's handed them to us. It's like he wants to give us clues to catch him, but then takes some of them away. Like when he wrote his initials on the wall where Kenny James was found and then scraped them off. Handing us this bloody watch and key and then getting David Smith to get them back.'

Anna got up and perched herself on the edge of the desk. 'Can I just say, you look knackered, mate. I mean, we're all knackered but you look like you haven't slept for a month. Are you alright?'

'I'm fine.'

'I know Andrew Longford's playing on your mind. How's he doing?'

'Not brilliant. I wouldn't be surprised if he's only got a few weeks.' She cleared her throat. 'And the cold-case team are no nearer to finding Matthew's killer. So, I have to resign myself to the fact that Andrew will die not knowing the truth about who killed Matthew . . . and that fucks me off.' Sheridan shook her head slowly, trying to move aside her feelings about Andrew.

Anna leaned across the desk and put her hand over Sheridan's. 'What can I do? Seriously mate, what can I do?'

Sheridan smiled. 'You can find out who JT is and bring him in.'

Anna smiled back. 'I meant to ask you, did you find out what the chief was doing here the other day?'

'No. I asked Hill, but she wouldn't say.'

Sheridan was emerging from the ladies toilet when Dipesh walked past her in the corridor, carrying a tall brass fan.

'Where did you get that from?' she asked, following him into CID.

'One of the antique shops I've just been to. They sell all kinds of cool stuff.' He set the fan down at the front of the office and plugged it in. It silently whirred round, sending a much-needed breeze across the office.

'Very nice,' Rob said, getting up from his chair and walking over to admire the new addition to the office. 'How much was that?'

'Forty quid.' Dipesh beamed proudly.

Sheridan narrowed her eyes at him. 'I hope you've got some news on this key, Dipesh. Or else I'm confiscating that fan.' She eyed the fan and thought it would look rather nice in the corner of her living room. A mental image came into her head of Maud lying in front of it, keeping cool in the sweltering heat.

'I have.' Dipesh turned the knob up on the fan and stood in front of it, lifting his arms up and turning slowly around, letting the air flap his shirt.

Sheridan crossed her arms, trying not to smile. Dipesh looked like a clumsy, sweaty ballerina, spinning around in a flat-footed pirouette.

He continued to turn as he spoke, much to the amusement of the team. 'I went to a couple of places, and they said that without the actual key it would be hard to say what it would have been used for. But one dealer said he knows a guy called Cameron John, who's not only a top antiques expert but what he doesn't know about old keys isn't worth knowing. I've been to his shop in London Road, but it's closed, so I've rung him and left a message asking him to call me urgently.'

Sheridan listened, a little distracted by the fan, admiring its brushed brass stand and subtle elegance. It really was a thing of beauty. 'Okay. Good work,' she said, noting how quiet the fan was as it oscillated.

Her phone pinged with a message from Sam: *Hi beautiful. Joni and Newman are coming over later for dinner and a few drinks, thought you could invite Anna and we can have a chilled night? I can order a take-out. Good idea or bad idea? xx*

Sheridan texted back: *Bloody brilliant idea. Should be done soon. xx*

Sam responded with a: *yay xx*

Sheridan sent a single kiss and stepped over to Dipesh, who stopped spinning and lowered his arms.

'How much do you want for the fan?' she whispered.

'It's not for sale.' He puckered his lips and shook his head.

Sheridan leaned her face towards his. 'I'll give you sixty quid. Cash.'

'Nope.'

'Seventy?'

'Nope.'

'Think of all the Lego your wife could buy with the money,' she said, before turning to leave.

Dipesh dramatically clasped his hands to his face. 'Oh, I hadn't thought of that.'

Sheridan turned back, expectantly. 'So, is that a yes?'

'Nope.'

Sheridan left, mumbling to herself about stupid people not knowing a good deal when they saw one.

CHAPTER 28

Juliet Hannigan was on her bed, flicking through a magazine, when her mobile pinged with a text from her father Frank: *Hi princess, how are you?*

She texted back: *I'm fine Daddy. You ok?*

He replied: *Yes, all good. I was just checking if you'd heard any more from that detective who was asking about Jake?*

Juliet messaged: *No, nothing.*

Frank: *Bit bad of her to come around asking questions and then leave you hanging. Jake's been on my mind since you told me about the police and I've not been sleeping very well. It just brought back so many memories of the day he died and I wondered how you were feeling? I'm worried about you.*

Juliet: *I'm ok Daddy, I have been wondering why she came round though, I told her when she was here that I know they wouldn't send a detective inspector round to talk about Jake if there wasn't more to it, but she just said they were checking nothing was missed.*

Frank: *Like what?*

Juliet: *I don't know.*

Frank: *Well I think it's a bit off that she's not explained exactly why she's looking into it. But that's the police for you.*

Juliet: *Yeah. Don't worry Daddy, I'm sure it's nothing, just the police with nothing better to do.*

Frank: *I'm sure you're right. Anyway, better go. I love you princess.*
Juliet: *I love you too.*

Frank Hannigan dropped his phone on the table and put his head in his hands. 'Fuck.'

Sheridan and Anna walked into the house, both ready to down a large glass of wine. Sam and Joni were out in the back garden with Maud and Joni's cat, Newman, lying under the garden table asleep in the sweltering heat.

Joni and Sam had met when they were seven. Joni had got herself into a fight at school – which she had been losing – when Sam jumped in to rescue her. They had been inseparable ever since, with Sam periodically reminding Joni that she probably saved her life that day. And Joni periodically replying that there was a distinct chance her life hadn't actually been in mortal danger.

Sam and Joni were best friends – like Anna and Sheridan – and all four women had formed a close bond, often sharing evenings at Sheridan and Sam's house and putting the world to rights. Usually while a little drunk.

They all sat outside under the large umbrella that gave them shaded respite from the evening sun. Maud got up, stretched and made her way through the conservatory and into the kitchen, where she slurped water from the bowl that Sam was keeping religiously topped up, ensuring Maud and Newman didn't become dehydrated. After managing to flick most of the water on to the kitchen floor, Maud collapsed in a dramatic heap. A moment later, Newman joined her, and they lay, mirror imaging each other, paws touching.

As the sun finally disappeared, the four women settled in the living room.

'Are you both back at work tomorrow?' Sam asked, re-filling Sheridan and Anna's glasses.

'Yeah. We're under the cosh on this case, so I don't think we'll be having any days off for a while.' Sheridan tilted her head. 'Sorry, sweetheart.'

Sam smiled. She knew the demands of Sheridan's job and how their life basically revolved around it. She'd understood that from when they first got together.

'Don't be sorry. You've got to catch this nutter,' Sam said as she topped up her own drink.

Sheridan often shared the details of cases she was working on with Sam, and Sam knew that whatever was spoken of within the walls of their home stayed there. She didn't pry, but just listened, letting Sheridan vent when she needed to and share her triumphs when a case was solved. Or her anguish when it wasn't.

Joni, on the other hand, although as trustworthy as Sam, was as nosy as fuck and asked questions about every case, in great detail.

Although Sheridan had no concerns about Joni discussing what was said outside of the safety of her home, she kept the detail short.

'So, Sam tells me this suspect of yours killed a homeless guy,' Joni said, her words slurred from the copious amounts of wine she'd consumed.

'That's right,' Sheridan replied with a grin, which she hid behind her glass. *Here she goes*, she thought.

Joni put a finger in the air. 'I was thinking. Maybe if you told me all about it, I could help. I mean, I knew a homeless guy once, I used to pass him on my way home and give him money. He said he used it to buy seed for the pigeons and one of them, called John, used to sit on his hand.' She looked at the three women in turn, who were failing to hide their amusement.

'Pigeon food, my arse,' said Sam. 'You were probably feeding his drug habit.'

Joni frowned and eased herself up from the sofa. 'Well, that's what he told me. Anyway, who wants another drink? I do. I'll get the bottle, you lot just relax.' A rambling Joni rather unsteadily stepped into the kitchen. 'Then you can tell me about this case and I bet I can solve it. Should have been a copper, me. Not a carer. PC Summers reporting for duty,' she mumbled to herself. 'I bet I'd look fucking fit in the uniform as well. I'd have fellas drooling all over me. Sexy Summers they'd call me.'

Suddenly, there was a loud clinking noise and Joni called out, 'Oh. Bollocks. Sorry.'

Sheridan got up and went into the kitchen to investigate, spotting water all over the floor.

Joni pulled a face. 'Kicked the cat's water over.' She looked down at the large puddle. Then she looked at Sheridan with a drunken smile on her face. 'At least it wasn't wine. I'll get some kitchen roll and clean it up. You relax. It's not a problem.'

Sheridan held her arm gently and ushered her into the living room. 'I'll sort it. You go and sit down. You'll never find the kitchen roll.'

Joni sat down. 'It's in the cupboard under the sink,' she called, winking at Sam who shook her head in amusement. She loved drunk Joni.

Anna got up to help Sheridan, who was on her knees, soaking up the water, when she suddenly stopped.

'You okay?' Anna asked, noticing Sheridan staring at the floor. She didn't answer, but slowly got up.

'I need to check something.' Sheridan walked back into the living room and flipped open Sam's laptop that was on the sideboard.

Joni watched her. 'Am I in trouble?' She put her hands out in front of her. 'It's a fair cop, Officer. Get the cuffs on and we'll be off to the clink. I just need a wee first.'

Sam burst out laughing as Joni unsteadily made her way upstairs. Sam followed her to make sure she got up there safely.

'What are you looking for?' Anna asked as she watched Sheridan quickly typing.

'Rob found a case from July 2008, where a family of four were found dead in their house. Parents and two adult disabled sons. They'd eaten poisonous mushrooms and had been dead for a week before the woman's sister found them.'

'And?'

Sheridan was reading as she spoke. 'And they had a pet dog, who was left outside, with no way to get in, but was fine.'

'So?'

'So, if the family had all been dead for a week, how did the dog survive?'

'It probably found something outside to eat.' Anna pulled up a chair and sat next to Sheridan, who pointed at the screen.

'It says here that a dog can survive without food for around three to five days, sometimes a little bit longer, depending on age etc.'

'So, it *could* have survived for a week,' Anna said.

Sheridan looked at her. 'Maybe. But it also says a dog can't survive without water for more than three days. It was July, don't forget. So, if the dog was fine when it was found, then who looked after it if everyone was dead?'

CHAPTER 29

Saturday 10 July

Sheridan and Anna had made it into work early, mainly because of Sheridan being keen to check out her theory about the dog. Anna went out to buy them a coffee while Sheridan waited for the team to arrive in CID, checking the file and finding the report from the first attending officers. She flicked through, looking for the reference to the dog. The report showed that when Janet Vickers had arrived at the property, the dog was outside. To ensure the dog did not enter the house, she placed it in her car. It appeared to be in good health and the attending officers confirmed that it did not require veterinary intervention. Janet confirmed that she would take the dog back with her to Cardiff.

Sheridan sat back just as Hill walked in.

'Morning,' Hill said, dumping her briefcase on a desk. 'You're in early.'

Sheridan told her about the poisoning case and her thoughts about the dog. Hill sat, cross-armed and stoic, as Sheridan went on to say that she wanted to look at the scene pictures and see if there were any signs that JT had been involved.

After carefully listening, without interruption, Hill finally spoke. And she didn't hold back. 'Explain this to me. What has any of this got to do with our suspect? So, the dog survived on scraps, and maybe there was a water supply outside, maybe a trough or something.' She raised her hands in the air. 'Maybe he lived off the vomit that was found all over the fucking house. Dogs eat *anything*. Even their own shit.' She sounded exasperated at what she'd been hearing. 'And, I repeat, what has this got to do with our other cases? Please explain, because right now I'm starting to wonder if you're going so far off-piste on this one, that you've finally flown over the fucking mountain.'

Sheridan took a deep breath. 'The dog had no way of getting into the house. I just find it odd that it was outside all that time in hot weather and wasn't dehydrated—'

Hill interjected. 'There's a million places it could have found water. And, like I say, dogs eat anything, they're survivors.'

'I still want to look at the scene photos,' Sheridan pressed.

Hill sighed heavily. 'Come on, Sheridan. None of it fits our other cases. And you've said all along that JT is targeting *lone* victims. This was the only potential suss death on Merseyside in 2008 around the same date as the other deaths, so you're trying to shoehorn it in. This is a family of four, in their own home, who sadly ate poisonous mushrooms that were growing on their land. There was a bowl of them in the fridge, for fuck's sake. It was a simple case of accidental death. Tragic, yes. Murder, no.' Hill swiped her briefcase off the desk.

Sheridan stood her ground, her voice slightly raised, but calm. 'I'm still going to get the scene photos . . .'

'Stop looking for things that aren't there, Sheridan.' Hill turned to leave.

Sheridan shook her head. 'I'm not looking for things that aren't there, Hill. I'm making sure that we check out every *single* potential death that could come back to JT. And I won't stop until I find them, even if it pisses you off.'

Hill turned back to face Sheridan. 'It doesn't piss me off. I'm just trying to keep you focused on the deaths that we *can* pin on JT and not go flying off trying to find ones that don't fit. You're all over the place . . .'

'No I'm not. I'm doing my fucking job.' Sheridan crossed her arms.

Hill took a deep breath. 'I had a call last night via the control room from Jake Hannigan's sister, Juliet. Let's just say she was a little bit annoyed.'

'About what?'

'About the fact that you rocked up at her house recently, asking all sorts of questions about Jake, about the day he died and about her father, Frank. She said that since then she hasn't heard from you, it's been playing on her mind and she's not sleeping.'

'Fine. I'll give her a call.'

'You don't need to. I covered for you . . . and she didn't want her mum finding out that she'd called, she just wanted to say her piece.'

'I don't need you covering for me. I'm quite capable of dealing with Juliet. I had a legitimate reason for visiting her and her mother and I'll visit them again if I feel it's necessary. There's nothing wrong with my bloody decision making . . .'

Hill took a deep breath. 'Alright. I'm going to say it. I know you've got a shitload of stuff going on in your head right now. This case, and the fact that your brother's best friend is dying. You want Matthew's case solved before Andrew Longford succumbs to his cancer, I get that. But, and you can tell me to fuck off if you want, I think your head is all over the place and right now, you're trying to make things fit that just *don't*. You're an exceptional police officer and I trust your judgement implicitly. But you need to focus, because otherwise, this case is going to beat us and if you're right and JT is killing people on the same day every year, then we've got twelve days to catch him. But maybe he doesn't kill every year, maybe he was in prison in 2008, who knows. So please, stop wasting time looking for things that aren't there.' Again, she turned to leave.

'Fuck off with your lecture about my brother.' Sheridan stabbed a finger into her own chest. 'I've been dealing with his murder for over thirty years. Has it ever come between me and my job? No. I give a hundred and ten per cent to every case I work on, in spite of the fact that Matthew's killer is still out there. I have never taken my eye off the ball.'

Hill put her suitcase back on the desk. 'I know that.'

'Do you? Because it doesn't fucking sound like it to me. I don't expect you to agree with every theory or idea I have. And, yes, I go off on one sometimes, but I do it because I don't ever want to miss something that we should have picked up on. That hunch, that gut feeling that tells me that something isn't right. Haven't I proved myself to you enough times?'

Hill inhaled deeply. 'Yes. You have.' She hesitated before continuing. 'And I'm going to tell you something now. I've been having meetings with the chief lately and do you know why?'

Sheridan didn't respond.

'Because he's asked me to head up a new team that's being put together at Potters Road nick. He wants me to be the DCI in charge of a team of detectives from the old Major Investigation Team. Which would mean that you'd be working with another DCI here and I wouldn't be working with you any more. Do you know what I told him?'

Still no response from Sheridan.

'I told him no. I told him no, because I don't want to work with anyone else. He went fucking mental and threatened all sorts of shit, but I still said no. So, don't you ever doubt how much I respect you and the way you work. Ever.'

A silence hung between them and for a moment they just looked at each other. Sheridan felt tears prick her eyes. She knew that Hill had an enormous responsibility being the DCI. It meant she had to make difficult, sometimes impossible decisions. She worked long, relentless hours, without comment or complaint. Sheridan knew Hill had to fight tooth and nail to draft in officers when a case started to spiral, and they needed boots on the ground. And in the midst of her workload, Hill also fought her own private demons. Losing her family so tragically and then being told that she had an inherited cancer gene that put her at high risk of developing breast and ovarian cancer. Having undergone a precautionary double mastectomy, Hill lived with the constant reminder of the cards that life had dealt her. A tough and unfair hand. She had told Sheridan about the cancer gene and the subsequent surgery when they'd first started working together. Neither were facts that she shared openly, but facts that made her the person she was. The person she had become through circumstance, not of her own choosing. Even when they butted heads, they shared a mutual respect that was impenetrable, solid and unspoken. Until this moment, Hill had never been so effusive about her respect for Sheridan, and Sheridan felt a strange warmth towards her. Even if Hill still annoyed the shit out of her with her bluntness.

'Are we done?' Hill asked, her voice soft and low.

'Yes,' Sheridan replied, her tone mirroring her boss's.

'Good. Then I'll do as you asked, and I'll fuck off.' She gave Sheridan an exaggerated smile. 'And we're . . . good?' She tilted her head.

'We're good.' Sheridan smiled.

'Oh. By the way, you've got egg down your top.' Hill pointed at Sheridan's chest. 'Best you sort it out before everyone sees what a fucking tramp you are.' Hill gave her a genuine grin.

Sheridan in turn pointed at Hill's chest. 'Your tits are wonky.' She shook her head and waved a finger. 'Best you sort them out before everyone sees what a fucking tramp *you* are.'

Hill deftly adjusted her bra inserts, picked up her briefcase and headed for the door.

'I'm still going to request the scene photos from the 2008 poisoning job,' Sheridan called after her.

'I know you are,' Hill called back.

They'd made their peace.

At that moment, Rob walked in, followed closely by Dipesh. Sheridan felt relief they hadn't entered any earlier to see the discord between her and Hill.

'Morning, boss,' Rob said, heading to the front of the room to fire up the brass fan, in preparation for what was forecast to be another punishingly hot day. 'Anything new happened?'

'Yeah. I need you to get me the scene photos and the file for the family who died of poisoning in 2008.'

Rob sat at his desk and logged on to his computer. 'Really? You think it's suss then?'

'I'm not sure.'

'What's that on your top?' Rob asked, squinting at her.

'Egg,' said Sheridan, before leaving the room to go and get changed.

CHAPTER 30

After a short briefing, the team continued working through their tasks. Dipesh left another message with the antiques dealer, Cameron John, before trying to locate a home address for him. If the key handed in by JT really was pertinent to the inquiry, then they had to know what it was likely to have been used for.

Sheridan had stressed to DC Bridie Sexton that locating David Smith was imperative, as he was the last person known to have had the key in his possession – unless, as the team suspected, he was working for or with JT. If that was the case, then locating both men was a matter of absolute urgency.

If Sheridan's theory was right, they only had twelve days before the killer would claim another victim. All his previous victims had apparently been chosen at random and they had – so far – found no connection between Annette Lennon, Jake Hannigan and Kenny James.

Sheridan stood at the window in her office, looking out towards the Albert Dock. The streets below were still fairly quiet; a steady but not solid flow of traffic had started to build up. Shoppers and weekend workers headed into the city centre. Any one of them could be next. Randomly selected by JT. Anyone, from any walk of life, doing any kind of job, just going about their day, could be dead in twelve days' time if she didn't find the killer. Was Hill right? Should she doubt her own conclusion that all the victims were alone? What about the family of four who died in 2008? Were they victims, too?

The MO didn't fit in that case. The cause of death didn't fit. There was no suspicion and certainly no evidence that it was suicide, or rather, had been made to look like suicide. Was she relying too heavily on the date? July 2008? She had to find something else. She had to find proof that JT had been responsible. That he'd left his mark at the scene – the same mark he'd left at other scenes. Maybe Hill was right, maybe he wasn't killing them every year, maybe in 2008 he was in prison. Or maybe he was abroad.

She closed her eyes, trying to stop a thousand questions of doubt filling her head. Bobby Stover's face came to mind. This had all started with him, with his insistence that Kenny James couldn't have killed himself. If Bobby hadn't come forward, then Sheridan and her team would never have known about JT. But was Bobby involved somehow? Why had he been in the PEO the same day that JT had handed in the bag? And more importantly, where the hell was Bobby now?

She switched off her computer and headed into town.

She spotted Bobby sitting on a bench near one of the escalators in Liverpool One shopping centre. A paper cup was on the floor at his feet. He was engrossed in a book and Sheridan noticed how battered it was. The cover was missing, and the pages were yellowed with age.

He looked up as she approached and smiled at her. 'Hello.' He glanced around quickly, before lowering his voice as Sheridan sat beside him. 'Do I call you Inspector, or Sheridan, or Holler? I don't want to say out loud that you're a police officer.'

Sheridan smiled back. 'You can call me Sheridan. I've been looking for you.'

'Oh. What for?'

The area was starting to fill with people and Sheridan didn't want to talk to Bobby out in the open. She stood up.

'Do you want to get some breakfast?'

'You still got that fancy bread that I had last time? The one with the seeds on it.'

'I meant a proper breakfast in a café, not at the custody suite.' Sheridan grinned. 'My treat.'

'Oh. Right, yeah, nice one. If they'll let me in.' Bobby picked up his cup and emptied out the lone pound coin, shoving his book into his pocket, before standing up.

They found a quiet seat in a nearby café, ignoring the scrutiny from the staff. They clearly looked like the odd couple. Sheridan, tall and head-turningly stunning, wearing suit trousers and a white shirt, her shoulder-length hair flicked back off her face, while Bobby was still dressed in the yellow tracksuit bottoms he'd been given out of the custody suite stock, over two weeks earlier. Sheridan noticed that he didn't smell quite as bad as he had when they'd first met.

She wanted to ask him about being at the police station at the same time as JT but had to pick her moment. If Bobby was involved, which Sheridan prayed he wasn't, she'd have to bring him in. She took a sip of coffee, choosing her words carefully.

'I meant to thank you,' she said.

'For what?'

'For coming into the station that day and telling me about Kenny.'

'I *had* to. I knew something wasn't right. Are you looking into it then?'

'Very much so.'

'That's really good.' He drank his tea. 'I thought you'd all laugh at me and not take me seriously. I came in a few times before, but there was always so many people in that I bottled it.'

'I thought you'd only come in once before, a few days before I spoke to you.'

'No, I'd been in quite a few times, but usually only got as far as the door. Then the first time I plucked up the courage to ask to speak to someone, there was some nutter in there preaching about God, so I gave up and left. And then the day I met you, I just couldn't leave without telling someone, I knew I had to do it, I had to tell the police about Kenny and so I gave me head a wobble.'

Sheridan smiled. *So that's why you were there the same day as JT*, she thought. Silently relieved that Bobby wasn't involved. But she'd still get Dipesh to check out the CCTV from the PEO. Just to be sure.

'Where do you sleep at night?' she asked, while Bobby tucked into a full English.

'If I get enough money, I stay in a hostel. It's ten pound a night, but you get a bed, a shower and hot food.'

'And if you don't?'

'Then I sleep in a doorway.'

She studied his face, while he chatted about his life. He was on a methadone script and felt like he was finally being weaned off the drugs that had controlled him. He talked about wanting to reduce his prescription gradually and sorting his life out. He dreamed of renting a room in a house where there were other people. He wanted to get a job, anything to do with cars. Although he'd never learned to drive, just the feel and look of them made him happy. He loved to read and had visions of filling his spare time surrounded by books. They were simple dreams and all of them were within his reach. He had a kind face, if a little ragged round the edges from

123

too many years of being battered by the elements. And an insatiable appetite for heroin.

She noticed he had kind eyes that sparkled when he smiled. His beard had started to grow back, and he'd decided to let it. As she listened, Sheridan realised she found him quite enchanting.

'What kind of books do you like reading?' she asked.

Bobby scratched his chin. 'Promise you won't laugh?'

'I promise,' Sheridan replied, intrigued as to where this was going.

'I like romance novels,' he whispered. 'I like to read about how people get together and find love. Romance novels pretty much always have happy endings.'

Sheridan didn't laugh, but she did smile. 'Is that what you're reading now?' She nodded at his pocket, and he pulled out the paperback, placing it on the table.

'Yeah. But I don't tell people I read romance, I say it's science fiction, makes me sound less of a dweeb.' He lifted the novel up. 'That's why I tear the covers off.'

And that was the moment that the soft spot she had for Bobby Stover grew a little bigger.

She told him how they were looking into Kenny's death and explained that she could give him little detail about the inquiry. Bobby understood and asked very few questions. She asked him if he'd ever been to the derelict building where Kenny's body was found. He told her he hadn't. Sheridan wanted to know if JT meant anything to him. It didn't ring any bells with Bobby and neither did the image of JT that she showed him.

It was clear from his reaction that although he was delighted the police were taking him seriously, he was somewhat surprised.

'When you're homeless and look like I do, people don't see beyond that. They just see a tramp who they look down on. A piece of scum that's lazy and has chosen to beg for money instead of going out to earn it. I get why they think that, but we all make mistakes in our lives and all I want to do is put that right. I'm forty tomorrow, and I really need to sort my shit out.'

Sheridan smiled. 'Happy birthday for tomorrow.'

'Cheers. Might celebrate with a bottle of champagne.' He laughed at his own joke.

'Please tell me you're not going to rob a bottle.'

Bobby grinned. 'No. I haven't shoplifted since that time I did it for Kenny.'

Sheridan's phone rang, it was Anna. She answered quickly. 'Yes, mate?' She stood up and walked to the back of the café, out of earshot.

'You okay to talk?' Anna said.

'Yeah, go for it.'

'Bridie's found David Smith on CCTV, after he picked up the bag. He's in a car and we've got the index number.'

'That's bloody brilliant. I'm on my way back.'

After discreetly handing Bobby a ten-pound note to pay for a hostel that night, she assured him that she'd keep in touch. He didn't have a mobile phone but told her he was easily found around Liverpool One, where he spent most days.

After walking back to his bench with him, she hurriedly made her way back to the nick. Adrenaline pumping through her body.

Were they about to find David Smith? And if so, was he then going to lead them to JT?

CHAPTER 31

Sheridan took the stairs two at a time. When she walked into CID, Bridie, Hill and Anna were huddled around a computer.

Sheridan joined them. 'What have we got?'

Bridie turned the screen towards her and replayed the CCTV of David Smith leaving the nick. She then moved forward to the recording from a different camera.

'Here.' Bridie pointed. 'He walks down this side road and goes off camera. Then, two minutes later, he's seen pulling out in a car. There's a car park at the end of that road, so he must have parked there before he came in to claim the bag. We're still checking CCTV to see where he goes after he leaves the car park.'

'Have you checked CCTV to see if JT is hanging around?' Sheridan asked.

'Yeah, but we can't spot him.'

'Okay. So, who does the car come back to?'

'Kyle Crane. Lives at an address in Bootle. He's known on PNC. Burglary in 1994 and handling stolen goods in 1998.'

Sheridan put her hands behind her head and sat back. 'So . . . if this Kyle Crane is the guy who came in to claim the bag, we need to speak to him as soon as.'

Hill turned to her. 'How do you want to play it?'

Sheridan sat forward. 'We need that bag. And we need to know if David Smith – aka Kyle Crane – and JT are working together.' She took a breath. 'If JT is going to take another victim on the twenty-second of July, then we're running out of time.' She looked at the three faces before her. 'I think we should pay Kyle Crane a visit. Just ask him about the bag and see what he says. We'll get his mobile number and check his phone records. I want to know who contacted him just before he walked into the PEO. We'll put a marker on his phone and see where he goes and who he contacts. Maybe he'll lead us to JT that way. I don't want to spook him, but we *really* are tight on time.'

Before they left to visit Kyle Crane, Sheridan tasked Dipesh, Bridie and two other DCs to check the CCTV from the PEO, hoping they'd find Bobby Stover on camera, confirming his account that he had visited there several times.

'And if he's not on there?' Dipesh asked.

'Then we've got a problem and Bobby's involved with JT,' Sheridan replied.

Sheridan drove slowly up the road where Crane lived. Spotting his car parked outside, she carried on past, parking by a row of garages.

She was out of the car first, followed by Anna. An unmarked police vehicle remained at the top of the road. Inside were two uniformed officers and Rob Wills, a precaution that Hill had insisted on.

Sheridan glanced at Anna before taking a deep breath and knocking on the door.

It was answered by the male they'd seen on CCTV – the one who'd come in to claim the bag under the name David Smith. He was taller than he appeared on the recordings, his short, cropped hair was wet and droplets of water ran down his bare chest. A grey pair of tracksuit bottoms hung around his waist.

Sheridan took the lead and kept her voice light and as un-police-like as she could muster.

'Hi, sorry to bother you. Is it Kyle?' She held up her warrant card, smiling.

'That's right.' He squinted at her ID.

'We're from Hale Street Police Station. It's nothing to worry about, we just need to check something, and we think you might be able to help. Can we come in for a second?'

'It's not really a good time right now. What's it about?' Kyle Crane said in a thick Scouse accent.

'We'd rather speak inside, if that's okay. It will literally take two minutes.'

Crane hesitated, before he opened the door fully and let them in.

The house was immaculate, if a little sparse. In the living room was a small sofa, a coffee table to the side and an old wooden cabinet against the wall, which was full of trophies. In the middle of the room was a set of weights, with a towel hung over them.

'I see you work out,' Sheridan commented as they stood in the room. 'And the trophies, are they yours?'

'They're my son's. He's a swimmer.' Kyle's response was cagey.

'He must be pretty good.' Sheridan stepped over to the cabinet. 'How old is he?'

'Seven. He lives with his mum. We're separated.' He watched Sheridan as she read the engravings on the trophies. 'Sorry, you said I might be able to help you with something?' he asked impatiently.

Sheridan turned to face him. 'Oh. Yes, you lost a bag recently and went into Hale Street Police Station on the thirtieth of June to see if it had been handed in.'

Kyle shifted his standing position and folded his arms, taking his time before responding. 'No idea what you're talking about.'

'You gave the name David Smith.'

Kyle's face flushed a little. 'Oh, yeah. So . . . what about it?'

'There was a key and a watch inside. Can we have a look at them?' Sheridan said.

'I haven't got them. I sold them.'

'Why did you sell them?'

'Didn't want them any more.'

'Who did you sell them to?'

'Some bloke in a pub in town.'

'What bloke? Which pub?'

'Can't remember which pub. And it was just some bloke. We got talking and he said he liked to collect old things. I showed him the key and he liked it, so I sold it to him. He took the watch as well, it was just a cheap one I'd had for a while.'

'How long had you owned the watch for?'

'I don't know. A few years.'

'Can you describe it to me?'

Kyle shook his head. 'It was a watch. Metal strap, that's it.'

'Were there any engravings or markings on either the key or the watch?'

'No. Don't think so.'

'How much did you sell them for?'

'Tenner.'

'Do you have a picture of them?'

'Why would I have a picture? What's this all about?'

'Where did you get them from in the first place?' Sheridan asked. *Don't fucking say 'some bloke in a pub'*, she thought.

'Some bloke in a pub,' Kyle replied. 'Seriously, what's this about?' He unfolded his arms.

'What was the name of the bloke in the pub?'

'No idea. Just a bloke. I don't know who he is. Why do you need to know?'

'I'm very interested in that watch and key, where they came from and where they are now.'

'Why?' He looked between Sheridan and Anna. 'What's so important?'

'I'm afraid I can't tell you that.'

Kyle shrugged his shoulders. 'Well, I'm sorry, but I can't tell you anything more, I swear down I don't know where they are now.' He glanced at the clock on the wall. 'Look, I need to get ready, I've got to get to work.'

'Why did you give a false name when you collected the bag?'

Kyle shrugged his shoulders again. 'I'm a private person. I don't like giving my details out. Look, I've really got to get to work.'

'What do you do for a living?' Sheridan asked.

'This and that. Just odd jobs for people.'

Sheridan took her card out of her pocket and handed it to him. 'That's my card. Kyle, please ring me if you think of anything, or remember anything about the guy you sold them to.' She took her pocket notebook and flipped it open.

'What's your mobile number?'

Kyle hesitated. 'Why do you need my number?'

'In case I need to speak to you again.'

'I don't know it off by heart.'

Sheridan spotted the mobile on the coffee table and picked it up. 'Call my number.'

Kyle bit down on his bottom lip and snatched it out of her hand. He read Sheridan's number and dialled it. As soon as it rang once, he cut the call off.

Sheridan smiled. 'That's great. Thank you for your time, Kyle. It's much appreciated. We'll let you get to work.'

He showed them to the door and closed it as soon as they were outside.

'Fuck,' he said under his breath.

He scrolled through his contacts and dialled the number.

'Hello?'

'What the fuck have you got me into with that bag?'

'What do you mean?'

'I've just had the bizzies at my door, asking all sorts of questions.'

'Shit.'

'Yeah. Shit. You said all I had to do was say the bag was mine and then you'd take it from there. I don't fucking need this. How did they find out my name and where I live?'

'I don't know.'

'Did you tell them? Have you grassed me up?'

'Of course not.'

'Well, we're both in the shit then. Because if they know who I am, then they'll come for you and trust me, I'll tell them everything. I'm not taking the hit for you.'

'Don't threaten me, Kyle.'

'Threaten you? I'll fucking batter yer.'

'No you won't. Look, where's the key and the watch now?'

'They're going in the Mersey.'

'No. Don't do that. I want the police to find them. It's important.'

'Not to me it isn't.'

The line went dead.

CHAPTER 32

Sheridan and Anna drove away from the house.

'Lying twat,' Sheridan said as they signalled to the unmarked car that they were heading back to the nick.

'What did you make of him?' Anna asked.

'As I said, he's a lying twat. He hasn't sold them for a tenner. He's in on it with JT, and they're fucking with us. We need to get his phone records – then we'll find JT. They *must* be in contact.'

'What do you think it is about this key and watch that made JT want us to have them?'

Sheridan took a moment to answer. 'I'm wondering now if it's just a red herring. Look how much time and effort we've put into trying to find them, when we could be concentrating on other things. Maybe they mean nothing, and JT just wants us to run around like a bunch of dickheads, while he merrily plans his next killing.'

Half an hour later, they were back in CID, where Sheridan briefed the team and tasked Dipesh with obtaining Kyle Crane's phone records as a matter of urgency, and placing a marker on his phone and car. Dipesh updated her that he'd left a further message for Cameron John to call him.

At the end of another long day, Sheridan was packing up her things to head home when Anna came into her office and flopped down on to a chair.

'Do you want to come to ours?' Sheridan asked. 'Joni's staying for the weekend, thought we might have a few drinks tonight. We've certainly bloody earned it.'

'I'd love to but I'm seeing Steve tonight. Just for a quick drink.'

Sheridan found herself hesitating about giving her response. She'd always hoped that the day Anna had thrown Steve out was the end of the relationship. Her doubts that he had hit Anna had remained with her and she couldn't shake them off. Sheridan had previously spotted the traits of controlling behaviour in Steve. The time he'd cut his wrist, knowing full well that Anna would find him. It had become more and more obvious that there were problems in the relationship, especially when Anna had confided in Sheridan that she was pregnant, a fact she'd hidden from Steve, along with her intention to terminate the pregnancy. Sheridan had accompanied her to the hospital for the procedure and made Anna promise that she would never, ever tell Steve. All the signs had been there. The relationship was a dangerous one and Sheridan silently prayed that Anna and Steve would never reconcile. So, now, as always, she chose her words carefully. 'Are you going to mention this time that you saw his profile on that dating site?'

Anna yawned. 'No. I don't think so. Because then he'll know that I've been on it as well.'

'So?'

'So, I don't want him to know.' She pushed herself wearily up from the chair. 'It's none of his business.'

As Sheridan drove home, her mind went over the investigation until she was going round in perpetual circles. She thought about her heated conversation with Hill. The thing she admired about Hill was that even when they came to blows and disagreed on something, Hill never dwelled on it. She just moved on, like Sheridan. A smile crept over Sheridan's face as she recalled what she had said to Hill that morning. There was a time, certainly early in her police service, when telling your boss to fuck off would have landed you in knee-deep shit. Things had changed, but it wasn't the rule books that came into play with her and Hill. It was their relationship. It suddenly dawned on Sheridan that she knew nothing about Hill's private life.

This made her recall talking to Dipesh, realising how little she knew about him, certainly not that his wife collected Lego.

She mentally went through what she knew of her team. She started with Rob. She'd met his wife, Jo, who was profoundly deaf, several times and they'd been out to dinner in the past. She thought about Bridie and remembered that she lived with her mother and had a dog, whose name escaped her.

Christ, Sheridan thought, *you don't know enough about the people you spend half your life with. You need to fix that.*

Her thoughts drifted back to Hill. Did she have friends who just rocked up at a moment's notice and stayed for as long as they wanted to, like her and Sam? Friends she could laugh with and whose company she loved. Did Hill have anyone? Someone she could talk to, someone she trusted. Or did she go home to an empty house and eat alone, sleep alone, stare out of the window and lose herself in the memories of her husband and twin daughters?

'Shit,' Sheridan said under her breath, feeling an overwhelming sense of guilt that she had the love of Sam, the love of her parents, Joni and Anna, where Hill apparently had no one.

She turned on to Bidston Hill and pulled over, before dialling Hill's number.

'Yes, Sheridan?'

'Hi, Hill.' Sheridan suddenly and inexplicably felt ridiculous and awkward. 'I erm . . . I was wondering if you'd like to come over to ours sometime. You know, for dinner or something.'

'You're feeling guilty about telling me to fuck off, aren't you?'

Sheridan put her head down and chewed her lip. 'Little bit.'

'Well, don't. And thank you for the offer, but no thank you.'

'I'd really like it if you did. And it wouldn't be out of guilt, it would be because . . . I like your company.'

'Have you been drinking?'

'No. I haven't been bloody drinking. I'm not even home yet.' Sheridan slowly shook her head.

'Fine. I'll be there shortly – I'll bring my guitar and we can sit round a fire and sing "Kumbaya".'

'Why do you have to be so sarcastic and awkward? I thought it was a nice gesture and—'

'Goodbye Sheridan. See you tomorrow.'

Hill had ended the call and Sheridan sat for a moment, a smile creeping across her face.

She looked to her left and realised she was parked by the allotment that Andrew Longford had mentioned. She wondered how many times she'd driven past it, not knowing that Andrew had a patch there. It had taken her several years to finally pluck up the courage to knock on his door. She always feared that he wouldn't want to speak to her about Matthew. So many times, she had parked down the road looking at his house and trying to force herself to walk up his path, knock on his door and introduce herself. She had known Andrew when they were children, but after Matthew died and the police investigation wound down, the contact diminished.

She glanced back at the allotment, tears stinging her eyes as a cloud of sadness descended over her. Memories came flooding back of the many times when Andrew and Matthew had happily played football together in the park before heading home at sundown. She could hear the joyful echoes of laughter from their childhood.

Life had been simple then, simple and uncomplicated. The innocence of children. An innocence so cruelly ripped apart the day her brother was murdered. Everyone around her had a cross to bear, her parents, losing a son, herself, losing her brother, Andrew losing his best friend and now quietly and bravely facing the end of his own life. Hill, her family also destroyed, all those years ago.

Families wrecked by events outside of their control, and yet they all continued to try and function in their everyday lives, quietly striving to act normal among those fortunate enough to have never been touched by tragedy. She slowly smudged the tears away, closed her eyes, and silently prayed to a God she had often struggled to believe in. She prayed for Andrew in his darkest hours. For her parents, and the hope that the truth would soon come. And for Hill – that one day she would find the courage to dismantle the defensive wall that she hid behind.

Shaking away dark thoughts, she headed home.

CHAPTER 33

Steve was already in the pub when Anna arrived. He kissed her on the cheek, then went to the bar to get her a drink.

On her way to meet him, she'd thought about broaching the subject of seeing his profile on the dating website. She'd battled with herself: should she just come out and say what she'd found? Be upfront with him? Or be more subtle and try to establish if he'd met someone?

Had seeing him on there made her want him back? A part of her still loved him, and she couldn't shake that off. Part of her despised what he'd done to her – the times he'd hit her and then cried in her arms, begging for forgiveness. She'd hidden what was happening from everyone, even Sheridan.

The day after she'd seen his face and profile on the dating site, she'd cancelled her own account.

Steve returned to the table, set the drinks down and sat opposite her, taking a sip of his tonic water.

'So, how have you been?' he asked.

'Yeah, good. You?'

'Really good. Life's good.'

As they chatted, Anna noticed how cheerful he seemed. Almost animated in the way he spoke, like he was putting on a show for her. Then, without warning, the words tumbled out of her mouth.

'So, are you seeing anyone?' She lifted her glass and instantly felt her face flush.

'No. Not really. You?'

She shook her head. 'No. I don't have time at the moment, work's mental.' She tried not to look at him. 'What do you mean by "not really"?'

'Oh. Well, there's just a woman I met recently. I think she likes me, and we might be going out for a drink at some point.'

'How did you meet her?'

'I joined a dating website. It's a bit weird and there are some proper cranks on there, but she seems okay.'

'Good for you.' Anna smiled.

Steve nodded at her. 'You should join one. You'd be snapped up.'

'Yeah, maybe . . .'

There was a silence between them and for a moment Anna felt like she was on an awkward first date with a stranger. She and Steve may not have had the perfect relationship, far from it, but they always talked, never running out of conversation. But suddenly, in this moment, no words passed between them.

Steve excused himself and went to the toilet.

When he returned, he asked her about the case she was working on. When they were together, she wouldn't have hesitated to spill the details of her job. But things had changed now, the trust she bestowed on him had gone. She told him it was a complex murder, but she wasn't allowed to talk about it.

As soon as she said it, the atmosphere between them changed.

'There was a time you'd tell me everything about a case you were working on.' Steve finished his drink and set the glass down purposefully. 'Sorry. It just makes me realise that we really are just mates.' He looked her in the eye. 'I just want you to know that although we'll never be together again, you can still trust me, Anna. I hope you know that.'

'Yeah,' she replied, with absolutely no conviction in her voice.

Steve stood up. 'Do you want another drink?'

Anna shook her head. 'No thanks.' She looked at her watch. 'Actually, I'd better go.'

After watching Anna drive away, Steve sat in his car, smiling proudly. He was playing her, and in his mind, he was winning. He'd recognised the look on her face at the mention of him being on a dating site. It was the reaction he'd hoped for. He'd joined several popular sites, hoping that maybe Anna would join one and see his profile. He'd waited and watched for two months, every night, scrolling through the pictures, ignoring any requests he'd had from other women to 'chat'. He didn't want to chat, he wanted Anna's face to come up. When it did, he knew the likelihood was that she would see his profile.

The way she'd questioned him tonight about meeting someone else sealed it for him. Anna wanted to know if he'd met anyone. It was perfect. His plan was working. He'd play on it now, each time they met – elaborating on the mystery woman. He'd tell Anna they were seeing each other, and things were going well. But there was no other woman and there never would be. He wanted Anna. And he was going to get her back. He'd kept up the pretence that he still wasn't drinking, always ordering a soft drink whenever they met up. Proving to her that he had changed.

Seeing her face and profile had made him sick to the stomach, even though he'd hoped to find her. So, she was ready to date again? Ready to put herself back out there?

There was not a chance in hell that he was going to let that happen.

Starting the engine, he pulled out of the pub car park and headed home. He needed to look at the screenshots of her profile again. And he needed a drink.

◆ ◆ ◆

As she walked into her empty house, Anna wished she'd taken up Sheridan's offer of spending the evening with her, Joni, and Sam. Instead, she opened the fridge and poured herself a glass of wine.

A cauldron of emotions enveloped her. Part of her was glad that Steve was moving on and had met someone, albeit only casually for now.

As she stood in the kitchen, the only sound to keep her company was the ticking of the clock.

She picked up the phone to call Sheridan. She *had* to tell her. She had to confide in her best friend that she was worried. Worried that Steve had met another woman, and maybe he'd do to her what he'd done to Anna. Lose his temper and hit her. How could she live with herself if that happened? She was a police officer; her job was to fight and prevent crime, to protect people. But how could she stop Steve from ever hurting someone again?

She needed to speak to Sheridan. She dialled her number and almost immediately cut the call off. Sheridan had enough on her plate, what with the inquiry into JT and the fact that Andrew Longford was dying. How could she put more on her?

Maybe when the inquiry was over and they'd caught JT and locked him away . . . maybe then she would confide in her.

She laid the phone on the kitchen table, picked up her glass of wine and made her way up to bed.

CHAPTER 34

Sunday 11 July

After making a pact with herself to find out more about her team, Sheridan sidled nonchalantly up to Dipesh.

'Hey mate. How's your wife's Lego collection going?'

Dipesh frowned and caught a glimpse of Bridie looking up at them from her desk.

'It's going . . . fine.'

'Good. So, you've been married, what . . . ten years now?' Sheridan picked up a pen and casually tapped it against her palm.

'Fourteen,' Dipesh replied, eyeing Sheridan suspiciously.

'Good, that's good.' She nodded.

'What's this about, Sheridan?'

'Nothing, just making conversation. Right, I'll let you get on.' Sheridan stood up, stretched her back and headed over to Rob who was on the phone. When he'd finished the call, Sheridan put her hand on his shoulder and sat down.

'I meant to ask you, how's Jo doing?'

Rob rubbed his chin and yawned. 'She's fine. How's Sam?'

'Fine. So, anyway, back to Jo, is she still erm . . .' Sheridan struggled to think of a question.

'Deaf? Yes, she's still deaf.' Rob flicked a look at Dipesh, who was grinning.

'No, I meant, is she still happy in her job?'

Rob sat back and put his hands behind his head. 'Which job? She's got two.'

Shit, thought Sheridan. 'Both of them, is she still happy in . . . both jobs?' she asked.

'Yes, she is.'

Sheridan stood up. 'Good. That's good to hear.'

Rob winked at Bridie. Sheridan didn't know that Dipesh had previously shared Sheridan's comment – that she knew so little about him – with the team. They'd discussed it and knew that this would play on Sheridan's mind. So they'd all waited for the day when she would try to fix it. And it was clear to them all that today was the day.

Bridie kept her head down as Sheridan approached her, pulling out a chair and sitting down opposite.

'So, Bridie. Bridie, Bridie, Bridie. How's everything?'

Bridie smiled. 'Good thanks.'

'How's the dog?'

'The dog died.'

Sheridan leaned forward slightly. 'Oh shit. I'm so sorry. Are you alright?'

'I'm fine thanks. It was four years ago.'

Sheridan swallowed. 'Oh.' She cleared her throat. 'How's your mum doing?'

'Good.' Bridie nodded.

'Is she still . . .'

'Catholic? Yes . . . as am I.' Bridie casually fondled the gold Maltese cross hanging from the chain around her neck.

'Good . . . That's good.' Sheridan tapped the desk and stood up. 'Right then, better get on.' She headed for the door.

As she reached it, she heard a high-pitched squeaking noise coming from behind her and turned to see Rob, whose face was bright red, tears streaming down his cheeks. Sheridan looked at Dipesh and Bridie in turn, who were both sucking in their cheeks, trying to keep straight faces.

'What's so funny?' Sheridan crossed her arms.

Rob composed himself before answering her. 'It's okay that you don't know everything about us. We still love you.'

CHAPTER 35

Monday 12 July

Sheridan's phone rang just as Rob walked into her office.

'Sheridan, it's Dipesh. We've checked through the CCTV from when Bobby Stover said he visited the nick. He's on there six times. On all but one occasion, he hovers in the doorway. On the twentieth of June, he comes in, stands in line, gets to the counter and speaks to Andrea. He then goes to sit on one of the benches next to a guy in beige trousers, with a beard and blue-rimmed glasses, but changes his mind and leaves. I checked and he didn't come back in. A minute later, some bloke walks in and points to the ceiling. He looks weird . . . But anyway, Bobby didn't return.'

'Yeah, the weird guy was some nut-job banging on about God. That's the day Bobby came in and left before I got to speak to him,' Sheridan said. 'What about the other times?'

'He just hovers by the door and doesn't go in. We've also got coverage from before and after the visits and he's always alone.'

Sheridan sighed with relief that Bobby's account panned out. 'Brilliant. Cheers, Dipesh.'

'And just to let you know I got a call from that antique key expert, Cameron John. I'm going out to see him now.'

'Great. Let me know what he says.' She glanced out of the window as a July rainstorm battered down outside.

She ended the call and gave Rob her full attention as he handed her a heavy box file. 'Got the scene photos from the family who died of poisoning. I've had a really quick look through the first few. Pretty horrible scene. I've sent you the digital copies as well.'

She opened the file and lifted some of the pictures out. The first one showed the outside of the property, which looked pleasant enough, but they soon got pretty grim.

As she sifted through them, she came to the ones that showed Freya Barker deceased on the sofa. She was a slight woman with pure-white hair, her face contorted and grey.

'We need to go through each of these carefully.' She looked up at Rob. 'If this was JT's work, then we're looking for a sign that he was there.' She put the photos back in the box file, and followed by Rob, she carried them through to CID.

As she walked in, she beckoned Bridie and Anna over and together with Rob, they each took a roughly equal share of photographs. And slowly, painstakingly, they looked through them.

Two hours passed, and with only a handful of photographs left to check, none of them had found the JT sign they were looking for. But Rob did spot something and pointed it out to Sheridan.

'What do you think that's for?'

The picture showed a solid wooden handrail to the right of the porch door. Secured to it was a thick metal ring.

'It could have been used to tie something to?' she said, studying the image. 'The report said that the dog was outside on the front porch when the victim's sister arrived. Maybe it was tied up.' Sheridan sat back, staring at the photograph, which she laid on the desk in front of her. 'And look closely . . . that's its water bowl. And it's practically full.'

Rob frowned. 'The family had been dead for a week before they were found. The doors were closed so the dog couldn't get inside the house, but if it was tied up outside for a week then how did it get anything to eat and how did its water bowl stay topped up?'

'My thoughts *exactly,*' Sheridan said. 'Unless, when Freya's sister Janet got there, she filled the water bowl.' She stood up. 'I need to get hold of her.'

CHAPTER 36

Sheridan was in her office with Anna with the door closed. She'd dialled Janet Vickers' number and put the call on loudspeaker.

'Hello?'

'Hello, is that Janet?' Sheridan asked, keeping her voice light.

'Yes.'

'Sorry to bother you. It's nothing to worry about. My name's Sheridan Holler, I'm a detective inspector based in Liverpool. Have you got a few minutes? I just want to have a chat with you about your sister, and what happened to her and her family. I know it must be extremely difficult to talk about, so I won't keep you long.'

'Do you need me to come to the station?'

'Oh, no. I wouldn't expect you to make the journey here. But if you'd prefer to talk face to face, I can come to you. Are you still living in Cardiff?'

'Yes. But I'm staying at my sister's house at the moment. I've been trying to sort the place out, before I sell it. There have been so many problems with probate and other things.'

Sheridan looked at Anna and put her thumb up. 'You're at the house right now?'

'Yes.'

'Can we come and see you?'

'Of course.'

Sheridan's eyes lit up and after she'd ended the call, she stood up. 'What a result. Now we might get some answers.'

Sheridan and Anna turned off the country lane and pulled into the track leading up to the Barkers' house. It was set within two acres of land, half a mile from Crosby beach. Sheridan stopped the car and took in the scene before her; the rain was easing a little and a rainbow arched itself serenely over the field before them. Two outbuildings stood to the right of the property. Wooden structures in need of repair.

'Hell of a big place for an elderly couple to look after, especially with two disabled sons,' Sheridan commented as she drove on up towards the house.

'Maybe they paid someone to help out?' Anna replied, undoing her seat belt as they pulled up next to Janet's car.

'I doubt it. They had a few financial problems.' Sheridan got out and walked with Anna towards the porch, spotting that the wooden handrail and metal ring were still there.

Sheridan was about to knock on the door when it was opened by a woman in her early seventies. Long grey hair rested in a neat cut around her shoulders. She was slightly built, with a weathered face, wearing smart but casual trousers and a short-sleeved top. By her side was a paunchy black Labrador whose tail was wagging furiously, making him look like he was doing a little happy dance.

'Inspector Holler?' Janet smiled.

'Yes. And this is my colleague, Detective Sergeant Anna Markinson.'

Janet ushered them in. 'Are you okay with dogs? Bouncer can be a bit over-friendly.' She kept hold of Bouncer's collar and walked him through to the kitchen, his paws tip-tapping on the tiled floor.

'No, he's fine,' Sheridan reassured her and secretly hoped that Bouncer would come and sit next to her.

The kitchen was bare, apart from a large wooden kitchen table, around which were four mismatched chairs. On the wall hung a small wooden cross. In the corner was a large upright fridge freezer, next to a 1950s-style dresser. On the shelves were a pile of cloths, and bottles of various cleaning products. The place smelt strongly of disinfectant.

Janet offered them both a drink which they declined. She was bright and chatty, which reassured Sheridan and Anna that they wouldn't have to drag information out of her. Without prompting, she dived straight in and told them all about her sister and the events leading up to the day she had found the family in the house.

In their younger years, Janet and Freya had never been particularly close. They had had little contact up until 2006 – two years before Freya died. Janet never had children and when her husband passed away, she found herself isolated and alone. And that's when she picked the phone up one day and called her sister. It took several months for the atmosphere between them to clear but as time went on, their conversations became more regular.

Janet had only visited the family once, in 2007. Freya and Brendan weren't social creatures, and kept themselves to themselves, but they had made her welcome during her short stay. Their two sons didn't react well to visitors, often becoming agitated and upset if a stranger entered the house. Even the sound of an unfamiliar vehicle pulling up outside would set them off, to the point where they got so distressed that the family had positioned their postbox at the end of the long driveway that led to the house. Brendan would also leave the refuse bins there, as even the bin lorry would upset the boys.

When Janet had arrived at the house for her first visit, the boys had responded badly, and it took several hours of Freya and Brendan calming them down before they relaxed in her company.

The couple's lives had revolved around their sons and they were devoted to them. Having fostered several children before Neil and Douglas came along, they loved having children in the house, and even when the boys became adults, their parents showed them unwavering love and compassion.

Janet went on to tell Sheridan and Anna about the day she had found the family dead in the house. As she spoke, Bouncer lay under the kitchen table, his tail innocently wagging the entire time.

'I couldn't get hold of Freya, and didn't know who I could contact to check if everything was alright. I didn't want to ring the police – it seemed a bit over the top – so before I left home on the day I found them, I left a message on their answering machine just to say I was a bit worried and was on my way to check in with them. When I arrived, Bouncer was lying on the porch.'

Sheridan didn't want to interrupt her, but was desperate to know if Bouncer had been tied up and his water bowl full when Janet arrived. There was just something about the whole scenario that unsettled her. She knew that Hill wasn't convinced the Barkers' deaths had anything to do with JT – and maybe she was right. But if Bouncer had been tied up for a week on a short lead, had no access to food and his water bowl was full, then something didn't add up.

Janet continued. 'I was a nurse my whole working life. I've seen and smelt death many times.' She studied her hands as she spoke, twisting her wedding ring around her finger. 'I knew I was walking into something awful. You can't mistake that smell and there was this eerie silence.' She looked at Sheridan. 'I found Freya first, laying on the sofa. Then I went to the boys' room and found them before I went upstairs and . . . there was Brendan.'

Sheridan could see that talking about it was becoming difficult for Janet. 'We've seen the photographs that were taken at the time. Please don't upset yourself if it's too hard to talk about.'

Janet wiped her mouth and looked down as Bouncer who was on his feet, his nose pressed into her lap. She stroked the top of his head and got up. 'I'll just give him a treat.' She stepped over to the dresser and opened the drawer, and off went Bouncer's tail again as he stood beside her excitedly.

Sheridan took the opportunity to ask the question. 'You said when you arrived that Bouncer was outside on the porch. Was he free or was he tied up?' she asked. *Please say he was tied up,* she thought, stealing a hopeful look at Anna who surreptitiously crossed her fingers.

Janet gave Bouncer a large chew stick, before answering. 'He was tied up.'

Yes, thought Sheridan. 'When you stayed with your sister that time, was Bouncer regularly tied up outside?'

Janet shook her head. 'Only when we ate dinner. Freya and Brendan didn't like him begging at the table, so they always put him outside at mealtimes.'

'Can you describe *how* he was tied up? How long his lead was, and if there was water in his bowl?'

Janet frowned. 'Why would you want to know *that*?'

'I just want to get a clear picture of what you saw when you first arrived.'

'Why is that relevant?' Janet watched as Bouncer devoured the treat she'd given him, smacking his lips loudly.

Sheridan knew that her questions made little sense in the scheme of things – a whole family were dead inside the house and here she was asking about the dog. 'Like I say, I just want to get a clear picture of the scene when you arrived. I know it seems irrelevant but if you could just go through it, that would be really helpful.' Sheridan smiled reassuringly.

Janet sighed. 'I already told the police all of this, but, alright . . . Well, when I pulled up, I could see Bouncer sitting on the porch. I got out of the car and went over to him. He was tied by his lead to the metal ring. His water bowl was full, but there was no food. I left him where he was and went inside and that's when—'

Sheridan put her hand up. 'Sorry I should have been clearer. You don't need to go over what you saw when you got into the house, I just need to know about Bouncer.'

Janet frowned, clearly a little confused as to why the detective was asking so many questions about the dog. 'Like I said, I left him where he was, until I came out of the house after finding them. I called 999 on my mobile and when they told me that the police and an ambulance were on their way, I went back inside to get some food for Bouncer. I found a box of dog biscuits, but he didn't want them, so I just put him in the car. I wanted him to be out of the way when everyone arrived. I didn't want him going into the house, for obvious reasons.' She looked at Sheridan. 'Does that answer your questions?'

'I'm surprised that he wasn't hungry. He couldn't have been fed for several days . . .'

Janet nodded in agreement. 'I put it down to him being traumatised, being left on his own. Believe me, he made up for it that evening and he's been making up for it ever since.' She paused. 'He loves his food. I've never had a dog before, so it took quite a lot of getting used to, but I wouldn't be without him now.'

Sheridan had all the answers she needed, except one. How long was the lead that tied Bouncer to the rail? She was desperate to ask, but hesitant at the same time. If the lead was long enough to allow him to venture far enough away from the house, then maybe, just maybe he'd found a food source.

Sheridan reached over to Bouncer's head and gave it a stroke. Then she asked the question that would help her make sense of everything. 'How long was Bouncer's lead?'

Janet looked at her, a little perplexed. 'What do you mean?'

'I just wondered how long his lead was.'

'Normal lead length. Why is that relevant?'

'I just wondered if he was able to roam around or not.'

Janet hesitated before answering. 'No. He wouldn't have been able to roam around. It was a short lead.' She placed her hands on the table. 'I think I know where you're going with this and so I'll say it. My sister loved that dog, and you might think him being tied up outside was cruel and the fact he couldn't have eaten for a few days, but they would never have treated him cruelly . . .'

'I'm not suggesting that for a moment.' Sheridan's voice was calm and quiet. 'I'm just trying to put the pieces together, and I wondered how Bouncer's water bowl stayed full if the family had all passed away several days earlier.'

'I can't answer that.' Janet swiped her hand up and down the table.

And neither can I, thought Sheridan. *But now I know someone else was there.*

CHAPTER 37

Sheridan stood up. 'Do you mind if we take a look around?'

'Be my guest,' Janet replied, clearing her throat, clearly still unsettled by having to relive what she'd gone through when she found her sister's family.

She followed Sheridan and Anna as they made their way from room to room. The house was practically empty, save for a few pieces of old wooden furniture. The carpets had been ripped out, exposing bare floorboards throughout most of the house. Janet explained that she'd arranged for the place to be emptied in an attempt to alleviate the smell that lingered for weeks after the family had died. The soiled sofa, carpets and beds had been the first to go, before she had begun the task of clearing personal items, most of which she had donated to charity.

The walls showed square light patches where pictures had once hung, and the wallpaper was aged and old-fashioned, some of it peeling away in the corners.

Each bare room had been scrubbed clean and each had a cross hanging on the wall. Even in the downstairs bathroom.

Janet talked them through the house, describing how it had looked before the family died. She painted a picture of happiness, of loving and doting parents besotted with their sons.

As she spoke, Sheridan and Anna listened, all the while scanning each room for any sign that JT had left his mark. As they came downstairs, Sheridan reluctantly concluded that even if this was JT's work, any sign he may have left was long gone.

'Can I ask you something?' Sheridan asked as they stood in the kitchen.

'Of course.'

'When you arrived in the house that day, was there anything you saw with the initials JT on it? Possibly scribbled or carved on something. I know it sounds an odd thing to ask, but it's the last question I have.'

Janet shook her head. 'No. Not that I recall. What's JT?'

'It's not important.' Sheridan smiled. 'We'll take a look outside if that's okay, and then we'll leave you in peace.'

Outside, Janet showed Sheridan and Anna where Bouncer had been tied up.

'So, the house was left to you?' Sheridan stood on the porch. The rain had ceased, and the air was filled with the sweetness from the apple trees and fruit growing nearby.

'No. Freya and Brendan hadn't made wills, but I'm the only living relative.' She turned to Sheridan. 'I'm not bothered about the money. If I'm honest, I'd rather not have to deal with all of this. Probate is taking forever to go through and there's an issue with the property's boundary lines.'

Bouncer trundled off ahead, eagerly sniffing everything in his path, as the three women walked towards the fence that separated the property from the field next to it. Upon reaching it, Janet pointed to a large overgrown area.

'Brendan put this fence up a few years ago, which makes it look like their land ends here. But it doesn't. There's another ten metres or so which is theirs too.'

'Why did he do that?' Sheridan asked.

'Because . . .' – Janet touched the leaf of a tall plant – 'this . . . is Japanese knotweed.'

She went on to explain that although the invasive plant was too far from the house to cause any concern, it had spread over the years, and any potential buyer would likely see it as an issue.

Remembering the photographs taken of the scene, Sheridan spotted the beech tree where the fatal death cap mushrooms had been growing. The thin wire fence that Brendan had secured was just in front of it, making it look like the tree was also not on his land.

'Did Freya and Brendan ever mention the death cap mushrooms to you?' Sheridan asked.

'No. But I *do* know they would never have touched them if they thought they were dangerous. They doted on those boys and would never have done anything to hurt them,' Janet said, raising her hand to shield her face from the sun that was now burning through the clouds. 'Can I ask you something?'

'Of course,' Sheridan replied.

'Their deaths were ruled as an accident. Is there a reason you're asking questions now? Is there anything I should know?'

Sheridan smiled reassuringly. 'It's just routine. We just want to make sure that nothing was missed.' She looked down, feeling Bouncer next to her and couldn't resist bending slightly to stroke him.

'It was two years ago. What could have been missed?' Janet asked.

'We know that Freya and Brendan had some financial difficulties, did she ever talk about it with you?'

'No. Not really.'

'Did she ever talk about being depressed?'

'Depressed? Where did you hear that?' Janet's reaction was immediate, and Sheridan sensed a marked defensiveness in her demeanour.

Sheridan shook her head slightly to calm her down. 'I didn't. I'm just trying to get a picture of the family and what they were like before they passed away.'

'They were a lovely family, good Catholics. I know they liked to keep themselves to themselves, but they were good people, kind people,' Janet replied, just as Bouncer started barking. 'He'll be wanting his lunch.' Janet smiled as Bouncer wagged his tail in recognition of his favourite word.

'Sorry, I know we're holding you up.'

'Not at all.'

Janet headed back to the house with Bouncer, leaving Sheridan and Anna to explore outside.

When she was out of earshot, Sheridan said, 'So, Bouncer *was* tied up on a short lead and his water bowl was full when Janet got here. He also wasn't hungry. I find all that very odd, don't you?'

Anna nodded. 'Yep. But I can't see how we link any of it to JT.' She raised an eyebrow. 'Unless Janet's hiding something?'

They walked the length of the fence and came to an area covered by thick foliage. Spotting a large wooden shed, Sheridan ducked under the fence and pushed through the dense undergrowth to reach it.

Anna reluctantly followed her, wishing she'd changed her shoes before they'd set out.

The shed was in reasonable condition and finding no lock on the door, Sheridan pulled it open. Giving her eyes a chance to adjust in the darkness, she stepped over to the window.

'Do I have to come in?' Anna asked, spotting a large swathing spider's web, as thick as a net curtain, draped in the corner.

Sheridan grinned, wiping the grimy window with her hand. 'Coward.'

'What are you looking for?'

'I don't know.' She peered through the clean gap she'd made and could see the house, spotting Janet emerge, lighting a cigarette, before looking in their direction.

'What do you make of her?' Sheridan asked.

'She got a bit weird when you asked about her sister being depressed.'

'Yeah. I noticed that.' Sheridan stepped back from the window and looked around. The shed was empty apart from an old cabinet, its top heavily marked with coloured circles left from paint pots. She brushed a cobweb from her hair and joined Anna outside.

'So, what do you want to do now?' Anna asked.

Sheridan stared at the house, watching as Janet stubbed her cigarette out on the ground, glanced back over in Sheridan and Anna's direction, before going back inside.

'Am I literally barking up the wrong tree here? Why do I keep coming back to the question about the dog?'

Anna looked at her. 'I think it's a bit weird too, the way he was able to survive. But I'm guessing there might be a simple explanation.'

As they made their way back to the house, Sheridan spoke her thoughts out loud. 'The thing is, on the face of it, what happened here looks like accidental death. Freya and Brendan were apparently happy. They loved their boys and wouldn't hurt them. They had a few money troubles, but nothing too bad. They were self-sufficient and private. So, let's say Brendan was the one who picked the mushrooms and Freya was the one who cooked them. Neither of them knew they were poisonous, or maybe they would have dug them up and got rid of them. They all became ill, and they all died. There was no medical intervention, because we know that the Barkers didn't ring for a doctor or ambulance. They didn't own a computer, so they couldn't even google their symptoms. I'm surmising here, but let's say they're all feeling ill and possibly died within a day or so of each other. We know they'd all been dead for a week before Janet found them. All of that makes sense, right?'

'Right,' Anna agreed.

'But I keep coming back to the dog. It just doesn't add up.'

'It doesn't mean that JT had anything to do with it though, and if I'm honest mate, I think this was just a tragedy.'

'I know, but isn't it strange that this is the only incident that occurred in July 2008 that could have been mistaken as a suicide? But none of it fits. Too many victims, and the more I come to think of it, how would anyone know about the death cap mushrooms and force the family to eat them? They didn't mix with other people.'

'Unless, like I said before, they employed someone to help out and just didn't tell anyone.'

'Yeah. But who? And if that was the case, then what happened to them? There's no one mentioned in the file . . .' Sheridan suddenly stopped in her tracks.

'What's wrong?' Anna asked.

'Hang on. There *was* someone. It *was* mentioned in the file. The Barkers used to foster children many years ago. Janet said that one of their foster kids had recently got back in touch and even visited them. Janet couldn't remember his name.' Sheridan continued towards the house, quickening her pace as she got closer, leaving Anna a few steps behind.

Janet was in the kitchen as Sheridan tapped on the open door, before walking in.

'Janet, you told the officers at the time that your sister and Brendan recently had contact from one of their foster children.'

'Yes. That's right.'

'Do you recall his name, or anything about him?'

'No. The police asked me that and I'm not even sure if Freya told me his name.' She stood in the middle of the room and crossed her arms. 'Is there something I should know?' Impatience creeping into her voice.

'What do you mean?'

'Well, for starters, you turn up here two years after all this has happened and start asking questions as if you doubt something. So, I'd like to know what's going on.'

'I'm just making sure that everything we have on record is accurate. That's all,' Sheridan tried to reassure her.

'I see. Well, like I said, I told the police everything at the time.' She picked up a cloth from the dresser. 'I really have to get on.'

'Sorry, we've taken up a lot of your time.' Sheridan took out a card and handed it to Janet. 'My number's on there. Please call me if you remember anything else.'

'Like what?' Janet looked at the card.

'Just anything that comes to mind.'

'Fine,' Janet replied curtly, placing Sheridan's card on the dresser.

After giving Bouncer a final stroke of the head, Sheridan and Anna left.

Janet watched from the porch as they drove slowly down the track away from the house. As they disappeared, she went back inside and stood in the middle of the kitchen; tears pricked her eyes as she looked at the cross on the wall.

'God forgive me.' She pulled a chair back and sat down, her legs shaking uncontrollably. 'I did it for *you*. I only did it to *save* you.' She sobbed. 'God please, please forgive me.'

CHAPTER 38

Hill looked up as Sheridan and Anna walked into CID.

'How did it go?' she asked.

Sheridan gave her a brief outline, called a team briefing and updated everyone with the details of their visit to Janet Vickers.

Hill agreed that although none of it appeared to be linked to JT, they should at least try to locate the Barkers' foster children, and Rob was tasked to find them.

Sheridan looked over at Bridie. 'Where are we with checking out the buildings across the road?'

Bridie shook her head once. 'We haven't got very far as yet. We know that if JT was watching the front doors to the PEO, he'd have to have either been standing outside, or across the road, but we've checked CCTV and he's not there. He could have been in one of the buildings along the road, opposite the nick. One's been turned into apartments, and the others are offices.' She checked her notes. 'There's a firm of solicitors, a private dental practice, accountants . . .' She looked up. 'The only other place he could have been was over by the Albert Dock. We're checking CCTV from some of the cafés and shops there, but it's going to take a while.'

'Okay. Thanks, Bridie.' Sheridan turned her attention to Dipesh. 'How did you get on with the antiques guy? What was his name? Cameron John?'

'He was really helpful, but without the actual key, he said it's hard to be sure what it was used for. Based on the photo we have of a similar key, it could be to a chest, or a door, but really too hard to tell.' Dipesh glanced at Rob who was grinning at him. 'What?'

Rob nodded towards the corner of the room and Sheridan turned to see a small black umbrella propped up against the wall.

'What's that?' she asked.

Dipesh shook his head. 'It was pissing down when I went to see Cameron John,' he explained.

'And?' Sheridan asked.

'And so . . . he sold me an umbrella.' He threw a look at Rob who was still grinning.

Sheridan stepped over to it and picked it up. 'Fucking hell, Dipesh. How old is this?' She flapped it up and down. 'Looks like something out of an old movie.' She studied it closer. 'It's very small for an umbrella. Are you sure it's not a parasol?' Her voice began to break.

Dipesh stood up and joined her, while the whole team looked on in amusement. He took it from her. 'It's all he had and anyway, I like it.'

'I need to stop sending you out to antiques shops,' Sheridan said, snatching it back. 'Oh lord, it's got a little lace frill around the edge.' She tipped her head at Dipesh. 'You'll look so pretty when you go to the ball,' she said in a mock American accent.

The whole room erupted in laughter and Dipesh turned to them. 'Yeah, yeah, very funny.'

Sheridan put her hand on his shoulder, steadying herself as she bent over, laughing, struggling to get her words out. 'How much was it?'

'Twenty quid. Bloody bargain.'

'Oh, mate.' Sheridan composed herself.

Rob piped up, 'Apparently this Cameron fella is very charming, and has one of those faces you can trust. Isn't that right, Dipesh?'

Dipesh threw Rob a frown. 'I didn't say that. I said he has a nice way about him.'

'Man crush,' Rob shouted out.

Dipesh put his hand out to Sheridan. 'Can I have my umbrella back please?'

'It's a parasol.' Sheridan slapped it into his open hand.

'It's an umbrella. A very *manly* umbrella.' Dipesh tucked it under his arm and, winking at Rob, he walked out of the office whistling the tune to 'Singing in the Rain', leaving laughter in his wake.

It was getting towards the end of the day and Sheridan was ready to head home, although she was still smiling at Dipesh's antics. It was moments like these that lifted the team when an inquiry was getting heavy.

She looked at the sheets of paper Blu-Tacked to her office wall. Studying them, like she did every day. She had drawn a large JT in thick black marker on one. Another was a countdown to 22nd July, when she believed – if her theory was right – that he would kill again. She stared at the copy of the note JT had posted to CID.

I'm surprised it's taken you so long. How many clues does it take to figure it out? You have the key to the answer. I'm sure at some point you'll turn things around. Then all you need to do is fill in the gaps. JT

She had read and re-read the words a hundred times, trying to make sense of them.

She had surmised that what he meant by '*fill in the gaps*' was some sort of reference to putting the key into a lock. And '*turn things around*' was the key itself. If you turn a key, it unlocks something. Is that what he meant? If that was the case, then the key was crucial to the inquiry. And they had no idea where it was.

As the fan in her office oscillated, the sheets flapped gently, like they were waving at her. Like JT was waving at her.

Her phone rang.

'Do you wanna pop through to CID?' said Anna. 'We've got Kyle Crane's phone records back.'

A minute later, Sheridan and Anna flanked Dipesh as he brought up the data on his screen.

From what they could see, Kyle Crane made and received a *lot* of calls and text messages.

Sheridan leaned forward. 'Scroll down to Wednesday the thirtieth of June at around 13.40, that's when he looked at his phone before he came into the PEO to collect the bag.'

Dipesh found the entry. The data showed that at 13.41 Kyle Crane had received a text message. Sheridan pointed at the screen. 'That one. We need to find out whose number that is.' She leaned back and crossed her arms. 'Because that, my friends, is highly likely to be JT.'

CHAPTER 39

Tuesday 13 July

Sheridan was up early, having lain awake most of the night. She'd crept downstairs in the early hours, trying not to wake Sam, and made herself a coffee. Sitting in the conservatory, with Maud on her lap, she'd watched the sun come up. Sam had woken and joined them, snuggling up with her head on Sheridan's shoulder. They had talked about the inquiry and how Sheridan feared they were running out of time. Nine days to catch JT and prevent him from killing his next victim.

'The worst part about it is that we have no idea who the next victim or victims are. There's no pattern to what he's doing.' Sheridan stroked Maud's head as she spoke.

'Is there usually a pattern in this kind of case?' Sam asked.

'Not always an obvious one, but there's usually something that connects the killings.'

'Like what?'

'Like the way the victims are killed, and the victims themselves. Sometimes the killer targets women, sometimes men, or the elderly. But this guy has no clear pattern. We've got Annette Lennon, a lone female on a railway platform, stabbed repeatedly in the face but left alive and told to give someone a message that he's just making a point. Possibly Jake Hannigan, a lone lad up on a rock, painting. Then the Barkers, poisoned in their own home. That last one might not be JT, but something's definitely not right about that case, and my gut says there's a connection. Then we have Kenny James, a homeless guy slashed with a razor blade and left to die.' Sheridan sighed. 'I really thought we'd see a pattern where the killer was making the deaths look like suicide, but if he is connected to the Barkers then he's not consistent at all. Their deaths don't show any hint of having been a suicide.'

'Maybe there really isn't a connection? Maybe he just sees someone and thinks, "They'll do"?' Sam said.

'I don't think so,' Sheridan said. 'For starters, he was prepared when he attacked Annette. He wore a hi-vis vest, he knew the train timetable and how to escape. He took the weapon he used with him. He knew the cameras wouldn't pick him up once he jumped over the wall. Then with Jake Hannigan, if this was JT, I think he'd seen him up there painting before, maybe he got talking to him and found out that Jake was there regularly.'

'But didn't you say that Jake was autistic? Would he have spoken to a stranger?'

Sheridan didn't respond, momentarily thinking about what Sam had said.

Then, she made the connection.

'They're all loners. Annette, Jake, Kenny and the Barkers. They're all people who like to be alone, or ended up alone through circumstance.' She kissed the top of Sam's head. 'Maybe JT's a loner too.'

'Possibly. And the way he stops walking when someone or something approaches him. Maybe this guy hates anyone being close to him if it's not on his terms.'

'Yes. That makes sense. He can control what *he* does, but he can't control others, like when someone comes towards him. He stops and steps aside. He even did it when a bloody cat walked past him.' Sheridan scraped a hand through her hair. 'I thought he was avoiding CCTV when he did that. But maybe it's not that at all.' She gently lifted a sleepy Maud from her lap and stood up.

'I need to get going. I've got to check something.'

◆ ◆ ◆

The early-morning sun was already warm as Sheridan parked up at Edge Hill train station, making her way to the platform where Annette Lennon had been attacked four years earlier. She remembered from the file that the CCTV at the time was located at the very end of the platform, a fair distance from where Annette had been standing. As she walked along the platform, she spotted the cameras, still situated in the same place. Ignoring the inquisitive looks from a group of teenage school kids, she walked the exact path that JT had taken to approach Annette, stopping at the point where he'd sidestepped before reaching her.

'Bollocks,' Sheridan said under her breath. The theory she'd had earlier suddenly didn't make sense. JT didn't sidestep because someone had approached him on the platform. The only two people who'd been there that night were him and Annette. And he'd approached her. His sudden movement to the side wasn't to avoid the camera, either. Maybe he'd stepped aside so that Annette didn't see him coming. Maybe he hadn't wanted to startle her.

She made her way back to her car and headed to the Dock Road, to the building where Kenny James had been found.

Twenty minutes later, she was walking the route that JT had taken after he'd been seen near the building two days before Kenny James was found. Again, she looked for cameras and what was around her. Absorbing everything, like Sheridan always did. Her mind trying to fit the pieces together. The link. The one thing that

JT always did, or didn't do. She got back into her car and started the engine, just as her mobile rang and Anna's number flashed up on her screen.

'Yes, mate?'

'Are you on your way in?'

'I'm five minutes away. What's up?'

'We've got the phone data back from the number that texted Kyle Crane's mobile, just before he came into the PEO.'

'And?'

'And you're not going to fucking believe it.'

CHAPTER 40

Sheridan flew up the stairs and burst into CID.

'Tell me you're sure,' she said, catching her breath.

'We're sure,' Anna replied, handing Sheridan a printout.

'Well, fuck me.' Sheridan raised her eyebrows. 'Let's go and get him.'

Anna followed her downstairs.

Sheridan stopped in one of the corridors. 'Let's check there's an interview room free first,' she said, just as Andrea appeared behind them, heading into the PEO.

They followed her. 'Is there a free interview room?' Sheridan asked.

'Yes, I think so. Let me just check.' Andrea looked under the counter before turning to Marcus. 'Where's the diary?'

He pointed to where she'd just been looking. 'Should be there.' He ducked down and reached back, pulling the A4-sized diary out and handing it to her.

Andrea flicked through it. 'Yeah. You're good to go, interview room two is free.'

'Thanks.' Sheridan looked past Andrea. 'Marcus. Can you come with us please?'

◆ ◆ ◆

Marcus Holt sat down, his leg shaking involuntarily. 'What's this about?'

He looked nervously at Sheridan, who closed the door and sat opposite him, next to Anna.

'Am I under arrest or something?' His voice broke and the colour drained from his face.

'No.' Sheridan went straight in: 'How do you know Kyle Crane?'

Marcus gave a slight shake of his head. 'Never heard of him.'

'You *have* heard of him. You sent him a text message at 13.41 hours on Wednesday the thirtieth of June.'

'Sorry, I don't know what you're talking about.'

'I'm going to repeat myself once and once only. How do you know Kyle Crane, and why did you send him that text?'

'I can't remember.'

Sheridan leaned forward. 'I'm dealing with a murder inquiry here, so I'll give you a minute to think.' She folded her arms and sat back. 'Take your time.'

Marcus focused on the table in front of him, breathing slowly in through his nose and out through his mouth. And then he spoke.

'He's a mate and I texted him to say the coast was clear.' He looked at Sheridan. 'I'm sorry. I'm really sorry. I had no idea it would be such a big deal.'

'The coast was clear? Explain,' Sheridan said.

'Clear for him to come in and claim the bag.' Marcus's head dropped.

'Explain *exactly* what you mean.'

Marcus shifted his position. 'I've been an idiot and I'm sorry.'

Sheridan didn't respond. She just let him keep speaking.

'When that bloke Justin brought the bag in, he asked how long he had to wait before he could come back if it wasn't claimed. I told him four weeks, and I asked him what he'd want with an old watch and key. That's when he said he thought it was valuable. I assumed he meant the watch, so, I knew I had four weeks before he might come back, and that's when I rang my mate, Kyle. I told him to come in and say the watch and key were his, sign for them and then we could get the watch valued. We were going to split the money if it was worth anything.' Marcus swallowed, shaking his head. 'I've been so stupid.'

'Did the Justin guy say anything about the date that he could collect the bag?'

'Yeah. He asked if four weeks meant four weeks exactly, or if it meant he could come back on the twenty-second of July.'

'What did you say?'

'I said either date was fine and he said he'd come back on the twenty-second.'

'Okay. Tell me everything you remember about the watch.'

'It was a Rolex.'

'Was anything engraved on it? On the back, maybe?'

'There was a name.' He looked down, trying to think. 'In memory of Tim . . . or Tom. I can't be sure.'

Sheridan noted it down. 'Think *very* carefully. Was it Tim or Tom and did it say anything else?'

Marcus gave it some thought, before replying. 'I'm really sorry, I can't remember.'

'What about the key? Anything engraved on that?'

'I don't think so.'

'Are you sure?'

'I don't remember seeing anything.'

'Where are the watch and the key now?'

'I think Kyle chucked them away.'

'You want me to believe he'd throw away a Rolex?'

'He rang me on Saturday and said the police had been round to his, asking about the bag. He was proper pissed off with me and said he was going to throw it in the Mersey.' Marcus's voice raised.

'I told him not to get rid of it. I knew it was important to you, and I bloody told him that I needed the police to find it. I was going to make sure you got it back, somehow.'

'Marcus. I need that bag. And I need it *now*.'

He put his hands out, palms up. 'I swear I don't know if Kyle got rid of it. I haven't spoken to him since Saturday.' He pulled his phone out of his pocket. 'I can ring him now if you want. He might still have it.'

Sheridan stood up. 'No. Don't call him. You don't need to speak to him. *I* do.'

Sheridan assigned a uniformed officer to stay with Marcus, while Rob and another uniform unit went to Kyle Crane's house, where they arrested him for theft, and brought him to Hale Street custody.

After declining a solicitor, he was interviewed and fully admitted his involvement in the ploy to claim the bag. He stuck to his original account that he'd sold the key and watch to some bloke he'd met in a pub. He couldn't remember which pub, which bloke, or when he'd sold them. He also stated that he couldn't remember if the watch or key had any engravings on them.

A Section 18 search warrant was issued, permitting a team to search his house and car.

Marcus was suspended, pending a decision by the force's Professional Standards department as to what action to take.

While the search was being carried out at Kyle Crane's house, Sheridan briefed the team.

'So, we know the watch has an engraving on the back, which reads, "In memory of Tim", or "Tom". So I'm guessing that's the name of our next victim. If we get the watch and key back, then we might just have JT. He told Marcus that they were valuable. Maybe the Rolex is, if it really is a Rolex, but I think JT meant valuable to *us* evidentially and not valuable as in monetary terms.'

Hill responded. 'So, are we now thinking that Marcus and Kyle are just two fucking dipshits and are nothing to do with JT?'

'I think so,' Sheridan replied. 'And if that's the case, then JT doesn't know that the bag's been collected, he still thinks that it's in the property store waiting for him to collect when the four weeks are up. JT handed in the bag on the twenty-second of June, so, four weeks after that date is Tuesday the twentieth of July, but he said to Marcus that he'd come back on the twenty-second of July. The same date he sticks to every time. The date he likes to kill people.' She paused. 'But when he handed in the bag, he *knew* that no one would claim it, because no one lost it in the first place. What he doesn't know is that Marcus fucked it up for us and now we don't have it.'

'But surely you're not thinking he's actually going to come in when the four weeks are up?' Hill asked.

'Not now I don't.' Sheridan sighed heavily. 'Because we put his bloody picture out there on the local news and we know he saw it because he posted us that fucking letter. He knows we're on to him and we know what he looks like, sort of. He won't risk it.'

The team sat in silence for a moment, processing this latest information.

Sheridan frowned, thinking. 'Back in a minute.' She left the room, making her way to her office. The sheets of paper that were Blu-Tacked to her wall had been blown on to the floor by the fan. She looked at the copy of the note that JT had sent her, cogs whirring in her mind and making connections, before racing back to CID.

Everyone looked up as she barged in and addressed the room. 'Listen to this. This is JT's letter to us. '"I'm surprised it's taken you so long. How many clues does it take to figure it out? You have the key to the answer. I'm sure at some point you'll turn things around. Then all you need to do is fill in the gaps. JT."' She looked up from the sheet of paper. 'We received this note on Monday the fifth of July.' She grabbed a whiteboard marker and wrote as she spoke. 'Let's go through the timeline. JT hands the bag in on the twenty-second of June. His picture goes out on TV on Wednesday the thirtieth of June, at which point he knows we're on to him. The letter was posted locally, so how long would it have taken to get here?'

Rob piped up, 'About a month – our postal service is shit.'

Sheridan allowed him the joke, which amused the rest of the team. 'Well, yeah. But let's say he posted it on the Friday, it would have got here on the Monday, is that fair to say?'

The team nodded in silence.

Sheridan continued. 'So, if JT *was* connected to Kyle and Marcus, he would have known that Kyle had collected the bag.'

Anna smiled. 'So why would he then say in the note to us that "you *have* the key"?'

Sheridan pointed at her. 'Exactly.' She nodded. 'He would have said, you *had* the key, not you *have* the key.' She held up the letter. 'Kyle and Marcus are definitely not working with JT. Like Hill says, they're just two fuckwits.'

'So, what now?' Hill asked.

'I think we need to be careful.' Sheridan addressed the whole room. 'We don't know for absolute certain that JT won't come back on the twenty-second of July and claim the bag. He doesn't yet know that we're aware of it. The problem is, we can't just wait and hope that will happen. We have to find him before that date and if we don't, then we'll have to hope and fucking pray that he comes in and we can nick him then. But the twenty-second is the day he's going to kill again. Even if he does come in on that date, he might have already killed his next victim, who we now believe

174

is called Tim, or Tom.' She rubbed her forehead. 'Let's hope the search team find the bag in Kyle Crane's house. Because right now, we've got little else to go on.'

Hill spoke. 'Let's play it safe here. I know we're concentrating on the twenty-second of July being the date that JT *might* come back for the bag. So, I'll speak to all the PEO staff and duty sergeants, make them aware that if someone does come in – anyone – then they're to alert us straight away. Even though JT knows that we know what he looks like, he could send someone else in at any time.'

The briefing came to a close and Sheridan returned to her office. Dipesh was right behind her as she walked in. 'Sheridan, sorry, I meant to ask, do you still want us to check out the buildings opposite? Now that we know JT wasn't the one that messaged Kyle, he probably wasn't watching the doors.'

'Good point. No, you can bin that.' Sheridan bent to pick up the sheets of paper that were still on the floor.

Dipesh crouched down and was about to scoop up one of the sheets when he stopped and stared at it.

'That looks a bit like the pi symbol,' he said, picking it up.

'What?' Sheridan asked, turning to see what he was referring to.

'Look.' He held the paper up. 'JT.' He turned the paper round. The thick black marker that Sheridan had used to write the initials had gone through to the other side, showing the initials backwards. TJ.

'What's the pi symbol? Isn't that some sort of mathematical thing?'

'Yeah. I'll show you.' Dipesh took out his phone and a moment later, he turned it to show Sheridan.

'It does look a bit like that actually. So, what is pi exactly?'

'It's the constant that's used when you're calculating the area of a circle. In other words, it's the ratio of a circle's circumference to its diameter and is approximately equal to . . .' Dipesh spotted the expression on Sheridan's face.

'How do you know all this?'

'I've got a maths degree. And I'm a geek.' He smiled, looking at the initials again. 'I mean it's not exactly like the pi symbol, but if you drew a line between the top of the T and the J, then it would be pretty close.'

Sheridan's eyes widened. 'Fuck.' She took out the note that JT had sent and read it out loud. "'*I'm surprised it's taken you so long. How many clues does it take to figure it out? You have the key to the answer. I'm sure at some point you'll turn things around. Then all you need to do is fill in the gaps. JT*".' She looked at Dipesh. 'Fill in the gaps. Could he mean fill in the gaps between the J and the T?' She read the note again. 'Fuck me, and he says "I'm sure at some point, you'll turn things around".' She looked up to the ceiling. 'That's it. All we had to do was turn the initials JT around, fill in the gap and there's the pi symbol.' She turned to Dipesh. 'Alright, you beautiful geek, tell me everything you know about pi.'

He pinched his forehead between his fingers, thinking. 'I don't remember the exact details. I'd have to look it up.'

Sheridan logged on to her computer and typed in pi. Dipesh stood behind her as she scrolled down.

A moment later, she flopped back in her seat. 'Oh my fucking God.'

CHAPTER 41

Sheridan and Dipesh stood at the front of the room and all eyes were on them. Sheridan took the whiteboard pen and wrote the word pi, explaining to the team how Dipesh had identified the pi symbol and the hidden clue in JT's note.

'We think that JT is using pi as a basis for the killings.' She turned to Dipesh. 'Our genius here worked it out.' She nodded, signalling for him to address the team.

He took the whiteboard marker from her and quickly wrote JT and the pi symbol on the whiteboard.

$$JT \leftrightarrow \pi$$

He then turned back to the room and explained what he and Sheridan had learned about pi.

'Basically, pi is the constant that's used when calculating the area of a circle. It's the ratio of a circle's circumference to its diameter and it's mainly expressed in two different ways, either as a decimal or a fraction. It always starts with three point one four, which is why some countries, including America, celebrate pi day on the fourteenth of March.' He looked at the attentive faces staring back at him and cleared his throat before continuing.

'Pi, as a fraction, is twenty-two divided by seven, 22/7, and the twenty-second of July is when "Pi Approximation Day" is celebrated in other countries, including the UK.'

Dipesh turned to the whiteboard and continued talking while he wrote.

'So, we have two patterns here for pi and for now, I've just written them out to ten decimal places and included the dates for when each pi day is celebrated.' He tapped the board for everyone to read:

Pi as the decimal 3.14, to 10 decimal places: 3.1415926535 – celebrated 14th March.

Pi as the fraction 22/7, to 10 decimal places: 3.1428571428 – celebrated 22nd July.

He gave them a moment to absorb the information, before continuing. 'Remember, pi is an irrational number, which means that it cannot be represented as an *exact* fraction. And more importantly for us, it means that the digits *after* the decimal point are never-ending.' He turned to Sheridan, checking that what he'd said made sense.

'Thanks Dipesh.' She looked at her team. 'Now, we know that JT is killing his victims on the twenty-second of July, which, if he's using *that* particular pi sequence, would suggest that he'd also use the pi sequence of numbers relating to *that* date, three point one four two eight and so on. However, if our theory is correct about the victims we've identified so far, then for some weird reason, he's following the decimal sequence, three point one four one five.'

'Christ,' came Hill's response. 'And he's killing them in order of the number?'

Sheridan nodded. 'Yeah. So, I was wrong when I thought Annette was his first victim.' She pointed to the first numbers of the pi sequence written on the whiteboard: three point one four one. 'He'd already killed three people, then when he attacked Annette, he told her to tell us he was just "making a point", by which he meant the point after the number three. Then if he *did* kill Jake Hannigan, that's *one* victim. Then, the Barker family, that's the *four* victims. Next was Kenny James, *one* victim. Three point one four one.'

Hill inhaled deeply. 'And the next number is five, which means on the twenty-second of July, we're looking at five victims.'

Sheridan looked her straight in the eye, hesitating before answering. 'Yes.' She faced the room. 'I need you all to think about the fact that pi doesn't end, it just keeps going and going. Which means that JT is never going to stop. Unless we stop him.'

No one answered, as the enormity of this realisation dawned on them.

Having summoned Sheridan and Anna into her office, Hill closed the door, and they all remained standing.

'I owe you an apology, Sheridan,' Hill said, her voice unusually soft and quiet. 'I think you're right about the Barker family, and probably Jake Hannigan. I should never have doubted you.'

Sheridan shook her head. 'None of that matters now, Hill. We just need to find this fucking monster and we've got nine days to do it.'

Hill crossed her arms just as her phone rang, which answered quickly. 'DCI Knowles.'

Sheridan threw Anna the same look that she had seen on the faces of her team. If they missed something, five people were going to die. Five men called Tim, or Tom. The police systems had been searched to see if anyone of those names had been reported missing, with a negative result. Officers were trying to find any connection between the names Tim, Tom and the number 5. A daunting task in the time they had left.

Hill ended the call. 'That's the search team at Kyle Crane's house. Nothing found in his house or car.'

'I know he's got that fucking bag,' Sheridan replied.

'What about his place of work?' Hill asked.

'He told us he does odd jobs for people. So, it'll be a nightmare to trace where he's been.'

'Haven't we pinged his phone?'

'Yeah. But so far, all we know is that it pinged off a mast about a mile from his house on Saturday the tenth of July and since then, he hasn't left the house. Or at least his phone hasn't.'

'What about his car? Has it turned up on any ANPR cameras?' Hill asked.

'No. So he's staying local.'

'Alright. Well, now that the search team have finished, let's charge and bail him. There's nothing to keep him in custody and we can keep tabs on him if he's out and about. Agreed?' Hill looked between Sheridan and Anna.

'Agreed.' Sheridan nodded once and left, with Anna in tow.

They headed back to CID. After a final team briefing, Sheridan was about to get into her car and make her way home, when her mobile rang. It was Ruth Manning from the cold-case team.

'Hi, Sheridan, you free to speak?'

'Yeah, go for it.' She climbed into her car and closed the door.

'I've found a witness who saw Stephen Tubby near Birkenhead Park on the day Matthew died.'

CHAPTER 42

Sheridan stared out of her windscreen. 'Really?'

'Yeah. But it's a bit complicated. This witness, John Riverstone, knew Tubby back then, from the local pub. Tubby was always talking about the fact that he liked watching the kids playing football. Apparently, Tubby used to go on about it, and John said that he thought it was a bit odd, but that Tubby was a bit odd, so he didn't think too much of it.'

'But he saw Tubby near the park that day? Why didn't he come forward at the time?' Sheridan asked.

'That's where it gets a bit tricky. Basically, John used to drop his fifteen-year-old daughter off at her friend's house on Saturdays, which is what he did the day Matthew died. Now, John would only tell me what he told me if I assured him he wouldn't be arrested. Basically, he'd been in the pub most of the day and left just before three p.m. Tubby had previously mentioned to him that he was working on a site a couple of miles away and so John, even though he was drunk, drove to the site in his van and robbed a load of copper piping. When he was driving back home, he passed Birkenhead Park and that's when he saw Tubby.'

'Where exactly *was* Tubby?'

'Coming out of the park itself.'

'What time was that?'

'Around four p.m.'

'Andrew Longford last saw Matthew around three p.m. that day . . .' Sheridan swallowed. She felt a palpitation in her chest. So many years had passed while she waited for a breakthrough and now suddenly it was happening. 'So, Tubby was there, at the park?'

'Yeah. I mean, John's not a great witness, and was quite reluctant to tell me anything in case I nicked him for drink-driving and theft.'

'From thirty years ago?'

'Exactly. I explained that we couldn't nick him now anyway. The problem is, he won't give me a statement and said he wouldn't go to court. To be honest, even if he did, a defence barrister would rip the shit out of him, especially as he'd just nicked a load of gear. They'd go down the route of unreliability and dishonesty.'

'But, even so, it puts Tubby right there at the right time. Does your witness remember what Tubby was wearing?'

'No. And he can't be sure if he had a beard or not. I've spoken to my DI, he doesn't think it's enough to nick Tubby yet, but I'm going to re-visit John in a few days to see if he changes his mind about a statement.'

A silence fell between them for a moment, before Ruth asked how Andrew Longford was doing. Sheridan told her that she'd been to see him the previous week and his palliative care was being organised.

'Have you told your parents about Andrew's condition yet?' Ruth said.

'No. But I think I'll have to soon.'

'Do you want me to visit Andrew and see if he remembers anything else?'

'No. It's okay. I'll go and see him.'

Sheridan thanked Ruth for all her hard work. After ending the call, she sat in her car, thinking about what she'd just been told.

Stephen Tubby was right there, leaving the park after Andrew went home. Andrew and Matthew had spotted the man in the brown coat, blue jeans with a beard. Surely, this was Tubby. But Andrew hadn't recognised him from his picture. Had his memory failed him? Tubby had mentioned that he liked to watch kids playing football. He'd lied to the police about where he was the day Matthew died.

Feeling a strange mixture of excitement and nerves, she started the car and made her way to Andrew's house.

◆　◆　◆

Andrew Longford shuffled into the living room after letting Sheridan in. They talked about the scorching weather and Sheridan told him about the brass fan Dipesh had bought and how she intended to steal it at some point.

But she didn't want to talk trivial matters with him. She wanted to ask him again about the man he'd seen hanging around Birkenhead Park that day. If this new witness was right, then she knew in her heart that Stephen Tubby truly was a strong suspect in her brother's murder. If not the *only* suspect. After making them both a coffee, she decided that with the little time Andrew had left, she had to bite the bullet and push him, just one more time.

'Andrew, I know I've asked you this so many times before, but the man you saw that day, the one with the brown coat, blue jeans and beard . . .' She hesitated for a second. 'It's just that the name that was put forward before, Stephen Tubby, well, we now think he was near Birkenhead Park the day Matthew died.'

'Really?' Andrew lifted his coffee cup to his lips and blew the steam off. 'So, what does that mean? Are you going to arrest him?'

'Not yet. But . . . and I'm sorry to ask you again, we know the man in the photograph is Stephen Tubby and I don't want to put words in your mouth, but is there any way that Stephen Tubby was the man you saw hanging around that day, the man watching you and Matthew?'

Andrew set his coffee mug down and placed his hands on his knees. 'I really don't know. I'm *so* sorry, Sheridan. I know you want me to say that it was him, but I really didn't see him closely. I just remember the beard, the brown coat and the blue jeans. I'm so sorry.'

Sheridan leaned over and placed a hand over his. 'It's fine. No need to be sorry. We'll keep looking for other witnesses. I promise you, there's a great detective working on it.'

'Is she better than you?' A brief smile touched Andrew's face.

'Well now, that's a question.' Sheridan returned the smile.

'How are your parents?'

'They're okay. I haven't told them that you're . . . poorly.'

'I understand. I'm the last link they have to what happened to Matthew. Maybe you should leave it until I've gone? I don't mind. You need to do what you think's best.'

'Yeah. We'll see . . .' Sheridan's voice drifted off for a moment. 'Anyway, how are you getting on with sorting out your affairs? Is there anything I can help with?'

'No. It's pretty much all done. The last thing was the allotment and that's sorted now.' His eyes welled up and he looked at her. 'Can I ask you something?'

'Of course, anything.'

'Will you come to my funeral?' He put his head in his hands. Sheridan saw his shoulders jolting as he began to sob.

She immediately got up and wrapped her arms around him, failing to fight back her own tears.

'Of course I will. Of course I will,' she said gently in his ear.

CHAPTER 43

Rosie Holler put a tray of tea on the coffee table. Sheridan's dad, Brian, was the first to grab at the plate of biscuits and Rosie slapped his hand away. 'Oi, let Sheridan and Sam have one first,' she tutted. He stuck his tongue out at her, earning him a gentle clip across the head.

'So, how are you two?' Rosie asked, settling herself on the sofa next to Brian, placing her hand on his knee.

Sam took the reins first, casually chatting about Maud, about school, and that she'd enrolled on a first-aid refresher course. Meanwhile, Sheridan was mentally preparing herself to tell them about Andrew Longford and Stephen Tubby. Whenever there was an apparent breakthrough in Matthew's case, she always worried that it would get her parents' hopes up. Although there hadn't been many in the thirty-three years since he'd been gone. As much as she never wanted them to give up on finding his killer, she also didn't want them to believe they were close, only to have their hopes crushed.

Sheridan watched their reactions to Sam's chatter, how they smiled and laughed at her stories about what the children in her class got up to.

'There's one kid, called Daisy. She's . . . well let's say she's a bit chubby, and some of the other kids pick on her. Yesterday, I walked in on her sitting on this kid – one of the bullies. Literally sat on top of him, with her arms folded, like a triumphant warrior. I asked her what she was doing, and she said, "I think it's obvious that I'm sitting on Harry Topping, miss."'

Rosie and Brian burst out laughing as Sam continued. 'I asked her why, and she said, "Because he called me fat and asked me how much I weighed. So, I sat on him, and now he knows. I weigh quite a lot".'

Rosie almost spat her tea out before asking, 'How long did you leave her there for?'

'A little bit longer than I probably should have.' Sam grinned. 'Harry Topping was starting to turn a funny colour.'

'This Daisy sounds like a real character,' Rosie said. 'It's a shame she gets bullied.'

'We try to stamp it out, but kids are kids and they can be cruel. We keep a close eye on the vulnerable children, but Daisy seems to have learned to deal with it in her own way. The sad thing is, she's super-intelligent and really funny, but sometimes people don't see that, because all they see is her size, but if they took time to talk to her and get to know her, they'd soon realise how cool she is.'

As Sheridan listened to Sam, she nervously prepared herself to tell her parents about Stephen Tubby and Andrew Longford. She'd tell them about Tubby first, how they had a witness that placed him at Birkenhead Park the day Matthew had died. Start with the positive. Then she'd tell them about Andrew.

When the biscuits had been devoured – mainly by Brian – Rosie got up to make another pot of tea. Sam quickly glanced at Sheridan, and she knew that was her cue. When Rosie rejoined them, waiting for the kettle to boil, Sheridan told them about Stephen Tubby.

'Goodness.' Rosie grasped Brian's hand. 'So, you can't arrest him yet? But it sounds very promising.'

'It does. And I know that Ruth, the cold-case detective, will keep going until she finds enough evidence to have him in.'

'That's really positive news.' Brian lifted Rosie's hand to his mouth and kissed it.

'I have something else to tell you, which is a bit sad though.' Sheridan tilted her head slightly. 'Andrew Longford is very poorly and . . . well, he's got cancer and it's terminal.' Before her parents could respond, she continued. 'I've been to see him a couple of times and he's being remarkably brave. He's got his affairs in order, and I met the lady who's going to be arranging his care and support.' Sheridan refrained from using the word 'palliative'.

'Oh, what a terrible shame. That poor man.' Rosie put her hand to her mouth. 'I expect you've been dreading telling us, haven't you?'

Sheridan tilted her head. 'Yeah, if I'm honest.'

'Of course you have.' Rosie got up and gave Sheridan a hug, before clasping her face gently in her hands. 'You beautiful girl. You worry too much about us, we're made of strong stuff, you know.'

'I know you are, but I still worry.'

Rosie kissed Sheridan on the cheek and went into the kitchen to see to the tea, quickly wiping her face with a hand towel, not wanting to show the tears that were threatening to crack her facade.

A moment later, she was carrying another tray of tea in, having replenished the plate of biscuits.

They chatted for an hour, before Sheridan and Sam left. Both relieved that the conversation had gone so well.

'Thanks for tonight.' Sheridan squeezed Sam's leg.

'What do you mean?'

'The way you lightened the mood with the story of the little girl, Daisy, the chubby one. I didn't want tonight to be all heavy and serious, and your story worked perfectly.' Sheridan smiled. 'She sounds like a proper little character.'

'She is. I've got a bit of a soft spot for her. Even though I'm not supposed to.'

As they pulled up on their drive, Sheridan turned the engine off and sat for a moment. Sam was taking her seat belt off. 'You okay?' she asked.

'Yeah. But I've just realised something about the victims that JT targets.' She turned to Sam. 'It was what you said about Daisy. It helped me connect everything in my head.'

CHAPTER 44

Wednesday 14 July

Sheridan stood in CID. Having got in early, the place was empty and she took the opportunity to update the whiteboard with her theory. Half an hour later, Anna appeared. 'Morning, mate.' She dumped her bag on a desk. 'What's happening?'

'I think JT gets to know the victims before he strikes.' Sheridan looked at the whiteboard. 'Start with Annette Lennon. He must have followed her before, he knows she's going to be on the platform at that time and day, the twenty-second of July. He can't have randomly just been there, hoping someone would come along to fit his victim profile. I think he must have spoken to her at some point earlier. Maybe she mentioned that she was going to catch that train. She used to work in a library . . . maybe that's where he met her.' Sheridan pointed to Jake Hannigan's name. 'Jake was autistic, but unless you spoke to him, you probably wouldn't know. He was a loner, didn't speak to strangers, so *if* he was pushed, then whoever got close enough to him to do it, must have gained his trust.'

Anna stepped in. 'And the Barkers. They were isolated, kept themselves to themselves. The only person who visited them was Freya's sister.'

'Exactly. So, unless you knew them or spent time with them, how would you get them to eat the poisonous mushrooms?' Sheridan paused. 'Let's not forget the foster kid who visited them before they died.'

'Oh yeah, of course. Christ you don't forget anything do you.' Anna sighed. 'Okay, so, what about Kenny James, our homeless guy?' she asked.

'That's the only one I'm not sure about. Because if JT had got to know Kenny, then he'd know he had little to no feeling in his hands.' Sheridan ran a hand through her hair. 'Bollocks. Am I doing that thing again?'

Anna smiled. 'Trying to shoehorn it all in so it fits? Maybe.'

The team began to arrive, and Sheridan shared her thoughts with them. Most agreed that her theory had legs. Hill stood silently at the front of the room, giving nothing away as she listened to the team bouncing ideas around.

'We need to really think about JT. What does he do? Does he work? He's using pi, so maybe he's a maths teacher or a lecturer. If he did kill the Barkers, then he made sure the dog was okay, so maybe he works in an animal sanctuary, or he's a vet?' Sheridan glanced around the room.

Hill finally spoke. 'Fucking hell, Sheridan, how are we going to narrow that down? There are hundreds of potential people who would fit that remit, and we're running out of time if you're right about when he's going to strike next.'

'I know we are, Hill. But we all need to be thinking about what sort of person JT is.'

'What about the names Tim or Tom and the number 5, have we got anywhere yet?' Hill asked.

'Not yet.' Sheridan looked at Rob. 'What about the Barkers' foster kids?'

'We haven't found their details yet. It's going to take a little while, because it's so long ago.'

'And what about our missing suspicious death from 2005, with three victims involved?'

'So far, I can't find one, but I'm still looking.'

Hill checked her watch. 'I'll leave you to it. I need to speak to the chief, he wants an update.'

With the briefing over, Sheridan returned to her office with Anna in tow.

Sheridan walked over to the window and looked down at the street below. 'How many cases have we worked on together?'

Anna joined her. 'Hundreds.'

'And what's the one thing I always say?'

'You ask us what we're missing.' Anna put her arm around Sheridan's shoulder. 'We'll catch him.'

'Will we? Maybe this is the one that beats us. This guy is smart, he plans, he gets close to the victims, they trust him and then he strikes. Maybe he's smarter than we are.'

'I don't believe that. You're smarter than him and the team will work their arses off for you, they always do. We'll catch him because of your brilliant mind. You see things that others don't, and you remember *everything,* every little detail of conversations. You miss nothing, and he'll make a mistake.'

Sheridan kissed her on the cheek. 'Maybe you're right.' She looked back out of the window. 'We need to go and see Annette and Jake's mum and sister again. We *have* to find out if anyone got close to them before the attacks.'

CHAPTER 45

With time against them, Sheridan delegated and sent Anna to visit Annette Lennon while she headed to Jake Hannigan's house. After calling ahead, Jake's mother confirmed she was at home and Jake's sister, Juliet, was at work, so Sheridan was surprised to see her BMW parked outside. Aware that Juliet had previously complained to Hill about her earlier visit, Sheridan prepared herself as she rang the doorbell.

'Oh, hi – your mum said you were at work,' Sheridan said cheerfully as Juliet answered the door.

'I was. But when Mum called to say you were coming over, I wanted to be here.'

Sheridan kept her voice low. 'I'm sorry if my previous visit caused you any concerns, I just . . .'

'It's fine.' Juliet stepped back, walking into the living room and moving a pile of papers from the sofa, for Sheridan to sit.

'So, what do you do for a living?' Sheridan asked casually, looking up as Stephanie walked in, wiping her hands on a tea towel.

'Hello, Detective,' Stephanie said. 'Can I get you a drink?'

'No. I'm fine thanks.'

'You said on the phone that you had some questions.' Stephanie sat on the armchair. Juliet stood beside her, with her arms crossed, having ignored Sheridan's attempt at small talk.

'Yes. I know I've asked before, but I wanted to check if Jake mentioned anyone he'd been talking to, outside of the family, before he died. Maybe someone who had befriended him?'

'No. And if he had, he'd have told me,' Juliet replied, looking at her mum, who nodded in agreement.

'Jake was always wary of people, he wouldn't have spoken to a stranger. Only us,' Stephanie said.

'If he *had* spoken to someone, would he have told his dad, maybe?'

'I don't think so,' Juliet responded. 'Jake and Dad weren't that close.'

Sheridan took out her pocketbook. 'I'd still like to speak to Frank anyway. Do you know where he is?'

Stephanie stood up. 'He's in Spain, and that's not far enough away. Will you excuse me?'

Sheridan watched her walk out of the room and heard her heading upstairs.

'Is she okay?' she asked.

'She doesn't like talking about him.'

'Have you spoken to him since he moved?'

'No.'

'Do you have a contact number for him?'

'No.'

'What does he do for work?'

'He runs some sort of security business, installing cameras and alarms.'

'What's the name of the business?'

'Hannigan Security. I think he sold it, though.'

Sheridan put her pocketbook away and got up. 'Thanks, Juliet. I'll be off. Please apologise to your mum if I've upset her and tell her to call me anytime.'

After Juliet watched Sheridan drive away, she shouted upstairs to her mother that she was going back to work. When there was no reply, she left the house and sat in her car. She dialled her dad's number.

He answered after a few rings. 'Hello princess. You okay?'

'Hi Daddy. Yeah, I'm fine. The police have been here again, that detective Holler. I think she's going to try and get hold of you. I told her we haven't had contact, and I don't have a number for you. And I said that I think you've sold the business. Anyway, are we still meeting up on Saturday?'

'Of course we are sweetheart. I've booked the same restaurant I took you to when I was over last year for your birthday. Only the best for my girl.' Frank hesitated. 'Was the detective asking about Jake again?'

'Yeah. She wants to know if Jake would have spoken to anyone before he died.'

There was a silence at the end of the line.

'You still there, Daddy?'

'Yeah. I'm still here.'

'So, where are you staying?'

'The Crowne Plaza.'

'The one by the airport?'

'No, the one near the Albert Dock.'

'I can't wait to see you.'

'Me too, princess.'

Sheridan arrived back at Hale Street at the same time as Anna, parking next to her.

'How did it go with Annette?' she asked.

'I had to apologise to her that we hadn't been in touch, but she was fine about it.'

Annette had told Anna that she couldn't recall telling anyone that she visited her friend, Clara, regularly, or that she was planning on catching a particular train. The only person who would have known was Clara, who Annette visited every other Saturday before taking the same train home. Annette and Clara had become distant since the attack and rarely had contact now, mainly due to Annette having isolated herself. She had spoken to a lot of people when she worked in the library, but she wouldn't have told any of them such personal information.

As Anna talked, Sheridan realised that she'd been so caught up in the investigation she'd practically abandoned Annette. The quiet, innocent victim living on her own, still in fear that her perpetrator was out there, possibly still watching her. Sheridan inwardly berated herself. Was it the fact that there were so many strings to the inquiry that she'd let one slip from her grasp?

'So, I guess JT must have followed her without her knowing,' Sheridan said as they headed up the stairs towards CID.

She briefed the team about Anna's visit and her own to Jake's mother and sister, tasking Bridie to locate a contact number for Frank Hannigan.

As Sheridan headed back to her office, Hill caught up with her in the corridor. 'I need to speak to you.'

They walked into Sheridan's office, and Hill closed the door behind them. 'The chief is doing his bollocks.'

'What about?'

'He's worried that we might be sensationalising this case by saying the killer is using pi as his basis for the killings.'

'Sensationalising? You're fucking joking. We *know* he's using pi. We've identified three point one four one. It's as clear as bloody day.'

195

'I know that – but he's not overly convinced.' Hill perched on the edge of Sheridan's desk. 'He wants us to re-think our theory and not make this something *fantastical*.' She air-quoted the word.

'He can fuck off, and then he can fuck off some more.' Sheridan exhaled loudly. 'What did you say to him?'

'I told him that if he thought we were sensationalising this case, then maybe he should speak to Potters Road CID, give them a full briefing on what we've discovered so far, set up a whole new team, set up a whole new inquiry with fresh eyes on it, and we all cross our fingers and hope that they find a better theory in the eight days we have left until JT kills five more victims. I then said that my only concern was that if Potters Road agreed with our pi theory and we ran out of time, then he needed to make sure the press office were prepared to explain that because the police had fannied and fucked about bouncing this job around, we would tell the media that we're very, very sorry and hope for forgiveness from the families of all those affected.'

Sheridan bit down on a grin. 'And what was his response?'

'He told me to carry on as we were. And then he told me to get the fuck out of his office.' Hill stood up, turning momentarily to wink at Sheridan before leaving.

By the end of the day, Sheridan couldn't shift the tension in her shoulders – the tightness that had travelled up her neck was throbbing in her temples.

She was about to log off her computer, when Anna walked in. 'You nearly done?'

'Yeah.' Sheridan turned the fan and computer off. 'How do you fancy staying at ours tonight and getting smashed?'

'I think that sounds like a fine idea. Takeaway?'

'Absolutely. Sam's got her first-aid refresher course, so we'll save some for her.'

Bridie appeared in the doorway.

'I found a number for Frank Hannigan, but it's no longer in service. His security business went into liquidation, but I'll do some more digging and see if I can track him down in Spain.'

'Thanks, Bridie. I know it's a real ball ache and we're so tight on time . . . but I really would like to speak to him.'

CHAPTER 46

Maud was gazing lovingly up at Anna and Sheridan as they sat at the kitchen table, tucking into their takeaway.

'Can she have some?' Anna asked and Maud let out a thunderous meow in response.

'Yeah, she'll have some naan bread,' Sheridan replied, draining her wine and getting up to refill their glasses.

Maud gently took the bread from Anna and made her way into the living room, settling under the coffee table with her own takeout.

'Have we actually got a night off, or are we going to talk about the case?' Anna's mouth was full of rice.

'I think we should have a night off.' Sheridan sat back down and took a sip of her drink. 'I walked the routes he took.'

'What?' Anna asked.

'Yesterday, I walked the routes that JT took.'

'I thought we weren't talking shop?' Anna raised her eyes to the ceiling.

'We're not.' Sheridan hesitated, before continuing. 'I went to Edge Hill station, then the derelict building where Kenny James was found, and the road JT walked to and from the nick when he delivered the bag.'

'Why did you do that?'

'I wanted to check the CCTV for myself, I think he knows where the cameras are and how to avoid them.' Sheridan ran her finger around the rim of her glass.

'Hence why he keeps his head down,' Anna said.

'Yeah. I think so.' Sheridan stretched out and put her head back. 'Why do you think JT leaves us clues?'

'Maybe he's enjoying it.'

'Maybe. I mean, he stabbed the JT initials into Annette's face and told her to say he was making a point. If he was responsible for Jake's death, then he left the same initials on Jake's painting and at the scene where Kenny James was found. Then he delivers a key and watch to us and the note. It's like he wants us to figure it out by leaving these cryptic clues.'

'You missed out the Barkers. He didn't leave any message there.'

'True.' Sheridan drank her wine. 'And the more I think about it, the more I wonder if I got that one wrong. Maybe JT didn't have anything to do with their deaths.' She eyed Anna over the top of her wine glass. 'I might have fucked up.'

'We know he's using pi, so the number of victims fits when it comes to the Barkers. But it could be that there's another case where there were four victims that we've missed.'

Sheridan didn't respond immediately, letting Anna's comment sink in.

'I know Hill believes that we've got pi right,' Sheridan said after she was finished considering. 'But maybe she was spot on when she said that I might be forcing Jake's and the Barkers' deaths to fit without any real evidence.' She sighed. 'Be honest with me . . . do you think I've taken my eye off the ball?'

Anna raised her eyebrows. 'I think you're distracted with the Andrew Longford business, but that's understandable. I also think that the closer Ruth gets to nicking Stephen Tubby, the more it's on your mind. In the past, you were always worried that your parents wouldn't live long enough to see Matthew's killer locked up, but that's switched to Andrew now.' She reached across the table and took Sheridan's hand. 'You've got a lot going on and you forget you're only human. You also forget that solving this case doesn't just lie with you, it lies with all of us. I know I've said that your brilliant mind will solve this case, although maybe I put too much on you when I say that. Even though you do have a brilliant mind.'

'Cheers, mate.' Sheridan squeezed her hand.

The front door opened, and Sam called out. 'Panic over – first aider, Sam Sloan, is here to the rescue.' Her smiling face appeared around the kitchen door. 'Evening, ladies.'

Sheridan puckered her lips and Sam bent down to kiss her and then held Sheridan's face between her palms. 'Do you feel okay? Any swelling? Chest tightness?' She pulled Sheridan's sleeve up.

'What *are* you doing?' Sheridan laughed.

'I'm checking that you're not having an allergic reaction to the meal you've just eaten.' She grabbed the remains of Sheridan's naan bread and shoved it in her mouth.

'First -aid refresher going well then?' Anna asked.

Sam pulled a beer out of the fridge. 'Let's just say, I am now officially trained in how to spot when someone is going into anaphylactic shock and how to use one of these.' She placed a plastic syringe on the table.

'What's that?' Anna picked it up and studied it.

'It's an EpiPen. You open the top cover, press it against the patient's thigh and the needle pops out and it injects adrenaline into the body. You can even use it through clothing. Clever, eh?'

'And they let you take these home?' Anna put the pen down. 'And inject someone?'

'No. We practised on an orange, and I nicked it.'

'You do know you live with a police officer, right?' Anna nodded at Sheridan.

'Ooh . . . you gonna arrest me?' Sam winked at Sheridan, who went over to the oven, taking out Sam's saved takeaway.

'I can't be arsed,' Sheridan replied as Maud, on hearing the oven door open, flew into the kitchen and skidded across the floor, bumping into the washing machine.

Sam scooped her up. 'You okay?' she asked as Maud tried to wriggle out of her arms.

'There's a woman on my refresher course that's allergic to cats. I mean, proper allergic. Can you imagine?' Sam kissed the top of Maud's head and plonked her down. 'They gave us a list of the main things people are allergic to, it's mental. Peanuts, milk, insect bites, latex, sesame seeds, fucking loads of things.' She turned to Anna. 'Have you got any allergies?'

Anna nodded. 'Yeah. Dickheads.'

CHAPTER 47

Thursday 15 July

Hill walked into CID eating a packet of crisps. She stayed at the back, while Sheridan was at the front of the room about to start the afternoon briefing.

Sheridan went around each officer, who updated the team as to where they were with their tasks. Hours of CCTV had been trawled through, trying to find images of JT when he'd left the police station after handing in the bag. None had been found so far. The Intel unit and PNC had searched their systems for anything that could indicate who JT was, with no results. The inquiry into the link between the names Tim or Tom and the number 5 had also come up blank.

Rob had checked all suspicious deaths on or around July 2005, trying to find an incident where three victims were involved, and had found none in the Merseyside area. He was still trying to obtain the details of all the children the Barkers had fostered and was hoping for results in the next few days. But they only had a few days left before JT was likely to kill again and as each officer spoke, the air of despondency was tangible. They hadn't lost hope of finding JT in the time they had left, but there was a clear feeling of having no direction and no leads that seemed positive.

Sheridan tried to rally them, throwing in idea after idea, each one a little weaker than the last. Finally, she came to her conclusions.

'If we didn't have a suss death in July 2005 that fits our remit, then maybe we need to be looking further afield? Another county? Maybe JT committed his first killing elsewhere and that's why we can't find it.'

Hill put her hands behind her head. When she spoke, her tone was unusually quiet and thoughtful. 'That's a mammoth task. It would take us months to get that information, and we only have days. We need to think of something else.'

After the briefing, Sheridan returned to her office, where she found herself once again looking out of the window over the Albert Dock. She tried to remember a case like this one and none came to mind. Not one. Every case came with its own pressures, she accepted that, but never had she known exactly what date a victim would be murdered, or in this case, victims. Five of them. She closed her eyes. Anna's words from the night before rang in her ears: *You forget you're only human. You also forget that solving a case doesn't just lie with you, it lies with all of us.*

Sheridan knew Anna was right, but it changed nothing. Every case, every victim, was personal to her. The job had rules and procedures that had to be followed, because if they were broken, the whole case could be lost, thrown out on a technicality. The unsigned statement, the misplaced evidence bag, the doubts as to whether forensics were gathered in line with the law. Rules and procedures. So many of them defiantly standing in the way of the one and only thing Sheridan ever wanted. Justice.

She opened her eyes, grabbed her bag and headed to her car. Fuck it. She didn't have time to play by the rules.

As Sheridan rang the bell, she could hear a child's voice shouting from inside. She looked up as the door was opened.

'Hello, Kyle. Can I come in?'

Kyle Crane folded his arms and flicked a look back down the hallway. Sheridan could see a little boy standing there, holding a football under his arm. 'Who's that, Dad?' he asked.

'No one, mate. Go back out in the garden, I'll be there in a minute.'

The little boy ignored him and bounced the ball. 'Do you like football?' he said, still bouncing it as he joined Kyle at the door.

'Yes, I do.' Sheridan smiled down at him. 'So, you're a swimmer and a footballer, eh?'

'Yeah. We've got a pool, do you want to see it?'

'A pool? Wow, that sounds cool.'

'Yeah. It's only a little one but you can come and play in it if you want.'

'I said go back into the garden, Chris.' Kyle touched the top of his son's head.

Chris bounced the football twice, before obeying his dad and walking back down the hallway.

'I only get to see him once a week on a Thursday, so whatever you want will have to wait.'

'What I need to speak to you about *can't* wait. It'll take two minutes.'

Kyle thought about it and stepped aside, pointing to the living room. Sheridan walked in and remained standing.

'Okay. You've got two minutes.' Kyle folded his arms again.

'I know you didn't sell that key and watch to some bloke in a pub. I can't tell you why I need them, but I will say this, they're crucial to my inquiry.'

'That's got nothing to do with me. I told you before, I sold them. They're gone.'

'It has *everything* to do with you. They'll lead me to someone who likes to kill people. So, if you've had them in your possession, then you can at least tell me about the name engraved on the watch.'

204

'I can't help you.'

'Was it Tim or Tom?'

'Can't help you.'

'Was there anything engraved on the key?'

Kyle gave a slight shake of his head. 'I've already been asked this. I didn't look at them that closely.'

'Yes, you did. It was a Rolex watch, so you *would* have looked at it closely.' Sheridan tried to keep the frustration out of her voice.

Kyle looked to the floor. 'I *didn't*. And you can keep asking me the same questions, but it will always be the same answer.'

Sheridan took a step closer. 'We know there was a name engraved on the watch. Either Tim or Tom.'

'So, if you already know that, then why the fuck are you asking me?' Kyle looked her in the eye. 'This is harassment, I told your lot everything and I was charged, so are you even supposed to be here asking me more questions? Because if not, then you need to go, so I can spend time with my boy.'

'I know you still have the key and the watch.'

Kyle moved towards the door. 'Goodbye, Officer.'

Sheridan followed him and as he opened the front door, she turned to him. She couldn't be certain that Jake Hannigan *was* a victim, but she was going to use his death to try and touch a nerve with Kyle.

'The man I'm looking for killed someone's son, their *only* son. He's going to do it again, he's going to kill again very soon and I might not be able to stop him if I don't have that key and watch.'

'Not my problem,' Kyle responded, as Sheridan passed him on her way out the door.

His comment made her turn round.

'It *is* your problem . . . if it's *your* son he kills.'

CHAPTER 48

Saturday 17 July

Frank Hannigan stood up as Juliet walked into the restaurant. She made her way over to him and they hugged.

'Oh, it's so good to see you, Daddy.' She kissed his cheek.

The waiter pulled a chair out and offered her a drink.

'I'll have a bottle of champagne, please.' Frank winked at Juliet. 'Only the best for my girl.'

They chatted as the champagne flowed. After they'd ordered their starters, Frank broached the subject of DI Holler asking questions around Jake's death. He put his glass down and wiped his mouth with a napkin. 'So, why are the police asking questions about Jake *now*? It was three years ago.' He cleared his throat.

'I don't know. This DI Holler just kept asking if Jake could have talked to someone before he died. It's all a bit weird if you ask me. But anyway, enough of that. What has Daddy bought me for my birthday?' She leaned across the table and took his hands in hers. 'I hope you haven't gone mad and spent lots of money on me.' She laughed and picked up her glass.

Frank smiled and slid a jewellery box across the table. 'Hope you like it.'

Juliet opened the box and put her hand to her mouth. 'Oh my God, Daddy. That's too much.' She stood and walked around the table, wrapping her arms around his neck and planting kisses on his cheek.

'You're worth it, princess.'

Juliet returned to her seat and took the necklace out, swiftly securing it in place. 'It must have cost a fortune.' She looked down at it. 'I bet it was at least ten grand.'

Frank clasped his hands together. 'Actually, double . . . But you're my princess and money doesn't come into it.' He sipped his drink. 'Are you getting the money okay every month?'

'Yeah. I'm saving most of it though.'

'Have you still got that second bank account?'

'Yeah.'

'And you haven't told your mum anything about the money?'

'No. She has no idea.'

'Good. And she still doesn't know that we're in contact?'

'No. No one knows.'

They talked through dinner and after Frank paid the bill, said their goodbyes outside.

'How long are you staying?' Juliet asked as her cab pulled up.

'Another week or so. I've got some business to sort out, then I'm heading back to Spain.'

She hugged him again. 'I wish I could see you more, not just once a year.'

'Me too, princess.' He brushed her hair away from her face. 'Keep me posted with this police thing. I want to know why they're so interested.'

'I will.'

He waved as she was driven away and then, tucking his hands into his pockets, he walked slowly, aimlessly towards the Albert Dock. The exorbitantly priced dinner he'd eaten was churning around his stomach and he took several deep breaths, trying not to be sick.

Feeling his head swimming, he sat on a bench, swallowing the bile in his mouth.

Why were the police asking questions about Jake? Had someone come forward to say they'd seen Frank there that day? The day Jake died. Had they heard the argument? Had they seen him leave? Everyone had believed his story that he was playing golf all day. No one had questioned it. Not even the police. They hadn't questioned it because Jake's death wasn't suspicious. He had simply jumped. He'd even left a suicide note. So, what were they looking for now, three years later? What would happen if they discovered that the last person to talk to Jake that day was his own father?

CHAPTER 49

Monday 19 July

Sheridan and Anna were coming out of the ladies toilet when Rob appeared in the corridor.

'Sheridan,' he called, waving a sheet of paper.

'What's that?' she asked.

'What we've been waiting for. The names of the Barkers' foster kids.'

Sheridan and Anna followed him into CID and Rob addressed the team.

'Okay, the Barkers fostered three children before they had the twins, who were born in 1977. Molly Frane, Carlton Devin and Emerson Corr.' He cleared his throat. 'The first child they fostered was Carlton Devin. He was three years old and stayed with them for two years from 1970 to 1972. The next was Molly, who was nine when she went to live with them in 1972. She stayed until she was adopted in 1976. While Molly was with the Barkers, they also took on Emerson, who was with them from 1972 until 1987. He didn't go back into care because he was an adult by then.'

Sheridan turned to her team. 'Okay everyone. We know that one of these foster kids was back in contact with the Barkers before they died. Freya's sister, Janet, told us that she couldn't remember the name but that it was a male, so let's concentrate on Carlton and Emerson.' She thought for a moment before continuing. 'Actually, let's find Molly as well, maybe she'd also been in touch with them and if not, she might be able to tell us about Emerson, seeing as they were in care together. You never know, he might be JT.'

Hill walked in and Sheridan brought her up to speed. 'I agree, we should concentrate fully on locating these three people.' Hill rubbed a hand down her face. 'As you're all aware, we're working on an operation to have officers in situ tomorrow in the PEO, which is one of the days that JT might come in to claim the bag. We know it's a long shot – but right now, that's all we've got.' She nodded at Sheridan and left.

CHAPTER 50

Tuesday 20 July

Sheridan felt her stomach jangling as she got out of her car. In the past five days, little progress had been made in the investigation. They had checked every lead, most of which had marched them down dead ends. They still didn't know who JT was, where he was or who he was going to kill next. All they were certain of was that they now had two days to find him. Two days to save the five men named Tim or Tom.

A meeting had taken place two days earlier between Sheridan's team, the local inspectors, sergeants and uniformed officers. It had been agreed there was a chance that JT would come into the PEO and claim the bag. The problem was they didn't know which day. JT had intimated to Marcus that he would return on the 22nd of July, but exactly four weeks from the day he had handed the bag in was the 20th.

Today.

A complex operation had been set in place. Andrea would be in the PEO, in her usual position. Working with her would be a male PC, dressed in the same civilian staff uniform. In the public area two PCs in plain clothes – one in a suit, making him look like a solicitor, the other in jeans and a cap – would blend in with the public. Across the road, two more plain-clothes officers would be watching, with four more on the roof scanning the street below for any sign of JT approaching. They had all been shown the images of him, from the attack on Annette Lennon and from where he was seen by the building Kenny James was found in, although they were grainy with little facial detail visible. The tech team had tried to enhance them with little success. Every officer involved was aware that JT didn't like to be near other people and would sidestep if he was approached. And this was the quirk that might just give him away. They also knew that he was smart and extremely dangerous and all officers taking part were armed.

As Sheridan walked into CID, the team were already present. She stood at the front of the room, next to Hill, ready for the final briefing before the PEO opened at 8 a.m.

She took a sip of water, and when everyone had congregated, she began.

'Good morning, everyone.' She went around the room, starting with Andrea. 'As you know, we don't have a clear image of what JT looks like, so the only way we'll know it's him is if he mentions the bag. Bearing in mind, he could send someone else. But whoever comes in is connected to JT because no one else knows about the bag. Are you okay with what you have to do?'

Andrea nodded. 'Yes. If he comes in and asks about the bag, I take the usual details, get him to describe it to me and I check the property log, confirm the bag hasn't been claimed and that lawfully it's his. I'll then tell him that I'm just going to go and get it out of the property store. That's when you lot drop him on his arse and nick him.'

A wave of amusement rippled around the room.

'Perfect,' Sheridan replied. 'This might be a long day, so bear that in mind. As previously agreed, we'll swap the two PCs that are positioned in the PEO every two hours, that way you get a comfort break and also if JT comes in to check the place out first, he won't suss out that you look out of place, having been there all day. We've got a dedicated airwaves channel, so everyone that's carrying a radio, please set them to PAT seven.'

At the end of the briefing, everyone left to take up their positions.

Sheridan's team of detectives sat at their desks. The room was eerily quiet as they took a moment for themselves. Was this the day they were going to catch JT? Was this their only chance to get him before he killed again?

After a few moments, they logged on to their computers and slowly but surely, they tried to get on with their day. Their radios crackled as the officers downstairs and on the roof confirmed they were in place.

Sheridan went to her office and looked out of the window, watching everyone on the street below. She clasped her hands together, feeling them shaking slightly. Every element of the investigation went through her head. She sat down and switched on her computer, staring blankly at the screen, before turning up her radio, immediately realising that little else would get done today.

By 6.45 p.m. there was still no sign of JT, and the PEO was due to close at 7 p.m. Fifteen minutes left. Sheridan felt frustration take over, and the doubts crept in. What if JT had spotted the officers in position? What if he'd realised they were waiting for him? If that was the case, then he would never come in. Not today. And not on the 22nd. She stood up and was about to head to CID when her phone rang.

She snatched at it, spotting Rob's extension number. 'Yes, mate?'

'Got an update on the three foster kids. You need to hear this.'

213

The whole team gathered round as Rob shared what information he had. 'I'll start with Carlton, first of all, he *can't* be JT.'

'Why?' Hill asked.

'Apart from the fact that he hasn't been back in the UK since he moved to Trinidad in 1992. He's Black.'

Sheridan crossed her arms. 'Okay. Let's rule him out. What about the other two?'

'We haven't found Emerson Corr yet, but Molly Frane went missing in 2005.' Rob looked at Sheridan. 'In *July,* 2005.'

Sheridan dropped her arms to her sides. 'That's the date we're missing. July 2005.'

'Yeah. She left her home in Norfolk with the woman she was living with, and they vanished.'

Sheridan swallowed. 'That doesn't fit the others. We're looking for *three* victims. It's the number three that starts off the pi sequence.' She looked at Rob. 'Any note left?'

'There was, but it wasn't a suicide note.' He looked at the sheet of paper in his hand. 'It read, "Mum, Dad and all our friends. We love you all so much, but we have decided that we want to be together, away from here, away to start a new life. Please don't worry about us, we'll be fine. We have everything we need. Maybe one day, we'll come back, but for now please don't look for us. This is what we want. Love Molly and Bethany".'

'So, were they a couple? Molly and Bethany?' Sheridan asked.

'Molly's adopted parents said at the time that they suspected they were a couple, but it was never discussed openly.'

'And it was just the two of them that went missing?'

'Yeah.'

'And what date did they disappear?'

'Sometime between the eighteenth and twenty-fourth of July.'

'The date fits but the number doesn't.' Sheridan bit on her bottom lip. 'Can you do a bit more digging? Let's see if we can establish another misper around the same date. Maybe they're connected to Molly and Bethany and that gives us three people. And let's keep looking for Emerson Corr.' She looked at the clock on the wall. 7.08 p.m.

The radio on the desk came to life.

'All units on PAT seven, the PEO is closing, and we have no sightings of the subject. Stand down. All units, stand down.'

CHAPTER 51

Thursday 22 July

Sheridan hadn't slept all night. She'd stared at the clock on her bedside table as it turned over to midnight. This was it. This was the day that JT was going to kill five people, and all they knew was that the victims were called either Tim or Tom. It was also the day that JT might come into the police station and claim the bag. Never had a case affected her quite like this one and the thought felt like a rock in her stomach.

She got up at 2 a.m. and crept downstairs, trying not to wake Sam. Maud woke up, too, and raced past her – very happy that she was likely going to get her breakfast early.

Sheridan hadn't been up for more than ten minutes and was sipping her coffee when Sam appeared round the kitchen door.

'Hey. You okay?' Sam kissed the top of her head and re-boiled the kettle.

'Yeah. I'm fine . . . actually, that's a fucking lie. I'm not fine, I'm angry at myself and I know I shouldn't be, but this bastard, JT, has outwitted us.'

'You still might catch him today.' Sam took a seat opposite her at the kitchen table and held her hand. 'No one is smarter than my girl. You know this case inside out, you know there's something about this guy that will catch him out. Something about him that's staring you in the face.'

'I know you're right. You know me and the way I work. But I've gone over everything, over and over and over and I can't figure it out, whatever it is that I haven't seen.'

They talked until the sun came up and Sheridan got herself ready. She had to be in early for the morning briefing, to go through the details of the operation in readiness if JT came in to claim the bag. The exact same set-up as two days earlier. Except this was their last chance.

As she got to the front door, she turned to kiss Sam. 'Wish me luck.'

Sam gently clasped Sheridan's face between her hands. 'You don't need luck. You just need to find the chink in his armour. His weakness. Because trust me, he has one. Remember, he's just a man, Sheridan.'

By 8 a.m., all the officers involved in what was now called Operation Pi were in position. Sheridan and her team sat quietly in CID, all reflecting silently on the fact that today was the day.

Hill addressed the room. 'Everyone's ready. So, let's hope he comes in,' she said. Muted nods came in reply. She turned to Sheridan. 'The chief wants a de-brief later. He knows that we're now expecting five bodies to be discovered, either today or in the next few days. The press officer is working on what's going to be released.' She tried to sound upbeat as she continued. 'You've all worked so hard and I'm proud of that. But I think we have to be prepared and face the fact that we're out of time. I'm sorry to say it, but that's the reality.' And with that, she quietly left the room.

Three hours had passed. Sheridan was in her office, once again staring down at the street. Anna came in and joined her, placing an arm around Sheridan's shoulder.

'We're not beaten yet. We might still get him.'

Sheridan turned to her, her voice breaking. 'I think we might have lost this one . . .'

At that moment, she heard running in the corridor and they both turned to see Rob.

'We've found Emerson Corr.' He caught his breath. 'He's registered at an address in Liverpool.'

Sheridan's eyes widened. 'Do we know if he's still living there?'

'No. But only because the electoral register can be well out of date. He's no trace on PNC, we're doing more checks on him, but so far all we've got is the address.'

'So, he's local and we know the Barkers were visited by an ex foster kid before they died.' Sheridan nodded. 'Right, we need to get round there. You, me and Anna will go in an unmarked car, and we'll have uniform to back us up.'

Sheridan, Anna and Rob made their way to Emerson Corr's address. Remaining in radio contact with the marked police van that followed them, they turned the sharp corner into the road. Three houses were all set back at the end of drives. The one where they believed Emerson Corr lived was at the other end, just before another sharp bend. As they passed the house, Sheridan slowed the car down and they looked to their right, spotting a male closing the back door of a grey Transit van parked at the end of the drive near the road. After locking the van, the male turned and walked down the road, carrying a bag. He kept his head down. He didn't look up as they passed. Sheridan radioed the police van behind them to keep driving and not stop.

'Who does that guy look like to you?' Sheridan asked as she reached the bend at the end of the road, parking up out of sight next to the police van.

'JT. He looks a bit like JT,' Anna replied, turning to look at Rob who nodded in agreement.

'He must have seen the police van,' Sheridan said. 'But he didn't look back at it.'

She radioed the control room, giving the description of the male, his location and direction of travel. The control room responded that the area wasn't covered by CCTV.

'Rob, you're going to have to follow him on foot,' Sheridan said.

Waiting until the male had disappeared around the corner, Rob got out of the car.

'Don't let him see you,' she said, and Rob nodded before heading off to follow him.

Sheridan looked over at the van, which was parked facing the road. From where she was, she couldn't see if there was any writing on the sides. She spoke into her radio. 'Charlie Delta six-six, I need a PNC check on a grey Transit van.' She gave the control room the index number of the vehicle.

She turned to Anna. 'I fucking hope that van comes back registered to Emerson Corr. Then we'll know this is his house and that guy we've just seen really could be JT.'

The radio crackled 'Control to Charlie Delta six-six.'

'Go ahead.' Sheridan felt the pulse throbbing in her neck.

'Vehicle comes back to a Martin Howlett, 46 Crimson Lake Road, Sefton.'

Sheridan responded. 'Can you check it again, please? And run Martin Howlett through PNC.'

A moment later the control room responded. 'Vehicle definitely comes back to Martin Howlett, registered keeper since 2001. He's no trace on PNC. 46 Crimson Lake Road is the registered business address of MH Painting and Decorating.'

'Fuck,' Sheridan said out loud, before replying. 'All received.' She turned to Anna. 'Maybe Emerson's having work done at the house.' She radioed the control room back and requested units to attend Martin Howlett's address.

She sighed heavily and shared her thoughts with Anna. 'If Martin Howlett answers the door at the Crimson Lake Road address, then he needs to tell us why someone else is driving his van. If he says he's lent it to a guy called Emerson Corr, then I think Rob's following the right guy. That could still be JT.' Sheridan closed her eyes for a moment.

Then the radio crackled and Rob's voice came over the airwaves. 'Sheridan, I've got eyes on him, but I'm having to stay back. He's turned into an alleyway off Clove Lane. He's put a grey cap on now.'

'All received,' she replied, resting her hands on the steering wheel. 'Why would he put a cap on?' She got out of the car and stepped over to the police van.

The uniformed sergeant in the passenger seat wound his window down. 'What's the plan?' he asked.

'We need to stay out of sight. If anyone's in the house, I don't think they'd see us from here.' She looked down the road. 'But I don't want to take any chances. Can you park up further away?' She pointed to a layby nearby. 'Park the van in there, out of sight. I'll give the order if I want you to make a move. We'll take it one step at a time.'

She returned to the car, just as Rob came through with an update.

'He's just entered Daisy's Flower Shop on Bright Street.'

Sheridan remembered the sidestep JT always made if he was approached, even by a cat.

She radioed Rob and asked the question. He hesitated before speaking. 'Three people walked past him, really close, but he didn't stop or sidestep them.'

Sheridan could hear the disappointment in Rob's message. 'Okay Rob. Keep eyes on him anyway.'

Three minutes of radio silence passed while the male remained in the flower shop.

Then came the message. 'Control room to Charlie Delta six-six. Officers are at Martin Howlett's address. There's a "sold" sign up outside and the place is empty.'

Sheridan acknowledged the update and put her head in her hands in frustration. 'Fuck's sake. So, we don't know if the guy we're following is Emerson Corr or Martin Howlett.' She put her head down. 'I'm not sure now if the guy with the cap on is JT. He *always* sidesteps when someone or something goes near him. But Rob's saying that three people have passed him and . . . nothing. No weird change in direction.' She looked at Anna. 'How much do you honestly think he looked like JT?'

'A bit. But we've never really seen his face, so we can't be sure. It did look a bit like him though.'

There was a pause.

And then the call came from the control room.

The call that everyone had hoped for, but none had expected.

'All units, all units, update to follow from officers in the PEO.'

Sheridan sat bolt upright, holding her radio close to her face. Waiting for the message. And then it came.

'All units on Operation Pi be advised, we have a male in Hale Street PEO who has claimed the bag. All units await further update.'

Sheridan snapped a look at Anna.

'Jesus. He came in. JT came in,' Anna said. 'Or he sent someone else in.'

Sheridan rubbed her forehead. 'Shit. Now we don't know who's who. Is that JT in the PEO, or is he the guy Rob's following . . . or . . .' She put her head back. 'Or are none of them JT? Has he set all this up just to mess with us?'

CHAPTER 52

Sheridan's heart was pumping so fast that she felt light-headed. But she had to concentrate. There was so much information coming through and she desperately needed to keep it all in her head.

Rob still had eyes on the flower shop that the male in the cap had entered . . . the male they now believed could be the registered keeper of the van, Martin Howlett. The male who coincidentally resembled JT.

The male who had entered the PEO to claim the bag had been taken to an interview room and Sheridan was waiting for an update. Was this it? Was it over? Was *he* JT? Had he really come back in to claim the bag on the date he said he would? Or had he sent someone else in? If that was the case, then he could lead them to JT. Or was he a decoy, just there to give JT time to kill his five victims?

Anxious minutes passed before Sheridan's mobile rang: it was Hill.

'I know you're up to your tits in it out there, but I've been downstairs and seen the guy who's come in to claim the bag.'

'Is it JT?' Sheridan asked, keeping one ear on the radio.

'I don't know. He's similar in height and build, but he's refusing to give his name. He keeps saying there's been a mistake.'

'Okay. I don't need to tell you this Hill, but don't take your eyes off him. If it is JT then he's smart, he'll have planned this to the last detail. Please Hill, don't trust him, not for a second.'

'Okay,' Hill replied. 'Are you still at Emerson Corr's place?'

Sheridan updated her that Rob was still following the male who looked like JT. 'But we don't know who's who. And maybe JT has set all this up to keep half of Merseyside police busy while he murders five people called Tim or Tom.'

The call ended and Sheridan closed her eyes, feeling a fury rising inside her. She wanted to cry out and scream until her lungs hurt.

Rob's voice came over the radio. 'Male has just left Daisy's Flower Shop with a bouquet. He's still carrying the bag, no longer wearing the cap, and he's now wearing a black top. Looks like he's heading back the way he came.'

Sheridan opened her eyes and turned to Anna. 'We're wasting our time. Whoever this guy is, it's not JT.' She stared out of the window. 'JT is laughing right now, because he's outsmarted us.' She gripped the steering wheel, turning her knuckles white. 'I told Sam this morning that JT had outwitted us.'

Anna sighed. 'We don't know that yet.'

Sheridan didn't reply but laid her head back, Sam's words echoing in her ears. *You know this case inside out, you know there's something about this guy that will catch him out. Something about him that's staring you in the face. You just need to find the chink in his armour. His weakness. Because trust me, he has one.*

'The chink in his armour,' she said under her breath, as her head swam with everything she knew about JT. Everything she'd picked up on. But what was his weakness? What was the chink in his armour?

Her eyes suddenly widened. *That's it,* she thought. *That's it. The chink in his armour.*

She quickly spoke into her radio. 'Rob, where is he now?'

'Heading back towards the alleyway, Clove Lane.'

She started up the engine and reversed back to where the police van was parked, out of sight.

She turned to Anna. 'Get in the driver's seat, keep the engine running.' She got out of the car and ran over to the side of the police van, sliding it open.

Anna, completely confused about what was happening, did as Sheridan had asked.

Seconds later, Sheridan emerged carrying a police enforcer, better known as the big red key. A fourteen-kilo piece of kit used by police officers to break down doors.

Sheridan, already out of breath, placed the heavy tool in the footwell and got back into the car. 'Drive me up the road, I'll tell you when to stop. I don't have time to explain.' She placed her earpiece in and clipped the radio to her belt.

Back in the police van, the sergeant stared in disbelief. 'Jesus Christ, she's going to the house, she's going to smash his bloody door in.'

Sheridan called up Rob. 'Where is he now?'

'About a hundred yards from the turning into his road.'

'Keep me updated every twenty yards.' Sheridan pointed as Anna drove. 'There. Stop right there, turn the car around, and get ready to drive away as soon as I get back in.'

She got out of the car, the adrenaline rushing through her and giving her the strength to lift the enforcer out.

Rob's voice in her ear. 'Eighty yards.'

She stood by the waist-high brick wall separating Corr's drive from the pavement and swung the enforcer as hard as she could. She felt the sudden jolt through her body as the enforcer struck the wall, cracking the bricks which came loose from the cement, the noise almost drowning out Rob's updates, and as she lifted the enforcer as high as her waning strength would allow, she let go.

Rob's voice in her ear. 'Twenty yards.'

Sheridan lifted the enforcer again, letting it drop to the ground again and again.

Rob. 'Ten yards.'

Sheridan heaved the enforcer back into the car and got in. 'Go. Go now!'

Anna put her foot on the accelerator and sped away. Just as they reached the bend at the end of the road, Rob came back on the radio.

'He's turned the corner.'

Sheridan tried to catch her breath as Anna pulled up, parking next to the police van.

'What the fuck was that all about?' Anna turned the engine off.

Sheridan's mouth was so dry she struggled to speak. 'I'll be back in a sec, keep listening to your radio.'

She climbed out of the car and crossed the road, stepping over a small wooden fence and disappearing into the trees. Anna could just make her out as she crouched down. Then Sheridan's voice came over the air, in a whisper. 'All units, radio silence. Wait for my signal. Rob, stay where you are, don't let him see you.'

From Sheridan's position, the male couldn't see her, and she watched as he walked up the road, carrying the bag and a large bouquet of flowers. 'Come on. Come on, please,' she said under her breath. 'Please.'

The man was closer now, his head down as he reached the spot at the top of his drive where Sheridan had used the enforcer. She tried to slow her breathing down, keeping her mouth slightly open, desperate not to make a sound.

She watched as the man suddenly stopped. Dead in his tracks. He slowly turned his head, looking at the cracked wall to his right.

Please, Sheridan thought.

And then he looked back down at the ground, took two steps to his left into the road, before continuing towards his house.

Sheridan let out a breath, as a huge smile took over her face. 'Hello, JT.'

CHAPTER 53

Sheridan carried on watching as the man turned into the driveway. 'All units, stand by, be ready to approach the house, the male has just walked up his drive. I haven't got eyeball on him.' She quickly made her way back through the trees and clambered over the fence, running towards the car. From their position they couldn't see the male, only the entrance to his drive. Sheridan approached the police van and the sergeant opened the window.

'That's our man. We need to—'

Rob's voice came over the radio. 'Sheridan, he's pulling out of the drive, he's in the van, he's turning left, towards me.'

'Shit.' Sheridan turned to the sergeant. 'You need to get into the house. Use caution and be aware that the whole place could be a crime scene. Keep me updated.'

The sergeant was about to answer her but she was already climbing into the car. 'Go, we'll pick Rob up on the way.'

Anna pulled away. 'What the fuck is going on? Is it JT?'

Sheridan turned to her, smiling. 'Yeah. It's JT.'

'How do you know?'

'I found the chink in his armour.'

Anna sped up as the grey van disappeared around the bend at the end of the road. Rob emerged and she pulled over to pick him up and he quickly got into the back of the car.

'I'll explain everything, but we can't lose that van.' Sheridan radioed the control room and updated them, requesting unmarked units to assist as she gave the location and direction of travel.

As they tried to catch up with the van it turned left into a side street, just as another car pulled out of a parking space in front of them.

'Get out of the fucking way,' Anna shouted, trying to manoeuvre around the car, but finding that the road was too narrow.

By the time they reached the end of the road, the van was gone.

'Which way?' Anna asked, as they looked in all directions.

'Go right, see if we can pick him up,' Sheridan replied.

They turned right, searching desperately, checking side roads as they went.

Five minutes passed and they were losing hope, when Rob shouted, 'Stop. There he is, coming towards us.'

Anna swung the car around and ended up two cars behind the van. Sheridan relayed their position over the airwaves and requested back-up vehicles to remain in the area.

'We don't know if he's already killed the five yet, but if he hasn't, he'll lead us to where he's going to do it.' Sheridan wiped her mouth.

And then her eyes widened. 'Oh, Christ, there's someone in the passenger seat. I can see an arm hanging out the window – someone smoking a cigarette.'

'Are we absolutely sure this is JT? Why's he buying flowers? Something seems off,' Anna said as they pulled up at the traffic lights, still two cars behind the grey van.

'You're going to have to trust me. It's him.' Sheridan bit down hard on her bottom lip.

As the lights changed, the grey van turned right on to the Dock Road and slowed down.

'Stay back, don't let him see us,' Sheridan said.

Anna pulled over and they watched as the van took another right and parked up.

No one got out and Sheridan radioed the control room. 'All units make for the Dock Road, subject has stopped outside the old Mayflower Joinery building. Silent approach.' She watched as a large metal shutter started to open and the van turned to face it.

'He's going to drive in there. We need to stop him.'

At that moment, a marked police car came around the corner and Anna pulled out, pointing out of the window to indicate that the van was now inside the building as the shutter began to descend.

'Go now, go now,' Sheridan shouted into her radio and the marked car headed for the shutter, which was halfway down. The police car drove at speed and the shutter crashed on to the roof, wedging it underneath.

Sheridan, Anna and Rob ran over as the two uniformed officers got out of the vehicle and headed into the building.

'Stop!' one of the officers shouted as the male jumped out of the grey van and started running.

He pulled open a heavy wooden door that led into a long corridor and came out into a large empty office. The officers were ten paces behind him as he turned left through another external door. The male was now twenty paces in front of them. They passed another derelict building, shouting all the while for him to stop. Then suddenly, he did stop, turned to face the officers and reached into his inside pocket.

Back inside the building, Sheridan cautiously peered through the passenger window of the grey van. Curled up in a ball was a slim woman, aged around twenty. Her pink hair was spiked up with gel. Sheridan slowly opened the door and reached in, just as the girl looked up.

'What's happening?' She uncurled herself and blinked at Sheridan.

'It's okay. You're safe now, we're police officers. What's your name?'

'Tara. Oh shit, am I getting nicked?'

'No.' Sheridan held out her hand and helped Tara out of the van, spotting the large bouquet of flowers on the seat next to her. The keys were still in the ignition and as Sheridan ushered Tara away from the vehicle, Rob took the keys.

As he unlocked the back doors, Anna joined him and they stole a look at each other, before pulling them open.

Sheridan, ensuring Tara couldn't see, watched as Anna and Rob reeled back.

'What is it?' she asked.

Rob reached inside and for a moment, Sheridan held her breath. Then he turned to her and slowly shook his head. 'We're too late.'

CHAPTER 54

The two officers remained motionless as the runner pulled something from his inside pocket, before throwing it as far as he could. Then he turned and ran again and the officers picked up the pursuit. As he turned a corner, he slowed down and when the officers had almost caught up with him, he came to a halt, and turning to face them, he threw his hands high in the air, then lowered them behind his head.

'I'm done,' he shouted loudly, smiling. 'I'm done.'

Sheridan's radio came to life and she heard a broken message over the airwaves. With the concrete walls making communication poor, she asked for the message to be repeated.

And then came the reply. 'One under arrest.'

She exhaled and felt her jaw tighten. Then she heard a clicking sound and turned to look at Tara, who was trying to light a cigarette.

'Have you got a light?' Tara asked.

Sheridan shook her head. 'No. But we'll get you one in a bit.'

Tara stood up. 'It's okay. Eddie's probably got one in the van.' She went to step over to where Anna and Rob were, but Sheridan put a hand on her shoulder, holding her back.

'You can't go over there.'

Tara sat back down. 'Bloody gasping,' she said, clearly still needing that cigarette.

Anna switched places with Sheridan, who went to join Rob. She could hear sirens approaching as she looked inside.

'Fuck,' she said under her breath. The sirens were now wailing outside as unit after unit arrived on the scene. She walked over to the shutter and ducked underneath it and approaching the uniformed inspector, requested his officers seal off the area and search the building.

Sheridan looked up to see the runner being led towards her, handcuffed. Her heart was drumming in her chest as they approached.

The runner spoke first. 'Detective Inspector Sheridan Holler,' he said, nodding in recognition.

'Emerson Corr,' she replied.

Corr's smile broadened. 'We meet again.'

Sheridan frowned. 'We've met before?'

'We certainly have.'

Sheridan's mind was going at a hundred miles an hour. What was he talking about? When had they met? She studied his face. Nothing. 'When?' she asked.

Emerson Corr took a deep breath. 'All in good time.' Refusing to elaborate further, he was led away.

CHAPTER 55

Sheridan was watching as Emerson Corr was driven off in a waiting police van. Anna emerged from under the shutter with Tara Brookes, who was placed in the back of a marked car.

Anna joined Sheridan. 'Tara's happy to give a statement, I'll get a quick account from her first.' She noticed the look on Sheridan's face. 'What's wrong?'

'He said we've met before,' Sheridan said, slowly shaking her head. 'I can't place him.'

She returned to the building. Inside the grey van was the body of a young woman. Her hands, feet and mouth were bound, wrapped in thick foam and tied with rope.

It was gone 12 p.m. and Sheridan knew that today, 22nd of July, was the day Emerson Corr had planned to kill five people. He'd succeeded in killing one, and Tara would have been number two. Lucky Tara had unknowingly escaped death by a literal miracle.

Sheridan took a moment for herself. Feeling her hands shaking, she placed her radio under her arm and clasped them together. Then it went off. 'Sheridan, it's Sergeant Holmes. We've searched Emerson Corr's address, there's no one here. Nothing to suggest foul play. The place is immaculate.'

'Okay. Let's get a seal on it and can you organise CSI to attend? I'll get a couple of my DCs over there.'

'Will do.'

Just then, the officer who had arrested Emerson Corr approached her. 'Sorry, I know you're busy, ma'am, but I wanted to let you know that Corr threw something away while we were chasing him. I've been back to the spot, but I can't see anything obvious.'

'Seal the area off and we'll get it searched thoroughly.'

The officer nodded and turned to walk away.

'Good job, by the way,' Sheridan called after him.

He turned back round. 'He's bloody fit, I'll give him that. He nearly outran me . . . and I was the 1500-metre county running champion two years running.'

Sheridan smiled and made her way over to Anna who was talking to Tara.

The twenty-two-year-old had disclosed that she had met 'Eddie', as he called himself, several times. Tara was a heroin addict, working the streets to fund her habit. He'd approached her, parking up in his car and offering to pay her if she got in and chatted to him. He'd brought her to the building they were currently at, and they'd sat outside. He'd told her he couldn't be seen with her as he was a man of the church, and he'd lose his job if it became known that he was picking up a prostitute. He never forced himself on her. Quite the opposite, according to Tara. He'd simply wanted to talk.

He asked her about her life and how she had ended up on the streets. And he paid her well for these conversations. Two hundred pounds just for an hour of her company. He seemed kind, was quietly spoken and she trusted him. Then, on one occasion, he had asked her if he could see her naked and she had agreed. He'd driven her inside the building, closed the shutter, and watched as she removed all her clothes. He hadn't touched her, just simply observed and then told her to get dressed, before driving her back to her usual patch. So that was why today, after he'd picked her up and said he'd like to see her naked again, she'd had no concerns when he drove to the disused Mayflower Joinery building. When she'd asked him why he was now driving a van and not his car, he'd told her he'd borrowed it to remove some items from the church.

Anna had asked her about the flowers and Tara explained that Eddie had an elderly mother who lived in a care home, who he visited every other day. The flowers were for her. Tara remembered that on the other occasions he'd picked her up he always had flowers with him.

After confirming that the names Tim or Tom meant nothing to her, and she didn't know of any other street workers who had recently gone missing, Tara agreed to be taken to Hale Street to give a formal statement.

After she'd got a light for her cigarette.

CHAPTER 56

Hill arrived on the scene and Sheridan updated her. The paramedics had been in attendance, and the girl in the back of the van was confirmed deceased. CSI were processing the body, and the building had been searched thoroughly with no sign of anyone else. Dipesh and Bridie were making enquiries to check who owned the place, one of many derelict buildings in the area which once hummed with thriving businesses.

The place where Emerson appeared to have thrown an object just before being arrested had also been searched, but nothing was found.

Hill placed her hand on Sheridan's shoulder. 'Great work.' She gave a slight smile. 'You saved four lives today. You caught him before he had the chance to kill his quota of five.' She winked. 'Tara was very lucky.'

Sheridan nodded. 'Yeah. She was.' She sighed. 'But he did manage to kill *one* before we caught him. And we got it wrong about the names Tim or Tom – I guess that was just a red herring.'

Hill squeezed her arm and looked up at the building. 'Do we think he owns this place?' she asked.

'If he doesn't own it, he has access to it. He used a key fob to get in,' Sheridan replied.

They both ducked under the shutter and Hill peered inside the grey Transit van. Her jaw tightened at the sight of the body of the unknown woman.

◆ ◆ ◆

When CSI had finished processing the body, the undertakers arrived to remove it. Sheridan felt a terrible sadness and looked away, stepping over to a large, heavy wooden bench near where the Transit van was parked. On top of it were three neatly cut lengths of thick foam, a roll of thin rope and a Stanley knife. Next to that was a small plastic holder which contained a number of fresh blades.

Hill joined her, looking at the scene before she said, 'I'm going back to the nick. The chief wants a briefing. I'll leave you to it. Really great job, Sheridan.' She turned to walk away.

Sheridan didn't reply, her eyes focused on the items lying on top of the bench.

Anna appeared next to her, listening as Sheridan spoke her thoughts out loud. 'He brought her here, placed the foam around her mouth, wrists and feet, then tied them with the rope. *Then* he killed her. He put her in the van, went home, parked up, went to buy the flowers before he headed into town to get Tara. He was going to bring her here and repeat the process.'

Anna looked at her. 'Three more times,' she said. 'But we got to him before he could do it.'

Sheridan remained silent for a moment and then she turned to Anna. 'What if we're wrong?'

'What do you mean?'

'Something doesn't add up. Why would he kill the first girl here and put her in the van? Why not leave her here while he goes to get the others? Why risk driving around with a dead body in the back?' She bit her bottom lip and looked at her watch. 3.06 p.m.

'What are the chances of him being able to find three more victims, convince them to get into his van, drive them here, tie them up and kill them by the end of the day?'

'Unlikely, he's more organised than that,' Anna replied.

'Exactly. He plans what he does well in advance.' Sheridan put her hand on her forehead. 'I'm missing something.' She looked to the floor. 'I'm bloody missing something.'

CHAPTER 57

Sheridan sent Rob back to Hale Street; she needed him and Bridie to urgently interview Emerson Corr, in the hope that he might disclose if there were other victims and more importantly, where they were. It was a long shot, but one they had to try. Since Emerson had been booked into custody he'd refused to speak and had declined legal advice. He had also declined food, accepting only a cup of water.

Half an hour later, Sheridan and Anna were sitting on a low wall across the road from the building, gratefully sipping coffee that one of the uniformed officers had brought them.

'So, come on, tell me. What was it?' Anna asked.

'What was what?'

'The chink in his armour.'

Sheridan took another mouthful of coffee. 'Cracked paving stones.'

Anna turned her head. 'What?'

Sheridan looked straight ahead as she spoke. 'I remembered walking the routes he took from when he was seen on CCTV near to where Kenny James was found. Then the platform at Edge Hill when he approached Annette Lennon and when he came to the nick and handed in the bag. I thought all along that the reason he has the strange sidestep was because he was avoiding cameras, or that someone was approaching him.' She turned to look at Anna, who was listening intently. 'But it wasn't that. He won't walk on cracked paving stones – he has to walk around them. *That's* the chink in his armour.'

'So that's why you used the enforcer to smash the pavement near his house.' Anna smiled. 'But why crack the wall as well?'

'Because Emerson Corr is no fool. He'd only left the house for a short time. He would have known something was wrong if, when he returned, *just* the paving stones were suddenly broken. So, I made it look like a car had come around the sharp bend, driven into the wall and caused the damage.'

Anna slowly shook her head. 'You really are quite special, Sheridan. That's bloody brilliant.' She tapped her coffee cup against Sheridan's and thought for a moment. 'When he went to the florist's, he changed his clothing before he came home, that's what was in the bag. Maybe that's why all along, we've never managed to catch him on CCTV, because once we spotted him, he'd turn a corner and, in that time, he looked different because he'd quickly changed his appearance.'

Sheridan nodded slowly. 'You're right. That's exactly what he's been doing.'

Just then, her phone rang. It was Rob.

'We've put a quick interview into him. He won't say anything other than he's already given us everything we need.'

'Okay,' Sheridan replied. 'Anything else?'

'Dipesh has run a check on the building you're at. Emerson Corr *does* own it, he bought it four years ago. We're checking if he owns any others.'

'Cheers Rob.' She ended the call.

'What do you think Emerson meant when he told Rob that we already have everything?' Anna asked, downing the dregs of her coffee.

Sheridan shook her head slightly. 'I don't know.'

They sat in silence a while longer. And then Sheridan stood up. 'Yes, I do. I *do* know what he bloody meant.' She stood up and took Anna's arm. 'Come on.'

'Where are we going?'

'To get the answers.'

CHAPTER 58

Sheridan knocked on the front door. A heavy police knock.

'Hello, Kyle.' She stepped forward as the door opened.

Kyle looked past her. 'What do you want? This is bloody harassment. My ex is on her way round with my boy. She doesn't know I was arrested and if she finds out she'll stop me seeing him.'

'I can fix that,' Sheridan replied, turning to see a car pull up outside the house.

'Fuck,' Kyle said under his breath. 'That's them, you need to go.'

'I'm not going anywhere until you give me the key and the watch.'

'I told you, I don't have them . . .' He spat his words out.

'Cut the shit, Kyle. I know you didn't sell them to some bloke in a pub.' Sheridan heard the car door open. 'Give them to me now and I won't let it slip to your ex that you've been charged with theft. Your choice.'

Kyle's face flushed red. 'Fuck's sake.' He looked up to see his ex-wife and son, Chris, walking up the path.

'Alright?' his ex said as she approached them, looking Sheridan and Anna up and down.

'Yeah, all fine,' Kyle said cheerfully.

'Who's this?' she asked, placing a hand on her son's head.

'She's a friend of Dad's,' Chris answered.

'No. She's not a friend . . .' Kyle hesitated. 'She's a police officer and she's just popped over to pick something up.' He looked at Sheridan. 'I'll just go and get it for you.'

'Get what?' said the ex.

'Kyle found something the other day, some lost property and was kindly going to bring it into the police station, but we were passing and said we'd pop over and pick it up. Save him the trip,' Sheridan replied, smiling.

'Oh. Right.' The ex pursed her lips before ushering Chris into the house.

Sheridan turned to Anna and winked.

A few minutes later, Kyle appeared at the door. 'There you are, Officer,' he said loudly enough for his ex to hear, at the same time handing Sheridan the bag containing the watch and the key.

'Thank you, Kyle. Very kind of you,' said Sheridan, just before he closed the door in her face.

'Wanker,' she said under her breath as she and Anna walked back to the car.

Sheridan reached into the bag and took out the key. It was just as Marcus had first described. Black metal and antique-looking. Across the barrel were letters and numbers. L208DA.

'Could be a vehicle index number?' Anna said, climbing into the passenger seat.

'Can you get it PNC'd?' Sheridan took the watch out of the bag. It was a Rolex, or at least carried the Rolex name. The glass screen was slightly scratched, but the face could be seen clearly. She turned it over. On the back was engraved: *In memory of TOM*. And underneath the name *TOM* was the number *5*.

'So, it was Tom, not Tim. And the number 5. That's the right number of victims in the pi sequence. But who the fuck is Tom?' Anna said, just before she radioed the control room to request a PNC check.

Sheridan stared at the watch for a moment. 'Christ knows,' she replied, as she started the engine and pulled away.

A moment later, the control room confirmed that no such vehicle index existed.

Sheridan screwed up her face. 'Hang on. What about a postcode? It could be a postcode.'

Anna grabbed her phone out of her pocket and typed the numbers and letters into it. 'Yeah. It is, it's a postcode.'

'Where?' Sheridan asked, a little excitedly.

Anna turned to her. 'Dock Road.' She looked back at her phone. 'Mayflower Joinery is one of the buildings in that postcode.'

'Okay. So, the key tells us the postcode for the address where he was taking the victims to.' Sheridan stopped at a traffic light. 'What about the watch?'

Anna read out the engraving on the back of the Rolex again. '*In memory of TOM 5.*' She looked out of the window. 'Maybe Tom is his son? And he died when he was five? It could be what started all of this – maybe he's angry.'

Sheridan pulled up in the backyard of Hale Street nick and turned off the engine.

Anna went to get out when she suddenly stopped. 'It's not a boy's name . . . it's prostitutes.'

Sheridan turned to her. 'What?'

Anna rested her head back. 'The five victims he was targeting are prostitutes.'

'How do you know that?'

'Because "Tom" is a nickname for them – prostitutes used to be referred to as "Toms".'

Sheridan undid her seat belt. 'Christ. Of *course* they were. Why didn't I make that connection? We always called prostitutes "Toms" back in the day.' She leaned over and kissed Anna on the cheek. 'You bloody legend. Right, we need to find out if any young women have been reported missing in the last few days. Because if they have and they're street workers, then Emerson Corr has been one step ahead and there are more somewhere.'

CHAPTER 59

Sheridan walked into CID and headed for Dipesh. She asked him to check if there had been any recent missing persons' reports, especially young women and those known to be prostitutes. It was common knowledge that due to the chaotic lifestyle of street workers, they were rarely reported missing to the police, and certainly not soon after they disappeared. They often lived on the streets. Those who did have accommodation regularly shared with others who didn't always expect them to return at the end of the day.

While Sheridan waited for Dipesh to make the enquiry, she went back to her office, feeling an uneasy tingling over her body. If no prostitutes had been reported missing, then maybe they had struck lucky. But if one had, or more worryingly, more than one, then they were probably too late, and Emerson could have already killed them and taken them *anywhere*.

She looked up as Dipesh appeared in her doorway. *Please say there aren't any*, she thought.

Dipesh cleared his throat and read from the printout in his hand. 'One misper report came in this morning. Female by the name of Dreya Marshall, nineteen years old. Medium height, slim build, shoulder-length brown hair, last seen wearing a peach-coloured T-shirt and short black skirt. Missing for two days. The caller, Dreya's flatmate, stated Dreya was a street worker, but it's very out of character for her not to come home. She'd tried calling her, but her mobile's switched off. The officer who's dealing with it tried calling it too, but it's still off. They tried to ping it, but no joy.'

Sheridan felt a strange and guilty moment of relief. From the description, she thought it could be the girl in the van. She was about the right age, with long brown hair, wearing tight blue jeans and a white sweatshirt. If the missing Dreya Marshall was the girl in the van, then there was hope that Emerson had only taken two girls. Her and Tara.

'That could be her.' Sheridan sat back. 'The clothes are different, but if her mate hasn't seen her for two days, she could be wearing different clothes.'

Dipesh turned the page of the misper report and frowned, before looking up. 'Was the girl in the van white?'

'Yes,' Sheridan replied. *Please don't say the misper's Black,* she thought.

Dipesh's shoulders dropped. 'It's not her. The misper's Black.'

Sheridan paced up and down her office, trying to focus, trying to think how Emerson thought, trying to get into his mind. She kept coming back to how organised he was, how he planned everything so well.

Now that they knew the girl in the van wasn't the misper, it left the investigation wide open. Was the misper another of his victims? Dipesh had been tasked with trying to find out if Emerson owned or had connections to any other properties. If he did, then this was probably where he took his victims after he killed them. So, if there *were* others, they were already dead, and Sheridan and her team would now have the unenviable task of finding their bodies. Two

DCs were checking CCTV and ANPR, trying to see if they could spot the van that Emerson had been driving in the last few days.

She walked out of her office and made her way to CID. Everyone was busy on phones, fingers tapping keyboards. Anna was sitting next to Rob and they both looked up as she approached them.

Anna leaned back in her chair. 'We're working on the interview plan. Who do you want to do it?'

'We will. Me and you.' Looking across to Dipesh, Sheridan asked, 'How are we getting on with the checks to see if Emerson owns any other properties?'

'I'm waiting for the details to come through. Shouldn't be much longer.' He nodded and looked back at his screen.

Sheridan walked over to the window and stared at the street, resting her hand on the water cooler. She closed her eyes, just for a moment. Everything was spiralling around in her mind. The dead girl in the van, bound with foam and rope around her mouth, wrists and ankles. Tara's face when Sheridan had found her. The derelict building. The bench where three lengths of foam and more rope had been placed on top, next to the Stanley knife. All in readiness for Emerson to bound and gag Tara. His second victim of the day.

Then it hit her.

She turned around. 'Tara *wasn't* number two. She was number *five*.'

Anna was the first to respond. 'How do you know *that*?'

Sheridan stepped into the middle of the room. 'Emerson doesn't kill them in the building he drove Tara to. He takes them there, gets them inside, puts foam and rope around their mouths, wrists and ankles and then he takes them somewhere else.' She paused. 'If he killed them *there*, then why would he have to tie them up?'

Anna stood. 'Of course. He wouldn't have to. If they were dead, there'd be no reason to do that. He ties them up in the first building and then drives them to wherever he does kill them.'

Sheridan swallowed. 'And we know that he plans everything well in advance. So, if that's the case, then why were there only three lengths of foam on the bench? I think it's because he only needed three more and they were meant for Tara. She was the last one, she's number five.'

Rob raised his hand. 'And he uses the foam to protect their skin before he ties them with the rope.'

It took a moment before Sheridan answered. 'Jesus, you're right. Because he makes his killings look like suicide, and so when these victims are found, if there was evidence that they'd been tied up, then we'd find that pretty bloody suspicious.' She shook her head. 'Christ, this guy's smart.'

CHAPTER 60

As the team waited for confirmation that Emerson Corr owned any other properties, the tension in the room was almost unbearable.

Sheridan scanned the faces of her team. Everyone had put their heart and soul into the case and now they were faced with the reality that somewhere, three women were dead. It was a recovery operation now. Emerson had won and Sheridan was consumed by a feeling of helplessness and defeat.

Bridie came in and picking up on the tension in the room, she hesitated before slowly walking over to Sheridan. 'Sorry, have you got a sec?'

'Sure,' Sheridan replied.

'I've interviewed the guy who came in to claim the bag,' Bridie said, perching herself on the edge of the desk, before going on to tell Sheridan and the team what had happened the night before.

Richard Hale and his mate, Greg Bliss, were at the bar of the Peacock pub in Liverpool. A man sat nearby and started talking, offering to buy them a drink. They chatted for a while and he introduced himself. Eddie told them he had arrived in Liverpool that evening from Aberdeen and was staying in the city overnight, waiting for the police station to open the next morning. Intrigued, Richard and Greg asked him why. Eddie said he'd been wanted on a warrant back in Scotland for a minor theft and a few weeks before had handed himself in at Hale Street nick. As he stood in the queue in the public enquiry office, he overheard a man in front of him handing in a bag containing a watch and key that he'd found by the Albert Dock. Eddie got a good look at the watch and realised it was a Rolex and likely very valuable. He was close enough to see the engraving on the back, which read *In memory of TOM 5*. He heard the exchange between the public enquiry officer and the man, and that the bag could be claimed in four weeks' time, if the owner hadn't come forward. Four weeks being the 22nd of July.

As they drank the pints he'd bought, Eddie told Richard and Greg that after he'd handed himself in, he was transported back to Scotland on the warrant and spent four weeks in prison. He'd been released that morning and rang the police station, claiming to be the man who had lost the bag, and was told he could come in and sign for it. He'd given the name James Thomas, telling the PEO that the watch had sentimental value.

By the time he'd arrived in Liverpool, the police station front counter was closed and so he was waiting for it to open in the morning.

After ordering another round, Eddie excused himself and went to the toilet. As he emerged, he was on his mobile, sounding upset and distressed. When he ended the call, he explained that his father had suffered a heart attack and was in hospital back in Aberdeen and his prognosis was poor. Eddie left his pint on the bar and told the two men that he had to go. He had a train to catch.

Now the two men had all the information they needed. They knew the bag hadn't been claimed. They knew about the key and watch, including the engraving on the back. Now that Eddie wasn't going to be able to claim it, they knew that all one of them had to do was walk into Hale Street police station the next day, give the name James Thomas and claim the bag. It was that simple. Richard had asked if the police would need some form of ID and Eddie had confirmed that he'd asked that question, and they had said that it wasn't necessary.

◆　◆　◆

Sheridan had listened carefully as Bridie relayed Richard Hale's account. 'I take it we've checked CCTV from the pub, just to confirm Richard's story?'

'Yeah. The images show Emerson Corr approaching them, talking and going to the toilet before he returns to them and then leaves.' Bridie paused. 'I don't think Richard Hale and his mate are anything to do with Emerson, they were just greedy and got caught up in his trick.'

'I agree.' Sheridan nodded. 'Emerson knew he couldn't claim the bag himself, but didn't want *us* to have it, so he fooled the two blokes into getting it. Where's this Richard Hale now?'

'He's still downstairs.'

'Okay. Kick him out,' Sheridan replied. 'Good work by the way.'

As Bridie left, she went back over to the window. Emerson Corr had planned everything to the very last detail. He took his time, he tricked people, played them, and even now, while he was locked up downstairs, he was winning. Tara had survived, so they'd prevented him from killing all five women he had planned to today, but only just. And if they couldn't find a link to him and any other property, then three dead women were hidden somewhere and it could take days, weeks, even months to locate their bodies.

She felt Anna's hand on her shoulder. 'You okay?'

Sheridan turned to look at her. 'No. He's beaten us. He was too clever.'

'We don't know for sure the other girls are dead, Sheridan. I know it's highly likely, but we can't give up.'

'Yeah. But how the fuck are we going to find out if they *are* alive?'

They stood in silence for a moment and Sheridan could feel tears of anger stinging her eyes. Sam's words came back to her. '*He's just a man, Sheridan.*'

She quickly looked around the room, before whispering to Anna, 'Stay here and call my mobile in five minutes, but don't speak.'

Before Anna had the chance to respond, Sheridan was already heading out of the office. For a second, Anna was tempted to follow her but resisted. She knew Sheridan well enough to know that whatever she was about to do, she wanted to do it alone. And she was probably about to break a shitload of rules.

CHAPTER 61

The custody sergeant was busy booking in a prisoner when Sheridan walked into the custody suite. The detention officer, Eve, smiled at her.

'Hello, ma'am.'

'Hi, Eve. I'm going to be interviewing Emerson Corr a bit later, so I'll just go and introduce myself.' She looked up at the cameras and noticed him standing in the middle of his cell, arms by his sides.

'He's been like that for an hour,' Eve commented. 'He's very quiet, so we're keeping him on regular checks. He's refused dinner and says he only wants water. I made him some toast earlier, but he's only eaten the crusts.' She put her hand on the cell keys that were attached to her belt by a chain. 'I'll take you to him.'

Sheridan put up her hand. 'It's okay. I'll go by myself.'

Eve gave her the keys and Sheridan went down the corridor to Emerson Corr's cell. She dropped the wicket.

'Step away from the door,' she said, and he immediately complied, taking three steps back.

Sheridan unlocked the cell and stood in the doorway, quickly checking to make sure that no one was coming.

'Detective Inspector Holler,' he said, with a wry smile on his face.

Sheridan didn't smile back. 'For a man who planned all of this so well, you missed something.'

'Did I?' Emerson crossed his arms, the smile still fixed and his eyes on hers.

Sheridan continued. 'I've been doing this job for many years, and along the way I've learned a lot about people, about the tricks they play.' She held his stare. 'Prostitutes.' She let the word hang in the air for a moment. 'Prostitutes are smart, they learn to think on their feet, they know how to survive on the streets, because they *have* to. And to do that, they need to learn the tricks of the trade. One of those tricks is how to hide things.' She paused, watching every muscle in his face, the vein in his neck, the slight change in his demeanour. She wanted to rattle him. And it was working. She pushed on.

'How do you think so many mobile phones get smuggled into prisons?' She didn't wait for him to reply. She also hoped he'd fall for what she was about to say. 'I'll tell you. In body orifices. And prostitutes are *absolute* experts in it.' She paused again. 'We got a 999 call from a young woman ten minutes ago. Her name's Dreya Marshall, a known local prostitute. She managed to tell the operator that she was taken by someone called Eddie, two days ago, and he took her to a derelict building called Mayflower Joinery, the building where you were arrested today. She said that once inside, you tried to rape her. She managed to fight you off, because she didn't want you to find the mobile phone she'd secreted in her vagina.'

Sheridan watched as Emerson's face burned red. She glanced down to see his fists clench, just before he put his hands behind his back.

She kept her voice steady as she spoke. 'Dreya said that she was then tied up and driven to another place, where she managed to free herself, but wasn't sure where she was. She was told to stay calm and stay on the line, so that we could trace her from her phone signal. I'm just waiting for a call to say that we've found her.' Sheridan cleared her throat. Just as her mobile rang – the pre-planned call from Anna.

She took the phone out of her pocket. 'DI Holler.'

She could hear Emerson's breathing becoming louder and more rapid. Looking to the floor, she stepped towards the door, her phone pressed to her ear. 'Where?' she said. 'Brilliant. Thanks, I'm on my way.'

She ended the bogus call and looked at him. 'I have to go, we've found Dreya.'

'She's lying.' His words were drenched in pure rage. 'I didn't try to rape her.'

'Why? Because she's Black?' Sheridan asked, wanting to convince Emerson that the police really had found her.

'No. Because she's a filthy little whore.' He turned his back and sat down, placing his hands on his knees.

Sheridan stepped forward and put her face near to his. 'Interesting . . . Sam was right, you *are* just a man.' She went to leave, bending to pick up the remains of the toast he'd left by the door. 'Aren't you hungry?'

When he didn't respond, she closed the cell door and hurried down the corridor back to the custody office. As she threw the toast in the bin, a brief image of Bobby Stover came to mind. *He would have loved this*, she thought, remembering his comment about liking the bread they served in custody, 'The posh stuff' as he'd called it. She allowed herself a smile as she ran towards the stairs, taking them two at a time.

A moment later, she strode into CID and everyone looked up. She caught her breath and said loudly, 'Dreya Marshall and the other girls are still alive.'

CHAPTER 62

Sheridan and Anna were standing in Hill's office.

'Why are you so convinced the other girls are still alive?' Hill asked, her arms folded across her chest.

Sheridan tried not to look at Anna. 'I went to introduce myself to Emerson in the cells and he told me that he . . .'

Hill put her hand up. 'Stop there, before you dig a massive fucking hole for yourself, Sheridan.' She stood up. 'Answer me this, did he make a significant statement that you documented and then asked him to sign?'

Sheridan shook her head. 'No.'

'Okay. Next question, did you threaten him?'

'No.'

'Last question.' Hill took an exaggerated deep breath. 'Are you going to come up with an elaborate enough lie about how you got this information, that's going to be believable enough for me to tell the chief, so that he doesn't totally lose his shit?'

'Yes. I'll definitely think of something.'

'Good.' She looked at Anna and Sheridan in turn. 'I don't need to know how you know this, but if these girls *are* still alive, then we need to find them bloody quickly. Dreya Marshall has been missing for two days and we don't know who the others are or how long ago he took them. But what we do know is time's running out.'

She eased herself from behind her desk. 'Let's hope Dipesh finds another property that we can link Emerson to, because that's where these girls will be.'

◆ ◆ ◆

While they waited in CID for any information to come through, a team of uniformed officers were placed on standby downstairs, ready to search any property that Emerson Corr had a connection to.

It was 6.09 p.m. when all eyes turned to Dipesh as he put his hand up, his eyes reading from his computer screen. 'Here we go. Okay, he owns . . .' He hesitated, leaning forward to read the information. 'Oh fuck.'

'What is it?' Sheridan asked.

Dipesh slumped back in his chair. 'He doesn't only own Mayflower Joinery on the Dock Road.' He looked at Sheridan. 'He owns the *whole* postcode.'

'What?' she blurted out.

'He owns every single building.'

'How many?' said Hill.

Dipesh put his hands on his head before he replied. 'Twenty-seven.'

CHAPTER 63

'Fucking bastard.' Sheridan felt her heart pounding in her chest. She closed her eyes tightly for a second, before turning to Hill. 'How the fuck are we going to search twenty-seven buildings in time to save these girls?'

Hill took out her mobile. 'I'll sort it.' She stood up and walked out of the office, her phone pressed to her ear.

The room fell silent as everyone tried to let the enormity of what they were facing sink in.

Half an hour later, Hill walked back in.

'I've got seven Police Search Advisors coming over, a tactical commander, dog units and officers coming in off rest days. We've agreed overtime for those about to go off duty and the chief is talking to other forces to see if they can help,' Hill said, her voice surprisingly positive in tone. 'The whole area is being cordoned off and the helicopter is being deployed.'

'Brilliant. We'll head out there now,' Sheridan replied and Anna followed her downstairs to their car. Sheridan handed Anna the keys and typed a message to Sam.

Hey gorgeous. I'm going to be really late or might not be home tonight. Sorry. I love you xx

Sam texted back: *No worries, just stay safe. I love you too xx*

Anna started the engine and pulled out of the backyard, behind four marked cars and two vans also heading to the Dock Road.

'What did you say to Emerson in the cell?' Anna asked.

Sheridan relayed her conversation.

'That might be a problem once he knows it was a total lie,' Anna responded. 'He could throw it back at you, or make a complaint that you coerced him.'

'I don't care, he can't prove anything. And if anyone wanted to check, all they'll see is me in his cell talking to him, none of it's on audio so there's no proof of what I said. Anyway, he's played enough games with us, so it's only fair that we play games with him.'

'Fair enough,' Anna agreed, turning to Sheridan. 'It was very clever, can I say? That's why I love working with you. You've got the biggest pair of balls of anyone I've ever known.' She smiled.

Sheridan raised her eyebrows. 'It will only have worked if we find these girls in time though.'

'Do you think we will?'

'I don't know. Twenty-seven buildings, all locked up, most of them boarded with no way of knowing which one they're in.'

Her mobile rang – it was Rob.

'Yes mate?' she answered.

'Sheridan, we've checked CCTV from the area where Emerson owns those properties. There aren't any that cover the actual buildings, only the main Dock Road, so we're not going to pick him up in the van at any specific location.'

Sheridan bit down on her lip. 'And because he owns the buildings, he's probably either removed any cameras or hasn't had any installed. Okay, cheers Rob.' She was about to end the call, when he added, hesitantly, 'I . . . thought it would be a good idea to check CCTV from when Emerson threw something away before he was arrested.'

Sheridan closed her eyes. She'd had the area searched and nothing had been found, but she'd totally forgotten to get the CCTV checked. Hill's words about her staying focused rattled around in her head.

'Nice one Rob. Sorry, I . . . forgot about that,' she said.

'It's fine, I'm only doing what you do, crossing all the t's and dotting all the i's. You can't remember everything, Sheridan,' he said softly.

Sheridan knew that her team always rallied in every case they worked on together. But it was usually her who was one step ahead. She missed nothing, but her mind had been in so many places working on this complex case, and knowing Andrew Longford was dying, that she'd been distracted. Her team knew it and now they were picking up the slack. She'd always supported her team, no matter what. Now it was their opportunity to support her.

'Thanks, Rob,' she said. 'Keep me posted if you find anything.'

It was almost 11 p.m. when Sheridan felt exhaustion kick in. The area was filled with specialist search teams and dog units, working their way painstakingly through each building, desperately trying to locate the women.

Darkness had fallen, but the area was floodlit by specialist equipment and the sheer volume of police presence.

Hill was liaising with the press officer, trying to keep the local reporters at bay. Social media was awash with rumours being circulated by armchair detectives that it *had* to be a bomb and everyone in the area should be prepared for Liverpool to be flattened by some enormous explosive device.

Sheridan had texted Sam again to let her know that whatever she might hear on the news was bullshit and although she was on the scene, she wasn't about to be blown to smithereens.

Sam had texted back: *Did you get him?*

Sheridan messaged: *Yes. Thanks to you, I found the chink in his armour. xx*

Sam sent back a single kiss. And a smiley face.

Sheridan looked up to see Hill approaching, carrying three cups of coffee, handing one to Sheridan and Anna in turn.

'Thought you could use one of these,' she said. 'How you both doing?'

'Fucking knackered, frustrated, pissed off. And I need a wee,' Anna replied, removing the lid from her coffee.

'And you, Sheridan?'

'What Anna said. Except the wee thing.'

Hill sat down. 'We put a quick interview into Emerson. We wanted to give him the opportunity to tell us where the girls are.' She paused. 'He was a little bit surprised at this. Apparently, he was under the impression that we'd already found Dreya Marshall . . . because somehow, she'd managed to hide a phone up her fanny.'

Anna blew on her coffee and tried desperately not to spit it out.

Hill continued. 'Then Dreya *miraculously* untied herself, made a 999 call, which we traced and then hey fucking presto, we found her.'

The three women mirrored each other as they quietly sipped their drinks. All staring straight ahead.

A whole twenty seconds passed before Anna broke the silence and plucked up the courage to ask, 'Did he say anything else?'

Hill stood up. 'Yes. He said to say "bravo" to you, Sheridan. And I don't think I want to know what he meant by that.'

At that moment, Sheridan was saved from commenting by her radio crackling with a message to all officers at the scene.

'All units, be advised, we've found something.'

CHAPTER 64

Sheridan, Anna and Hill stood in the derelict building. Once a thriving paper supply company, the walls now crumbled with neglect. A hole in the roof let in an eerie light from the moon. In one corner of the room was a pile of empty boxes, in the other was an old brown leather sofa, its innards spilling out like a child's over-loved toy. Two low wooden tables stood in front of it, one covered in old paint, the other, tilted slightly, nursing a broken leg. Magazines with curled edges and old newspapers were piled high and a selection of half-burned candles were positioned around the place. Boxes of matches and a scattering of lighters were all over the floor, and among them were hundreds of hypodermic needles.

As Sheridan took in the scene, Hill joined her. 'Looks like a drug den to me. The place wasn't locked, so anyone could get in.'

Sheridan nodded. 'Yeah.' She looked at her watch. Midnight.

'What if we're looking in the wrong place?' Anna said as the three women went back outside, standing in the street on tired and aching legs.

'What do you mean?' Sheridan asked.

'Well, apart from Dreya Marshall, we don't know how long ago he took the others. They could be lying somewhere dying and we're all scrabbling around here looking for them. Maybe they're not in any of the places he owns and by the time we do find them, they're all dead.'

Sheridan looked to the sky. 'You could be right.' She dropped her head and walked away slowly. 'You piece of shit, Emerson Corr,' she said under her breath.

Anna and Hill shared a look, leaving Sheridan to wander off down the road, alone.

As she walked, Emerson's words resonated around her head. *I've already given you everything you need. I'm sure at some point you'll turn things around.*

She thought about it. They had already turned things around. The JT initials, which, when turned around, resembled the pi sign. She took her phone out of her pocket and looked at the pictures she'd taken of the watch and the key. The key that held the postcode of all the buildings Emerson owned. She flicked to the photo of the watch, the engraving on the back. *In memory of TOM 5.* Again, they'd already figured out that "TOM" referred to the prostitutes and the number 5 was how many of them he'd planned to kill.

'What are we missing?' Sheridan said to herself. Then, she looked again at the engraving on the back of the watch.

And then she saw it.

Anna and Hill looked up as Sheridan went running past them.

'What's wrong?' Anna called after her.

'Get in the car. I know where the girls are.'

Two minutes later, with Sheridan driving, they scoured the area, looking for the building.

'There.' Hill pointed.

They all got out and Sheridan gave directions over the radio to the search commander. She impatiently rattled the shutter, looking for any way into the place.

A police car flew around the corner and came to a grinding halt, two officers jumped out and using bolt croppers they snapped off the padlock. A moment later they were inside the building, torch lights flashing left and right.

'Hello?' Sheridan called out, straining to listen for any sign of life as more officers arrived on the scene.

In front of them was a large Transit van, bigger than the one Emerson had been driving that day. Sheridan tried the driver's door, which was unlocked. She saw the keys were in the ignition, but the front cab was empty. From the front of the van, there was no way of seeing what was in the back, as a heavy wooden board had been placed there. She tried the back doors which were locked, and spotted a heavy chain attached to a tow bar. At the other end of the chain was a large, metal, T-shaped bar.

Grabbing the keys out of the ignition, Sheridan took a deep breath before unlocking the van doors, while Anna, Hill and the uniformed officers watched.

Sheridan pulled the doors open. The back of the van was empty.

'Shit,' she said, looking around the derelict room. A stepladder was propped up against the wall. She instinctively looked up. 'What's the ladder for?'

Everyone in the room looked at the ceiling. Heavy wooden beams were criss-crossed above them. It was impossible to make out any detail in the darkness, even with police torches scouring the area above their heads.

'It's nowhere near tall enough to reach the rafters,' she observed.

Sheridan felt sick. Had she made the wrong call? Had she mistakenly dragged officers away from searching the *actual* building that the girls might be held in? Had she wasted more precious time? Time the girls might not have.

'Fuck,' she said, walking around the van.

Her foot clipped something, and she crouched down.

'I need your torch.' She held her hand out to a nearby officer who slapped a Maglite into it.

The van was parked on top of what appeared to be an inch-thick solid sheet of metal.

'Get this van moved, now!' Sheridan stood up.

Hill stepped forward. 'What have you seen?'

'This is an old MOT testing station. I think it's an inspection pit.'

The van was driven slowly off the sheet, the heavy chain and T-shaped bar scraping along the concrete floor. Once the van was out of the way they could see a pipe, about six inches in diameter, that had been fed through a hole in the sheet of metal. Sheridan's eyes followed it, spotting that it ran along the ground and into the brick wall.

'What the hell is that?' she said, now joined by Hill and Anna.

One of the Police Search Advisors appeared next to them. 'Wherever that pipe leads to, it's in the next room.'

'Then we need to get in there. It could be pumping something into the pit,' Sheridan replied.

The officer quickly organised his team as they desperately tried to find a way to gain entry.

Sheridan felt helpless as she looked at Anna and Hill. 'What if the girls are in the pit? What if whatever's being pumped in there is killing them?'

Two officers were kneeling on the heavy metal sheet where the van had been parked. One put his mouth close to the pipe and shouted, 'Hello?'

Everyone held their breath, listening.

Nothing.

He tried again. This time, as he called out, he pulled gently on the pipe.

Nothing.

'Be careful. We don't know if this is a trap,' Hill said.

Sheridan knew she was right. Emerson could have set anything up here. If they pulled at the pipe, would it set something off? Until they knew its purpose, they had to wait. But while they waited, time was running out.

She closed her eyes. Thinking.

And then came the call on the radio. 'The pipe leads all the way outside.'

Sheridan opened her eyes and glanced back over at the stepladder.

And that was the moment she made the final connection.

CHAPTER 65

Sheridan watched with her heart in her mouth as the POLSA officer slowly and carefully pulled at the pipe. Her heart was beating so fast she could see white spots dancing in front of her eyes. As the end of the pipe was pulled through the space, the officer threw it to one side and put his face to the six-inch hole, peering in. Sheridan joined him, kneeling down. The smell hit her first and she swallowed, trying not to react. Ignoring the stench, she grabbed the torch and shone it down into the pit.

'Hello?' she called, not being able to see anything.

No response from within.

She stood up. 'We need to move this metal plate.'

A team of officers tried unsuccessfully to shift the heavy sheet, its sheer weight and size beating them.

Anna turned to look at the van, parked up a few metres away. 'The chain and T-bar,' she said, pointing to it.

Sheridan smiled. 'Yes.'

A few moments later, the van was reversed, so that the T-shaped bar at the end of the chain reached the hole in the metal plate. Then, turning the T-bar so that it fit in the hole, the metal plate was pulled, the T-bar acting like an anchor.

Once in position, the van was driven forward, and the plate slowly but surely was dragged off the inspection pit.

Everyone held their breath, partly because of the smell from the pit and partly out of dread for what they might find. They had all prayed to find alive the first three victims that Corr had abducted before the girl in the van and Tara. The five innocents that he had planned to kill. The next number in the pi sequence.

Sheridan was the first to step forward, inching her way to the edge. With the torch in her shaking hand, she looked down.

'What the fuck?'

'Did we get it wrong?' Anna asked as she sat in the hospital with Sheridan and Hill. 'Pi, I mean.'

'I don't know,' Sheridan replied. 'But something isn't right.'

Inside the pit, there were four women, not three. They had foam around their mouths, wrists and ankles, tied in place with rope. Just like the girl in the back of the van. They were all dehydrated and had soiled themselves, hence the stench. But they were alive. Barely, but alive.

After discovering the girls in the pit, Sheridan realised that Corr had left the stepladder in the room so that he could carry the girls down. What he intended to do with them after that remained a mystery. The pipe fed through the sheet had turned out to be a source of oxygen, Emerson's way of keeping them alive until the time was right.

It all made sense, except for the number. If Sheridan's theory was correct, there should only have been three girls. So the question remained, why four?

Sheridan had worked out that Emerson's message about 'turning things around' didn't only mean turning JT to make the pi sign, but turning around the message on the back of the watch.

TOM. Turn around TOM and it spells MOT. Of all the buildings Emerson owned, only one was an old MOT testing station.

'It *has* to be pi,' Sheridan said eventually, resting her head back. 'Anyway, the main thing is, we got the girls out in time.' She turned her head to look at Hill, who had a rare smile on her face.

'Once we know the girls are going to be okay, I think we should all go home. We've got an early start tomorrow.' Hill tapped Sheridan's leg. 'Because you get to interview Emerson Corr.'

CHAPTER 66

Friday 23 July

Sheridan and Anna were setting up in the interview room, having read Emerson Corr's custody record. He'd continued to decline food, only accepting water, and had maintained his stance on refusing legal advice.

'Do you think he's on some sort of hunger strike?' Anna asked.

'Don't know, don't care,' Sheridan replied.

A minute later Emerson was brought into the room by the detention officer. He took his seat and looked around.

After the initial introductions, Sheridan reminded him that he was still under caution.

As she was about to ask her first question, Emerson spoke.

'I know you're going to ask me many things, but before that, I have a question for *you*.' He clasped his hands together as if in prayer.

Sheridan tilted her head to one side. 'Go on.'

'As a detective, how would you describe the perfect crime?' he asked, his eyes fixed on hers.

Sheridan didn't want to engage in petty conversation, she had a million questions to get through, but allowed him this.

'I guess the perfect crime is one where the perpetrator leaves no evidence, or certainly not enough to prove they've done it.'

Emerson slowly shook his head. 'You're so *very* wrong.'

'Enlighten me,' said Sheridan.

'The *perfect* crime is when there is no evidence that a crime has even been committed.' He drummed his fingers on the table. '*That* is the perfect crime.'

Making the deaths look like suicide, Sheridan thought. 'So, is that what you believe? That you've been committing the perfect crimes?'

'It's not what I believe, it's what I *know*.' He smiled.

'Using pi.' Sheridan didn't wait for him to respond. 'Three point one four one five.'

Emerson clapped his hands together in mock applause. 'I'm glad you finally figured that out. You see, I believe that pi is the perfect number. It's perfect because it never ends. It combines the two things I revere. Infinity . . . and perfection.'

'When you were arrested, you said it was nice to meet me again. *When* have we met?' Sheridan asked.

'All in good time, Detective.'

Sheridan tapped a pen on her interview notepad. 'Okay. Let's start at the beginning. The number three.' She sat back.

To date, they hadn't managed to find the three victims that would have started the pi sequence back in 2005. They *had* discovered that Molly Frane, who had been fostered by the Barkers, had gone missing with her girlfriend that year, but, if Emerson had anything to do with her disappearance, then who was the third person?

Emerson Corr placed his hands flat on the table. 'Molly.' He shook his head slightly. 'Shame, because I liked her. Until she showed her imperfection.'

'You and Molly were fostered by Freya and Brendan Barker and lived together with them for a number of years. Why were you put into foster care?'

Emerson sighed heavily. He went on to tell Sheridan and Anna that his own mother was an alcoholic and he was taken from her and placed in several foster homes, before going to live with the Barkers. He was an only child and a very intelligent one. He found it difficult to make friends as he wasn't interested in playing football or climbing trees like the other local kids. Instead, Emerson desired mental stimulation – he needed to feed an insatiable appetite for knowledge, which he found in books. He became a ferocious reader of academic literature, studying every subject from science to mathematics. And it was then that he discovered pi. It fascinated him, the concept of a never-ending number that had always baffled the greatest minds. But he had no one to share this passion with, no one to debate with and it frustrated him. He made up games that only he understood, but he lacked an opponent. His mother never understood him, never paid him attention. He never knew who his father was. When he was fostered by Freya and Brendan in 1972, Molly was already living with them. Everything was fine at first – the two children adored each other. Molly was smart, but even she struggled to keep up with Emerson, although she tried, listening to him talking about subjects normally only discussed among the brightest of minds. She wasn't a worthy opponent, but at least she listened to him. Then, Molly was adopted by another family in 1976, leaving Emerson as an only child again. He missed her but they kept in touch by letter, writing to each other regularly over the years. The Barkers doted on Emerson. They were good Catholic people and his life with them was a happy one. A perfect one.

One day Freya and Brendan sat Emerson down and told him that Freya was pregnant. With twins. That in itself wasn't an issue, and Emerson looked forward to having other children in the household again. But when the twins were born, everything changed. Born blind and severely disabled, they required all of

Freya and Brendan's attention and slowly but surely, Emerson began to feel neglected.

And that was when his hatred of imperfection began. Because it was the twins' imperfection that caused him to feel totally abandoned.

'Okay,' Sheridan said, 'we'll come back to Molly. You left the Barkers' home in 1987, but you returned to visit them in 2008. Tell me what happened.' *How did you kill them? Because I know you bloody did,* she thought.

'I cooked dinner for them.' Emerson smiled broadly. 'You see, when I was a kid, Brendan always told me to stay away from the beech tree. He said that not everything that grew on their land was good for you. I remembered seeing these mushrooms and realised that was what he'd referred to. So, when the time came and I needed four victims, I hid up near their house and when it was dark, I picked one of the mushrooms. Turns out they were death caps and highly poisonous. The next day, I disguised myself by dressing as a delivery man and took a parcel to their house. Brendan didn't recognise me. The parcel was just an empty box but I told him it had been ordered online and he said it couldn't have been, because they didn't have a computer, or mobile phones.' Emerson stretched out his legs. 'That's when I knew I could trick my way back into their lives and kill them all.'

'How?' Sheridan asked, looking up from her interview notes.

'I turned up on their doorstep, this time without the disguise. I told them who I was and that I'd never forgotten what they did for me, how they'd brought me up right and were such loving parents. They invited me in, and I weaved a tale of how I'd qualified as a doctor and travelled the world. They believed every word. They felt comfortable, because even the twins recognised me and didn't react like they usually did with strangers. They even offered to let me stay for a few days.'

'And you knew they couldn't check out your story about being a doctor, because they didn't have access to the internet.'

'Exactly.'

'The boys were blind. How did they recognise you?' Anna asked.

'When they were small, I used to gently run my hand down their faces, it made them smile. So, that's all I did, and they knew it was me.' Emerson raised his palm. 'Would you like me to show you?'

'No. I wouldn't,' Sheridan replied and waited for him to lower his hand before asking her next question. 'How did you get them to eat the mushrooms?'

'That was very simple. When I was little, Freya used to let me help out in the kitchen, she actually encouraged it. So, on the second day I was there, I went into town, bought all the fresh ingredients for a stew, then threw the death caps in. I'd kept them in my car, but the Barkers just assumed I'd bought them in town.'

'But if you all ate together, how come you weren't ill?'

'When I dished up, I set the alarm on my phone to go off and told them I'd been called to the hospital. By the time I got back that evening, they'd already eaten dinner.'

'Talk me through what happened after they'd eaten them,' Sheridan said.

'It was around midnight, and I heard Freya being sick. An hour or so later, Brendan was the same. By the next morning, they were getting disorientated and dehydrated. I told them it was a bug and encouraged them to drink plenty of water.'

'Did they ask you to call an ambulance? Or ring the GP?'

'No. They trusted me, because they thought I was a doctor.' Emerson grinned. 'The boys were in bed all day, puking and messing themselves. I told Freya and Brendan that the boys were okay, but not a lot of what I was saying got through. Freya and Brendan were out of it and by that evening, Brendan was dead.' Emerson put his hand over his mouth and yawned. 'Freya died a couple of hours later.'

'And the boys?'

'They lasted a bit longer. Douglas died two days after he ate the mushrooms, and Neil went a few hours after him.'

'You like your victims to die on the twenty-second of July. But the Barkers didn't die that day.'

'True. But they ate the mushrooms on the twenty-second, so they were as good as dead from that moment on.'

'So once the family were all dead, what did you do?'

'I stayed there. You see, they had a dog, Bouncer, a lovely Labrador, and I wanted to make sure he was okay. I knew it might take some time for the family to be found, and I was worried about him. Freya's sister kept ringing and leaving messages on the answerphone. She sounded more and more worried that they weren't answering the phone, and then on the Monday morning, the twenty-eighth, she left another message to say she was coming to check on them, and she'd be arriving around midday.'

'Where were you when she arrived?'

'There's a shed at the end of the field, it's got a window in it, and you can see the house and driveway from there. So, I watched and saw her arrive. I was still in there when the ambulance and police turned up.'

'Tell me more about the dog,' Sheridan asked. Was he about to confirm her theory?

Emerson rested his back. 'I had to make sure he was alright. You see, animals fall into my perception of perfection. They do what they need to do to survive. They're loyal, trustworthy and never let you down. I may have killed a lot of people in the last few years, but I would never harm an animal, quite the opposite. I have a hatred of anyone who raises their hand to a dog, or *any* animal.' He paused. 'I kept Bouncer tied up outside, so he didn't go in the house. He was used to it because Freya and Brendan always tied him up out there on the porch when they were eating, so I knew he'd be okay.'

'You fed him?'

'Of course. Every day.'

'And you topped up his water bowl?'

'Yes, every day. Sometimes twice a day. It was July and a hot one. I didn't want him to get dehydrated. Dogs can only survive a few days without water.'

Sheridan felt Anna's leg pressing against her own and looked down to see the note she was surreptitiously writing.

YOU REALLY ARE THAT GOOD

Sheridan hid a smile and continued. 'We know at all the other scenes where you murdered your victims, you left your mark. The initials, JT. You made them look like suicides, but not with the Barkers. Why was that?'

'Well, therein lies the mystery.' Emerson took a sip of water. 'I *did* leave my mark. I left a suicide note on the kitchen table. But when it was on the news about the family being found dead, I followed the case and there was never a mention of suicide. So, I always wondered what happened to the note. Maybe the police missed it? I was quite annoyed because I'd made sure everything was in place. I'd left the remaining mushrooms in the fridge, kept Bouncer safe outside and left the suicide note, but the deaths were never recorded as suicide.'

'What did the note say?'

'Just can't take any more.' He grinned.

The same message you left on Jake Hannigan's painting, thought Sheridan.

'Capital J, capital T,' she said. Remembering that she'd believed the letter T was capitalised.

'Yes. Clever, eh?' Emerson smiled.

Sheridan didn't respond. Instead, she pressed on. 'Let's go back to Molly Frane and her friend, Bethany, who both went missing in July, 2005. What happened to them?'

Emerson ran a hand through his hair. 'I didn't intend to harm Molly, not until she showed her imperfection. I actually had three other victims in mind, but then Molly wrote to me and asked if I'd like to visit her in Norfolk and stay for a few days.' He took another sip of water. 'When I arrived at her house, she introduced me to her *friend*.' His jaw tightened. 'Then she told me that her *friend* was actually her lover.' He looked Sheridan in the eye. 'It's not normal, is it? Two women together. It's imperfect, it should *never* be that way. It's disgusting to think that a woman would touch another woman. And so, Molly and her lover deserved what happened to them.'

Sheridan held his stare. *You dickhead,* she thought. 'Where are Molly and Bethany?' she asked.

'At their house.'

'What do you mean?'

Emerson smiled again. 'A lot of properties in Norfolk have something that other places don't have.' He raised an eyebrow, waiting for Sheridan to answer. 'Any ideas?'

'Tell me.'

'Septic tanks. Molly and Bethany are in the septic tank. They've been there the whole time.'

Sheridan felt her stomach turn. 'But the pi sequence starts with the number three. Molly and Bethany are only two.'

Emerson laughed and put his hands behind his head. 'And . . . baby makes three.'

'What baby?' Sheridan asked.

Emerson grinned. 'Molly was pregnant.'

CHAPTER 67

Sheridan was staring at her own reflection in the mirror when Hill walked into the ladies toilet.

'He's something else, isn't he?' Hill joined her and stood tidying her hair. She'd been watching the interview remotely until the chief had called her for an update.

'Yeah.' Sheridan ran the tap and splashed water on her face. 'Fucking piece of shit. I've met some monsters in this job, Hill. But this guy beats them all.'

'Did he say why he didn't make Molly and Bethany's deaths look like suicide?'

'Yeah. He didn't come up with that idea until after he'd killed them. He'd thought that their deaths were the perfect murder, but then realised he could be even cleverer. At some point, he realised that making the deaths look like suicide was a better plan. So, he used that as his MO going forward.' Sheridan shook her head. 'The note that was found in the house, telling everyone that Molly and Bethany had planned to move away and start a new life, was written by *him*. He perfected her handwriting, copying it from all the letters she'd sent him over the years. After he'd put them in the septic tank, he went through the house and found all the letters he'd sent her, then took them with him. Molly had told him that they were thinking of selling up and starting afresh somewhere nearer a city, possibly London. They hadn't told Molly's adoptive parents about their plan. They hadn't even told them they were a couple, or about the pregnancy. She was only a couple of months gone and they didn't want to say anything in case something went wrong. She hadn't even been to her GP, she just took a pregnancy test.'

'Who was the father?'

'A friend of Bethany's. Him and Molly had sex purely so she could get pregnant. It was a mutual agreement that they never told anyone. He was an American, and by this time he was back in the States.'

Anna's face appeared around the door. 'There you are.' She stepped in. 'Just been on to the hospital, the girls are all doing okay. Bridie and a couple of the DCs are there now getting statements. Dreya Marshall wanted to discharge herself, but they've persuaded her to wait.'

Hill put her thumb up and turned to Sheridan. 'Are you going back into interview now?'

'Yeah.' Sheridan adjusted her top.

'Okay. I'll speak to Norfolk Police and sort out getting the septic tank emptied.' And with that, Hill left the room.

Back in the interview, Anna pressed the record button as they restarted. Emerson leaned back in his chair and folded his arms.

Sheridan began. 'So, you've told us about Molly and Bethany, their unborn child, and the Barkers. We know the pi sequence includes a point. Three point one four one five. Tell me about the point.'

Emerson tilted his head to one side. 'The hideous fat girl on the railway platform.' He closed his eyes. 'How does someone allow themselves to become so obese? It's repulsive. And imperfect.'

'You targeted her because she was overweight?' Sheridan asked.

'Imperfect,' he said.

'Had you seen her before?'

'Yes. Several times. I was thinking of ways to target a single victim, and I used to sit on the platform at Edge Hill train station, watching. I hadn't come up with a way of making a point, but while I was working on it, I thought I'd plan how to kill a single person and pushing them in front of a train seemed so easy. I knew she caught the same train on the same day and was always alone. She also always stood at the far end of the platform. The only problem was, the CCTV would have caught me if I pushed her, so I couldn't make it look like suicide. So, I chose *her* to make a point.'

'You stamped the initials JT into her face over and over with a litter grabber. How did you adapt it so that it was shaped like JT?' Sheridan asked.

Emerson held out his hands and inspected his fingernails. 'I improvised with a cookie cutter. Just had to make a few adjustments to it.' He cleared his throat. 'In fact, it was the fat girl who gave me the idea about making all the subsequent deaths look like suicide. You see, the day I gave her the message to tell you I was making a point, she'd been looking down at the tracks, like she was going to jump.' He looked at Sheridan. 'Did she end up killing herself? Please say yes.'

'No,' Sheridan replied.

'Shame. She really ought to have. She has no place on this earth.'

Sheridan resisted the urge to throw the table at him. 'Let's move on to the next number, the next killing in 2007. One person.'

'Ah, yes.' Emerson raised a finger. 'The painter.'

'Tell me about him.'

'He used to sit at the top of Thurstaston Cliffs. Alone. Always alone, painting. I knew it would be fairly easy to throw him over the cliff, but I didn't know if he had an imperfection. Not until the day his father turned up.'

Sheridan looked up from her notes. 'His father?'

Emerson continued. 'Yes. It was a couple of weeks before I killed him that his father turned up and I heard them talking. The lad was sitting on one side of a big rock. I was the other side. I heard a voice and realised someone else was there. I couldn't see them, and they couldn't see me, but I heard *every* word.'

CHAPTER 68

Sunday 8 July 2007

Frank Hannigan stopped as he reached the top of the rock and looked out towards Wales. The sun was creating shimmering light beams on the water and for the first time ever, he realised his son had captured its beauty in so many of his paintings. Frank had been to his local golf club that morning, ready to play his usual Sunday game with a group of friends. As he'd arrived, several members were congregated outside, talking quietly. Frank had joined them and that was when they told him about one of the member's sons. Harry was nineteen years old and had recently been diagnosed with a brain tumour. He'd died that morning. The golf game was cancelled, and Frank had sat in his car, thinking about Jake. How he rarely, if ever, showed any love for him. Knowing Jake would be painting at Thurstaston, Frank drove there, deciding that the time was right to have a father–son talk.

He spotted Jake, paintbrush in hand, sweeping across the paper and creating cloud shapes.

Frank walked over to him, causing Jake to jump slightly. 'Hello, son.'

'What are you doing here?' Jake snapped at him, put the paintbrush down and wiped his hands on a cloth.

'I wanted to talk to you. Just me and you.'

'What about?'

'You do know that I love you, don't you?' Frank leaned back against the rock.

Jake didn't reply.

'I know I never talk about your autism, or ask you how your day was, but I do love you. I'm just not very good at showing it.'

'Yeah. Whatever.' Jake picked up his paintbrush and continued to work.

'Well, I just wanted you to know.' Frank turned and walked away.

On the other side of the rock, out of sight, was Emerson Corr, who had heard everything and now knew that Jake had an imperfection: autism. That was the moment when Jake Hannigan's death was sealed. And he'd be dead in exactly two weeks' time.

◆ ◆ ◆

Sunday 22 July 2007

Emerson had arrived at Thurstaston Cliffs early. The sun was high and heavy in the sky as he took up his position and waited for the young painter to arrive.

An hour later, he peered around the large rock and could see him heading to his favourite spot, carrying his easel, fold-up chair and box containing his paints and brushes. Emerson breathed in and allowed himself a smile. Not long now.

Ten minutes passed and the young man was set up. Emerson would wait a few minutes before approaching him, but as he was about to go for it, he heard a voice. The same voice he'd heard two weeks earlier. The young man's father.

Emerson held his breath, listening.

'Hello, son.' Frank Hannigan appeared next to Jake.

'What are you doing here *now*?' Jake's voice was tinged with anger.

'I thought I'd surprise you, maybe watch you paint for a while.'

'I don't want you here. I want to be on my own,' Jake snapped.

'Don't be like that. Come on. We can talk while you paint.'

Jake threw the paintbrush on the ground. 'Just go away, Dad. You don't really want to be here, so don't pretend you do. Just fuck off and leave me alone.'

'Don't you dare use that language with me, I'm your father and you'll watch your mouth.'

'Fuck off, fuck off, fuck off.' Jake's voice grew louder.

'You little bastard. I'm trying to be your friend, and you talk to me like that.' Anger seeped into Frank's voice.

'I don't want a friend. I wanted a dad, and you were never one. I know you love Juliet and not me. I know you hate that I'm different, well I can't change that. So, just leave me alone and stop pretending.'

There was a silence between them as Frank tried to think of what to say. When no words came, he turned to leave.

'I'm sorry you feel that way, son.'

'Just go away.'

Emerson waited until he was sure that the lad's father had left, before carefully and quietly making his way around the rock. He moved silently, every step taking him closer. Just as he reached him, his foot cracked down on a dry twig and the painter suddenly shouted, without turning around.

'I said leave me alone!'

Emerson was right behind him now. He took a deep breath, before he wrapped an arm tightly around Jake's throat.

And then he broke his neck.

Sheridan and Anna listened as Emerson went on to describe how, after Jake was dead, he knew he had to move him in order to throw his body off the cliff. From where Jake had set up his easel, it was almost impossible to push his body over the edge, as just below was a thick bramble bush and Jake's body would have got stuck in it.

Emerson had dragged Jake around the other side of the rock and laid him on the ground, before re-positioning the easel, paints and Jake's little chair. Because the note he'd left at the Barkers' property, 'Just can't Take any more', clearly hadn't been found, Emerson felt safe using the same words which he wrote across Jake's painting. Once everything was in position, Emerson lifted the lad's body and threw him over the cliff.

CHAPTER 69

While Emerson was taken back to his cell for a toilet break, Sheridan and Anna remained in the interview room.

'You were right about Jake Hannigan all along.' Anna leaned back in her seat and put her pen down. 'That's why his easel and paints were found in that position.' She looked up at Sheridan, who was standing with her back to the wall. 'You knew something wasn't right and you were bang on.'

'There was nothing in Jake's file to say that his dad, Frank, was there that day. Juliet told me that Frank was playing golf and found out about Jake's death when he got home, and the police were there.' Sheridan sighed. 'I bet Frank Hannigan had always thought that Jake jumped because he was upset about their argument.'

Anna yawned. 'Yeah. And that's why he never told anyone that he'd visited Jake up on the rock. He didn't want anyone to know he'd been there, because his wife and daughter might have blamed him.'

There was a tap on the door and the detention officer opened it, escorting Emerson back in.

When they'd taken their seats, Sheridan continued.

'So, we've covered three point one four. Tell us about the next victim, the one that represents the next number. This would be the twenty-second of July 2009.'

Emerson rubbed his hands together. 'The filthy tramp.' He nodded. 'I'd watched him for a while. He was easy to spot because he always wore the same red coat.'

Sheridan made herself a note. *Bobby Stover always wore a red coat, not Kenny.*

'Why did you target him?' she asked.

'Because like the others, he was imperfect. Tramps are a vile, useless drain on society. They choose to live on the streets and beg for what they should be working for. They take drugs and steal to feed their habits. Is that enough reasons, or would you like me to go on?' He raised his eyebrows.

Sheridan readjusted her position. 'Tell us what happened to him.'

'Like I said, I'd watched him for a while, he slept in the same doorway most nights, sometimes with another tramp. They looked like brothers and would lie there in their sleeping bags, drinking bottles of wine together. I knew I had to pick one of them, because that was the next number in the pi sequence. So, I picked the one who always wore the red coat, because he did something that no person should *ever* do.' Emerson inhaled through his nostrils and shook his head slightly.

'What was that?' Sheridan said.

'He tore the cover off the book he was reading. That was why he was the one I had to kill.' He placed his hands flat on the table. 'Books are sacred, they bring knowledge, power and it's incomprehensible that someone would deface them.'

Sheridan made herself a note: *He meant to kill Bobby Stover, not Kenny.* Deciding to save this piece of information until later, she let Emerson continue.

Emerson took a sip of water and went on to describe how he'd noticed that one day the tramp with the red coat had gathered up his few belongings and walked down the street. Emerson followed him until he reached the Dock Road and disappeared into one of the derelict buildings. Emerson had waited until after dark and returned, watching as the tramp settled down for the night after finishing his bottle of wine, letting it slip from his hand as he fell asleep. An hour later, Emerson stood over him, listening to his breathing. He'd said 'hello' loudly several times, but the tramp was comatose. Emerson knelt and touched his hand. Nothing. He then lifted his arm into the air and let it drop. Still nothing. And that was when Emerson knew that the tramp in the red coat was his next victim.

'I went back a few times after that and did the same thing each time, but he never woke up and so I knew slashing his arm would be easy.' Emerson lifted his own arm in the air and ran a finger down it. 'I cut him from here, to here. It was messy but effective. He was dead within minutes.'

'Why did you lift his arm in the air, then let it drop?' Sheridan asked.

'I wanted to be certain that he was out of it. I didn't want him to wake up while I slashed him. Come on, Detective, surely you know by now that I'm always very prepared when I carry out my killings.' He held Sheridan's stare, only shifting his gaze to Anna when she asked the next question.

'Did you leave the JT sign on the wall before or after you killed him?'

'After. And I left it there long enough for you lot to find it, but it appears you didn't.' He slowly shook his head, waving a finger at the same time. 'I left you clues at *every* scene and when you didn't figure out it was murder, I took some of the clues away.'

'Like scraping the JT sign off the wall behind Kenny James,' Sheridan replied.

Emerson pointed a finger at her and grinned. 'So, you did spot it. I'm impressed.'

She turned the page of her interview notes. 'Now tell us about the girls.'

'They're not girls, they're whores.' Emerson wiped his mouth with the back of his hand. 'They sell their disgusting bodies to men, purely because they have no control over their lives. Then they use that money to buy drugs like heroin and inject it into their veins.' He looked at Sheridan. 'What purpose do they serve in life? None. They are imperfect in every single sense of the word. When I planned to kill five people, the next number in the sequence, picking them was ideal. Five less useless whores on the streets.'

'Tell us how you managed to take them, and what you planned to do with them afterwards.'

Emerson stretched out his back, before describing how, for six months, he had visited the areas of Liverpool where prostitutes hung around. Selecting them from a distance, he made a mental note of the slightly built ones, so they'd be easier to overpower and carry down into the inspection pit. Once he selected the first girl, or whore, as he referred to her, he picked her up one evening, telling her he was a priest. She'd laughed at this initially, until he offered her two hundred pounds just to talk. He had driven her to the run-down building, Mayflower Joinery, a property he owned, and they sat outside in his car. He told her he couldn't risk being seen by one of his parishioners. On the back seat he'd placed a bouquet of flowers, telling her they were for his elderly mother who was in a nursing home.

'Why did you do that?' Anna asked.

'It made me more trustworthy. Taking flowers to your mother . . . it gives the impression of a doting son. The whores felt safe with me. If I was off to see my mother and take her flowers, there was little chance I was going to hurt them. And it worked, every single time.'

He went on to describe how he needed to figure out how to get the girls into the building, how to build their trust, so that when the day came when he tied them up, it would be so easy. The first was a Black girl called Dreya. They'd talked on several occasions, and she'd told him how she'd left home at sixteen and moved into a small flat with a friend. She'd started working the streets of Liverpool soon after, turning to prostitution to pay her rent and feed her heroin addiction. Emerson picked her up several times, calling himself Eddie, and she began to trust him. He never touched her, never asked for sex, just wanted to talk. He always drove her to the same building, where they sat chatting. Then one day, he told her he wanted to see her naked, and although the area had little footfall or passing traffic, there was always the risk that someone might see them. So, he raised the shutter and drove inside, where Dreya got out of the car, removed her clothes and stood in front of him. A moment later, he told her to get dressed and they got back into the car. He then opened the shutter, drove out and took her back into town, ensuring he dropped her down a side road, again so he couldn't be seen. After placing two hundred pounds into her hand.

Dreya trusted him. And eventually, so did the other four girls that he targeted. He carried out the same routine with them over several months, until the date of 22nd July loomed. He knew he had to ensure that each girl was in position, so separately, he asked them to be at a certain place at a certain time, two hours apart. He pre-warned them that he wouldn't be in his car, but had hired a van as he was moving items from the church. The first girl, Hannah, turned up on time and didn't hesitate to get in. He drove her to Mayflower Joinery, where, as he had done before, he said that he wanted to see her naked. She agreed without reservation. Once she'd put her clothes back on, he overpowered her, and using the foam and rope, he bound her up before placing her in the back of the van and taking her to the next building. The old MOT testing station, where he carried her down into the inspection pit.

Having prepared the pit weeks earlier, ensuring there was an oxygen supply through the tube, he left Hannah there and went back out to collect the other girls. One by one.

Once all five were in the pit, all he had to do was wait for two days until the 22nd of July and then he could load them into the van and move them to where he would finally end their lives. All together.

'Where were you planning to take them?' Sheridan asked.

'You're probably aware by now that I own several buildings along the Dock Road.' He looked at Sheridan, who nodded. 'Well, I'm sure at some point you'll find one that's been set up to look like a drug den. There's a sofa in there and some tables, a few magazines and newspapers scattered around. Along with a nice collection of needles.'

Sheridan felt Anna's leg push against hers again.

'Yes. We found the place. So, you planned to take the girls there and then what?'

'Whores. Not girls.' He sighed. 'I had enough heroin to make sure they all died from an overdose. Heroin mixed with brick dust. Once they were all injected and dead, I was going to untie them and position them so that it looked like they'd all died from an overdose of bad drugs.'

'How do you know about mixing brick dust with heroin?'

'I read up on that one. Dealers mix them together to bulk out the heroin . . . with wonderfully lethal consequences.'

'Where's the heroin that you were going to inject them with?'

Emerson smiled. 'Have you not found it yet? Well, I'm sure you will eventually.'

'Where did you get it from?'

'A local dealer. I don't know his name.'

'What did you throw away before you were arrested?' Emerson looked to the ceiling and smiled again. 'Was it drugs?' Sheridan asked.

He leaned forward slightly. 'Yes. It was.'

Sheridan picked up on the slight change in Emerson's tone. There was something in the way he'd answered this particular question that stood out. She mentally banked it, turning the page on her interview notes. 'Tell me why you used foam before tying the girls up with rope.'

'I didn't want to leave marks on them. If they had rope marks, then the police would find that a bit suspicious. I thought that was obvious, Detective Holler.'

'It *was* obvious. I just wanted to hear it from you.'

'Then, very well worked out, Detective.' He tipped an imaginary cap towards her.

Sheridan put her pen down for a moment. 'So, you had the five girls tied up in the inspection pit. But when we caught you, there was a deceased girl in the back of your van, Tara in the passenger seat and four girls in the pit. That makes six. Explain that to us.'

Emerson cleared his throat and took a sip of water. 'The whore in the back of the van was Hannah. I'd gone to check on them the night before, on the twenty-first, and she was dead. And before you ask, no I didn't kill her. I guess she died of natural causes, which was very inconvenient, because I then had to go and get another whore to take her place.'

'And that would be Tara?'

'Yes. Tara. I'd picked her up a few times before, so she knew me. She was my backup in case one of the other girls didn't show up when I'd arranged to meet them.'

'What did you intend to do with Hannah's body?'

'I'm sure I'd have thought of something.' Emerson chewed on the inside of his cheek, biting down on a smile.

Sheridan checked her notes, not wanting to look at Emerson while he wallowed in his own arrogance.

She took a breath. 'You left a lot of clues along the way. The JT sign, the note you sent us, telling us that all we had to do was turn things around and fill in the gaps. The postcode engraved on the key and the word TOM and the number 5 on the watch. Why did you do that? Why give us so many clues? Did you *want* to get caught?'

'No. Absolutely not. I wanted to carry on playing the game while I committed the perfect crimes. The clues were my way of having fun while I did it. I wanted to prove that not only could I get away with it, but I could also do it even when I gave you everything you needed to catch me.'

'And we did.' Sheridan glanced at Anna.

Emerson leaned forward slightly. 'Eventually. But I wouldn't go patting yourselves on the back too hard, Detective. Count the dead. Count how many lives I took before you caught me.' He spread his fingers out. 'I even gave you my photograph, fingerprints and DNA.'

'When?' Sheridan asked.

'On the two occasions that I visited your public enquiry office.'

Sheridan knew that Emerson had been into the PEO once on the 22nd of June, to hand in the bag, but when was the other time? He'd said to her after his arrest that it was nice to see her again. A comment he hadn't elaborated on.

'So, apart from the twenty-second of June when you handed the bag in, when was the other occasion?'

'Two days earlier.' Emerson watched her face carefully.

Sheridan sat back, thinking. The 20th of June. A Sunday. The day that Bobby Stover had come in but had left by the time Sheridan had got to the PEO. It was the day that the weird God man was in there chanting the words, 'We are all here only because God allows us to be.' She recalled the man sitting on the bench, wearing beige trousers, his hair scraped forward and his blue-rimmed glasses halfway down his nose as he watched, amused by God man's antics. Sheridan remembered he'd looked at her and smiled. And she had smiled back. *Christ,* she thought. *You were right there.*

'You were sat on a bench, wearing beige trousers. You had a beard and blue-rimmed glasses, you dropped them, and I picked them up and handed them back to you. You were watching the guy that came in shouting about God.' She nodded slowly. 'I remember you spoke to me, you said my name because you'd heard me introduce myself to the guy talking about God.'

Emerson Corr put his hands behind his head and laughed. 'No Detective, that wasn't me.' He raised his hands into the air and stood up, looking at the ceiling. 'We are all here only because God allows us to be.'

Anna followed Sheridan into the ladies toilet. The interview had been suspended after Emerson requested a comfort break.

Sheridan placed her hands on the sink. Leaning forward slightly, she took a moment to study her own reflection, as if she was about to have a conversation with herself. If Emerson Corr hadn't turned out to be the worst serial killer she had ever encountered, the situation would be comical. The fact that not only had she spoken to him, she'd told him to leave the police station. She had no way of knowing at that time who he was, or that a series of unsuspicious deaths were about to be uncovered as murders, but it still choked her.

Anna was patiently waiting beside her. She always knew when Sheridan needed a moment.

'What's he talking about?' Anna eventually asked.

Sheridan told Anna about her encounter with God man.

'He was there, he was right there and I let him go.' Sheridan fiddled with the cold-water tap. 'I spoke to him, I told him I'd nick him if he didn't leave.' She looked at Anna. 'He said he was hungry and was going to get a piece of pie.' She sighed heavily. 'I had him right fucking *there.*'

'A piece of pie, P-I. He was playing with us even back then,' Anna added.

'I'm so mad at myself that I'd forgotten about him.' Sheridan turned the cold tap on and splashed water on her face. 'Let's get back in there.'

Back in the interview room, Sheridan tried to hide her annoyance that Emerson had played her, continuing with her questions.

'Tell us why you were in the PEO on the twentieth of June, chanting about God.'

'I was checking out the cameras.'

Sheridan recalled watching the God man when he had stood in the middle of the PEO, arms raised as he looked to the ceiling. He'd turned ninety degrees, still looking up. Then again, turning ninety degrees. That was how he'd disguised what he was doing. Just a lunatic chanting about God, but all the while, he was checking out where the CCTV cameras were, so that when he came in to deliver the bag containing the watch and the key, he knew how to avoid his face being seen.

'Why draw attention to yourself? Why not just come in and check out the cameras without behaving like that?' Sheridan asked.

'I thought it would look suspicious if I walked in and someone saw me looking at where your cameras were, so I thought I'd have some fun.'

'And what about your fingerprints and DNA? You didn't leave them there that day,' Sheridan said.

'No. That was when I handed in the bag.'

Sheridan remembered the CCTV footage of Emerson reading a newspaper and sipping a cup of coffee, before licking the rim of his cup. *Shit. So that's what you were doing,* she thought. 'I see,' she replied, looking down at her interview notes. 'Why did you buy a whole postcode? Why buy twenty-seven buildings?'

'I bought myself a playground, Detective. Imagine the possibilities when you have access to that many properties. I was going to have so much fun carrying on the pi sequence.' He sighed. 'I would have had the privacy to hide away my victims, play with them, prepare them.' He looked at Sheridan. 'The possibilities were endless. Just like pi.'

'How did you make your money?' Sheridan asked. 'I mean, you're clearly a very wealthy man.

'Property. I bought an old property when I was twenty, did it up, sold it and kept doing that. I liked finding derelict places that were falling down and imperfect. Because once I'd had them renovated, they were perfect again. I always hated those sad buildings along the Dock Road. So much industry went on back in the day and then one by one, they closed down and were just left to rot, so I thought I'd fix that.'

'Why did you choose the twenty-second of July to kill your victims? The pi sequence you were following refers to Pi Day, which is celebrated on the fourteenth of March, so why not use *that* date? Why kill them on the twenty-second of July?'

'I was going to pick the fourteenth of March, but I thought the police might figure out that date too quickly. So, I chose the July date. I didn't want to make it *too* easy for you.'

'And you targeted your *victims* because you saw them as imperfect?'

Emerson shrugged his shoulders. 'Of course.'

Anna looked down at her notes and then asked, 'You explained that you wanted to commit the perfect murders, that you revere infinity and perfection, and that's why you targeted those you saw as imperfect. Do you think *you're* perfect, Emerson?'

'I *did*.'

'Did?'

'Yes.' He folded his arms across his chest. 'I *did*.'

'As in past tense?'

'You'll see.' He grinned. 'You'll see.'

Sheridan sat back and held Emerson's stare. He'd played his game and almost won. He was smart. Probably the smartest killer Sheridan had ever encountered. And if he didn't *know* that, he certainly *believed* it.

He hadn't wanted to get caught. He'd wanted to keep going, to keep killing, to never let it end. Just like pi. But, even after all his ingenuity, intricate planning and deceit, he had been brought down by *one* simple mistake. And Sheridan was about to reveal it to the monster sitting opposite her. While she felt some triumph in what she was about to tell Emerson, it was heavily cloaked with a burning sadness for all the innocent victims that had been lost. So, this . . . was for them.

She took a sip of water, before purposefully placing the cup down. And then she began.

'Emerson, you said that you chose the homeless man in the red coat, as opposed to his friend, because he tore the covers from the book he was reading, and you didn't like that.'

Emerson nodded once, stony-faced with not a hint of emotion.

'His name is Bobby Stover,' said Sheridan.

Emerson firmly shook his head before he smugly responded with his trademark air of disturbing arrogance.

'*Was*. His name *was,* not *is,* Detective. *Past* tense. Tut-tut . . . now you really are getting sloppy.' Emerson draped the last word with his typical patronising tone.

And Sheridan was about to fix that.

'His name *is* Bobby Stover. The homeless man you actually murdered was called Kenny James.' As Sheridan let that bombshell hang in the air for a moment, she noticed a subtle shift in Emerson's cocky composure. As a tiny furrow of confusion crossed his smug face, Sheridan cranked it up a notch.

'You made a *huge* mistake, Emerson. One mistake that ultimately led to your downfall.'

Corr shifted slightly in his seat, his swaggering arrogance finally starting to slip. 'What mistake?'

'Bobby Stover was the man who always wore a red coat, the man who tears the covers off books. You see, what you didn't notice was that Bobby and Kenny swapped coats and when you followed who you thought was Bobby to the derelict building, you were actually following Kenny. Then, as you've told us, you waited until he was unconscious through alcohol consumption and lifted his hand to see if he would wake up before you slashed him. But you see, Kenny James had a medical condition, he'd practically lost the feeling in his hands and forearms. He wouldn't have woken up when you touched him, because he couldn't feel you.'

Appearing to be regaining some of his supercilious confidence, Emerson replied, 'Why does this mean anything? I killed a tramp. One less scumbag on the street.'

'You're still not getting it, are you?' She slowly shook her head, as if trying to explain a simple fact to a child. 'Let me spell it out for you. It means that had you *actually* killed Bobby Stover, you would possibly never have been caught. You could have carried on with your plan, you'd still be out there now, plotting your killings for the twenty-second of July next year. But you made a mistake and you

299

killed the wrong man. Here's the thing, Emerson . . . Bobby Stover was the only person who knew about Kenny's condition. When he discovered that Kenny had apparently committed suicide by slicing his own arm and bleeding out, he knew that Kenny wasn't physically able to do that. So, he came to the police station and told me all about Kenny and how it had to have been someone else who killed him.' Sheridan leaned forward. 'And *that mistake* is why you were caught.'

With no response from Emerson, Sheridan terminated the interview and casually started to gather her notes together. While Anna switched off the recording equipment, Emerson glared at Sheridan, watching her every move. He started to nervously tap his fingers on the table, his body slightly swaying from side to side, as if trying to figure out his next move. Except he was out of moves. It was game over. And Emerson Corr had lost.

Emerson remained silent as Sheridan escorted him back to his cell, only speaking as she was about to close the door on him. 'So, what happens now, Detective Holler?'

'In the morning, we'll present the case to CPS.' She lowered her voice before adding, 'And then we're going to charge you with so many offences that you're going to die in prison.' She smiled at him.

Emerson Corr took a step forward, his face inches from hers. 'That's where you're wrong, Detective Holler.'

'Am I? How am I wrong?'

'You're not going to be charging me with anything. You see that cell door? I'm going to walk right out of it . . . and there's nothing you'll be able to do to stop me.'

CHAPTER 70

It was 4 p.m. by the time Sheridan and Anna walked into CID to a round of applause from the team. Both exhausted from the hours spent interviewing Emerson Corr, which showed on their faces.

'Great job everyone.' Sheridan gave a weary smile, looking around the room. 'According to Emerson, we're not going to be charging him with anything and he's going to walk right out of here.'

A wave of amusement rumbled through the team.

'However, just because he's a smart fucker, the custody staff are keeping a very close eye on him in case he tries anything.'

Hill made her way over to Sheridan and stood beside her, addressing the team. 'The chief is delighted with the result. And so am I. I've sorted out an extension on Emerson's custody clock, so seeing as we were all up half the night and back in first thing this morning, you all deserve an early knock-off. Go and do whatever it is you do when you're not here. Go for a beer, go home to your partners, get some sleep. We'll crack on first thing in the morning.' She put her thumb up.

Rob raised a hand. 'Just an update. We've tracked down Martin Howlett, the guy who's the registered owner of the van Emerson was driving. He was in the process of moving house and was selling the van after giving up his painting and decorating business. Apparently, Emerson told him he was a priest and the day he collected the vehicle was the day Martin was moving out. So, Emerson said he'd take care of the documents and save Martin the trouble. That's why the vehicle is still in Martin's name.'

'The same bullshit story about being a priest that he fed to the girls,' Sheridan replied.

Bridie stepped forward. 'Talking of which, we've been out to the hospital to see them. They're all doing okay and have given statements. They all say the same thing, that they'd known Eddie for a few months and trusted him . . . because he never laid a finger on them, paid them well and was . . .' She looked around the room.

'A priest,' the team said in unison.

As everyone began to pack away and head home, Anna's phone pinged. A message from Steve.

Fancy a quick drink?

Anna looked up at Sheridan who was busy updating the whiteboard. 'Are you off home?' Anna asked.

'I certainly bloody am,' Sheridan said. 'I need to sink a large glass of wine and then another. What about you?'

Anna decided not to tell Sheridan about the text. 'Yeah, off home for a very early night.' She put her hand on Sheridan's shoulder. 'We got him.'

Sheridan kissed her on the cheek. 'We did.' She smiled, before heading back to her office, getting ready to head home. After logging off, she stood at her office window looking down at the streets that in the last few weeks had seemed unsafe and vulnerable, and a feeling of relief washed over her. But now Emerson Corr was locked away, Liverpool seemed to breathe a little easier.

As she drove home, the tension in her head began to dissipate. She'd texted Sam to tell her she was on her way and to make sure there was wine in the fridge, and as she sat in the queue of traffic heading out of Liverpool, her mobile rang.

'DI Holler.'

'Sheridan, it's Ruth Manning.'

'Hi Ruth. You okay?'

'We've got him, Sheridan. We've got Stephen Tubby.'

Sheridan couldn't stop her hands from shaking as she pulled the car over. 'What do you mean?' She felt her mouth dry up.

'Do you remember the guy we found, John Riverstone?' Ruth asked.

'Yeah. The one who said he saw Tubby leaving Birkenhead Park on the day Matthew was murdered.'

'Yes, him. As you know, he told me that he'd dropped his fifteen-year-old daughter off at a friend's house before he went to the pub that day. Well, his daughter wasn't visiting her friend, she was meeting up with her nineteen-year-old boyfriend in Birkenhead Park . . . for sex.'

Sheridan exhaled slowly. 'Okay.'

'So, while she's having a fumble with her boyfriend behind a bush, Stephen Tubby turns up and he stands right near them, but doesn't know they're there. He stays there for a while, just staring straight ahead. They didn't move in case Tubby spotted them, but when he eventually walked away, they got dressed and noticed Tubby walking across the other side of the park. Then he stood near a tree, out of the boys' sight just watching them playing football. The daughter and her boyfriend then saw Tubby walk around a corner and disappear for a short while. They stayed where they were for about five minutes and then Tubby ran past them and out of the park. Once he'd gone, they left.'

'So, the three boys playing football were Matthew, Andrew and Chris.' Sheridan's voice broke a little.

'Yes.'

'How has this only come to light now?'

'After I spoke to John Riverstone, he told his daughter, and she rang me. She's in her late forties now and a mother of two. She couldn't tell anyone about that day because she was terrified that her dad would find out about her being in the park having sex with a lad much older than her. She kept it to herself all those years, as did the boyfriend.'

'Is she sure it was Tubby?'

'Positive. She knew him because he used to drink with her dad. She has no doubt it was him and she's made a full statement.'

Sheridan couldn't respond at first, her mind spinning with this new information.

'You still there, Sheridan?' Ruth asked.

'Yeah. I'm still here. I just . . .' Sheridan felt tears fill her eyes and she blinked them away. Her voice broke again. 'It's not enough to arrest him though.'

'No. But we're going to have him in tomorrow voluntarily. He's lied and lied to us, saying he was working away and was nowhere near Birkenhead Park. But now we have him *right* there.'

Sheridan cleared her throat. 'I want to speak to Andrew Longford. He's so poorly, Ruth. I won't tell him any details, but can I at least say we're close?'

'Of course. I trust your judgement on what you say to him, Sheridan.'

They ended the call and Sheridan sat for a moment, giving herself a little time to let it sink in. Was this it? Was this real? Stephen Tubby was right there, watching Matthew playing football when he'd told police that he was two hundred miles away. He'd maintained the lie for so long, but now they had a witness to show he was there. Was it enough? Would he finally admit to having been at the park? She wiped a rogue tear from her cheek and sent a text to Sam.

Hey beautiful person. I'm popping in to see Andrew Longford on my way home. Won't be too late. I have news. Will explain everything when I get home. I love you so much xxx

Sam texted back: *Hey you. Good news I hope? I love you too, more than you know xxx*

Sheridan sent back a single kiss before pulling into the line of traffic.

CHAPTER 71

Anna walked into the pub, immediately spotting Steve in the corner. He stood as she approached him, and he kissed her on the cheek.

After getting the drinks in, he began fiddling with a beer mat. 'So, how have you been?'

Anna felt an unease about his demeanour. 'Fine. You?' She sipped her drink.

'Yeah, all good. I wanted to talk to you about something.' He put the beer mat down. 'I've . . . met someone.'

'The woman you told me about?'

'Yeah. We're getting on really well and . . . she's asked me to move in with her.'

'That's very quick,' Anna replied, realising her response was abrupt. 'I mean, you've only just met her.'

'I haven't said yes yet.'

'What does she do?' Anna lifted her glass to her mouth and then put it down.

Steve told Anna that his new girlfriend, who was thirty-four, lived in Speke, worked in a card factory and didn't have children. She was looking to settle down and have children, once she'd met the right man.

As he talked, Anna felt an uneasy veil of concern for this other woman. What if Steve moved in with her and returned to his old ways? Steve's violence towards Anna had escalated over time, like so often in cases of domestic abuse, especially after a couple started living together. But was it possible that he really had changed and would never raise a hand to another woman again? Or was this new girlfriend about to become his next victim? If that was the case, then Anna had good reason to be worried.

Steve was still talking, but little was getting through as Anna thought about Sheridan. Her best friend. The friend she had no secrets from, except this one. After excusing herself to use the toilet, she stood looking at her reflection in the mirror, noticing a poster on the wall behind her. She turned and read the words.

IF YOU OR SOMEONE YOU KNOW IS EXPERIENCING DOMESTIC ABUSE, YOU ARE NOT ALONE. YOU CAN CALL THE HELPLINE IN CONFIDENCE.

She didn't need to call the number on the poster. She just needed to call Sheridan.

Sheridan tried to hide her concern as she sat in Andrew Longford's front room. He had lost more weight and was unsteady on his feet. The palliative care nurse was going to be moving in during the following week, because although he could still feed and wash himself, everything was becoming an effort now. As he talked about how he didn't fear the end of his life, Sheridan felt overwhelmingly sad. Trying to stay positive, she buried her own emotions and smiled when he tried to crack a joke, and although the person she had come to know was disappearing before her eyes, there was still that cheeky grin.

He got up to use the toilet and Sheridan felt a fluttering in her stomach as she prepared herself to tell him about Stephen Tubby.

When he was settled back in his chair, she cleared her throat.

'I have some news.'

Andrew blew his nose. 'Go for it.'

'I can't say too much, but we're closer to making an arrest in Matthew's case.'

Andrew reached for the cup of water on the table next to him. 'Really? What's happened?'

'We have another witness who has come forward saying she saw a man in Birkenhead Park, watching you, Matthew and Chris playing football. She's named him and we'll be speaking to him . . .'

'Will he be arrested?' Andrew asked and Sheridan noticed tears forming in his eyes. Then he said: 'Is it Stephen Tubby?'

Tubby's name had come up several times over the years. It wouldn't take much for Andrew to put two and two together. But still, Sheridan had to be cautious. Even though Andrew didn't know Tubby and was unlikely to discuss their conversation with anyone, she still had to adopt her police head and not disclose too much to a potential witness, especially as it might damage the case. In the few seconds that had passed since Andrew had asked the question, he hadn't taken his eyes off her. 'I know you can't say . . . and I understand.'

Sheridan gave a half smile. 'Thank you.' She stood up. 'Shall I pop the kettle on?'

'What will happen to him? If he says he was in the park that day? What evidence do you need to . . .' Andrew suddenly stopped speaking.

Sheridan was about to walk into the kitchen when she heard a loud, uncontrollable sob and turned to see Andrew with his head in his hands.

'Hey.' She stepped over and knelt down, grabbing both his hands and holding them in her own. 'Hey. I'm sorry, I didn't mean to upset you, I just wanted to share the good news with you because . . .'

'Stop. Just stop, please Sheridan.' He pulled his hands away. 'I beg you to stop.' His words were barely audible.

'I'm sorry, I just wanted you to know that we're making progress and there's a chance that we'll have the answer soon . . .'

'Enough!' Andrew blurted out. 'Enough now.' He didn't bother wiping the tears that tumbled into the creases of his face.

Sheridan eased herself up. 'I'm so sorry. We won't talk about it any more.'

Andrew looked up at her. 'Stephen Tubby didn't kill Matthew.'

Sheridan took a moment to answer, eventually responding. 'What are you talking about?' Her voice had fallen to a whisper.

'It was *me*, Sheridan. It was me. *I* killed Matthew, I killed your brother.'

CHAPTER 72

Anna left the pub and sat in her car. Taking out her mobile, she sent a text to Sheridan.

Hi mate. Is it ok if I pop over? I'll bring wine x

She waited for a response. When none came, she decided to head to Sheridan's house anyway. If she didn't talk to her *now* about her concerns surrounding Steve, then she might talk herself out of it.

After picking up two bottles of wine, she checked her phone; still no reply from Sheridan. She dialled her number, and it went straight to voicemail. Leaving a message, she carried on her journey.

Emerging out of the Kingsway Tunnel, she tried the number again, still voicemail. She called the house phone.

'Hello?' Sam answered cheerily.

'Hi Sam, it's only Anna. Is Sheridan there?'

'No, she's gone to see Andrew Longford, she shouldn't be too long. You okay?'

'Yeah, fine. Is it alright if I pop over? I've got wine.'

'Of course it is. See you in a bit.'

Anna felt an unexpected sense of relief, knowing that she was finally going to open up about Steve. It wasn't going to be easy, but Sheridan would know what to do. Sheridan always knew what to do. Little got past her, so it was likely that she already had her suspicions, and all Anna had to do was confirm them.

Anna thought about the Emerson Corr case and how the whole team had been lifted by his arrest, Sheridan included. Today was a good day, a positive day.

She turned on to Bidston Hill and let a smile come across her face. Her best friend would fix it. Sheridan could fix *anything*.

◆　◆　◆

Every part of Sheridan's body was shaking. She thought she might collapse, but somehow she managed to remain on her feet.

Andrew Longford was crying so hard that he looked like he was going to have a heart attack. His face burned red and every word he spoke was virtually incoherent.

Eventually, he caught his breath. 'I've wanted to tell you for so long. Every time you've come to see me, I was so close to just saying it, to telling you what happened that day.'

Sheridan didn't speak. She just listened in disbelief at the words tumbling out of her brother's best friend's mouth.

'When Chris went home, I carried on playing football with Matthew.' Andrew squeezed his eyes shut. 'He called me fat, he kept saying it, over and over. He started to run away, towards the trees, shouting back at me that I was too fat to catch him. I started running after him and I caught up and . . .' Andrew coughed, a heavy, dying man's cough. 'I picked up a lump of wood . . . a broken tree branch. It was so heavy, and I swung it at him. I was so angry . . . He fell down instantly, and I just stood there looking at him. He wasn't moving. I knew it was bad, I think I even knew he was dead. He just lay there, still and quiet, his eyes were slightly open, but I don't think he was breathing. I just panicked. I didn't know what to do, so I checked to see if anyone was around, if anyone saw me, but there was no one there.' He lowered his head so he didn't have to look at Sheridan. 'I ran home, I didn't know what else to do. So, I ran home and told my dad, he told me to stay indoors and not go anywhere and then he left. I waited for ages and when he eventually came home, he told me that Matthew was dead. He'd hidden his body under a massive pile of wet leaves after he took his clothes off in case they could find something on them that showed he'd been there and touched Matthew. He said the police would come and want to speak to me.' Andrew moved slightly in his chair, pausing momentarily, looking back up at Sheridan who was still standing, stunned and motionless in the middle of the room.

'It was my dad who told me to say that I'd seen a man hanging around, watching me and Matthew. He made me memorise three things, so I got my story straight. Blue jeans, brown coat and a beard. I just had to remember BBB.'

Sheridan closed her eyes, as tears streamed down her face. BBB. The three initials that Sam had picked up on.

Andrew continued. 'I don't have any words to say how sorry I am. I told you that God works in mysterious ways, so I guess the cancer is my punishment for what I did.'

'God has nothing to do with this, so don't you fucking dare use your cancer as penance for what you've done.' Sheridan's voice was barely audible. 'What happened to his clothes?'

'I don't know. I honestly don't know.' Andrew wiped a hand down his face. 'I know you can't forgive me. I know you hate me, and I don't blame you. I just don't want Stephen Tubby to go down for something he didn't do. He wasn't even there.'

Sheridan clenched her fists together and spoke through her tears. 'You fucking bastard. You complete fucking bastard. My family have lived with this pain for thirty-three years and now you're dying, you decide to tell me the truth. Yes, I do hate you. I hate you more than you could ever contemplate.'

The pain in Sheridan's chest made her wince. The pain of grief she had felt all these years for Matthew was with her now, and she couldn't ignore it. Thirty-three years filled with the agony of not knowing what had happened to him suddenly overwhelmed her. She opened her mouth to speak, but not a single word came out.

The silence in the room was only broken by her phone pinging in her pocket. Ignoring it, she lifted her head, stepped over to Andrew, and towering over him she finally spoke.

'Andrew Longford, I'm arresting you for the murder of . . .' She had to stop mid-sentence, a cry emitting from deep within her which filled the air. 'Oh, God . . .' She swallowed, before the words came. 'I'm arresting you for the murder of . . . Matthew Holler.'

CHAPTER 73

Sam and Anna were at the kitchen table chatting.

'Are you okay?' Sam asked, noticing that Anna seemed distracted.

'Yeah, I'm fine. Why?' Anna felt her stomach flip. She was going to tell her best friend that she'd lied to her, she'd kept the truth about Steve's violence from her. Anna adored Sam and trusted her implicitly, but she wanted Sheridan there when she finally revealed her secret. Sheridan and Sam. Her two best friends.

'You seem a bit . . . quiet.'

Anna inhaled. 'I'm alright, honestly,' she replied, cheerfully.

Sam glanced at the clock on the wall. 9.16 p.m.

'I wonder if something's happened,' Sam said, feeling Maud pushing her face against her leg. 'To Andrew, I mean. Sheridan's been there for hours and she's not answering her phone.'

'Shall we try calling her again?' Anna got up to refill their glasses.

At that moment, the front door opened, and Sam smiled. 'Ah. Here she is. We were getting worried about you,' she called out as Sheridan walked into the kitchen.

Sam went to give her a hug and noticed the look on her face. 'What's wrong?' she asked, taking Sheridan's hand in her own. 'Is it Andrew?'

Sheridan stared at her as if she hadn't heard the question, eventually answering, 'Yes.'

Anna stood and put an arm around Sheridan's shoulder. 'Oh, mate. I'm so sorry. Come and sit down, I'll pour you a drink.'

Sheridan looked at Sam and Anna in turn. 'Andrew was the one who killed Matthew.'

A look of astonishment fell across their faces.

'What?' said Sam.

Sheridan took a deep breath. 'Andrew admitted to killing Matthew. It was him who killed my brother.' She put her hand on the kitchen table, feeling nauseous and a little unsteady. Sam pulled out a chair and eased her down on to it, throwing a look at Anna.

'What happened?' Anna asked.

Sheridan told them about the conversation she'd had with Andrew Longford, and how, after arresting him, he was taken by uniformed officers to Potters Road custody suite. Because of Sheridan's association with the case, it was inappropriate for him to be booked in at Hale Street.

Andrew had been seen by the force's medical officer and deemed fit to be detained, with a further assessment to take place the following morning before he was interviewed. Ruth Manning had been updated and was appointed to be the officer in the case. Sheridan told Sam and Anna about the new witness coming forward, placing Stephen Tubby at the scene, and how this now didn't make any sense.

'Christ.' Sam slowly shook her head. 'I don't know what to say. I mean, it's brilliant that you now know who did it, but . . .' She touched Sheridan's face. 'How do you feel?'

'Numb.' Sheridan burst into tears. 'I feel numb . . . and angry that he waited this long. He'll die before he gets anywhere near a prison cell. I hate him. I fucking hate him, he's put us through so much . . .' Her voice trailed off.

'When are you going to tell your parents?' Anna said gently.

Sheridan wiped the tears away and cleared her throat. 'Not yet. I want to wait until he's charged. Then I'll tell them.'

'So, this witness, the one who saw Tubby at the park that day, what's that all about? Do you think she was mistaken or is there something else going on?' Anna asked.

Sheridan rubbed her face. 'Fuck knows.' She took a sip of wine. 'Anyway, what are you doing here?' She smiled, silently glad that her best friend was there.

'I fancied a celebratory drink with me bessie mate.' Anna smiled back. 'We nailed Emerson Corr today and I thought that deserved a cheeky drink.' She raised her glass. 'And now you know the truth about what happened to Matthew.'

Anna knew from the moment Sheridan had told them about Longford that she couldn't burden Sheridan with her concerns about Steve and his new girlfriend. She'd wait, until the time was right, whenever that might be.

CHAPTER 74

Saturday 24 July

Sheridan was in her office when Hill came in, closing the door behind her. She sat opposite Sheridan, her face and voice soft and full of concern.

'Are you sure you're okay to be here? You can take some time off if you need to.'

'I want to be here. Anna's putting everything together for CPS and then we get to charge Emerson Corr.' Sheridan put her palm up. 'I'm fine, Hill. Ruth will keep me posted on Andrew Longford and . . .' She blinked away a tear and stood, turning to face the window.

Hill joined her. 'I can't comprehend what you're feeling. And . . . I know I don't do emotion, but I do do practical, and if there's anything and I mean *anything* that you want or need, you just say the word.' She leaned closer to Sheridan, their shoulders touching.

They both looked out across the Albert Dock and several seconds passed before Sheridan replied. 'There is one thing you could do for me.'

Hill turned to her. 'Whatever you want.'

Sheridan stayed looking straight ahead. 'Tell me your real name. I mean, seriously, what is it?'

Hill allowed a grin to take over her face. 'Well, I know you put a tenner on it being Hilda in the ongoing office bet. Well, it's not that.'

Sheridan dropped her head. 'How did you know about the bet?'

'Rob keeps a running list in his office drawer. There's an envelope in there marked, "Guess boss's real name" and two hundred quid bet money.'

'And . . . has anyone guessed right?' Sheridan asked sheepishly.

'Nope.'

'So, are you going to tell me what it is?'

'Nope.'

Sheridan walked into CID and made her way to the front of the room. 'Morning, everyone.'

A quiet 'good morning' came the reply from her team. Hill had briefed them all about Andrew Longford's arrest.

'I just want to say that I know you're all aware of what's happened, but I've got a job to do, and I need to get on with it.' She paused. 'We'll be charging Emerson Corr later today, once Anna's spoken to CPS. According to custody, he's still refusing food, just water, so they're still keeping a close eye on him.' She nodded once and everyone got on with their work.

She returned to her office and half an hour later, her phone rang. 'DI Holler.'

'It's Rob. I've been going through the CCTV from when Emerson threw something away before he was arrested.'

'You found something?'

'Yeah. And you really need to see this.'

Sheridan sat next to Rob as he brought up the CCTV recording of Emerson Corr running from the uniformed officers.

'Okay. Watch as he stops, reaches into his pocket and then throws whatever it is away.' Rob leaned back.

Sheridan squinted at the screen. 'I can't see him throw *anything*. He looks like he does, but—'

'That's because he *doesn't*.' Rob moved his mouse and clicked on the next recording. 'Now, watch *this*. This is when he stops running, throws his hands in the air in surrender and gets nicked.'

Sheridan's eyes widened as Rob played the images, over and over, until she saw it.

She pointed at the screen. 'There. *That's* when he chucks something, as he throws his hands in the air.' She sat back. 'Little fucker.'

'What do you think it is?' Rob played the recording again and paused it as the item flew out of Emerson's hand, over his head and landed in the doorway of one of the derelict buildings.

Sheridan stood up. 'I know *exactly* what it is. We asked him in interview what he threw away before he was arrested. He said it was drugs. But there was something odd about the way he answered the question. We need to get over there, because if that's heroin, then it's laced with brick dust. And if someone finds it and it gets out there, we could have more bloody deaths on our hands.'

CHAPTER 75

As Rob drove to the Dock Road, he asked Sheridan how she was feeling. He'd worked with her long enough to know he could broach the subject and not shy away from it. There was no awkwardness between them.

Sheridan rested her head back. 'It feels weird. After all these years, it was Andrew all along. I feel so angry that he fooled me. And even more angry that he'll die before he sees a prison cell. I'm confused about the witness who saw Stephen Tubby there.' She sighed. 'And I'm absolutely terrified of telling my parents. When they find out it was Andrew, it's going to devastate them.'

'I'm here if you need me, Sheridan. You know that don't you?' Rob glanced at her.

'I know.' She looked out of the window. 'You're a good friend.'

He pulled into the street where Emerson had thrown the object. 'Right, let's go and root round a dirty doorway and look for some dodgy heroin, shall we?'

Sheridan grinned. 'You certainly know the way to a girl's heart.'

Rob parked up and they got out, both snapping on latex gloves. Sheridan grabbed an evidence bag out of the boot and joined Rob, who was bending down, carefully moving away pieces of paper, empty cans and sweet wrappers that had gathered in the doorway.

Moving aside an empty plastic bottle, Rob reached for something. 'There's no drugs here. Just this.'

He held it up and Sheridan took it from his hand, examining the object carefully.

Suddenly, her eyes grew wider. 'No, no, no! Fuck.' She swallowed. 'Oh fuck.'

◆ ◆ ◆

Sheridan reached into her pocket and grabbed her mobile, dialling the number for the custody suite. No answer. She tried again. 'Come on, come on,' she said impatiently. Still no answer. 'We need to get back to the nick.'

They jumped in the car and Rob screeched into a U-turn, pulling away at speed. It was a short drive back to Hale Street.

Sheridan was on the radio. 'Charlie Delta six-six to control, urgent call.'

The reply came immediately. 'Charlie Delta six-six, go ahead.'

'I need to get through to Hale Street custody urgently, no one's answering the phone.'

'They've got a major incident . . .'

'What's happening?' Sheridan flicked a look at Rob, who was weaving his way between the traffic.

'We're not sure at the moment. I'll try to get an update. My colleague has been asked to call an ambulance.'

'For a prisoner or member of staff?'

'Stand by. I'm just trying to find out.'

As Sheridan waited with the radio to her ear, Rob pulled into Hale Street and drove down the middle of the road, swerving into the backyard.

Sheridan was out of the car first, running to the door, the item that Emerson had thrown away grasped in her hand as she frantically entered the code to get in. She pushed the door open and raced along the corridor towards the custody suite. Her heart was thumping in her chest and as she ran down the corridor towards the cells, it all came together. All the signs. Every clue that had been right in her face the whole time.

Emerson Corr's words echoed around her head.

'You're not going to be charging me with anything. You see that cell door? I'm going to walk right out of it . . . and there's nothing you'll be able to do to stop me.'

The detention officer's comment: *'I made him some toast earlier, but he's only eaten the crusts.'*

Bobby Stover's smiling face as he'd mentioned the decent food he'd been served in custody. *'Proper bread?'* Sheridan had asked him.

'Yeah. The posh stuff, got seeds in it.'

And then the night Sam had come home from her first-aid refresher course. *'They gave us a list of the main things people are allergic to, it's mental. Peanuts, milk, insect bites, latex, sesame seeds.'*

As Sheridan reached the cells, she could see the crowd of officers on their knees around Emerson Corr. His cell door was open, and he lay on the floor outside in the corridor. His face was swollen, and his breathing was no more than a wheeze.

'Get back!' Sheridan shouted, dropping to her knees next to Emerson.

And then she removed the cap and pressed the EpiPen into his thigh through his clothing. A slight click and the adrenaline was forced into his body.

Reversing the effects of Emerson Corr's life-threatening allergy to sesame seeds.

CHAPTER 76

Hill walked into Sheridan's office. 'Emerson's going to be fine. They're going to keep him in hospital overnight. We'll wait until he's back in custody and then we'll charge him. CPS have had a field day, he's getting the lot thrown at him.'

Sheridan nodded. 'Good.'

Hill perched herself on the edge of the desk. 'How the fuck did you know about his allergy?'

Sheridan smiled. 'I just put two and two together. He removed the crusts from his toast and waited until he was ready before he ate them. That's why he threw the EpiPen away – he didn't want us to know about his allergy.' Sheridan rolled a pen between her fingers. 'He told me that he was going to walk right out of the cell and there was nothing we could do to stop him. He pressed his cell buzzer and when the detention officer opened the wicket, Emerson put the crusts in his mouth and started reacting almost straight away, so she opened the cell door . . . and he walked out.'

'And then collapsed,' Hill added.

'Yeah. But technically he *did* walk out.'

'Well, good job. That would have really pissed me off if he'd managed to top himself. Prick.' Hill stood up. 'Oh. They found the heroin by the way, it was hidden behind a loose brick in the building where we found the girls.'

Sheridan's phone rang and Hill got up to leave with a wave of her hand.

'DI Holler.'

'It's Ruth Manning. You free to speak?'

'Yeah.'

'Andrew's been interviewed. He's made a full and frank confession. CPS have agreed to charge him with murder. He'll be kept in custody until the next court on Monday. But, I will warn you, the court might well bail him, due to his condition.'

'I know,' Sheridan replied. 'Thank you, Ruth. Thank you so much.'

'The press have got hold of it and the press officer has batted them away so far. I told her you need to speak to your parents first, before it's made public.'

'I'll go and see them this evening.' Sheridan ended the call and rested her head in her hands, just as Anna came in.

Sheridan updated her about the call from Ruth.

'Why don't you go home *now*? Go and see your mum and dad, don't wait until tonight,' Anna said.

'No. I'll do it later.' Sheridan stood up.

'Why are you putting it off?'

'Because I'm scared. I'm scared and elated all at the same time and I just need to get my head around it, so that when I tell them, I don't fall apart.'

Anna wrapped her arms around Sheridan. 'Fair enough.'

Sheridan squeezed Anna tightly. 'Anyway, we've got someone *else* to go and see.'

◆ ◆ ◆

Sheridan and Anna sat in Annette Lennon's living room, politely accepting the cup of tea she'd offered.

'We have some good news,' Sheridan said, smiling.

Annette clasped a hand to her mouth. 'Oh God, have you caught him?'

'Yes. We have.'

'What's his name?' She exhaled loudly as if she'd been holding her breath.

'Emerson Corr.'

'Is he in prison?' Annette asked, tears rolling down her face.

'Not yet. But he will be.'

Annette wiped her mouth with a tissue. 'That's brilliant. I can't believe you've actually caught him.' She smiled, and then her head dropped. 'But, how long will he get? I mean, you can't lock him up forever.'

Sheridan sat forward. 'He'll get life.'

Annette looked at her, searching her face. 'Life?' She nodded slowly. 'He did something really bad, didn't he? I mean, worse than what he did to me.'

'Yes. He did something really bad. But you can now do something for me.' Sheridan stood up and took Annette by the hand, leading her over to the window. 'You can open your curtains. Let some light in. Because he's not out there.'

Annette burst into tears, and Sheridan didn't hesitate to wrap her arms around her.

When she'd composed herself, Annette Lennon threw the curtains open. 'Fuck you, Emerson Corr.'

After sitting back down, Annette asked why Emerson had targeted her and what he'd meant by the message that he was just making a point.

Sheridan delicately explained Emerson's reasons, deciding to omit, for now, that Annette was targeted because she was overweight, and stressing that it was because she was alone and looked like she was going to jump in front of the next train.

As they sat chatting, Sheridan noticed the obvious and almost complete change in Annette's demeanour. Her body language had shifted from a frail, scared victim to a strong, warm and confident woman. She didn't ask about the details of Emerson Corr's other crimes. But she did ask how they had managed to capture him. Sheridan told her about Bobby Stover, and how he'd been convinced that his friend, Kenny, couldn't have killed himself. And it was that conviction that drove Bobby to pluck up the courage and approach the police.

'I'd like to meet him,' Annette said. 'I'd like to meet Bobby Stover. I want to thank him personally.'

Sheridan glanced at Anna who was smiling. 'We could arrange that.'

As they got up to leave, Sheridan hesitated by the door, surreptitiously indicating that she wanted to speak to Annette alone. As Anna walked back to the car, Sheridan turned to Annette.

'Do you mind if I ask you a question? You don't have to answer it.'

'You want to know if I was going to jump in front of the train that night.' Annette's eyes filled with tears. 'Yes. I was.'

'But since then, you haven't felt like that?' Sheridan asked.

'Strangely, no. After it happened, something changed in me and I realised that if I killed myself, then I'd never see the day that the man who attacked me was caught. I can't explain how it feels, it's like you so desperately want this person caught that it takes over your whole life. You literally wake up every day and wonder if it's the day you're going to find out he's been arrested.' She looked Sheridan in the eye. 'Can you imagine how that feels?'

Sheridan felt her jaw tighten and blinked down on a tear. 'Actually, yes, I can. I know *exactly* how that feels.'

CHAPTER 77

Sheridan walked into CID and approached Bridie, pulling out a chair opposite her.

'Can I ask you a personal question?' Sheridan said.

Bridie smiled. 'Go for it.'

'How is suicide viewed in the Catholic religion?'

Bridie sat back. 'Well, it depends. There are those who believe it's still a sin and those who have relaxed their views.'

'So, a devout Catholic might still feel that it's sinful?'

'Absolutely.'

Sheridan stood up. 'Thanks Bridie.' She made her way back to her office.

A moment later, she was heading out the door when she bumped into Anna.

'I'm going to see Janet Vickers. I'll see you later.'

'Why can't I come with you?' Anna asked.

'I just need to do this on my own. Trust me.' Sheridan winked.

Twenty minutes later, Sheridan pulled up at the Barkers' property. Bouncer was on the porch and got up, stretching, before wagging his tail all the way over to her car.

Janet appeared at the door. 'Hello. Come in.' She forced a smile as Sheridan followed her into the kitchen.

Pulling two chairs out, they sat at the kitchen table.

Sheridan tentatively explained how Emerson Corr had been responsible for the deaths of Freya, Brendan, and their two sons. How he'd tricked his way back into their lives. She left out the detail of the other killings but confirmed that Emerson had admitted to several other crimes, and would spend the rest of his days in prison.

As Sheridan spoke, Janet remained silent, gently stroking Bouncer's head.

'I know this is a lot to take in, but if there's anything you need, any support, please just let me know,' Sheridan said, feeling Bouncer's tail flicking against her leg.

'I'll be fine, thank you,' Janet replied. 'I just feel so . . . sad . . . and yet, relieved that we now know the truth about their deaths.'

Sheridan stood, placing a hand on Janet's shoulder. 'You have my number. Call me anytime.' She glanced at the cross on the wall. 'They were good Catholic people, weren't they?'

Janet followed Sheridan's gaze. 'Yes. Yes, they were.'

'Emerson told us that he'd left a note on the kitchen table for the police to find. He wanted their deaths to look like suicide. I know that suicide is frowned upon in the Catholic Church, so maybe it was a blessing that the note was never found and everyone thought they died accidentally.' She glanced down at Janet, who had clasped her hands together.

Sheridan continued. 'My guess is that when you arrived that day and opened the door, the note somehow flew off the table and you just didn't see it. Maybe with all the police activity that day, it just got lost.'

Janet looked up at her. 'I guess you could be right.'

Sheridan gave Bouncer a last stroke. Janet followed her to the door and as she was about to leave, she touched Sheridan's arm.

'Thank you.'

Sheridan smiled. 'You're welcome.'

328

As Sheridan's car disappeared down the lane, Janet returned to the kitchen. She recalled the day she'd entered the house and found the note on the table. It was the first thing she'd spotted. *Just can't Take any more.* After the shock of finding Freya, Brendan and the boys, she'd returned to the kitchen and picked up the note. And that was the moment she decided to protect their reputation. She didn't want them to be remembered as the parents who had killed their own sons and then themselves. It went against everything they believed in, as good Catholics. Because *that's* what they were.

Sheridan knocked on Stephanie Hannigan's door. Juliet answered and showed her inside. Sheridan went through the same process she had with the others, carefully explaining how Jake hadn't killed himself, but was a victim of Emerson Corr.

Stephanie remained silent, the shock of what she was hearing slowly sinking in. 'Why my boy? Why Jake?' she asked, her voice broken with emotion.

'He targeted people he believed were imperfect,' Sheridan answered. 'He knew that Jake was autistic, and in his warped head, that was enough to target him.'

Stephanie wiped her face with a tissue. 'How did he know Jake was autistic?'

And that was the question that Sheridan was expecting. And the one she had to answer very carefully.

'You said that you're not in touch with Jake's dad, Frank. Is that still the case?'

Stephanie nodded, and so did Juliet, but Sheridan saw her face flush red.

'Well, according to Emerson, Jake's dad had visited him up at Thurstaston Cliffs a couple of times and he'd heard them talking. He overheard Frank mention Jake's autism. And apparently Frank was there the day Jake died.'

Stephanie snapped a look at Juliet. 'Frank never said anything about that. He never said a bloody word, did he?'

Juliet stayed silent and Sheridan noticed how uncomfortable she looked.

'Did he ever mention it to you, Juliet?' Sheridan asked.

'No.'

After explaining the next steps, that Emerson would be charged and held in custody, Sheridan promised to keep them updated. Juliet showed her to the door.

'Thank you, Detective Holler.' Juliet held out her hand and Sheridan shook it.

'We've tried to locate a number for your dad, but we haven't found one yet. If you do hear from him, please let him know I'm happy to discuss the case with him.'

Juliet bit her lip. 'I will. If I ever hear from him.'

And with that, Sheridan left.

Juliet went back into the living room. 'I'm going for a drive, just to clear my head. Will you be okay?'

'I'll be fine. I might go for a lie-down.'

A moment later, Juliet was pulling away from the house, parking up just around the corner before dialling her father's number.

'Hey, princess. You okay?' he answered.

'The police have been here again.' She told him about Sheridan's visit and the details of Jake's death.

'Christ,' Frank replied.

'You never said you were with Jake the day he died,' Juliet said.

There was a silence down the phone.

'Daddy?'

'Yeah. I'm here.' He paused. 'I never told you because I thought I'd upset Jake that day and that's why he killed himself. I've always thought it was my fault. I'm so sorry I lied to you.'

Juliet could hear the emotion in her father's voice. 'It's okay, Daddy. It's okay. We know now that Jake didn't kill himself. He was murdered. It wasn't your fault.'

'But it *was* my fault. The only reason this Emerson guy knew about Jake's autism was because he overheard me saying it.'

'Daddy, listen to me. We can't change anything, and I don't want you to blame yourself. Please.'

'Thank you, princess. I never want you to hate me.'

'I could never hate you, Daddy. I love you so much.'

'Are you going to tell your mum that we've been in contact all this time?'

'No. Of course not, that's our secret. That has to stay our secret.'

She ended the call and rested her head back, smiling.

Juliet Hannigan had never lost contact with her father. Why would she? He sent her money every month, and an added bonus on her birthday. All she had to do was to play up to her 'princess' persona and her father would keep the money coming. As long as her mother never found out they were in contact, then she could remain living in her mother's house, rent free. Until she'd saved enough money to buy her own place. When Sheridan Holler had visited and asked what she did for a living, Juliet had managed to swerve the question. The truth being, she didn't have a job because she didn't need one. Unbeknown to her mother, she spent her days going to the gym, lunching with friends and going shopping, dipping into the money her father sent her every month. She'd played her parents perfectly, using her brother's death as a tool to gain their attention, as they would do anything for their daughter. The daughter who was now their precious only child. All Juliet had to do was keep playing the game.

CHAPTER 78

Exhaustion kicked in as Sheridan walked through town. Everyone had been updated, except Bobby Stover. She checked his usual haunts, but with no sign of him she decided that she'd run out of excuses. No more delaying telling her parents about Andrew Longford. She had to do it. And she had to do it now.

She headed back to the nick and was collecting her things from her office when Hill walked in.

'I'm going home,' Sheridan said, switching off her computer.

'Home or to your parents'?' Hill asked.

'Home first to get Sam and then to my parents'.' Sheridan felt a fluttering in her chest.

Hill took her gently by the arms. 'They've been waiting for this for thirty-three years. But now the healing can start. For all of you.'

Sheridan nodded. 'I know. Thanks, Hill.'

She walked slowly to her car.

Sam put her hand on Sheridan's leg as they pulled up outside Rosie and Brian's house.

'I feel sick,' Sheridan said, taking deep breaths.

'You'll be fine. Remember that you're about to end this for them. And I love you.'

Sheridan smiled. 'I love you too.'

They walked up the path to the front door, which was opened by Rosie. 'Come in, come in, the kettle's on.'

They hugged. As Rosie went to make the tea, Brian came in from the garden.

'This is a nice surprise.' He kissed Sheridan and Sam in turn, before arranging the kitchen chairs for them all to sit.

'So, how's work?' Brian asked.

'Fine,' Sheridan replied.

'How's the big case?' Rosie said.

'Fine.' Sheridan felt her stomach turn.

Rosie placed a tray of biscuits on the table. 'You're very quiet, is everything alright?'

'I have some news. About Matthew's case.'

Rosie sat down and Brian took her hand. 'What news?'

'We got him, Mum.' She couldn't hold back her tears. 'We got the man who killed Matthew.'

Brian pulled Rosie to him and she buried her head in his chest. They cried openly and Sheridan joined them, wrapping her arms around her parents.

Sam watched as the three people she loved the most shared this moment. The moment they had waited and prayed for, for so very long.

When Sheridan took her seat, she reached across the table and held her parents' hands.

Her mother was the first to ask, 'Who is he? What's his name?'

Sheridan took the longest breath. 'It's . . . It was Andrew Longford.'

Rosie looked at Brian and back at Sheridan. 'Matthew's best friend? But . . . he was just a boy . . .' Her voice trailed off.

Sheridan took her time, carefully relaying the account that Andrew had given about what had happened that day. Stopping every now and then to let the details and the enormity of it all sink in.

It was late in the evening by the time she and Sam got up to leave. She'd warned her parents that Andrew's arrest would likely be on the news the following day.

As they got to the door, Rosie grabbed Sheridan. 'We love you so much. Our beautiful girl.' She turned to Sam and touched her face. 'You look after her.'

Sam smiled and they headed back to the car. Few words were spoken as Sheridan drove the short journey home. As she turned on to Bidston Hill, approaching the allotments, she recalled the conversation she'd had with Andrew Longford over two weeks earlier.

'I didn't know you had an allotment.'

'Yes. My dad had it from the early seventies. We used to spend a lot of time there together when I was a kid.'

Sheridan pulled the car over.

'What's wrong?' Sam asked.

Sheridan got out and stepped over to the fence, staring at the allotment plots. 'It can't be,' she said under her breath.

CHAPTER 79

Sunday 25 July

Sheridan walked into Hill's office to find her on the phone. She remained standing as Hill finished the call.

'That was Norfolk Police. They've found remains in the septic tank. Just bones, but hopefully DNA will confirm it's Molly and Bethany.'

Sheridan nodded. 'Anna's going to be charging Emerson Corr this afternoon. He's back in custody from hospital, so we can add them to the charges once we know for sure.'

Hill leaned back in her seat. 'How did it go with your parents?'

'They were . . . fine. Shocked that it was Andrew, but relieved it's all over.' Sheridan rested a hand on the back of the chair in front of her. 'Andrew Longford had an allotment, he took it over when his dad died. I want it searched.'

Hill pursed her lips. 'I'm sorry, I don't understand, what are we looking for?'

'Matthew's clothes. Andrew said that when he ran home after he killed Matthew, his dad went to the park and was gone for ages. It was his dad who removed Matthew's clothes, but he had no idea what his dad did with them. I think they might be buried in the allotment.'

Hill tapped her fingers on the desk. 'Leave it with me. I'll get it sorted.'

They made their way to CID together and updated the team about what had been found in Norfolk.

'I know this job has taken it out of you all, but we're there now.' Sheridan smiled. 'You did a great job and hopefully you can all now catch up on your other cases.'

A light groan came from around the room, a reminder that there was no rest in CID.

After going through everyone's workloads, the team knuckled down, and Sheridan returned to her office.

She typed Bobby Stover's name into the crime system. Having not seen him for a couple of weeks, she wondered if he'd been arrested recently. He hadn't been in his usual spot when she'd walked into town of late. He was the only one who hadn't been updated about Emerson's arrest and she felt a pang of guilt. He really needed to know. It was his bravery in coming forward that had led to the whole inquiry, after all.

After the crime system and PNC showed that Bobby hadn't been arrested, Sheridan headed back to CID and made a beeline for Dipesh. She had a job for him. A job that only Dipesh could carry out.

Bobby Stover turned the page of his book and took a bite of the sandwich a passer-by had handed him. Every now and then, he lifted his eyes from the page, always on the look-out for any trouble. Being on the street meant you had to stay alert. One minute a kind member of the public could be handing you a cup of coffee or a few loose coins, and the next a group of shit-bags could approach you and spit in your face. He watched as Sunday shoppers ambled past, before returning to concentrate on his book. A moment later, a dark shadow covered the sun that was beating down on him and he looked up, squinting.

'Bobby?'

'Yeah. Who are you?'

'You need to come with me.'

Bobby looked around. 'No. You're alright, mate.'

'You *have* to come with me.'

Bobby felt the freezing water hit his face and he winced as it sent a chill over his naked body. He stood shivering on the hard, cold, concrete floor. Placing a hand on the wall, he could hear screaming outside the door and turned his head to listen.

Half an hour later, he was sitting on a chair, the small, unfamiliar room making him feel claustrophobic. He looked down at the clothes he was wearing. Everything felt alien. He could feel his hands shaking slightly as he touched the crisp wrapping of the bouquet of flowers that lay on the table next to him. He couldn't remember feeling this nervous before. Maybe the first time he'd been sent to prison.

He took a couple of deep breaths, trying to calm himself.

And then the door opened.

'Hello, Bobby.'

'Hello, Detective Holler.' Bobby grinned.

Sheridan sat down and glanced at the flowers. 'Did my colleague, Dipesh, explain what's happening?'

'Yeah.' Bobby nodded.

'Let's see you then.'

Bobby stood up and held out his arms. The brand-new suit fitted him perfectly.

After tasking Dipesh to go into town and find Bobby, Sheridan had told Dipesh to take him clothes shopping. She'd suggested a pair of casual trousers and a shirt. But Dipesh, the connoisseur of smartness, had decided to take it one step further and got Bobby kitted out in a very nice suit.

'You look really smart.' Sheridan smiled at him. 'And you've had a shave, I like it.'

'Not that I'm complaining, but that shower in custody is freezing.' Bobby sat back down. 'And it sounds like you've got a right nut-job in there.'

'We had a young girl brought in for shoplifting and she's been kicking off, screaming blue murder down the cells.' Sheridan stood. 'Anyway, I like the flowers, they're a nice touch. I'm sure Annette will love them.'

Bobby stood and wiped a hand down the front of his chest. 'And she really wants to meet me?'

'She does. She wants to thank you, because you're the one that led to her attacker being caught. She'll be here in about an hour.' Sheridan paused. 'But I wanted to talk to you first.'

Sheridan told Bobby how Emerson had targeted Kenny. How he'd noticed the homeless man in the red coat and watched him, deciding that he would be his next victim. How he'd seen him alone in the derelict building and waited until dark, until he was unconscious through drink, and how he'd made sure he was out of it by lifting his hand and letting it drop.

Bobby listened and Sheridan could see tears forming in his eyes. 'So, it was *me* he'd been watching,' he eventually said. 'The guy in the red coat was me. I swapped my coat with Kenny before I went shoplifting for his wine that day. The day I got arrested, the last time I ever saw him.' He looked at Sheridan. 'Kenny wouldn't have felt his arm being lifted in the air, because he'd lost the feeling by then.'

'I know,' Sheridan replied.

'If I hadn't gone to rob that wine for Kenny, he'd still be alive, he would've stayed in town, sharing a doorway with me. This Emerson bloke wouldn't have killed him.' Bobby shook his head. 'It was my fault.'

Sheridan leaned across the table and touched Bobby's arm. 'Kenny was very ill. He had undiagnosed heart failure and cirrhosis of the liver. He really didn't have long to live and the way he died, he wouldn't have felt a thing. None of it was your fault, and you coming forward has prevented a man from going on to kill others and he would never have stopped. We may never have realised that all the deaths he was responsible for were murders. He could have gone on and on and on, he was *that* clever. The only thing you're responsible for is bringing him to our attention and that's how we caught him.'

Bobby quickly wiped tears away with the back of his hand and puffed out his cheeks. 'Okay. Well, good on yer, boss. You fucking got him.'

'We did. Anyway, are you ready to meet Annette?'

'Yeah. Yeah I am.'

CHAPTER 80

Anna walked Annette into the room and Bobby put his hands behind his back and then down by his sides, clearly unsure what to do with them.

'Hello.' Annette smiled at him and he smiled back. 'Is it okay if I give you a hug?' she asked.

'Of course.' Bobby held out his arms and as Annette stepped towards him, she looked away.

'I hope you can fit them round me.'

'I'm sure I can, my arms are quite long, I mean not that they have to be long to go round you, I just mean . . . I brought you some flowers.' Bobby's nerves had got the better of him and he spoke at a hundred miles an hour.

Sheridan threw a look at Anna. 'Why don't we all sit down. I'll get us some teas and coffees.' Sheridan put a reassuring hand on Bobby's shoulder before she left the room, returning ten minutes later with a tray of drinks.

Bobby talked openly about being homeless and how he was trying to put his life back together. Annette remarked on how smart he looked in his suit.

'I'll be the best-dressed homeless guy in Liverpool,' he joked, making Annette laugh.

Annette told him how she missed working in the library, and their shared love of books gave them cause for a comfortable and natural conversation.

Sheridan and Anna sat back, just listening. Every now and then stealing a look at each other as Bobby and Annette, two strangers, thrown together in the most tragic of circumstances, appeared to be bonding.

After an hour, Annette got up to leave and Bobby handed her the flowers. 'Thank you, Bobby. And thank you for meeting with me. I hope you know that what you did was amazing. I feel so different already. I'd hardly left my flat and now I can, because he's not out there.'

'It was nothing. I did it for Kenny. I had no idea that there were others out there. I hope you'll be okay now.'

'I think I will. Thanks to you.'

They hugged again. Anna showed Annette out of the station, leaving Sheridan with Bobby.

'That went alright, didn't it?' Bobby asked, rubbing his hands together.

'It was perfect. You did really well.'

'Thanks Detective Holler. It was really nice meeting Annette. She's sound.' He squinted and rubbed his stomach. 'Built up a right appetite. Any chance of grabbing some of that posh bread you give out in custody?'

Sheridan shook her head. 'No. They don't serve that any more. Apparently, some dickheads are allergic to sesame seeds.'

She showed him out of the station and noticed the confident swagger in the way he walked down the road. Bobby in his new suit. And a twenty-pound note in his pocket to treat himself to lunch.

Anna met Sheridan back in CID. 'Well, what do you think?' She grinned.

'I think I saw a twinkle in Annette's eye,' Sheridan said, raising an eyebrow.

'Me too. Anyway, I've got to go and speak to CPS, we're ready to go through the charges.' Anna left the room.

Hill walked in. 'Sheridan, we've got a search warrant for the allotment. They're going out there now. Do you want to be there?'

Sheridan took a deep breath. 'Yeah.'

CHAPTER 81

Sheridan and Hill remained back as they watched the search team digging up Andrew Longford's allotment patch.

The area had been cordoned off, and the main road that ran alongside the allotment was closed to traffic, but the police presence had drawn attention from locals who were lined up by the cordon.

Hill stood shoulder to shoulder with Sheridan. 'You okay?'

'I just keep thinking about how I've driven past this place every day on my way home from work for so many years. And the whole time it might be the place where Matthew's clothes have been buried.' She pinched her forehead between her thumb and forefinger.

'Have you thought about the fact that we might not find anything?' Hill asked.

'Yeah. But then at least I'll know they're not here. Andrew's dad could have burned them or thrown them in a bin.' Sheridan's voice broke as she said the words. The thought that her little brother's body had been stripped naked and buried under a pile of leaves was enough to break her, but the fact that his clothes could have been discarded like trash made her feel intolerably sad. She remembered his smell, how his hair had felt when she ruffled it. How the black plimsolls he'd been wearing that day had a little hole in the toe. His favourite red shorts, the ones that Sheridan's mum had sewn the Liverpool football badge on to. His white T-shirt and red sweatshirt.

Sheridan tried desperately not to burst into tears. Andrew Longford's father had tried to protect his son by hiding what he'd done. By giving him a story of the man in the park, the man with the beard, the brown coat and blue jeans. The man who was never there.

Hill glanced at her. 'You can let it out, you know,' she whispered.

'No, Hill. I can't, I just can't.' She swallowed.

Hill noticed Sheridan's hands were shaking and felt she should put her arms around her. But Hill rarely did emotion and so she stood there, awkwardly trying to find the right words.

At that moment, an officer from the search team looked over at them and raised his hand.

Sheridan took a deep breath. 'They've found something.' She went to step forward, but Hill held her back.

'You can't go over there, Sheridan.' She could hear Sheridan's breathing getting faster, her eyes fixed on the sudden activity around the deep hole the search team had dug. Hill put her hand out. 'Can I borrow your phone?'

'What for?'

'My battery's dead. I need to make a call.'

Sheridan handed her mobile to Hill, who stepped away out of Sheridan's earshot.

A few moments later, she returned. They stood watching, waiting. Ten long minutes passed before one of the CSI officers came over to explain what was going on.

'We've found a plastic bag, we're clearing the dirt away around it.' He looked at Sheridan. 'We'll let you know as soon as we know what it is. Shouldn't be too long.'

Sheridan nodded, biting down on her tears. She folded her arms across her chest and then unfolded them.

'If his clothes *are* here, they won't smell of him anymore, will they?' Sheridan asked the question, already knowing the answer.

Hill was watching the search team as she replied. 'It's been a long time, Sheridan.' She hesitated and several minutes passed before she spoke again. 'The girls' clothes smelt of my perfume.'

Sheridan snapped a look at her. Hill never talked about her family.

'Ralph had bought me a bottle of my favourite one for my birthday. The girls used to sneak into our room and spray my perfumes all over themselves. When I got their clothes back, I could smell it. I never wore the same one again.'

'I'm so sorry . . .' Sheridan said.

'We've both lost something very precious.' Hill turned her head to look at Sheridan. 'But we're not bonding, you know? Because I don't do that.' The hint of a smile showed on her face.

'Of course not. God forbid.' Sheridan grinned, despite her sadness.

Hill kept looking past Sheridan to the road by the side of the allotment, seeing a marked police car pull up. She turned back to see the search team carefully lifting a black plastic bag from the ground. The CSI team carefully opened it, before one of them looked over and put his thumb up as he made his way towards them.

'Oh God,' Sheridan gasped, putting a hand to her mouth, taking a step forward.

'We've found them. We've found Matthew's clothes,' the CSI officer said and Sheridan burst into tears. Her whole body started shaking and heavy tears fell down her face.

Then, from behind, she felt arms around her and turned to see Sam there. 'I've got you,' Sam said. 'I've got you.'

Sheridan let Sam lead her over to the police car, where they sat in the back. Sheridan laid her head on Sam's shoulder. 'What are you doing here?' she asked, tilting her head to look at Sam.

'Hill called me from your phone. She said you probably needed a hug and that she was sending a police car to the house to pick me up.'

At that moment, Hill opened the back door of the car. 'Nice to meet you, Sam.'

'Nice to meet you, Hill.' Sam smiled. 'I've heard a lot about you.'

'All bad I expect.' She bent down to look at Sheridan. 'How are you doing?'

'I'm okay.' She squeezed Sam's hand. 'Thank you for bringing Sam here.'

'No problem.' She cleared her throat. 'So, now you have some closure. I hope you can take comfort in that, Sheridan. We know Andrew Longford killed Matthew, we know why he did it and how he did it. And now we have Matthew's clothes. It doesn't take the pain away but at least you can start the process of putting it to bed.'

Hill's mobile rang.

'I thought your battery was dead?' Sheridan asked with a raised eyebrow.

'I lied. I just needed your phone to call Sam.' She pressed the answer button. 'DCI Knowles.'

'It's Anna. Is Sheridan with you?'

'Yes. Do you need to speak to her?'

'No. I need to speak to *you*.'

Hill straightened herself up and walked away from the car, out of Sheridan's earshot. 'Go ahead.'

'We've got a massive problem.'

'What kind of problem?'

'Stephen Tubby has turned up at Hale Street PEO.'

'What does he want?'

'He says we've got the wrong man in custody. He wants to confess to Matthew Holler's murder.'

CHAPTER 82

Hill marched into CID and headed towards Anna. 'What the actual fuck is going on?'

Anna stood up. 'Tubby's downstairs, he doesn't want a solicitor, he just wants to tell us what happened. Ruth Manning and her colleague are on their way now to interview him.'

'For fuck's sake, I thought this job was done and dusted. What's Tubby playing at?' Hill's hands were on her hips. 'I haven't told Sheridan yet. She's taken the afternoon off to visit her parents with Sam.' She turned to leave. 'Have you charged Emerson Corr yet?'

'Yeah. Ten counts of murder, six counts of kidnap, GBH on Annette and possession with intent.'

'Good job.' Hill put her thumb up. 'I'll update the chief about that first to put him in a good mood and then I'll tell him about Tubby.' And with that, she left.

Ruth Manning and her colleague, DC Gliss, arrived in custody and set themselves up in an interview room. Stephen Tubby was brought in a few minutes later. After the formal introductions, Ruth began.

'Stephen, you've handed yourself in today to confess to the murder of Matthew Holler. Is that correct?'

'That's correct,' Stephen Tubby answered clearly with a pronounced nod. He was short in stature, with a distinct pot belly which bulged over his trousers and stretched the buttonholes of his shirt. His thinning hair was cut short and neat, and a heavy gold chain sat tightly around his neck. He sat upright and made direct eye contact as he listened to Ruth's next question.

'As you know, we have someone in custody for Matthew's murder . . .'

'Yes. I'm aware that Andrew Longford has admitted to killing the lad. He might have thought that he killed him, but he didn't. *I* did.'

'You've been asked by me on several occasions if you were in Birkenhead Park the day Matthew Holler was murdered, and you've always denied it.'

'Yes. I lied. I *was* there.'

Ruth asked him to describe the events leading up to the day that Matthew died.

Stephen Tubby took a sip of water and began to tell his story.

'I used to spend a lot of time in Birkenhead Park. I liked to watch the lads playing football most weekends. I know that people thought I was a bit odd, some sort of weirdo, infatuated with little boys. But it wasn't like that. It wasn't like that at all.'

There was a short silence before Ruth said, 'Tell us what happened the day Matthew Holler died.'

Stephen readjusted his position. 'I'd been watching Andrew playing with the other two lads, one was called Chris and the other was Matthew. I stayed back out of the way, so they didn't see me. I saw Chris leave and Andrew and Matthew carried on playing for a while, maybe about half an hour or so. Then I heard Matthew shouting something to Andrew and run away. Andrew

348

ran after him and I had to move from where I'd been standing, to just around the corner. That's when I saw Andrew pick up the lump of wood and hit Matthew across the head. Matthew fell to the ground immediately and Andrew stood there for a while, just staring at him, he kept looking around but there was no one nearby. He didn't see me. Then he ran away.'

'What happened next?'

'I went over to where Matthew was, and I knelt down. There was blood pouring out of his ear and his nose. His eyes were still a bit open. I thought he was dead. Until he made this sound, like a gurgling noise from his throat and he opened his eyes wider. He looked straight at me and . . .' Stephen paused. 'He tried to say something, but only this loud noise like a squeal came out and I panicked. I put my hand over his mouth to keep him quiet. I don't know what came over me, but the next thing I know, I . . .' He hesitated again. 'I can't believe I did it, but I just kept my hand there, over his mouth, until he stopped breathing.' He swallowed and looked to the floor.

'Take your time,' Ruth said.

Stephen continued. 'I looked around to make sure there was no one there, and I tried to think of what to do with his body. I didn't know if I should leave it there or move it.'

'Did you remove his clothes?'

Stephen shook his head. 'No. Barry Longford did that.'

Ruth looked up from her interview notes. 'Andrew's dad?'

Stephen Tubby nodded. 'While I was trying to figure out what to do, I heard someone coming and hid out of the way. That's when I saw Barry Longford turn up. He went over to Matthew and put his head near his face. I guessed he was checking if he was breathing. He looked distraught and I remember he kept putting his head in his hands, like he was sobbing. He kept looking around then looking back at Matthew, he was on his knees, rocking back and forth, like he didn't know what to do. Then, he took Matthew's clothes off and shoved them inside his coat, before he covered Matthew up with loads of leaves. And then he left. I waited a few minutes and then I ran until I got to the park gates. And then I walked home.'

'How did you know it was Barry Longford?'

'I'd seen him at the park when the lads played football. He used to take a lot of photographs, always had a camera in his hand.'

'Why didn't you come forward at the time?'

'I was just so scared. I was scared for Andrew, and I was scared for myself. Then as time went on and no one was ever arrested, I thought we'd got away with it. Until this morning when I saw on the news that Andrew had been charged.'

'And that's why you've come forward now? To put the record straight?'

'Yes. I know I couldn't live with myself if Andrew wound up spending the rest of his life in prison for something he didn't do.'

Ruth snatched a look at her colleague, knowing full well that Andrew Longford probably had less than a few weeks to live. A fact that Stephen Tubby was obviously unaware of.

Ruth paused the interview for Stephen to have a break. She also wanted to go over what the interview had thrown up. While Tubby was out of the room, she said: 'Everything Tubby has told us so far was public knowledge at the time. It was reported in the news and the papers that Matthew had been playing football with two friends, who were both named. It was reported that Matthew suffered a significant head injury and that his clothes were removed. There's nothing he's said yet that only someone who really *was* there would know.' She sat back.

DC Gliss removed his glasses and rubbed his eyes. 'What about the fact that he said that it was Andrew's dad who removed Matthew's clothes? How would he know that?'

'We know it was either Andrew or his dad because the clothes have been found at Andrew's allotment. So, I guess that's one thing. But he could have just guessed that. We need something else. Something more solid that only Tubby would know.'

Ruth thought for a moment and then sat up straight. 'The mark on Matthew's hand. He had a line down his palm, like his hand had been caught by something.' She was flicking through the photographs of Matthew's body. 'There.' She pointed to a picture. 'We never knew what caused it, and Sheridan and her parents stated at the time that they weren't aware of any injury before he went to play football that day. And it was never part of what was made public.'

DC Gliss put his glasses back on and picked up the photograph. 'That could have been caused by *anything.*'

'Yes, but if Tubby *was* there that day and he tells us that he saw it, then I think that's enough.'

Stephen Tubby was brought back into the interview room and placed his cup of water on the table in front of him.

Ruth began. 'Stephen, you've told us your account of what happened that day. I want to ask you a few more questions.'

Tubby nodded. 'Okay.'

'Apart from when you placed your hand over Matthew's mouth, did you touch any other part of his body?'

'No. I'm not a pervert if that's what you're implying,' he replied angrily.

'I didn't mean that. There's no suggestion of that. I'm just asking if you noticed anything else, any other injury apart from the blood coming from Matthew's ear and nose.'

Tubby slowly shook his head, picked up his cup of water and took a sip. 'Only the mark on his hand.' He looked at Ruth. 'I'm sorry, I forgot to say . . . he grabbed my coat.'

'Your coat?'

'Yes. When I first put my hand over his mouth, he reached up and grabbed my coat. I had to pull it free. My coat was open, and it had a zip on it and when I pulled his hand free, it left a mark on his palm. A red mark from the zip.'

Ruth sat back. *You were there*, she thought. 'Thank you, Stephen,' she said.

Tubby clasped his hands together. 'Is that everything?'

She looked at him. 'I have one more question. Andrew Longford has been charged with killing Matthew Holler. So, why come forward now and say it was you?'

'Like I've already said, I don't want him going to prison for something he didn't do. I've never done anything for him in his life and so the least I can do now is to protect him.'

'Why?'

'Because that's what you do for your children, you protect them. You protect them no matter what.'

'But why are *you* protecting Andrew? He's not *your* son.'

Stephen Tubby held Ruth's gaze. 'Yes, he is. Andrew *is* my son.'

CHAPTER 83

Stephen Tubby went back to before Andrew was born. He had been in a relationship with Andrew's mother, Michelle, when they were in their late teens, but as they grew older, the relationship ended, albeit amicably, and they remained in touch, often sharing nights together in his little flat. Even when Michelle met Barry Longford, she and Stephen still got together on occasion, totally unbeknown to Barry.

When Michelle became pregnant, she told Stephen that Barry was never to know. She said she would maintain the lie that Andrew was Barry's son. And so, they kept the secret. It suited Stephen – he was a young man, working away a lot of the time as a trainee plasterer and earning good money for a lad his age. He didn't want the responsibility of a child. When he wasn't working, he was out with his mates, supping pints down the pub and chatting up girls.

Then, when he was in his mid-twenties, his life changed. He met a woman several years older and moved in with her. After a year, she became pregnant with a daughter and the little family were happy together.

Then one day, Stephen came home from work to find their daughter crying in her high chair, and his girlfriend unconscious on the kitchen floor, having suffered a brain haemorrhage. She was rushed to hospital but died the following morning.

Stephen was left to look after their daughter and although he tried his best, the responsibility was too much, and she eventually went to live with an aunt. Stephen visited her as often as he could, and this was around the same time that he began watching Andrew play football with his friends in Birkenhead Park, making sure he was walking by when they were, sometimes taking a paper and pretending to read it so he didn't look suspicious.

'So, Andrew doesn't know that you're his father?'

'No.'

'Have you had contact with him over the years? Or recently?'

'No. I've never spoken to him. I just watched him play football whenever I could.'

'Are you positive he's your son?'

'Absolutely. There's no question he's mine. And for all those years I wasn't able to have contact with him, I should have put my foot down and told Michelle that I wanted the truth to come out. But I didn't. I kept my promise to her and never told a soul about being Andrew's dad. Even though I wanted to be a part of his life and do what dads do for their sons. But now I *can* do something for him. I can let him live his life as a free man. I know he might be in trouble for hitting Matthew, but Andrew didn't kill him. I did.'

Ruth concluded the interview and made her way to Hill's office. She updated her with the details of Tubby's confession.

'Let's see what CPS have to say,' Hill said.

'When do you think we should let Sheridan know about Stephen Tubby's confession?' Ruth asked.

Hill looked at her watch and tapped her desk. 'Speak to CPS, and then we'll go and see her together.'

CHAPTER 84

Monday 26 July

Sheridan parked up in the backyard and remained in her car for a moment. Hill and Ruth's visit from the night before was still playing over in her mind. She'd listened in disbelief as they told her how Stephen Tubby had described his involvement in Matthew's death. How he was still alive when Tubby had placed his hand over his mouth. Sheridan knew the details of Matthew's case well enough to know that the injury from the blow to his head alone would have been fatal. Tubby's actions had simply brought his death forward by a few moments. After Hill and Ruth had left, Sheridan and Sam had driven to her parents' house and gently told them. They had sat up until the early hours, processing all the information that had come to light in the last few days. They now knew the absolute truth about Matthew's last moments.

After two hours' sleep, Sheridan felt remarkably awake. Today was the day that Emerson Corr, Andrew Longford and Stephen Tubby would all appear at Liverpool Magistrates' Court. And Sheridan intended to be there. But first, she wanted to speak to Emerson Corr.

She hesitated as she walked past Tubby's cell. Her urge to open the door and look him in the eye was overwhelming, and it took everything for her not to. Instead, she dropped the wicket to Emerson's cell door. He stepped back as she unlocked it.

'Detective Holler. How nice to see you.'

'I take it you're feeling better now?' she asked, her voice drenched in sarcasm.

'I don't think you came here to ask me that.' He sat on the bench and placed his palms on his knees. 'So, what can I do for you?'

'I just came to say goodbye. You're off to court this morning and then you'll be remanded in custody. You'll go to prison and that makes me very happy. Knowing that you'll spend the rest of your pathetic life behind bars.'

'I'm sure you're not supposed to say things like that to me. But it's okay. I like you, Detective Holler.' He weaved his fingers together. 'Do you smoke?'

'No.'

'I assume you don't take drugs, but do you drink?'

'That's none of your business.'

'I only ask because you strike me as being perfect. You're slim, healthy, you work hard, you're smart. I can't see one imperfect trait. And that's why l like you.'

'I have a question for you, about being perfect.'

Emerson smiled. 'Fire away.'

'When we interviewed you, you said that you "*did*" believe you were perfect, as in the past tense. So, I figured that when you first discovered your allergy and how life-threatening it was, you became angry. You became angry because up until then, you thought you were perfect.'

Emerson slowly clapped his hands together. 'Bravo.'

'Is that why you started killing everyone you saw as imperfect?'

'Yes. But had I met you, you would have been safe. You are the epitome of perfection.'

Sheridan took two steps forward and leaned down, her face just inches from his. 'You really aren't as clever as you think you are.'

'What makes you say that?'

Sheridan dropped her voice to a whisper. 'I *am* . . . according to your warped theory, one of the imperfect. You targeted a girl who was overweight, a family who had disabled sons, a homeless man, a young lad with autism, prostitutes and . . . a woman who loved another woman. I'll leave you to figure it out.' She stepped back and watched Emerson's face flush with anger. 'Have a nice life in prison.' She closed the cell door and winked at him through the wicket, before snapping it shut.

Making her way back down the corridor, she hesitated outside Stephen Tubby's cell. Her hand touched the wicket. Behind the heavy metal door was the man who had seen Matthew take his last breath. The man who had placed his hand over Matthew's mouth and watched him die. The man who never came forward and left her family to suffer for over thirty years.

She felt her hand shaking as she dropped the wicket.

Stephen Tubby was sitting on the cell bench. He looked up when he heard the wicket open.

Sheridan clutched the keys in her hand and felt the pulse in her neck throbbing.

And then she opened the door.

Tubby remained sitting. 'I'm so sorry.' He dropped his head. 'I'm really very sorry.'

She didn't reply but stood motionless for a few moments. Motionless and without words.

'I have to protect Andrew. If you were a parent, you'd understand.'

Sheridan stepped back and slowly closed the door, taking one last look at Tubby through the wicket, before closing it.

357

It was 4.30 in the afternoon by the time Sheridan and Anna walked back into CID, having spent all day at court.

The whole team looked up and stopped what they were doing, waiting for Sheridan to speak.

'Emerson Corr has been remanded in custody for four weeks to the Crown court. Andrew Longford and Stephen Tubby were both bailed, which we expected.' Sheridan looked around the room. Her team not quite knowing if they could celebrate the Emerson Corr result while all still reeling from the events leading up to Andrew Longford's and Stephen Tubby's arrests.

Sheridan allowed herself a smile. 'You *can* all celebrate, you know. It's fine. We got Emerson Corr locked up and saved a shitload of lives.' She paused. 'And my family and I now know what happened to my brother.' She nodded once. 'It's all good.'

For a moment, no one spoke. Until Rob piped up. 'Thank fuck for that, because I was beginning to worry that we weren't getting cakes.'

And that's when the team applauded. And Sheridan threw her pen at Rob.

CHAPTER 85

Two weeks later – Monday 9 August

Stephen Tubby was watching Andrew Longford's house. He'd parked as close as he could, so he had a view of the front door. Looking down at the package on the passenger seat, he touched it once, before checking no one was around. He knew he was breaching his bail conditions by being here, but he didn't care.

He turned his face away as a woman passed with a dog. When she was gone, he glanced up to see the nurse leaving Andrew's house and watched as she closed the front door and walked down the road, getting into her car and driving away.

After one last check that she hadn't turned back, Tubby got out of his car and approached the front door, the package gripped tightly in his hand.

Andrew answered it a minute later and stood back. 'Come in. Did anyone see you?'

'No.' Tubby followed him into the living room and placed the package on the sofa, before sitting down. 'How long have we got?' Tubby asked.

'She'll be back in an hour.' Andrew coughed and wiped his mouth with a tissue. 'Is that the stuff?' He nodded towards the package.

'Yes,' Tubby replied. 'Are you sure about this? I mean, are you *absolutely* sure?'

'Yeah. I'm sure. Are *you*?' Andrew asked.

'Yes, I'm positive. It's the only way.'

Andrew coughed again and put a hand to his chest, his face etched in pain. His mouth was open and a rasping sound emanated from his throat. 'How long will it take?' he said, putting his head back.

'Not long.'

'Then let's get it over with,' Andrew replied, taking a deep breath and closing his eyes.

Andrew's palliative care nurse, Nancy, lifted the shopping bag out of the boot and locked her car. She'd bought a cake and a packet of Andrew's favourite biscuits. His appetite had diminished, but he still managed to enjoy the odd treat. She'd make him comfortable, and they'd settle down in front of the TV with a cuppa.

Having learned about Andrew's arrest and subsequent charges, her bosses had made it clear that she didn't have to remain Andrew's palliative care nurse. But she'd weighed it up and knew Andrew was no threat to her. As a carer, she had to put her own feelings aside, just as anyone in health care had to. Medical staff in A&E couldn't choose who they treated, they couldn't refuse to try to save the drunk driver whose victim lay dead on a trolley in the room next door. Nancy had been shocked by what she had learned about Andrew but chose to carry on. Until the end. Because that was her job.

She opened the front door and called out, 'I'm back.'

No reply came and she dropped the bag of shopping on the kitchen table, before walking into the living room.

'Andrew?' she said, her voice soft and low. 'Andrew?' she repeated, stepping over to him.

His head was dropped to his chest and thick, yellow vomit stained the front of his T-shirt.

She touched his shoulder, shaking it gently, before stepping back and reaching for her mobile, dialling her boss's number.

'Hello?'

'It's Nancy Brett. Andrew Longford has passed away.'

CHAPTER 86

Annette Lennon felt her legs shaking as she stood in the witness box. Because Emerson Corr had pleaded guilty there had been no trial, but this was her opportunity to do the one thing that had kept her going in the years since he'd attacked her. This was her opportunity to face him. Reading out her victim impact statement was her chance to get the closure she needed.

The courtroom was silent as she took a deep breath and began to read.

'Four years ago, I was standing on a train station platform with only one thought in my head. To jump. I was in a bad place back then and felt that my life was worthless, that I was worthless and couldn't think of a reason not to end it. Then you attacked me, and you did it because you saw me as imperfect, like all your other victims. My imperfection in your eyes was that I'm overweight, I was *then* and I still am now. I'm sure that in the last four years you've given me little thought, well, I've thought about you, every single day. I lost my job and was too scared to leave my flat, in case you were out there, watching me, waiting for me.' Annette paused and raised her head to look at Emerson Corr, who sat in the dock, flanked by two prisoner custody officers, with a broad smile on his face. Annette felt tears sting her eyes and she blinked down on them, determined not to let him see any weakness. Her eyes moved to where Sheridan was sitting and she saw the slight nod, encouraging Annette to stay strong and keep going.

'The thing is Emerson Corr, you targeted me because I was imperfect, and you thought that I didn't deserve to be on this earth. You hoped that I eventually *did* end it, that one day I made the jump and threw myself in front of a train. Well, as you can see, I didn't, and I have *you* to thank for that.'

Sheridan glanced over at Emerson Corr and spotted that the smile had gone, replaced now with pure anger. His chest was rising and falling sharply as he listened to Annette's words.

Annette looked down at her statement, to the last lines which she knew off by heart, and raising her head, she looked him in the eye.

'I hope I'm in your thoughts *every* day. I'm only here because of *you*. I have everything in life now that I could ever have dreamed of. So, thank you for saving me. You saved my life and I hope you spend the rest of *yours* remembering that.'

Annette Lennon stepped down from the witness box and made her way across the courtroom towards her seat, next to Sheridan. As she passed the dock, where Emerson Corr sat, she smiled at him and stuck her middle finger up.

CHAPTER 87

One month later

Sheridan's desk phone rang. It was Rob's extension number.

'Yes, mate?'

'Can you come to CID? We've got a problem.'

Rob waved her over as soon as she walked in.

'What's up?' she asked, as he opened his desk drawer and pulled out the white envelope containing the details of who had placed bets on Hill's real name. He unfolded the sheet of paper and showed it to her.

'Someone's written the word "wrong" next to every guess . . . and the money's gone.' Rob pulled a face. 'I think Hill's rumbled us.'

'Ah . . .' Sheridan replied, biting down on her bottom lip. 'Well, never mind, eh?'

'Never mind? Is that all you've got to say? She's going to kill us.' Rob quickly shoved the envelope and sheet of paper back in the drawer as Hill walked in.

'I need everyone's attention.' Hill scanned the room before pointing to Dipesh. 'Let's start with you, Dipesh. Does the name Hill Billy ring any bells?'

Dipesh's eyes widened and he tried to sink lower in his seat. "Hill Billy" was his guess. Along with his ten-pound wager.

'Er . . . well.' He stumbled over his words.

'Okay, let's try you, Rob. "Hillman"?'

Rob pursed his lips and covered his mouth with his hand.

'I know you've all been placing bets on my real name, well, you've all guessed wrong. So, the betting can stop now.' She stepped over to Rob and held out her hand. He pulled the drawer open and handed her the envelope.

'Thank you, Rob.' She screwed up the envelope and threw it in the bin. 'Oh, and by the way. I took the two hundred quid. Cheers.'

And with that, she left the room, a huge smile forming on her face as she returned to her office.

They all looked at each other but no one said a word.

Sheridan was about to leave too, when Dipesh mumbled, 'She can't just take the money. Can she?' He looked at her for an answer.

Sheridan shrugged. 'It went to a good cause.'

'What good cause?' Dipesh asked.

'What do you think paid for Bobby Stover's new suit?' Sheridan raised an eyebrow and left.

A moment later, she peered round Hill's office door. 'That was fun,' she said.

Hill grinned. 'It was, wasn't it.'

'So, are you going to tell me your real—'

'Nope.'

At the end of the day, as the team were packing up, ready to head home, Dipesh still hadn't stopped complaining about losing his tenner.

A face appeared around CID's door. 'Hi, I'm from Estates, I just need to do some PAT testing, if that's okay?'

Dipesh waved a hand. 'Fill your boots.'

The electrician stepped over to the brass fan at the front of the room. He unplugged it and opened his toolbox, removing the back of the plug, tutting to himself.

Dipesh looked up. 'That's *my* fan.'

'It's not safe, the wiring's out of date. I'll have to take it away, I'm afraid.'

Dipesh looked around the room and realised everyone had left. He hadn't brought his car to work, having caught the train. 'But, it's mine. I can take it home . . . just not today.'

The electrician shook his head. 'Sorry, regulations. I need to decommission it and check that it hasn't damaged the wall plug. Once it's deemed safe, you can have it back.'

Dipesh looked to the ceiling. 'Fine.' He grabbed his jacket and left, mumbling to himself about losing a tenner and his beloved brass fan all in the same day.

Sheridan came out of her office, spotting the electrician coming out of CID carrying the fan. 'Did he fall for it?' she asked.

'Hook, line and sinker. Where do you want it, Sheridan?'

She handed him her car keys. 'I've put the back seats down, should fit in there nicely.' She smiled, admiring her lovely new fan.

CHAPTER 88

Emerson Corr sat on his bunk, reading a book. The noise from outside his cell was familiar to him now. The heavy boots of prison officers as they went about their duties. The shouting between prisoners, goading each other, followed by laughter. The clanging of metal gates as they were opened and shut. All day, every day, the same sounds, the same routines.

He'd read the newspaper coverage of his crimes and how the police had caught him. How they had stopped him carrying on killing his victims using the pi sequence. How they had saved so many lives, as the sequence never ends, hence the belief that he would never have stopped. But Emerson had taken his failed suicide attempt as a sign that he wasn't meant to stop. He'd been given a second chance to carry on with the sequence. The papers had called him the pi man. The pi man who bought himself a playground. He liked being called that. Pi never ends. And Emerson Corr was never going to stop.

He spent most days quietly reading in his cell, sometimes venturing out into the corridors, where he watched the other inmates interacting with each other. And Emerson Corr watched them *very* closely.

A voice made him look up from his book. 'Alright?' The prisoner stepped into Emerson's cell.

Emerson nodded once.

'I'm Dougie Pinner. I hear you're quite the celebrity.' He placed a hand on the top bunk, looking around the immaculate cell. 'They call you the Pie Man, don't they? Word around this place is that you chopped up your victims and put them into pies. Is that right?' Dougie Pinner laughed. 'That's proper fucked up.'

Emerson didn't respond.

'Well, don't you be asking for a job in the kitchens, eh?' Dougie quipped.

'What's your misdemeanour?' Emerson asked, closing his book and placing it on his lap.

'Murder.'

Emerson studied the man before him. He was six feet tall – muscular, with short, perfectly cropped hair. His clothes were immaculate, and Emerson realised he didn't have the common smell of body odour like most of the other prisoners. 'Were you under the influence of drugs or drink at the time?' Emerson asked.

'What sort of question is that?'

'Just a question.'

'No. I wasn't. I don't do drugs and I'm teetotal. I don't even smoke, I hate it, terrible habit.'

No imperfections yet, thought Emerson. 'Do you have mental health problems?' he asked.

'What's with all the questions? If you're trying to build me a defence, you're too late, my barrister tried all that, and I still got fifteen years.' He laughed again.

Still no imperfections, Emerson thought again. 'Who did you kill?' he asked.

'My neighbour. Found out he was a nonce and had been watching my kids out of his window. So, I knocked on his door one day and kicked him to death.'

Fair enough, thought Emerson as he picked up his book.

Dougie yawned. 'And then I kicked his dog to death.'

Emerson put the book down and looked at the man, tilting his head to one side.

And that was the moment that Dougie Pinner became the next name on the list of five imperfect inmates Emerson Corr was planning to kill on the twenty-second of July, the following year.

After Dougie left, Emerson lay down on his bunk and smiled to himself. Sheridan Holler may have taken him off the streets of Liverpool, but she had no control over him now. Emerson closed his eyes, imagining her face when, in nine months' time, she got to hear that Emerson Corr had managed to murder five inmates. Five inmates with imperfections. She might be smart, he thought, but he was fucking smarter.

◆ ◆ ◆

Dougie Pinner was heading back to his cell when he heard his name being called. He turned to see one of the prison officers waving him over.

'Pinner, the governor wants to see you.'

'What the fuck for?' Dougie raised his hands.

Behind him, jeers from the other prisoners rang around the wing.

'Who's been a bad boy?' one of them called out and Dougie stuck his middle finger up. More jeers and laughter echoed around as he made his way to the gate, where the officer let him through.

They walked in silence to the governor's office and the officer tapped on the open door.

'Come in.'

Dougie stepped inside and the officer closed the door behind him, leaving Dougie and the governor alone.

'Have a seat.' The governor pushed the phone on his desk towards Dougie, who dialled the number.

'DI Holler,' Sheridan answered.

'Hi Sheridan, it's DC Alfie Flane.'

'Hello mate, how's it going?'

'You were right. He's planning his next killings. And he's just added me to his list. That story about killing a dog was perfect – he looked bloody furious.'

'Thought he might. He hates anyone who hurts animals.' Sheridan paused. 'Okay. Great job, I'll speak to the governor now. Cheers Alfie.'

Undercover police officer DC Flane handed the phone to the prison governor.

'Hello Sheridan, how you doing?'

'I'm all good thanks, Bob. So, now we know that Emerson Corr is planning to kill five inmates next July, what's *our* plan?'

'I can wait until nearer the date and put him in segregation. He'll be on his own and nowhere near any other inmate.'

'But how many times can you do that?'

'As many times as I like.'

'You're a legend, Bob.'

Sheridan ended the call and sat back with her hands behind her head, smiling. *You might be smart, Emerson Corr,* she thought. *But we're fucking smarter.*

EPILOGUE

Juliet Hannigan continued to receive money from her father every month until an investigation was carried out into Frank's business dealings. All the money he had been sending her was linked to an international money-laundering syndicate. When Juliet was initially interviewed by police, she vehemently denied having any contact, stating that they hadn't spoken since Jake had died. She also denied having received any money from him, happily showing the police her bank statements. The investigation soon established that she had *two* accounts, in one of which a substantial amount of money had been deposited every month by her father for the last three years. Her mobile phone records showed the weekly contact and text messages between them, which included several where she had thanked him for the money, promising him she had told no one about the second bank account. And that it would remain their secret, seeing as she was and would always be his princess.

On learning about the lies Juliet had told, her mother Stephanie banished her from the house and refused to ever speak to her again. Suddenly needing to earn her own money, Juliet applied for several jobs, but with the ongoing investigation hanging over her, she still can't secure employment. No longer the rich girl that her friends took advantage of, Juliet is now living in her car.

The package that Stephen Tubby took to Andrew Longford's house on the day he died was a DNA testing kit. The results came back two weeks later, and having spent his life believing he was Andrew's father, the test showed conclusively that Stephen Tubby was *not* in any way related to him.

Tubby still maintained the account he gave to the police of his involvement in Matthew Holler's death. He was sentenced to life imprisonment with a recommendation that he serve a minimum of fourteen years before he is eligible for parole.

Emerson Corr was handed a whole-life sentence. He will never be released from prison. Oblivious to the fact that the police and prison governor are aware of his plan, Emerson is still working on his list of five.

Anna continues to meet up with Steve. He changed his story about moving in with his new girlfriend, telling Anna that he agreed it might be too soon and wants to take things slowly. The truth remains that there is still no new girlfriend and never will be. Steve continues to work on his plan to trick Anna back into his life. And he will never give up.

Anna is still waiting for the right time to tell Sheridan of her fears.

Andrew Longford – who succumbed to his cancer the day Stephen Tubby visited him – was buried next to his father. His *real* father, Barry Longford. Sheridan did not attend his funeral.

Janet Vickers eventually sold the house where her sister and family had died. She donated half the money to the Catholic Church and the other half to an animal sanctuary. She still has Bouncer.

After plugging in her lovely new fan at home, Sheridan discovered that Maud was absolutely terrified of it and hid under the bed, refusing to come out. The fan was returned to CID the following day.

Marcus Holt was investigated by the Professional Standards Department. He resigned from his position as public enquiry officer.

Kyle Crane's ex-wife never found out that he'd been arrested for theft. The charges against him were dropped.

Bobby Stover came off his methadone script and is drug free. He now works mornings at a car wash and loves it. He continued to meet up with Annette Lennon, who finally found the courage to return to her job in the library.

Bobby spends most afternoons there reading romance novels. He doesn't tear the covers off.

Annette still lives in her little flat, where during the day the curtains are always open. It's Bobby who closes them at night, just before they go to bed, where he sleeps with his arms around her. Annette still has the scars from the attack, deciding not to have surgery, as Bobby loves her just the way she is. Perfect. Bobby still has his suit.

The deceased girl in the back of Emerson Corr's van was identified as twenty-year-old Hannah Lavers. The week before she'd got into Emerson's van, she had contacted her parents in Devon asking if she could move back in with them. Her parents had agreed immediately, telling her that her room would be ready when she returned. Knowing that 'Eddie' would pay her his usual two hundred pounds, she'd planned to use it to pay for her train ticket home.

The four surviving girls that were found in the pit all made a full recovery. Three of them returned to the streets of Liverpool, where they still get into strangers' cars.

Tara Brookes didn't return. She moved to Newcastle where she is slowly being weaned off the drugs and lifestyle that almost killed her.

Dreya Marshall also didn't return to a life on the streets. She now volunteers for a charity that supports vulnerable women.

Thirty-three years after Matthew Holler's murder, Sheridan and her parents have finally found their peace.

Hill's real name is . . . still a mystery. For now.

ACKNOWLEDGEMENTS

And now here we are . . . the acknowledgements, where I get to thank everyone who has helped me along the way. So, grab yourself a coffee, tea (or not tea) and settle down, this might take a while. Why? Because as I've said before, I'm just the storyteller and there are a lot of other people involved in this process.

So, who's first? YOU of course, the readers: so many of you have contacted me to say how much you love Sheridan and the team and trust me, it never gets old. I had a crazy dream many years ago of writing crime fiction and seeing my books out there, and now here I am, doing just that. But it's only happened because you, the readers, buy the books. I've had the absolute pleasure of meeting some of you over the past year or so at various events and hope to see you again. You can bring Jaffa Cakes, but it's not obligatory.

Next up, Susie, my incredible wife: you know I couldn't do any of this without you. And I wouldn't want to. You're there every step of the way on this unbelievable journey.

Can I just say one thing though, it's your turn to make the coffee. Jeez, woman, how long do I have to wait for you to put the kettle on? Then when you do . . . you're off putting up a random shelf (which we don't need) or ordering Tupperware (which we don't need) or rearranging a room, which is fine, but then I get disorientated and start bumping into things. And can I say, I counted the number of pens we have in the house recently. One hundred and six. WE DON'T NEED ANY MORE PENS. And . . . seriously, what's with all the pairs of scissors? WE DON'T NEED ANY MORE SCISSORS.

But when you're not doing all your weird and wonderful stuff, you're helping me plot these books, often late into the night and at weekends, when I should be taking you dancing.

You make me smile every day. Never change. I love you just as you are. You're perfect.

Right, on to my gatekeepers, Michael Doherty, Breda Byrne, Lorraine Burns, Katharine Robinson and Jane Edwards: I need to find other ways to say thank you. You lovely lot are my first faithful readers and give up your precious time to point out all the stuff that you love . . . and all the stuff that you don't. As always though . . . there is a disclaimer in that you're still not getting paid. I would pay you, but Susie has spent all our money on bloody pens and scissors. Seriously though . . . thank you. You're all wonderful.

Next up is Supt Sonia Humphreys: you not only advise me on a lot of the technical police procedures, you're also a fabulous human being. I can't tell you what a joy it was to finally see you again after so long. Catching up on all the times we worked together is a memory that I'll treasure. Especially when we both recalled the woman who invited us into her house to see her snails. I think I saw some wine shoot out of your nose when I reminded you of her. Thank you for all your help, as always.

Joanne Farrelly, senior probation officer: Jo, once again you have been gold dust. Thank you for all your advice on sentencing etc. I'll be back to pick your brain (bug you) when I start book five. Cheers, lovely!

Professor James Coulson, Honorary Consultant Physician, Clinical Pharmacologist & Toxicologist, Cardiff University/

Cardiff & Vale University Health Board: James, when I contacted you asking for advice on death cap mushrooms and toxicology, I expect you were a little concerned at first. But, once you knew I wasn't about to wipe out half of Merseyside, you were more than happy to help. Your knowledge is sublime and you answered all of my strange questions in such a way that they made sense in my tiny brain. Thank you so much for your time. I will no doubt be back in touch for future books.

Paul Sturman: my firearms and search advisor (and mate, of course). What would I do without you? Even if you did want to re-write one of the scenes in *This Ends Now*, because you thought the police officer was based on you. What was it you wrote? . . . Oh yeah . . . *'The tall dark handsome sergeant assessed the scene, his cool smouldering grey eyes missing nothing, his muscular arms resting upon his impressive chest. He walked towards the vehicle, his female colleagues admiring his firm buttocks.'*

When you suggested this, I laughed so hard that I nearly coughed up a kidney. You are very funny, but don't give up the day job. Do you even have a day job now? Anyway, apart from all that . . . thank you again for all your help . . . you big beefcake of a man.

John Cameron, antiques expert: John . . . what can I say, except . . . 'Aren't you that bloke off the telly?' Your knowledge of all things antique was priceless when writing this book. Cheers, mate. However, when I asked if you'd like to be a character, I think you wanted me to portray you as a smouldering hunk. Well, I didn't, but I did describe you as . . . well . . . read the book and you'll see. Thank you for all your help, not only do you know your stuff, you tell me so many interesting facts about antiques . . . and only you could make a story about chests of drawers sound fascinating. Let's meet up for that beer we promised each other, when you're next this way. Drinks are on me.

Fraser Ritchie: senior crime scene investigator. Hey Fraz, can you believe we're on book four? You have been so helpful with this one, as you have been with all of them. I love your reactions when I ask you questions that only a serial killer should be asking. Cheers mate, you're a legend.

Next up, my totally fabulous agent, Broo Doherty: good grief, Broo . . . what's going on? From the moment you signed me to now, I've been bouncing. It just gets better and better and here we are now . . . book four is done and I get to keep writing. You are truly very special and I know you don't believe it, but trust me, you really are. Oh, hang on a sec . . . Susie's calling from the living room, she says to say 'hi' and sends her love. God knows what she's getting up to in there, but I can hear nails being hammered into walls. If our house falls down, can I come and live with you? I'll bring Jack.

Vic Haslam, my wonderful editor: I've said it before, but I'm allowed to say it again and you can't stop me . . . you believed in me and continue to do so. I had to have a little celebratory drink when I got the call to say you wanted four more Sheridan Holler books. Okay, it was a fairly large drink. Okay, okay . . . it was huge and there was more than one. Oh, for heaven's sake . . . there was a copious amount of alcohol consumed and there may also have been a happy dance. But seriously, thank you for everything.

Right, on to Russel McLean, my dev editor: the picky one. Yes, you're picky but you love Maud, and anyone who loves her is alright in my book. Not my book, as in THIS book, but alright as in . . . oh, you know what I mean. Anyway, thank you for all your hard work, I know I make your head hurt sometimes and you never complain, but I only do it to wind you up.

To everyone at Thomas & Mercer: you're all wonderful. Thank you for everything, you really are a fantastic team. I know I am part of the amazing T&M family, with your unerring support that has never wavered. I know we will continue this journey together and I am immensely proud to have you behind me all the way.

Helen Edwards: translation rights genius and quiet assassin. I still don't know how you do what you do. But you do. Please don't worry about trying to explain it to me, just tell me where to sign. Cheers, lovely.

Lynn Parsons: so proud to call you our friend. Your support is unwavering and it's our turn to buy lunch next time. Just a small salad for you? . . . hahaha . . . seriously though . . . you really are quite wonderful. Oh and by the way . . . Gloria and Doreen are going to get even naughtier . . . just sayin'.

To the totally wonderful team at Pritchards Bookshop, Crosby. Amy, Mitch, Alex, Angie, Lu and Kristian: you have supported me so much and continue to do so. Thank you for everything . . . you are such incredible advocates of the DI Sheridan Holler series and . . . your bookshop is awesome. If anyone is reading this who hasn't yet visited Pritchards, please pop in if you're in Crosby. It's a great place and the staff are amazing.

Heather Bleasdale: audio book narrator: ah . . . Heather . . . the voice of Sheridan Holler and her team. I literally don't know how you manage to nail every character and bring them to life, but you do. Thank you for continuing to be brilliant.

Graham Bartlett: hang on a minute, how did you get to be in the acknowledgements? Let me think . . . oh that's right . . . I remember now . . . you're bloody ace. Not only do you write exceptionally good crime thrillers, you've supported me and this series and provided some rather wonderful endorsements. May we continue to appear together at future book events, even the ones where I'm dressed as a police officer and you nick someone for . . . what was it? . . . reporting their three TONNES of cannabis being stolen. Seriously, how was I supposed to keep a straight face at the

'You're Nicked' event? Hilarious. I don't think anyone noticed that my 'CS canister' was actually a Sherbet Dip Dab.

Next up: The Coven: you know who you are. The best, maddest, most supportive and wonderful group of women I still haven't met. It will happen. Bring cats. And chips. And not tea . . . lots of not tea.

My Twitter friends: you know I love interacting with you all. Thank you for sticking around. You're all lovely.

My copy-editor, proofreader, cold reader and cover designer: never think for a moment that I don't appreciate what you do. Thank you so much for all your hard work.

Lex Brookman at Team Tandem: what an absolute pleasure it is to work with you. You're amazing and you save me every time I'm about to give away spoilers for my own books. I've loved doing all the podcasts and readalong stuff, what a total blast. Let's do it all again!

And finally, the incredible human being that is Stu Cummins (The Stu): mate, your total passion for the Sheridan Holler series is tangible. You are such an amazing advocate, a fantastic blogger and a bloody lovely person. Thank you for everything. Legend.

I really hope I haven't missed anyone.

So, that's it from me. As you can see, there are so many people involved in this process, and this is my way of thanking them.

A final note from me: I love basing the series in Liverpool and the Wirral and only ever want to portray them as the fantastic places that they are. When I'm writing scenes, I do sometimes make up a street name or tweak how an area looks, but I only do this because it fits the story better.

In this book I have referred to Thurstaston Cliffs, which, if you know the area, is also known as Dee Cliffs. Having visited there while researching this book, I spoke to locals, who agreed it is generally known as Thurstaston Cliffs, hence my reference to it.

Oh . . . almost forgot . . . as you can see from the acknowledgements, I have a great team of professionals who make sure I get the procedural stuff right, but again, sometimes I'll use a bit of artistic licence, so any discrepancies are mine.

Right, I'd better go, because Susie is banging around in the loft and I dread to think what she's doing up there.

Catch you soon.

Tina

xx

ABOUT THE AUTHOR

© 2023 John McCulloch @ Studio 900

T. M. Payne was born in Lee-on-Solent, Hampshire, and now lives on the Wirral with her wonderful wife.

She is the bestselling author of the Detective Sheridan Holler series. Her debut novel, *Long Time Dead*, went to number one in crime fiction in both the UK and Germany. The second book in the series, This Ends Now, also became a number-one bestseller, as did her third in the series, Play With Fire.

She has spent most of her working life in the criminal justice system, starting out as a store detective (when she once got thrown in a river) before becoming a prisoner custody officer (when she once carried a prisoner out of the courtroom single-handedly after he started hallucinating butterflies).

She has worked in practically every London court, including the Old Bailey and Court of Appeal, and has been handcuffed to murderers, rapists, and dealt with some of the most violent prisoners to pass through the court system. In 2001, she joined Norfolk Police as a detention officer, working in the custody suite, before joining the Domestic Violence Unit as a police case investigator. In her fourteen years in that role, she dealt with thousands of victims of domestic abuse, with one of her cases earning her a chief constable's commendation. She now writes full-time.

T. M. Payne is crazy about animals and if you walk past her with your dog she will probably ask if she can pat it on the head. Or take it home with her. Or both.

She hopes to one day have seven dogs, fifteen cats and a penguin (or three).

She loves laughing, Christmas, playing golf (badly), walking along New Brighton beach (not walking her dog because she hasn't got one yet), snow, sunshine, sunsets, family and friends.

She dislikes beetroot.

Follow the Author on Amazon

If you enjoyed this book, follow T. M. Payne on Amazon to be notified when the author releases a new book!
To do this, please follow these instructions:

Desktop:

1) Search for the author's name on Amazon or in the Amazon App.
2) Click on the author's name to arrive on their Amazon page.
3) Click the 'Follow' button.

Mobile and Tablet:

1) Search for the author's name on Amazon or in the Amazon App.
2) Click on one of the author's books.
3) Click on the author's name to arrive on their Amazon page.
4) Click the 'Follow' button.

Kindle eReader and Kindle App:

If you enjoyed this book on a Kindle eReader or in the Kindle App, you will find the author 'Follow' button after the last page.

Printed in Dunstable, United Kingdom

72232571R10231